DALEN &GOLE

SCANDAL IN PORT ANGUS

MIKE DEAS

ORCA BOOK PUBLISHI

*Thank you to Nancy. From story ideas to long hours coloring,
you really made this project possible.*

Library and Archives Canada Cataloguing in Publication

Deas, Mike, 1982-
Dalen and Gole : scandal in Port Angus / by Mike Deas.

Issued also in electronic format.
ISBN 978-1-55469-800-4

I. Title.
PS8607.E374D35 2011   JC813'.6   C2011-903460-3

First published in the United States, 2011
Library of Congress Control Number: 2011929254

Summary: Dalen and Gole, refugees on Earth from the distant planet of Budap,
must solve the mystery of diminishing fish stocks and save their home planet
from an evil plot.

Disclaimer: This book is a work of fiction and is intended for entertainment purposes only. The author
and/or publisher accepts no responsibility for misuse or misinterpretation of the information in this book.

Orca Book Publishers gratefully acknowledges the support for its publishing programs provided
by the following agencies: the Government of Canada through the Canada Book Fund and the
Canada Council for the Arts, and the Province of British Columbia through the BC Arts Council
and the Book Publishing Tax Credit.

Cover and interior artwork by Mike Deas
Image coloring by Mike Deas and Nancy Deas
Cover layout by Jasmine Devonshire
Author photo by Erik Lyon

ORCA BOOK PUBLISHERS   ORCA BOOK PUBLISHERS
PO Box 5626, Stn. B   PO Box 468
Victoria, BC Canada   Custer, WA USA
V8R 6S4   98240-0468

www.orcabook.com
Printed and bound in Hong Kong.

14 13 12 11 • 4 3 2 1

CHAPTER 1

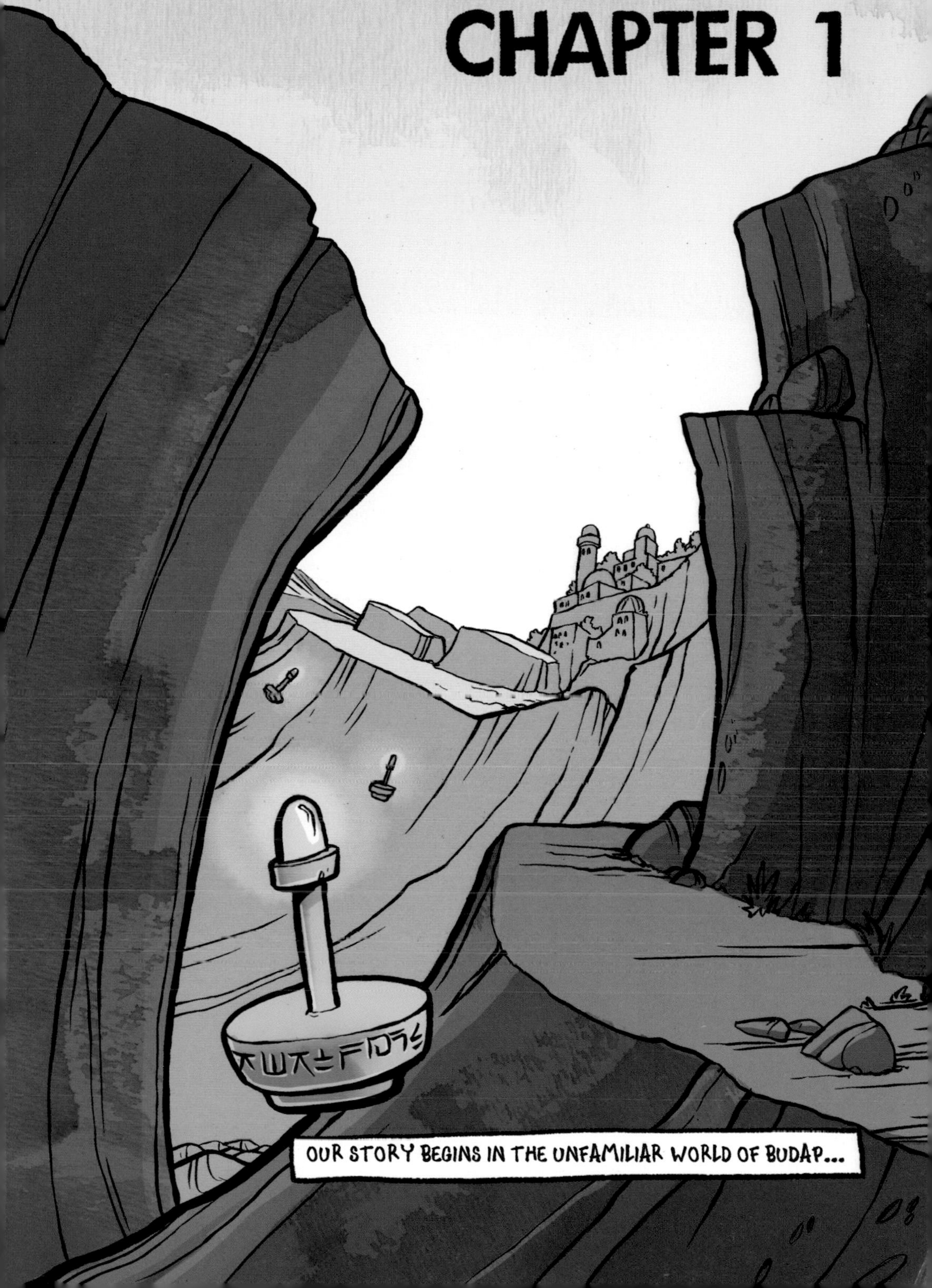
OUR STORY BEGINS IN THE UNFAMILIAR WORLD OF BUDAP...

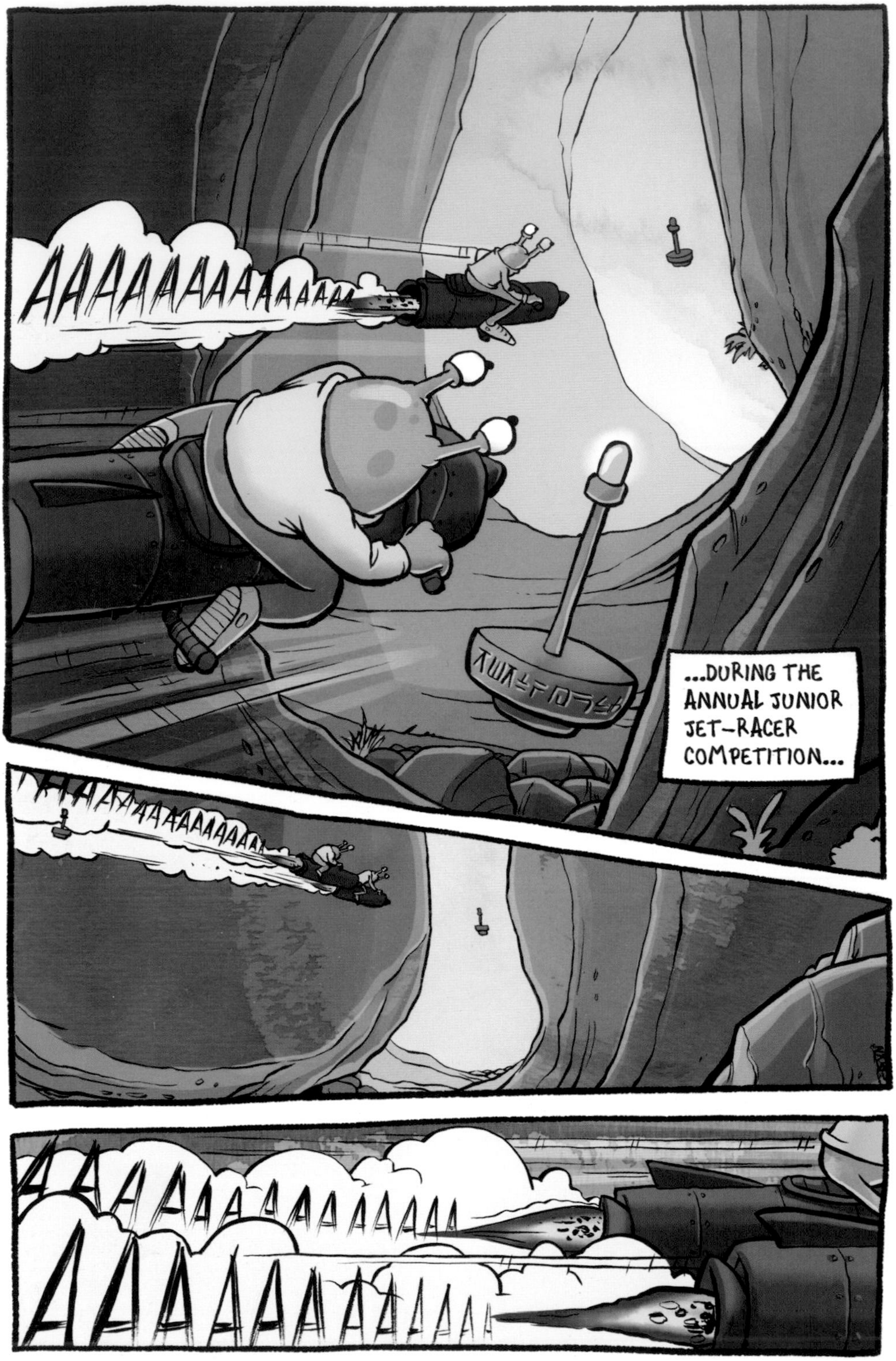
AAAAAAAAAAAAAA
...DURING THE ANNUAL JUNIOR JET-RACER COMPETITION...
AAAAAAAAAAAAAAA
AAAAAAAAAAAAAAA
AAAAAAAAAAAAAAAAAA

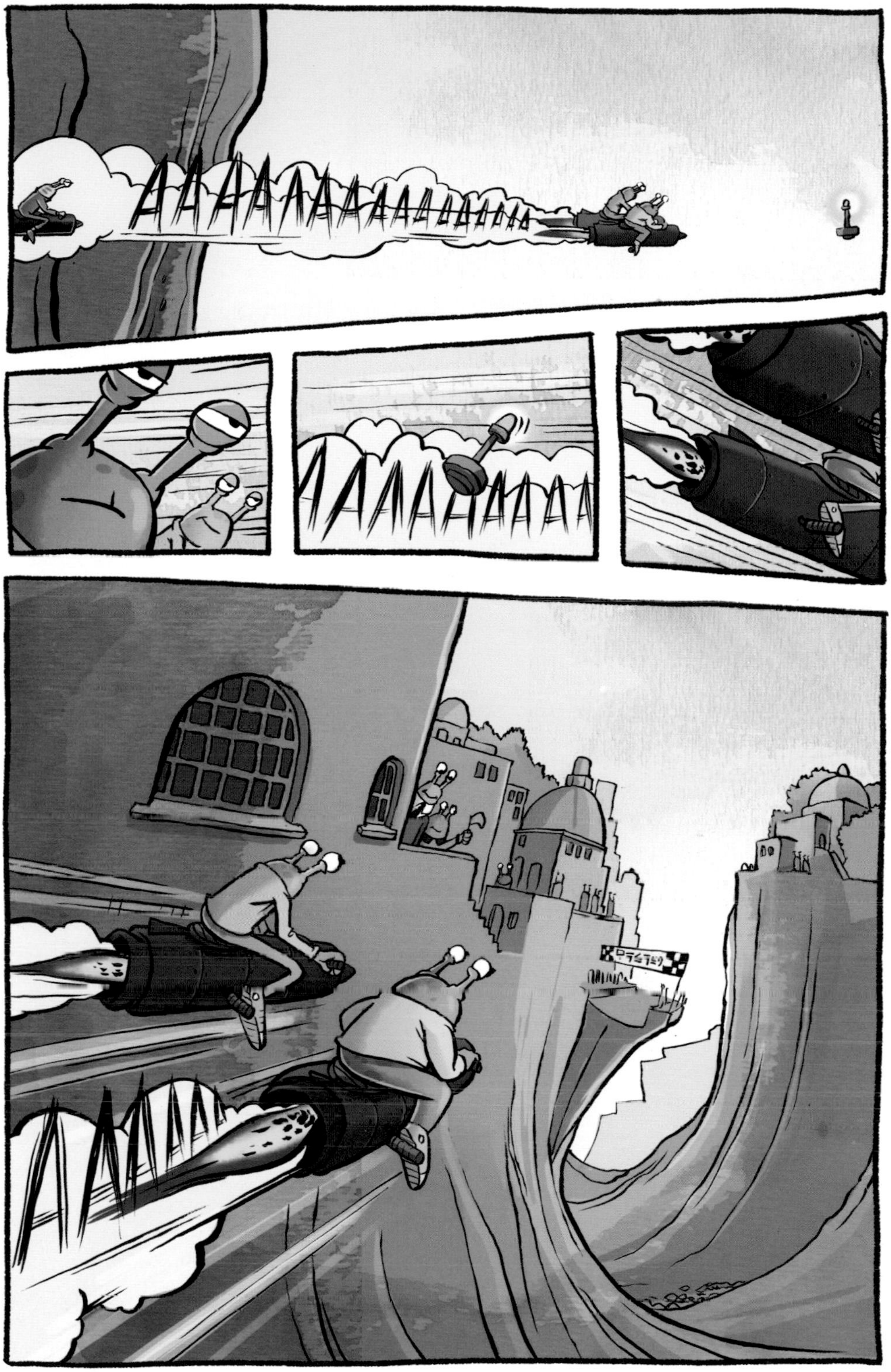

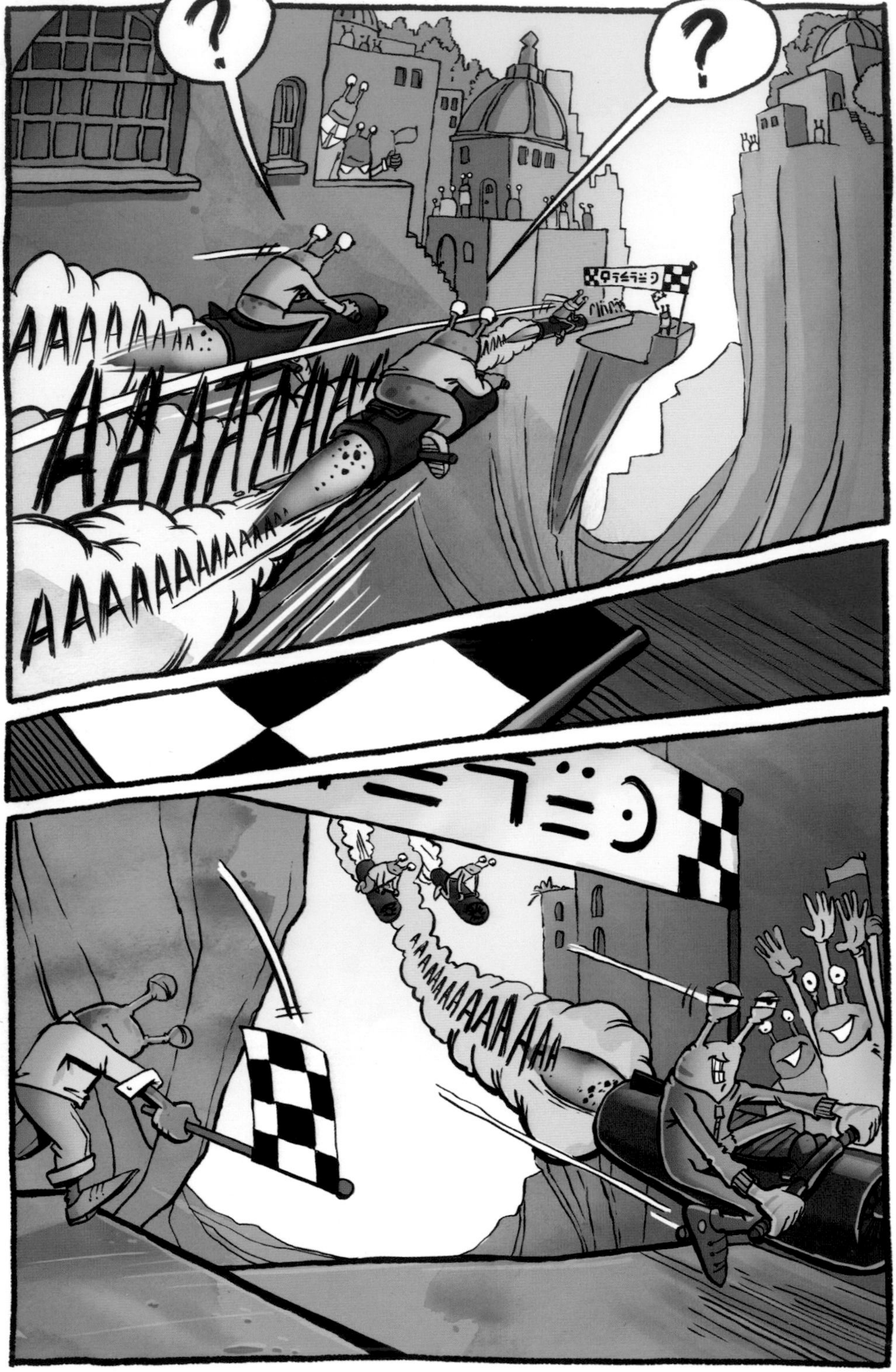
?
?
AAAAAAAAA
AAAAAAAAA
AAAAAAAAAAAAA
AAAAAAAAAAAAAA

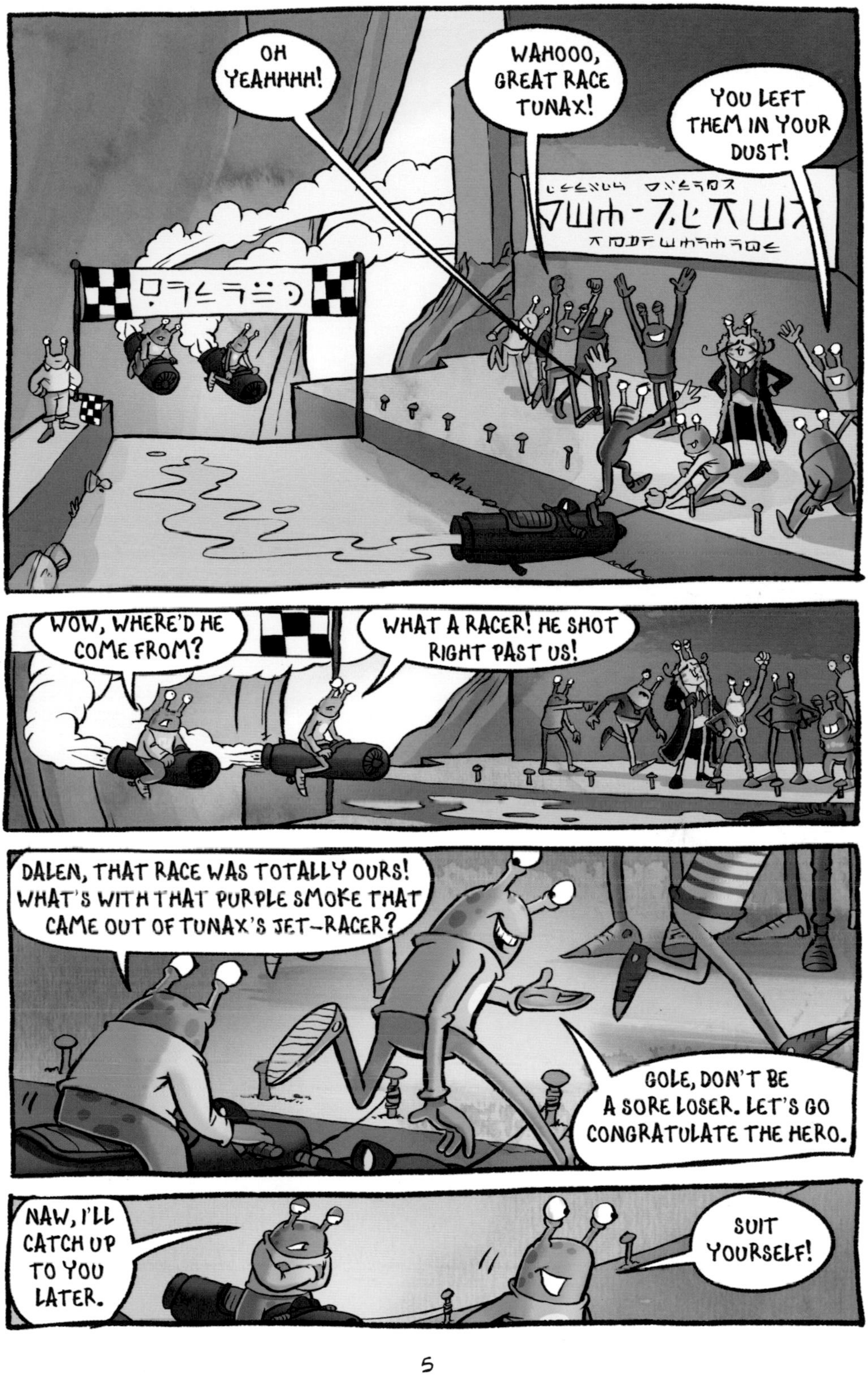
OH YEAHHHH!
WAHOOO, GREAT RACE TUNAX!
YOU LEFT THEM IN YOUR DUST!
WOW, WHERE'D HE COME FROM?
WHAT A RACER! HE SHOT RIGHT PAST US!
DALEN, THAT RACE WAS TOTALLY OURS! WHAT'S WITH THAT PURPLE SMOKE THAT CAME OUT OF TUNAX'S JET-RACER?
GOLE, DON'T BE A SORE LOSER. LET'S GO CONGRATULATE THE HERO.
NAW, I'LL CATCH UP TO YOU LATER.
SUIT YOURSELF!

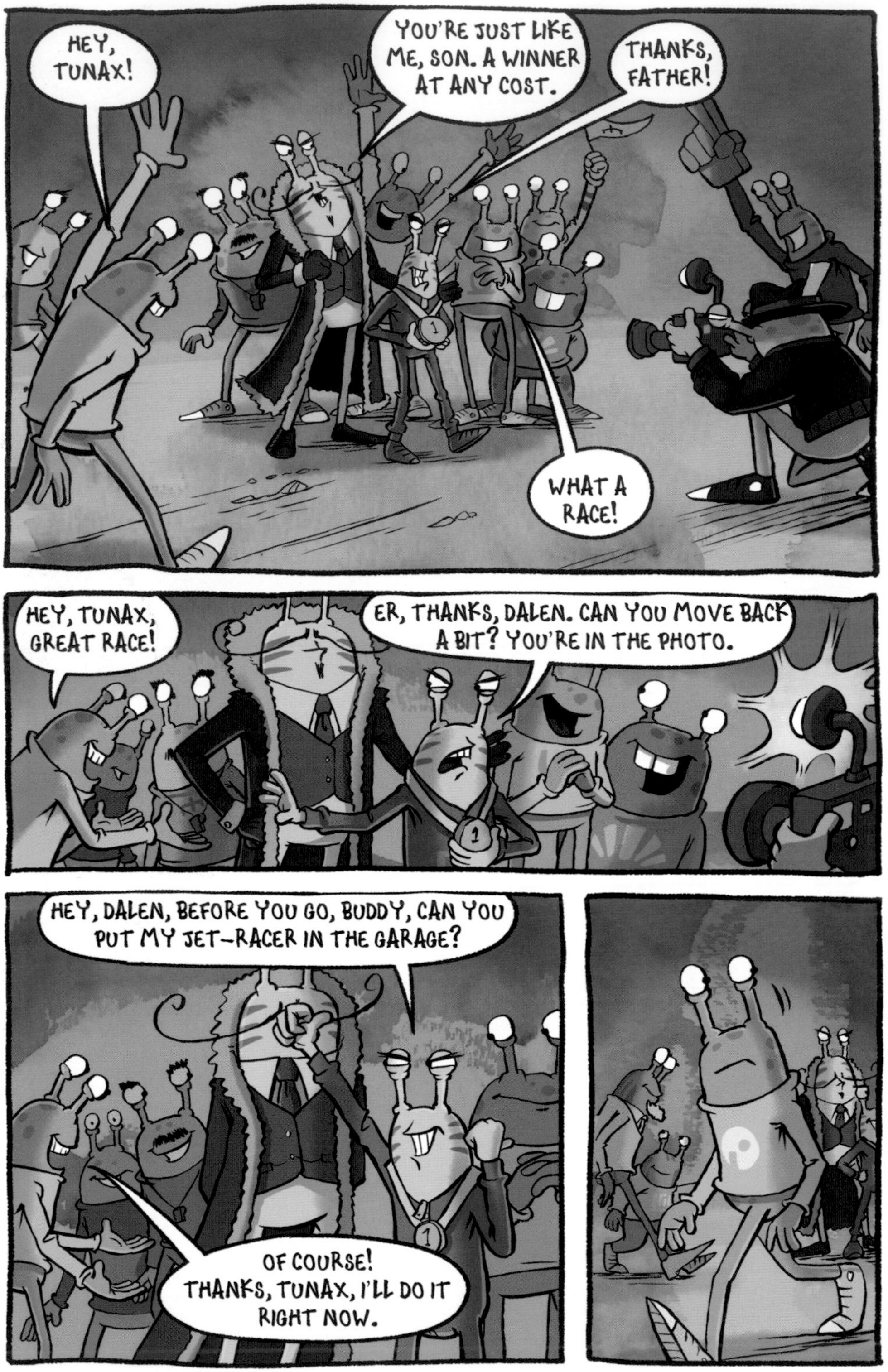
HEY, TUNAX!
YOU'RE JUST LIKE ME, SON. A WINNER AT ANY COST.
THANKS, FATHER!
WHAT A RACE!
HEY, TUNAX, GREAT RACE!
ER, THANKS, DALEN. CAN YOU MOVE BACK A BIT? YOU'RE IN THE PHOTO.
HEY, DALEN, BEFORE YOU GO, BUDDY, CAN YOU PUT MY JET-RACER IN THE GARAGE?
OF COURSE! THANKS, TUNAX, I'LL DO IT RIGHT NOW.

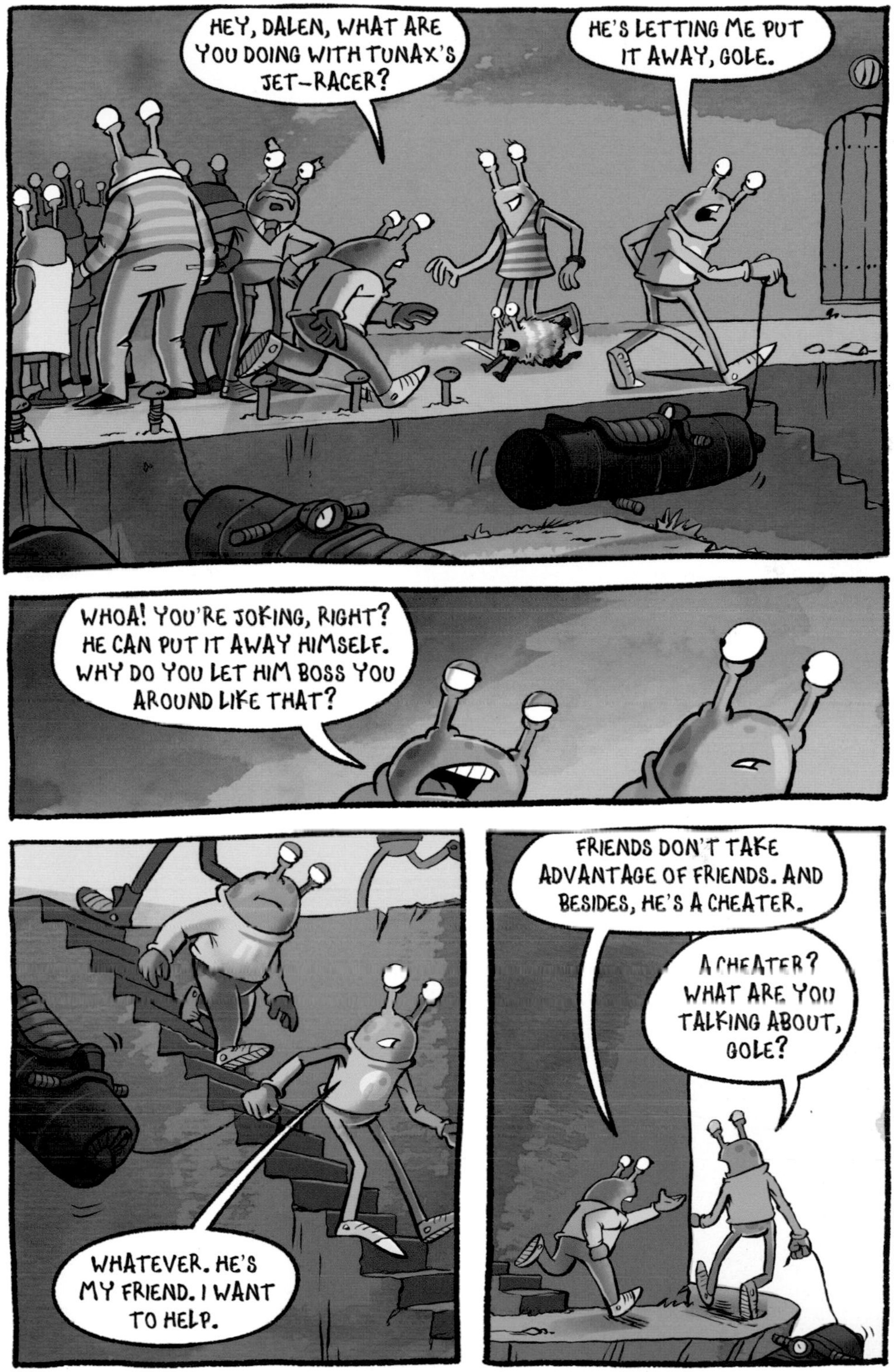
HEY, DALEN, WHAT ARE YOU DOING WITH TUNAX'S JET-RACER?
HE'S LETTING ME PUT IT AWAY, GOLE.
WHOA! YOU'RE JOKING, RIGHT? HE CAN PUT IT AWAY HIMSELF. WHY DO YOU LET HIM BOSS YOU AROUND LIKE THAT?
WHATEVER. HE'S MY FRIEND. I WANT TO HELP.
FRIENDS DON'T TAKE ADVANTAGE OF FRIENDS. AND BESIDES, HE'S A CHEATER.
A CHEATER? WHAT ARE YOU TALKING ABOUT, GOLE?

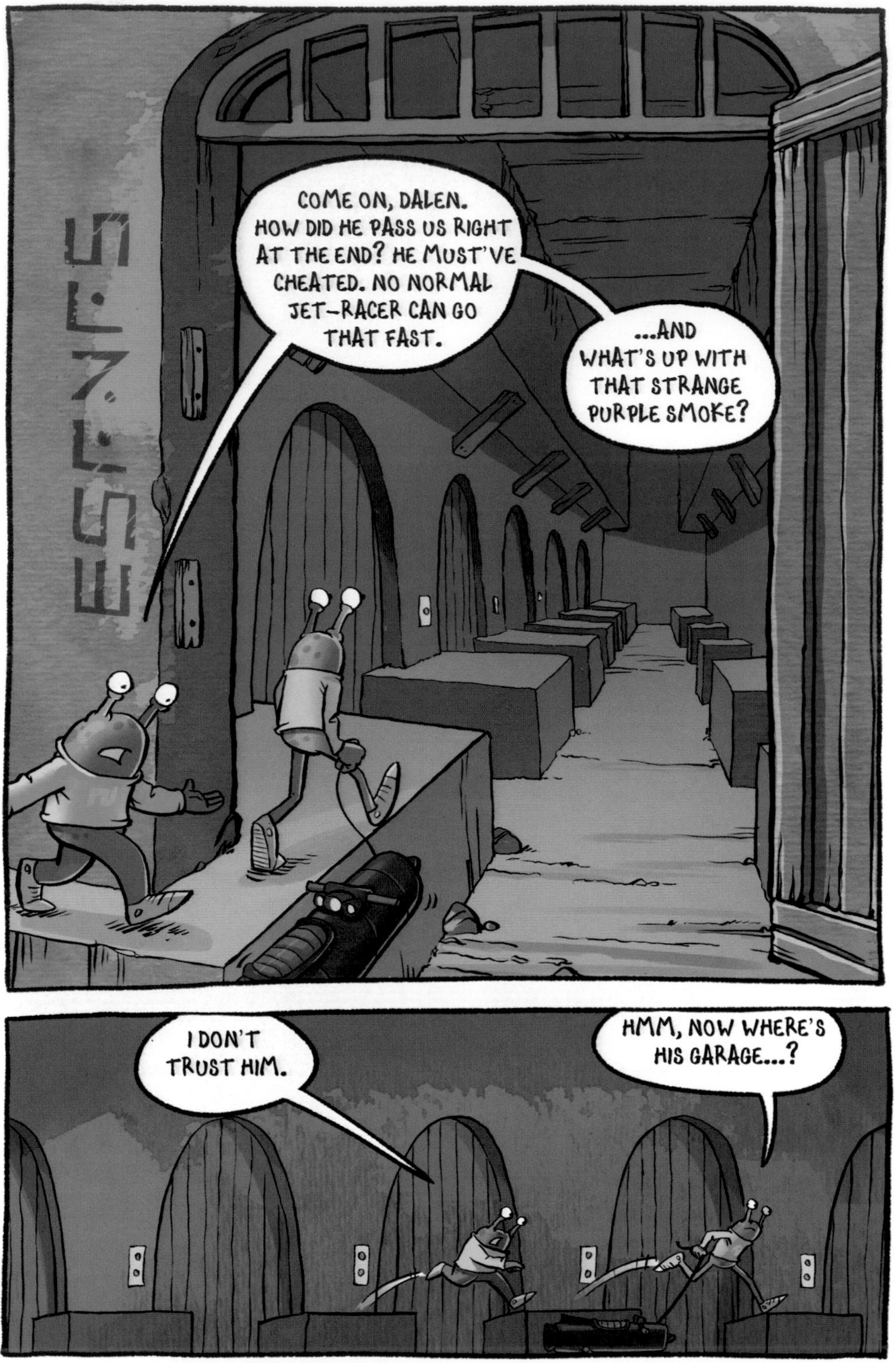
COME ON, DALEN. HOW DID HE PASS US RIGHT AT THE END? HE MUST'VE CHEATED. NO NORMAL JET-RACER CAN GO THAT FAST.
...AND WHAT'S UP WITH THAT STRANGE PURPLE SMOKE?
I DON'T TRUST HIM.
HMM, NOW WHERE'S HIS GARAGE...?

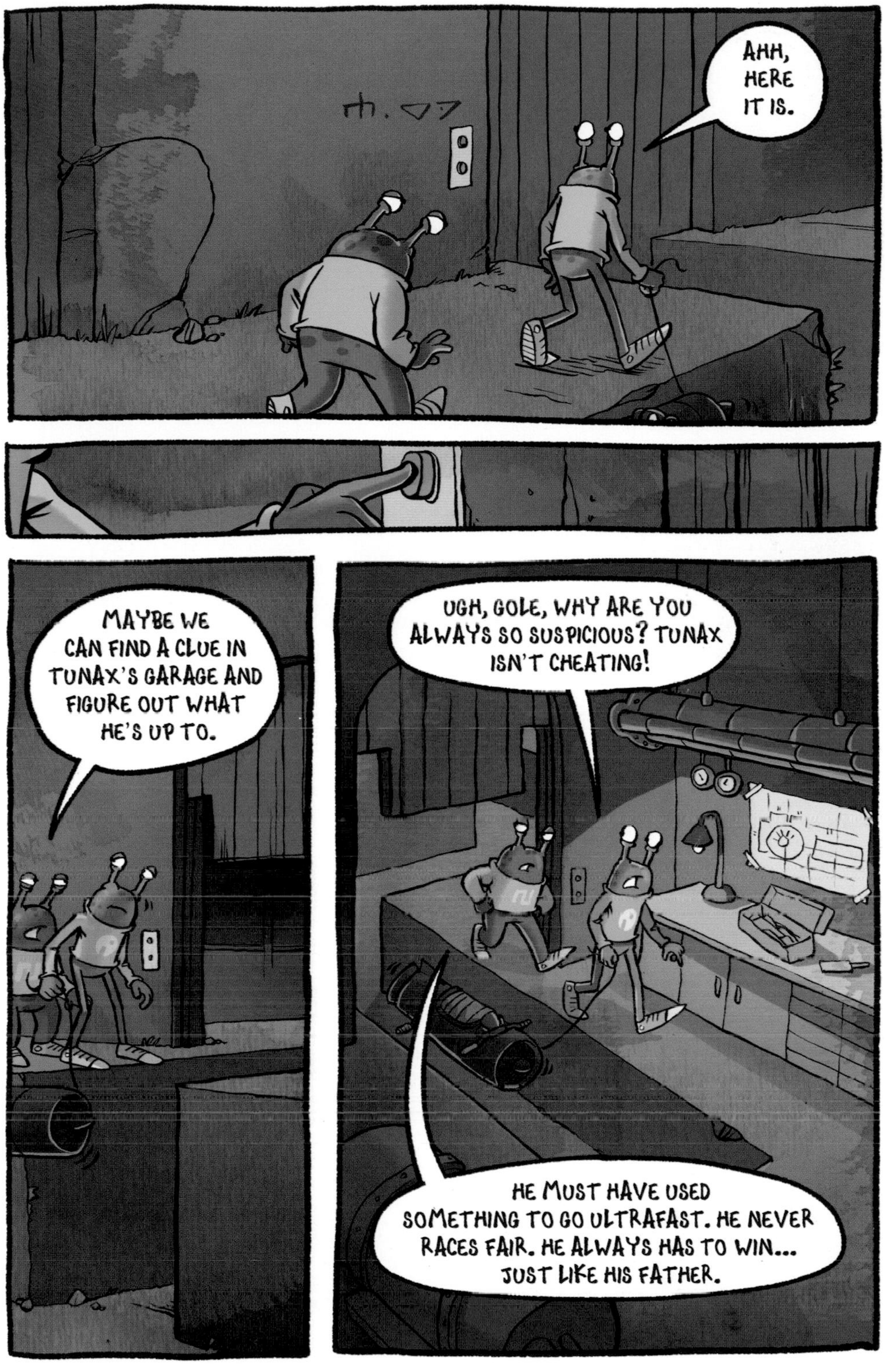
AHH, HERE IT IS.
MAYBE WE CAN FIND A CLUE IN TUNAX'S GARAGE AND FIGURE OUT WHAT HE'S UP TO.
UGH, GOLE, WHY ARE YOU ALWAYS SO SUSPICIOUS? TUNAX ISN'T CHEATING!
HE MUST HAVE USED SOMETHING TO GO ULTRAFAST. HE NEVER RACES FAIR. HE ALWAYS HAS TO WIN... JUST LIKE HIS FATHER.

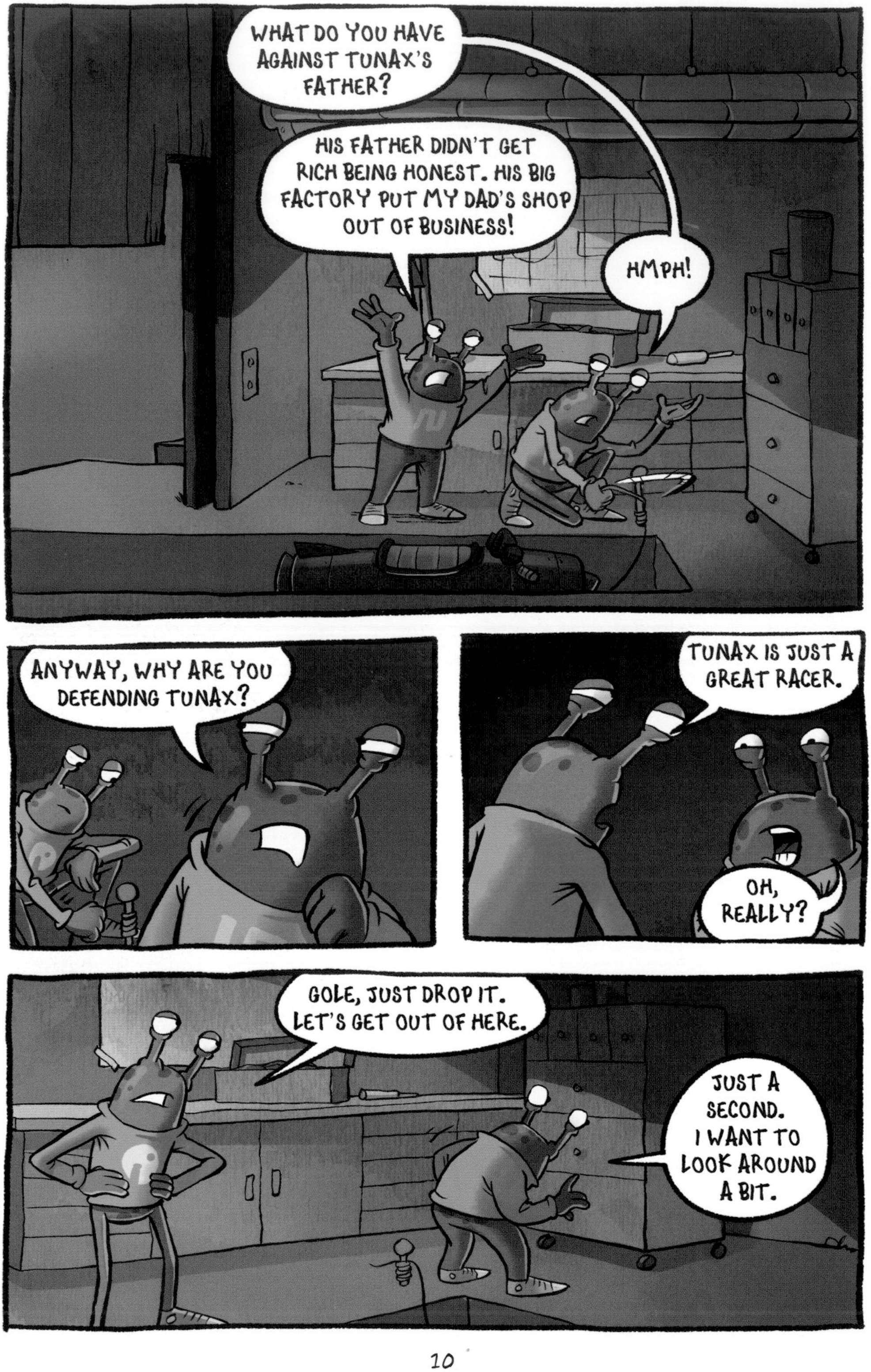
WHAT DO YOU HAVE AGAINST TUNAX'S FATHER?
HIS FATHER DIDN'T GET RICH BEING HONEST. HIS BIG FACTORY PUT MY DAD'S SHOP OUT OF BUSINESS!
HMPH!
ANYWAY, WHY ARE YOU DEFENDING TUNAX?
TUNAX IS JUST A GREAT RACER.
OH, REALLY?
GOLE, JUST DROP IT. LET'S GET OUT OF HERE.
JUST A SECOND. I WANT TO LOOK AROUND A BIT.

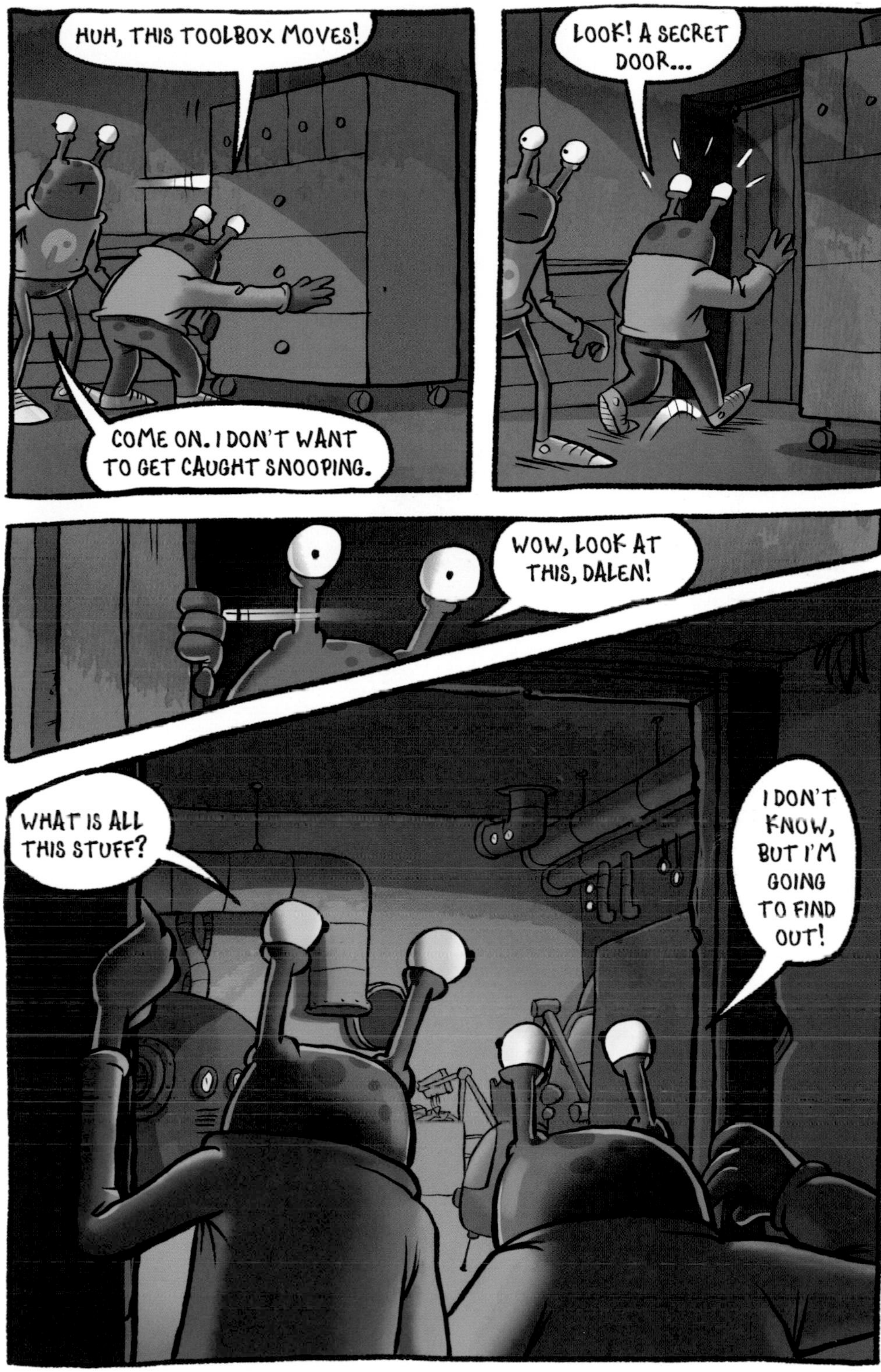
HUH, THIS TOOLBOX MOVES!
COME ON. I DON'T WANT TO GET CAUGHT SNOOPING.
LOOK! A SECRET DOOR...
WOW, LOOK AT THIS, DALEN!
WHAT IS ALL THIS STUFF?
I DON'T KNOW, BUT I'M GOING TO FIND OUT!

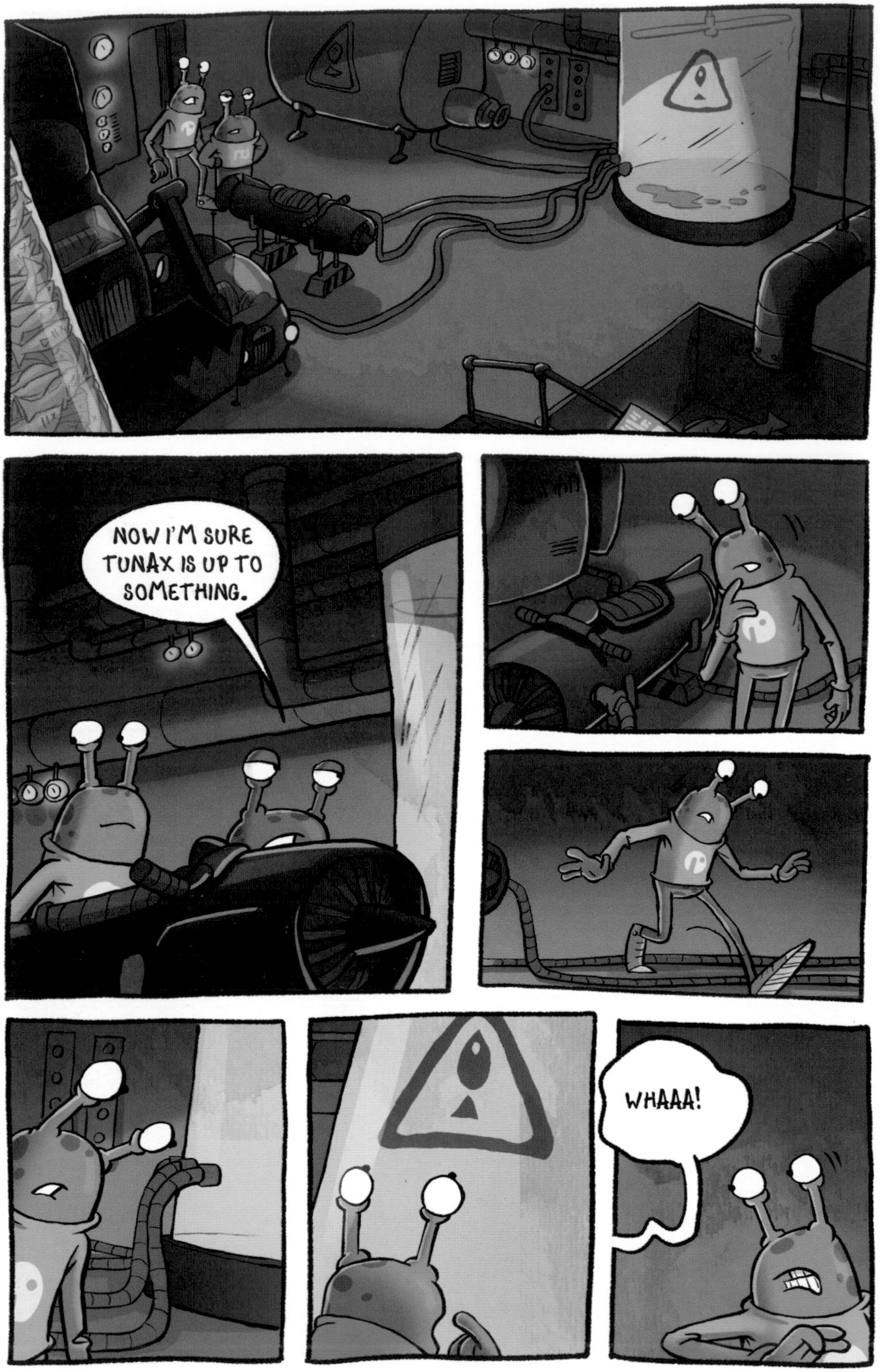
NOW I'M SURE TUNAX IS UP TO SOMETHING.
WHAAA!

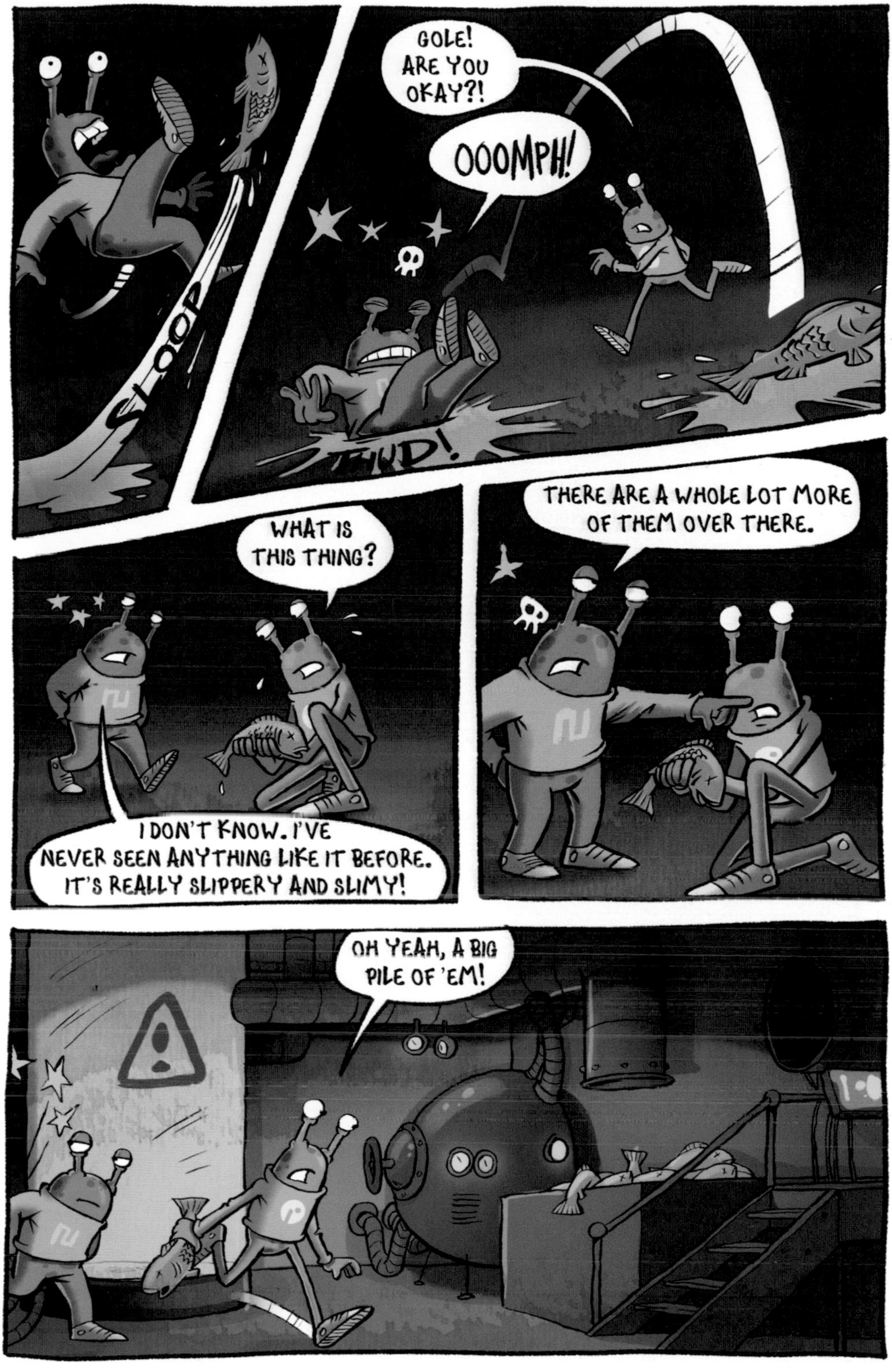
SLOOP
GOLE! ARE YOU OKAY?!
OOOMPH!
THUD!
WHAT IS THIS THING?
I DON'T KNOW. I'VE NEVER SEEN ANYTHING LIKE IT BEFORE. IT'S REALLY SLIPPERY AND SLIMY!
THERE ARE A WHOLE LOT MORE OF THEM OVER THERE.
OH YEAH, A BIG PILE OF 'EM!

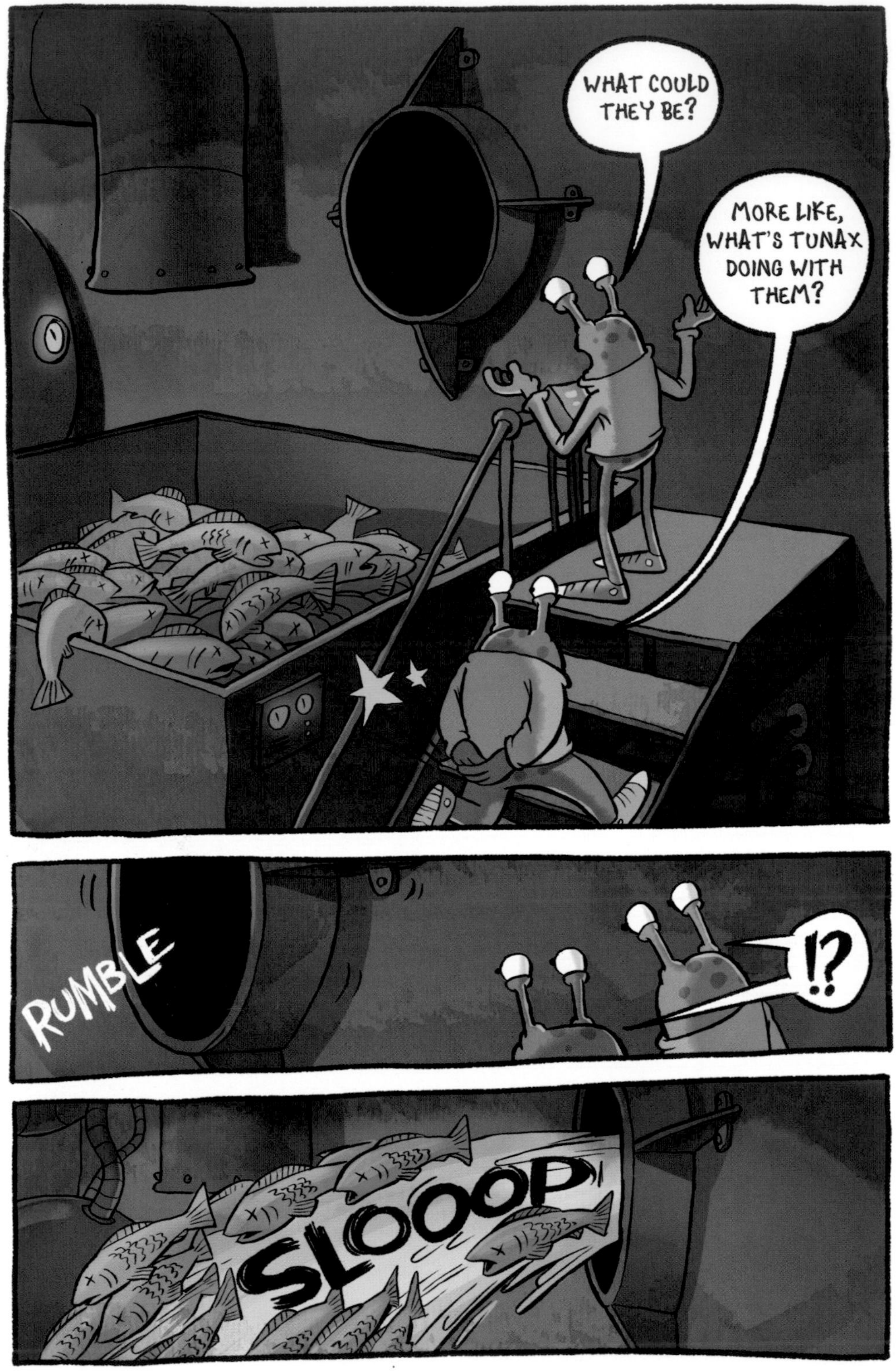
WHAT COULD THEY BE?
MORE LIKE, WHAT'S TUNAX DOING WITH THEM?
RUMBLE
!?
SLOOOP

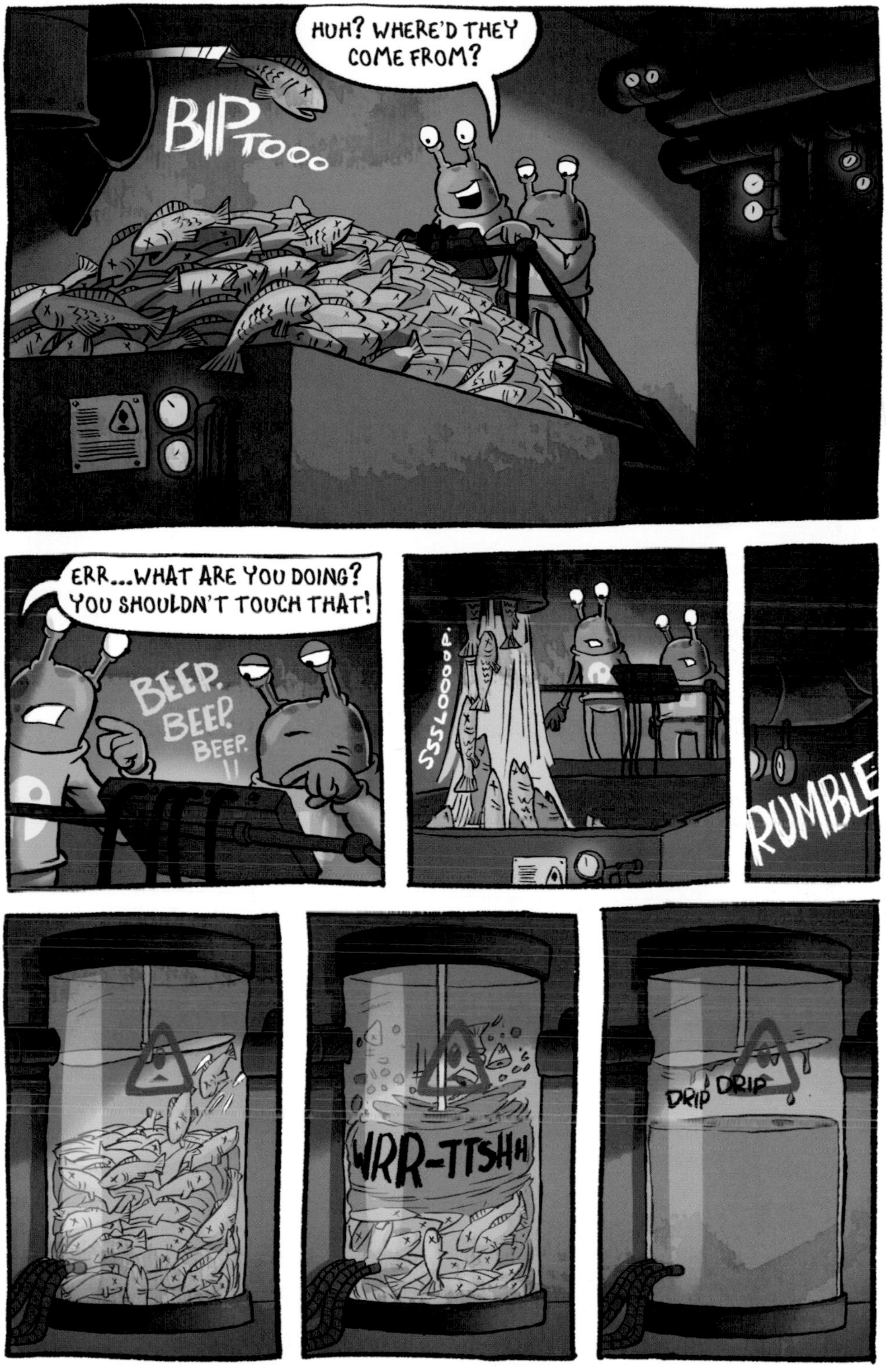

BIPTOOO
HUH? WHERE'D THEY COME FROM?
ERR...WHAT ARE YOU DOING? YOU SHOULDN'T TOUCH THAT!
BEEP. BEEP. BEEP.
SSSLOOOOP.
RUMBLE
WRR-TTSHH
DRIP DRIP

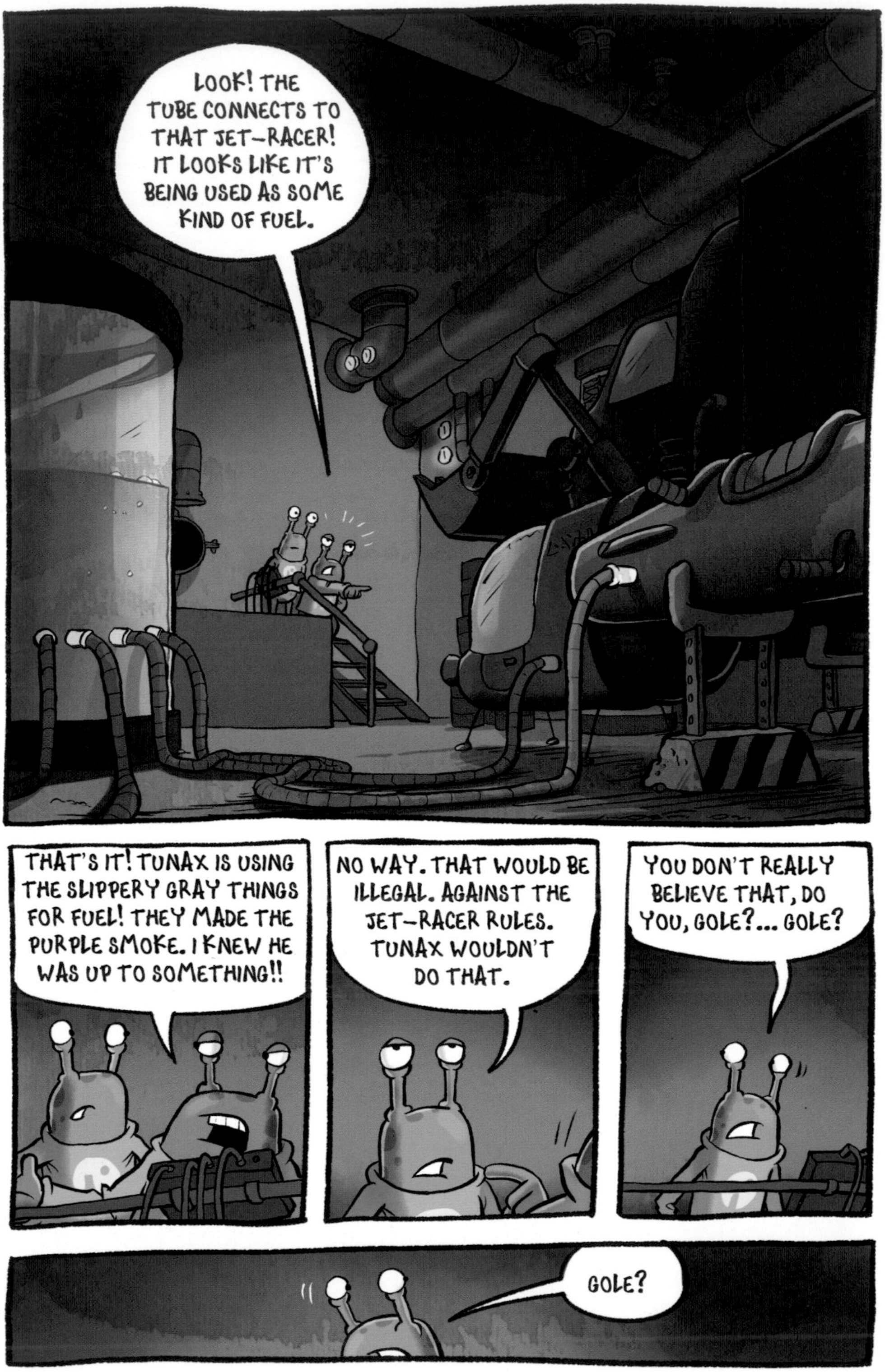
LOOK! THE TUBE CONNECTS TO THAT JET-RACER! IT LOOKS LIKE IT'S BEING USED AS SOME KIND OF FUEL.
THAT'S IT! TUNAX IS USING THE SLIPPERY GRAY THINGS FOR FUEL! THEY MADE THE PURPLE SMOKE. I KNEW HE WAS UP TO SOMETHING!!
NO WAY. THAT WOULD BE ILLEGAL. AGAINST THE JET-RACER RULES. TUNAX WOULDN'T DO THAT.
YOU DON'T REALLY BELIEVE THAT, DO YOU, GOLE?... GOLE?
GOLE?

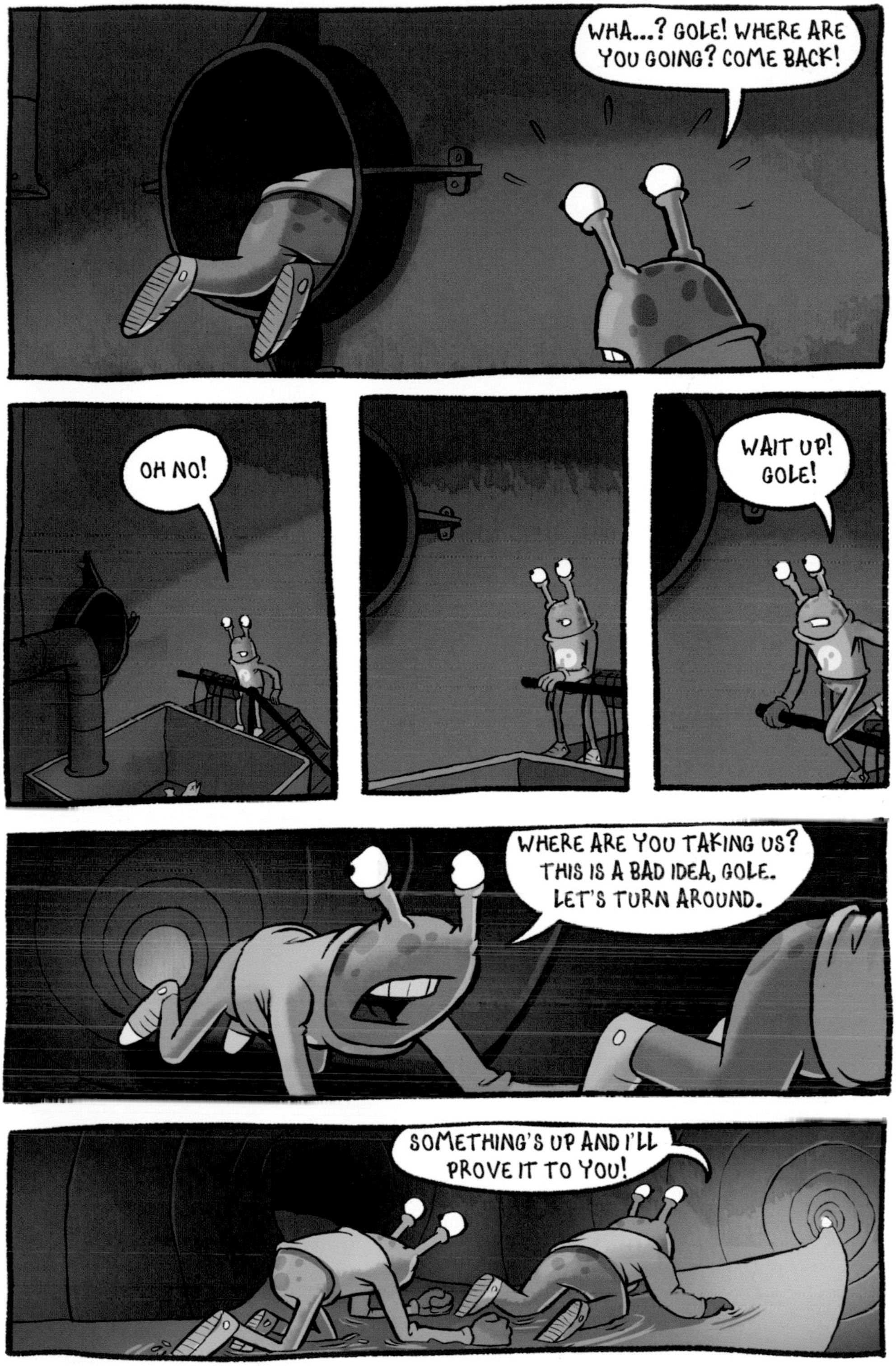
WHA...? GOLE! WHERE ARE YOU GOING? COME BACK!
OH NO!
WAIT UP! GOLE!
WHERE ARE YOU TAKING US? THIS IS A BAD IDEA, GOLE. LET'S TURN AROUND.
SOMETHING'S UP AND I'LL PROVE IT TO YOU!

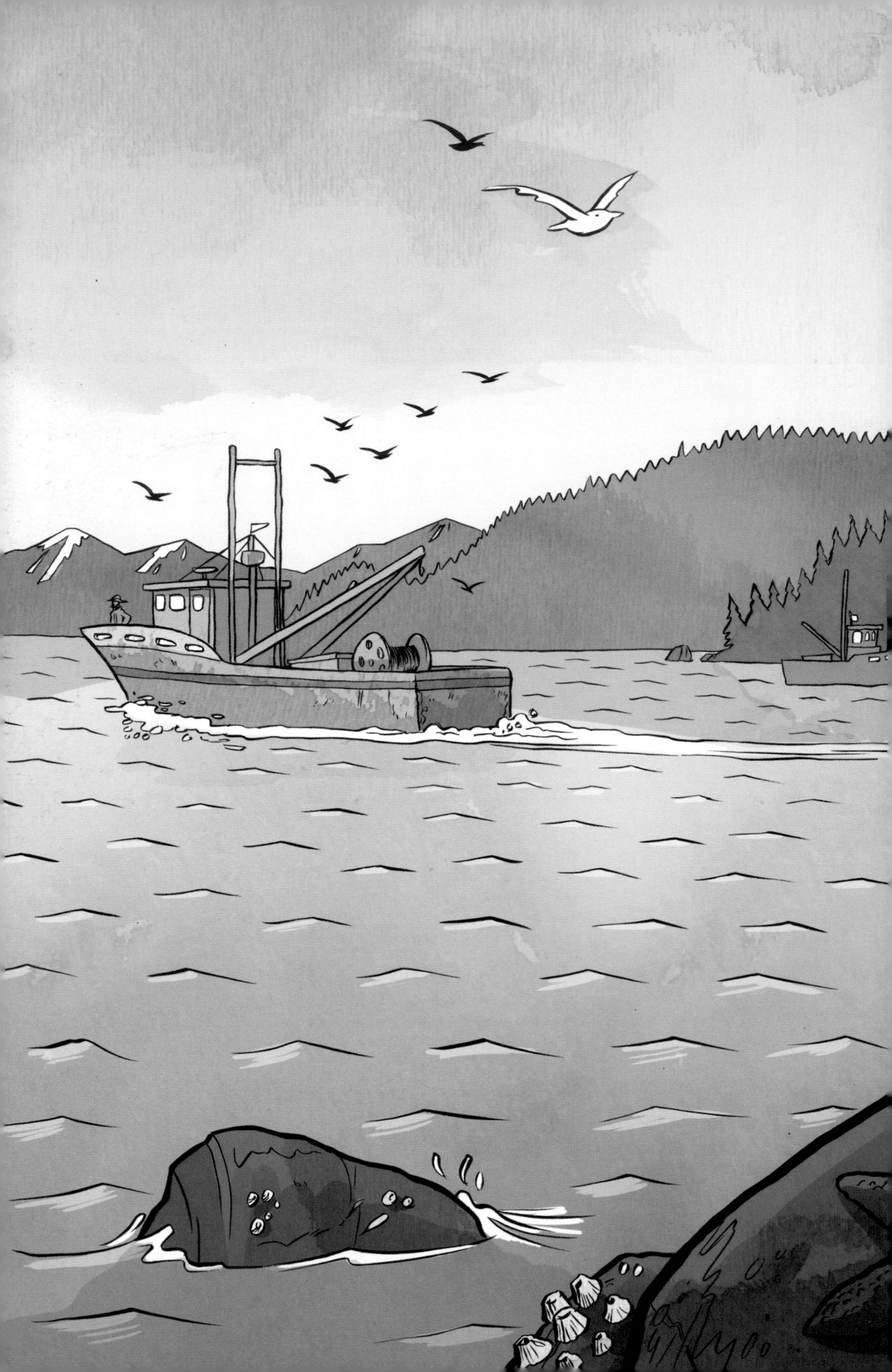

CHAPTER 2

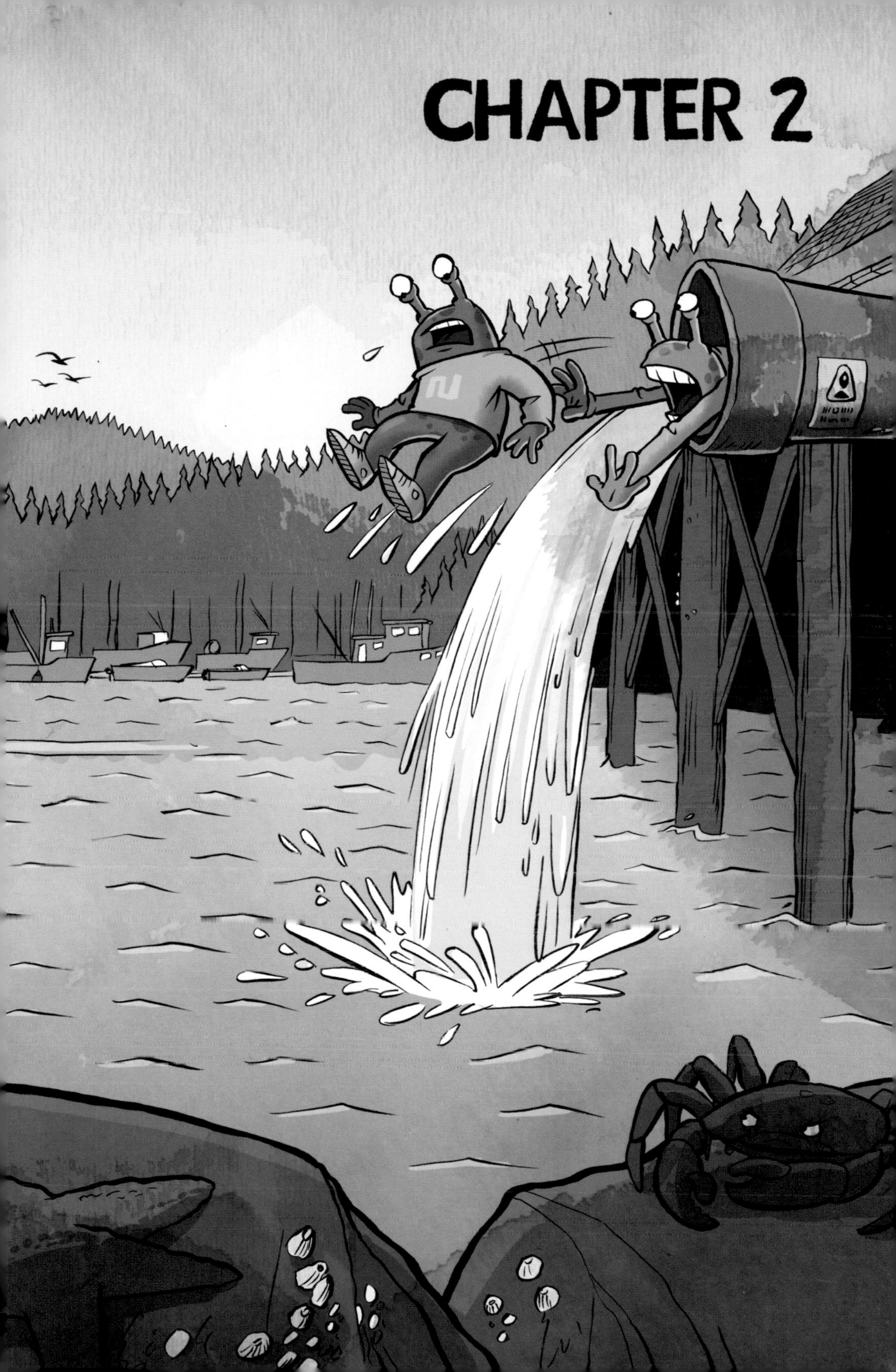

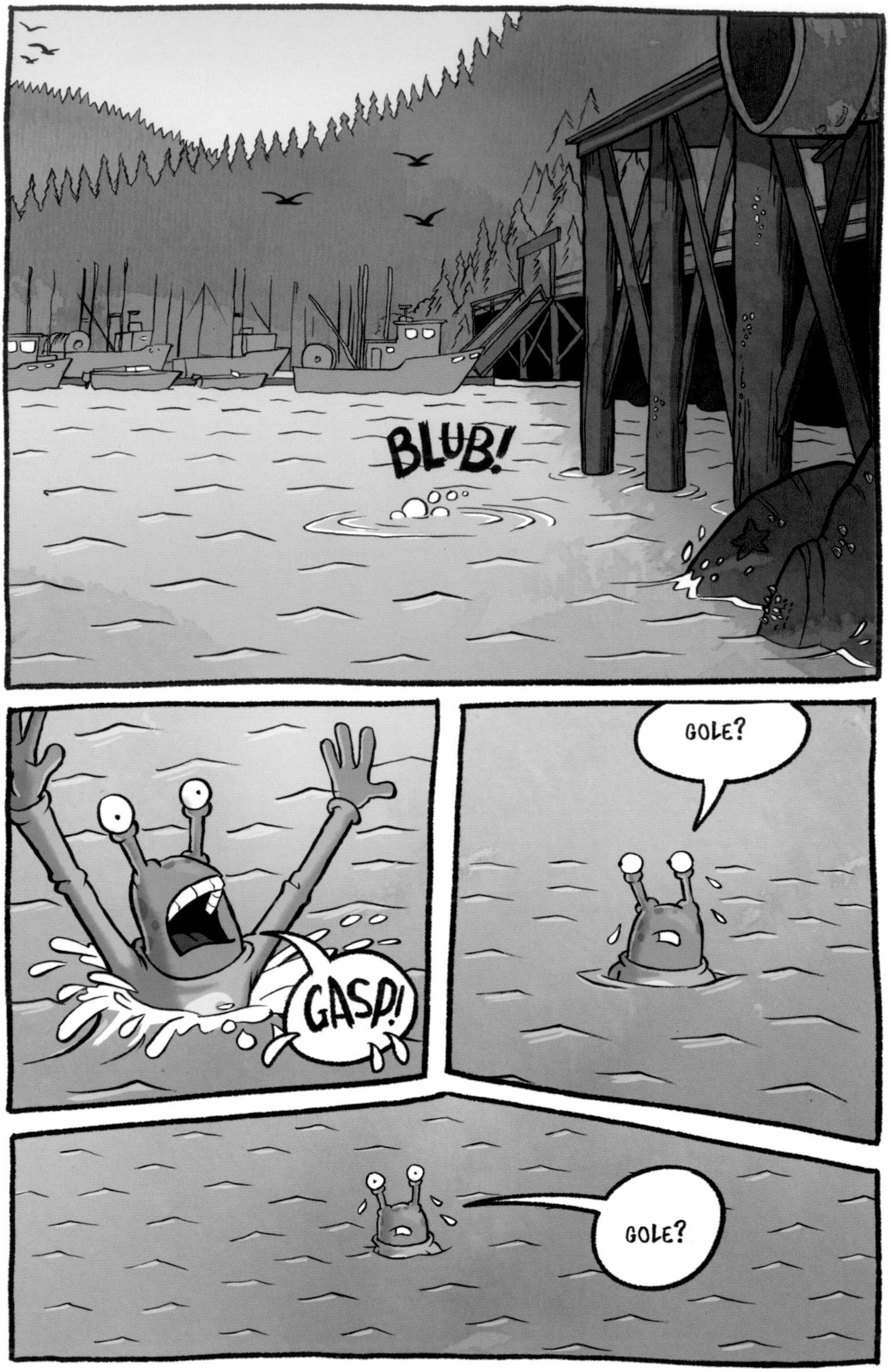
BLUB!
GASP!
GOLE?
GOLE?

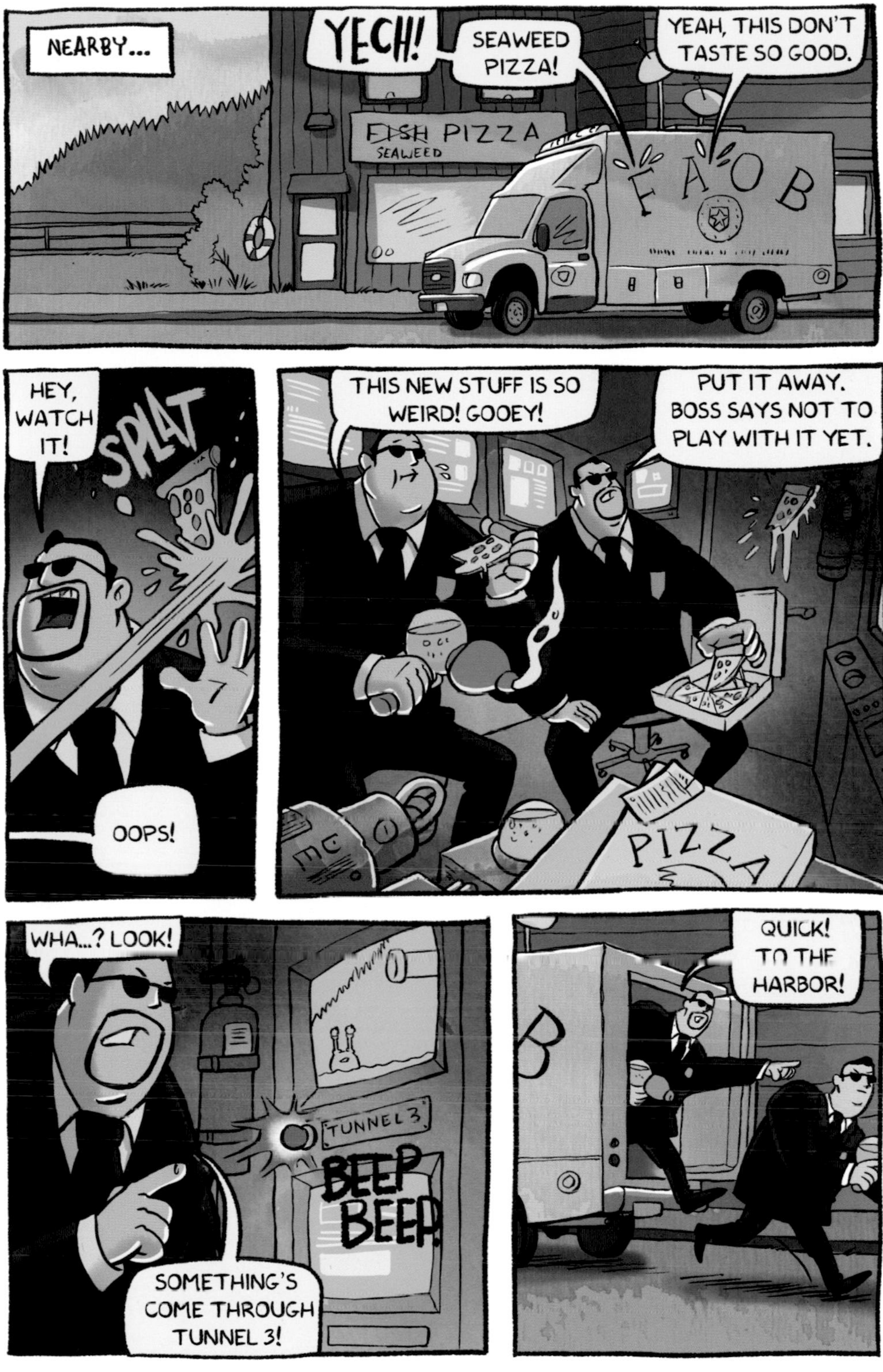
NEARBY...
YECH!
SEAWEED PIZZA!
YEAH, THIS DON'T TASTE SO GOOD.
FISH PIZZA
SEAWEED
F A O B
HEY, WATCH IT!
SPLAT
OOPS!
THIS NEW STUFF IS SO WEIRD! GOOEY!
PUT IT AWAY. BOSS SAYS NOT TO PLAY WITH IT YET.
PIZZA
WHA...? LOOK!
TUNNEL 3
BEEP BEEP
SOMETHING'S COME THROUGH TUNNEL 3!
QUICK! TO THE HARBOR!
B

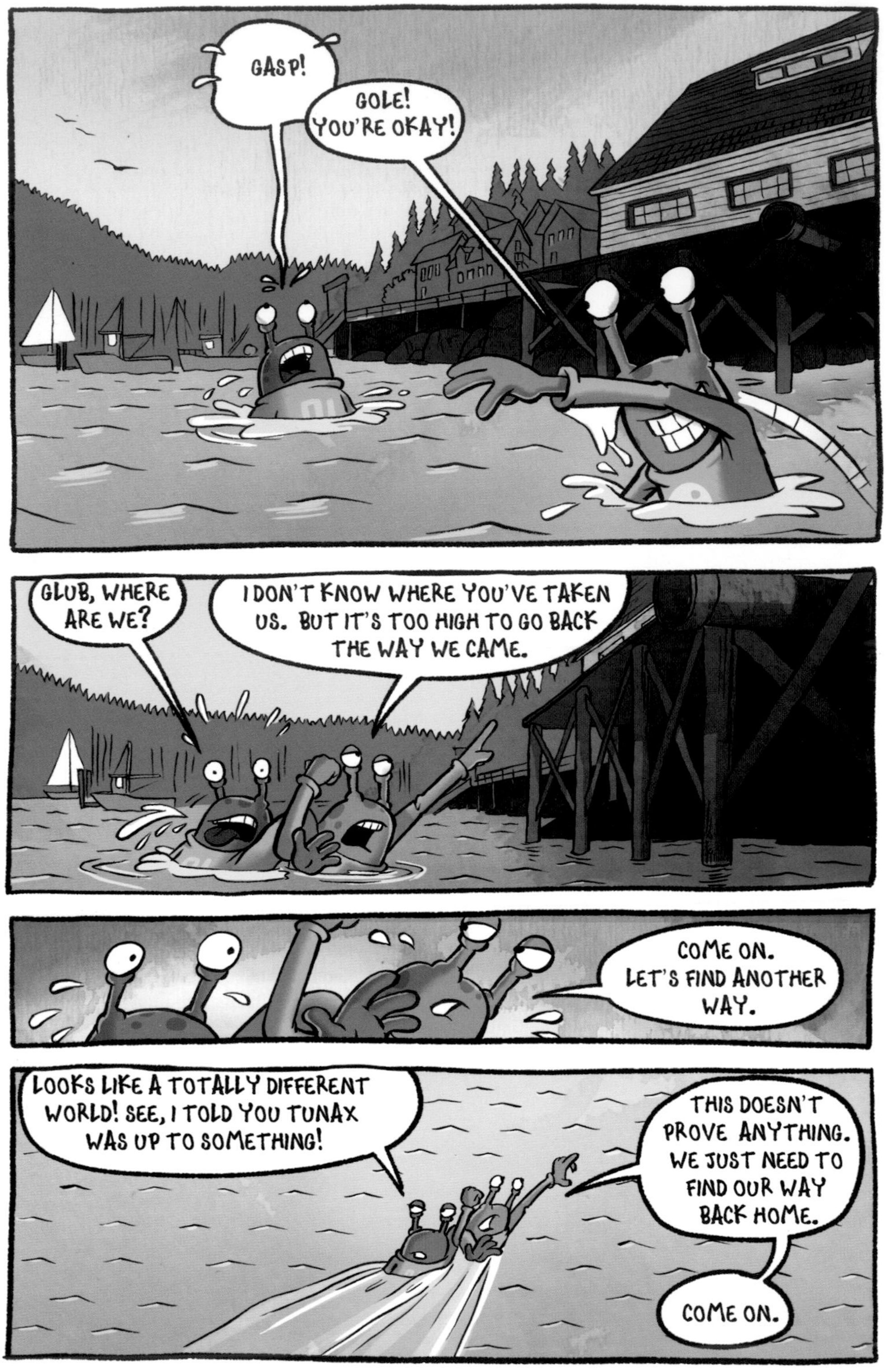
GASP!
GOLE! YOU'RE OKAY!
GLUB, WHERE ARE WE?
I DON'T KNOW WHERE YOU'VE TAKEN US. BUT IT'S TOO HIGH TO GO BACK THE WAY WE CAME.
COME ON. LET'S FIND ANOTHER WAY.
LOOKS LIKE A TOTALLY DIFFERENT WORLD! SEE, I TOLD YOU TUNAX WAS UP TO SOMETHING!
THIS DOESN'T PROVE ANYTHING. WE JUST NEED TO FIND OUR WAY BACK HOME.
COME ON.

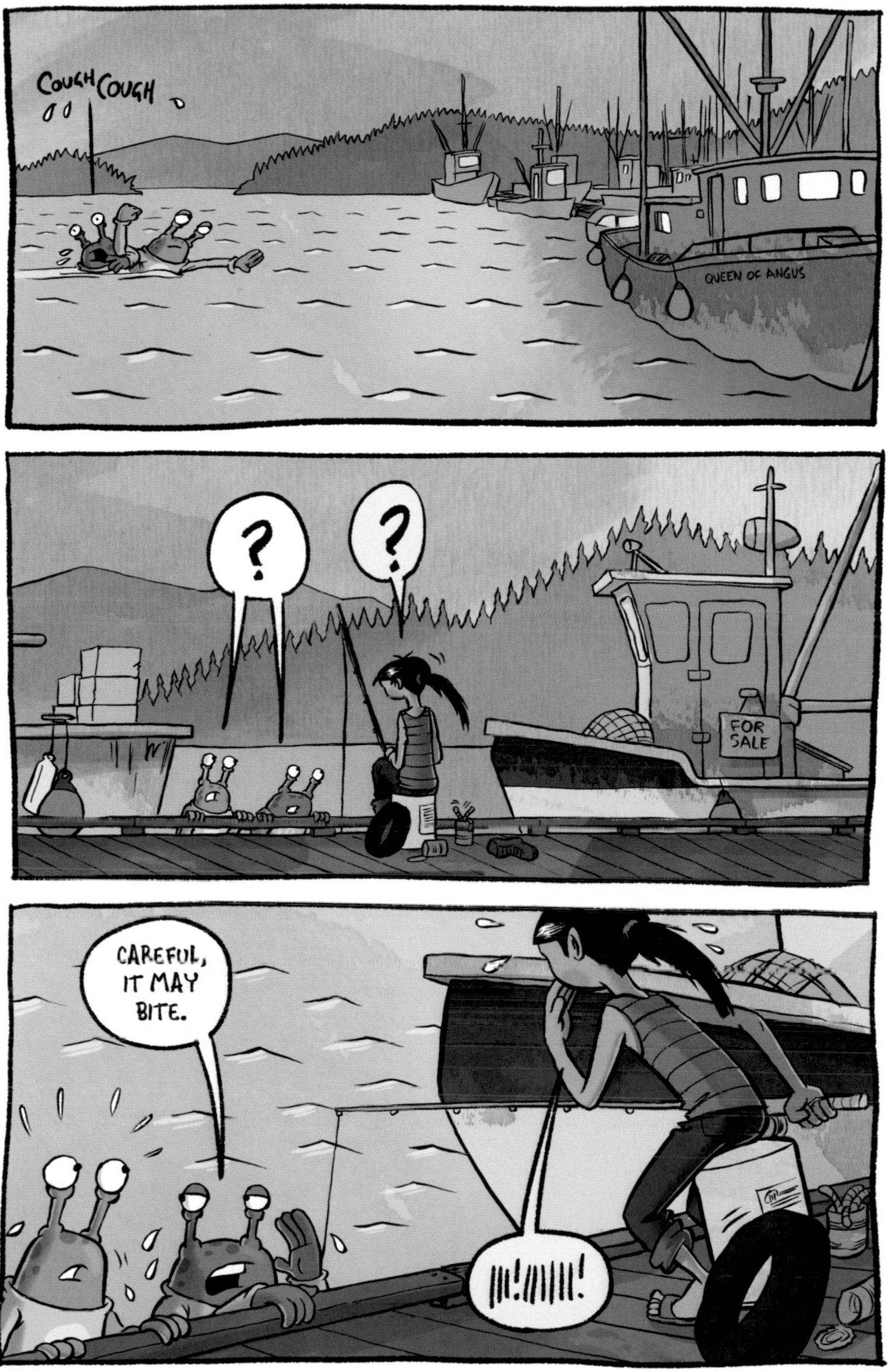
COUGH COUGH
QUEEN OF ANGUS
?
?
FOR SALE
CAREFUL, IT MAY BITE.

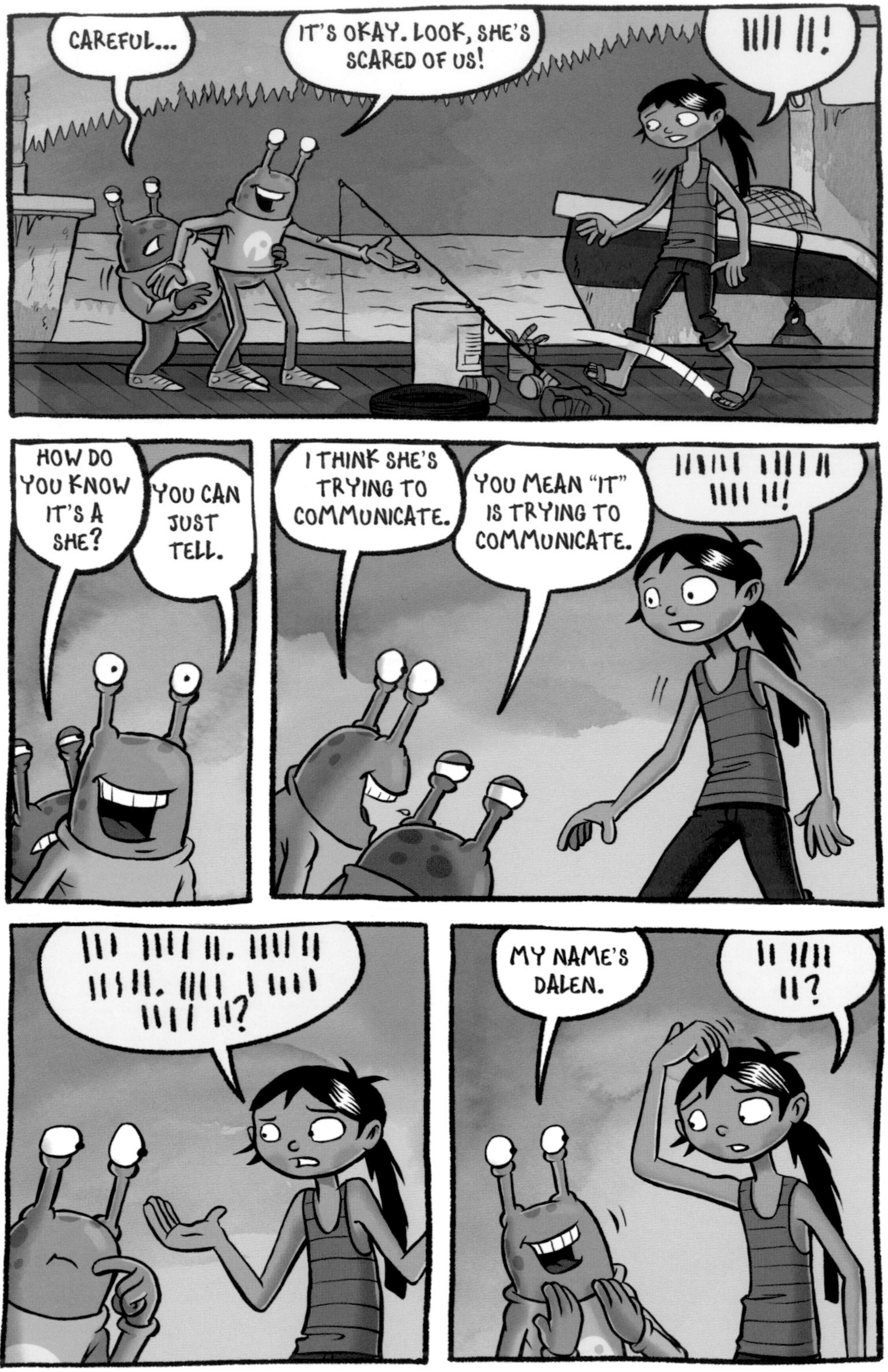
CAREFUL...
IT'S OKAY. LOOK, SHE'S SCARED OF US!
IIII II!
HOW DO YOU KNOW IT'S A SHE?
YOU CAN JUST TELL.
I THINK SHE'S TRYING TO COMMUNICATE.
YOU MEAN "IT" IS TRYING TO COMMUNICATE.
IIIIII IIIII IIII II!
III IIII II. IIIII II IIIII. IIII IIIII IIII II?
MY NAME'S DALEN.
II IIII II?

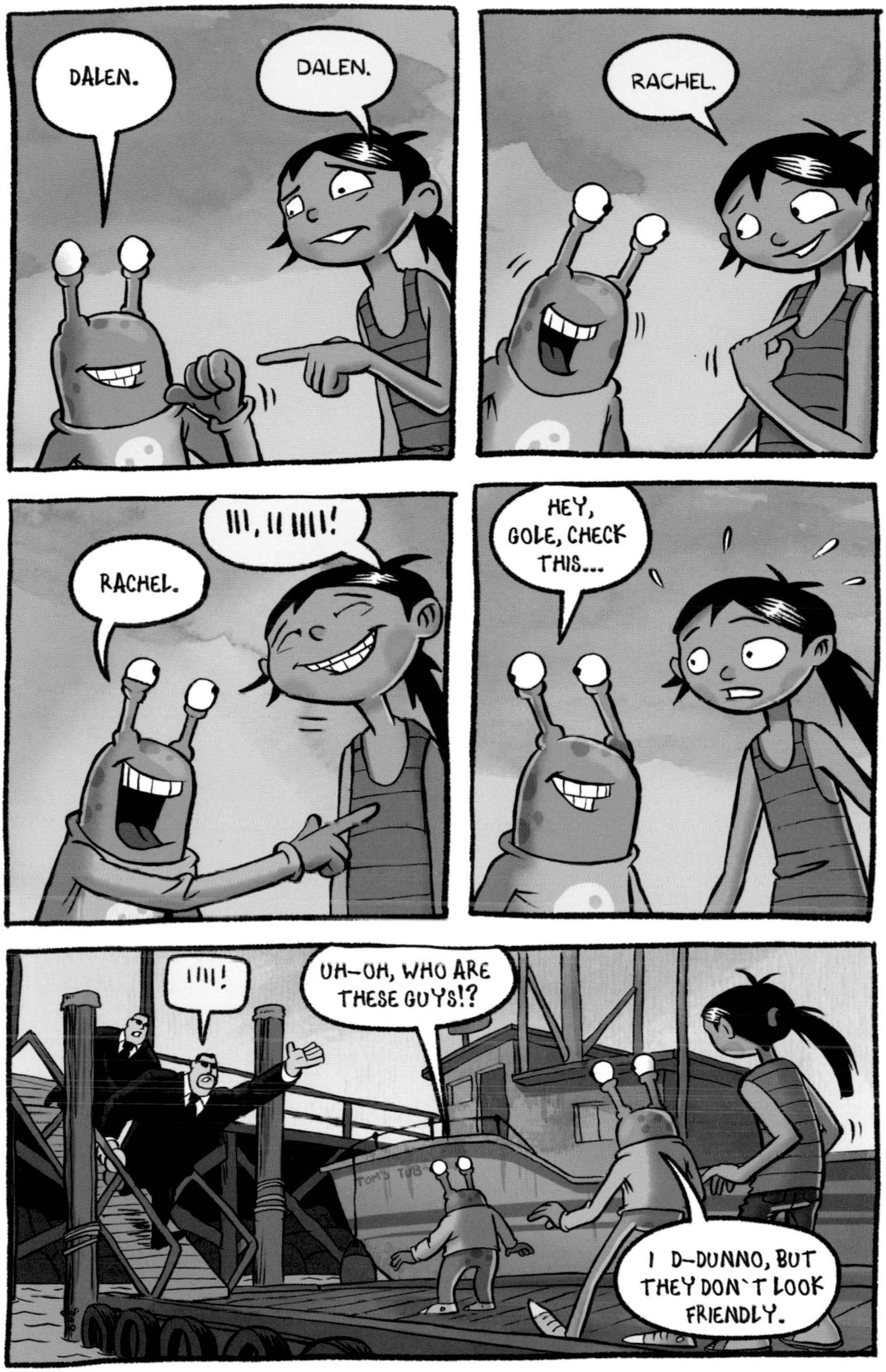
DALEN.
DALEN.
RACHEL.
RACHEL.
|||, || ||||!
HEY, GOLE, CHECK THIS...
||||!
UH-OH, WHO ARE THESE GUYS!?
TOM'S TUB
I D-DUNNO, BUT THEY DON'T LOOK FRIENDLY.

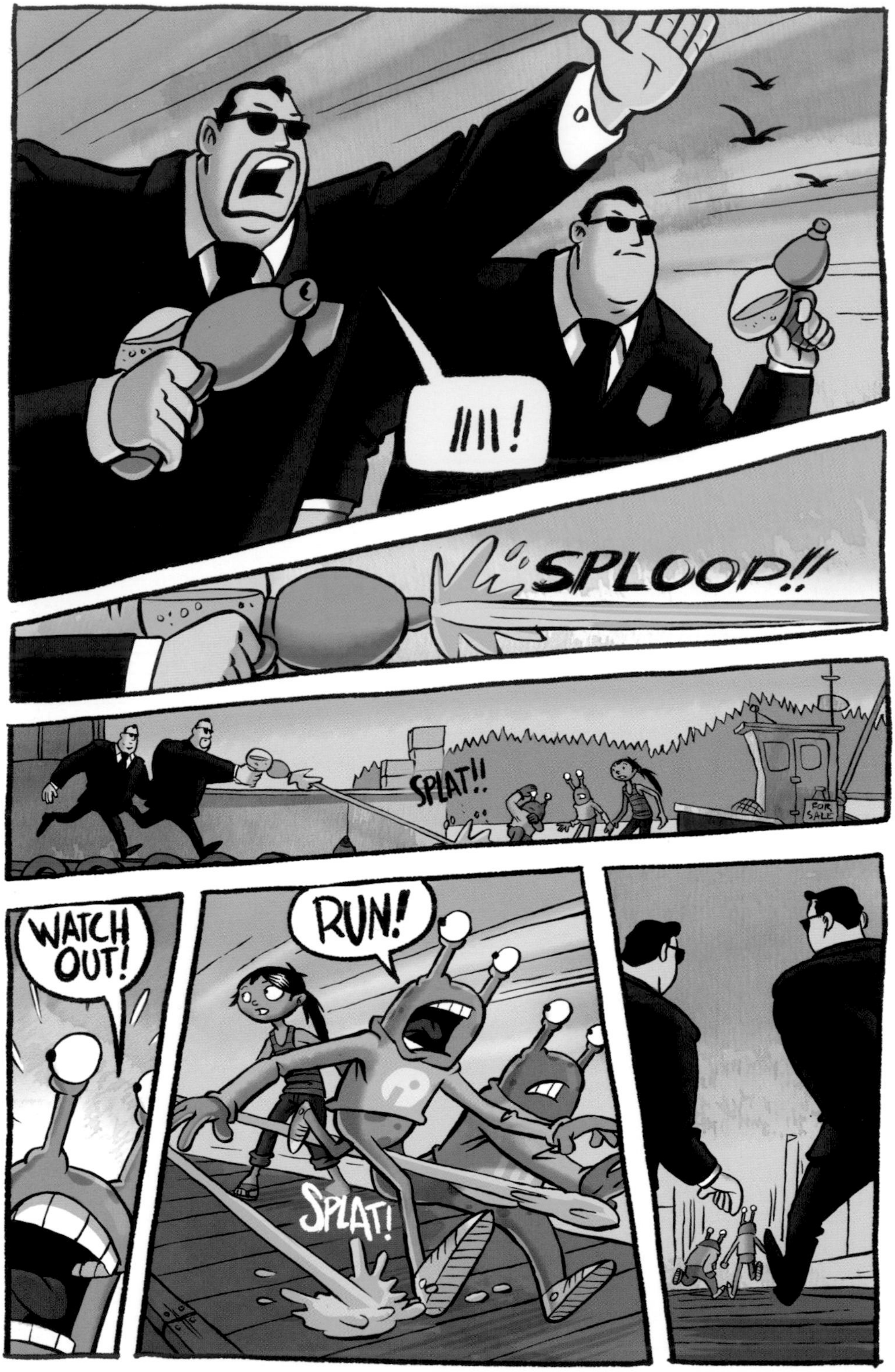

!!!!!
SPLOOP!!
SPLAT!!
FOR SALE
WATCH OUT!
RUN!
SPLAT!

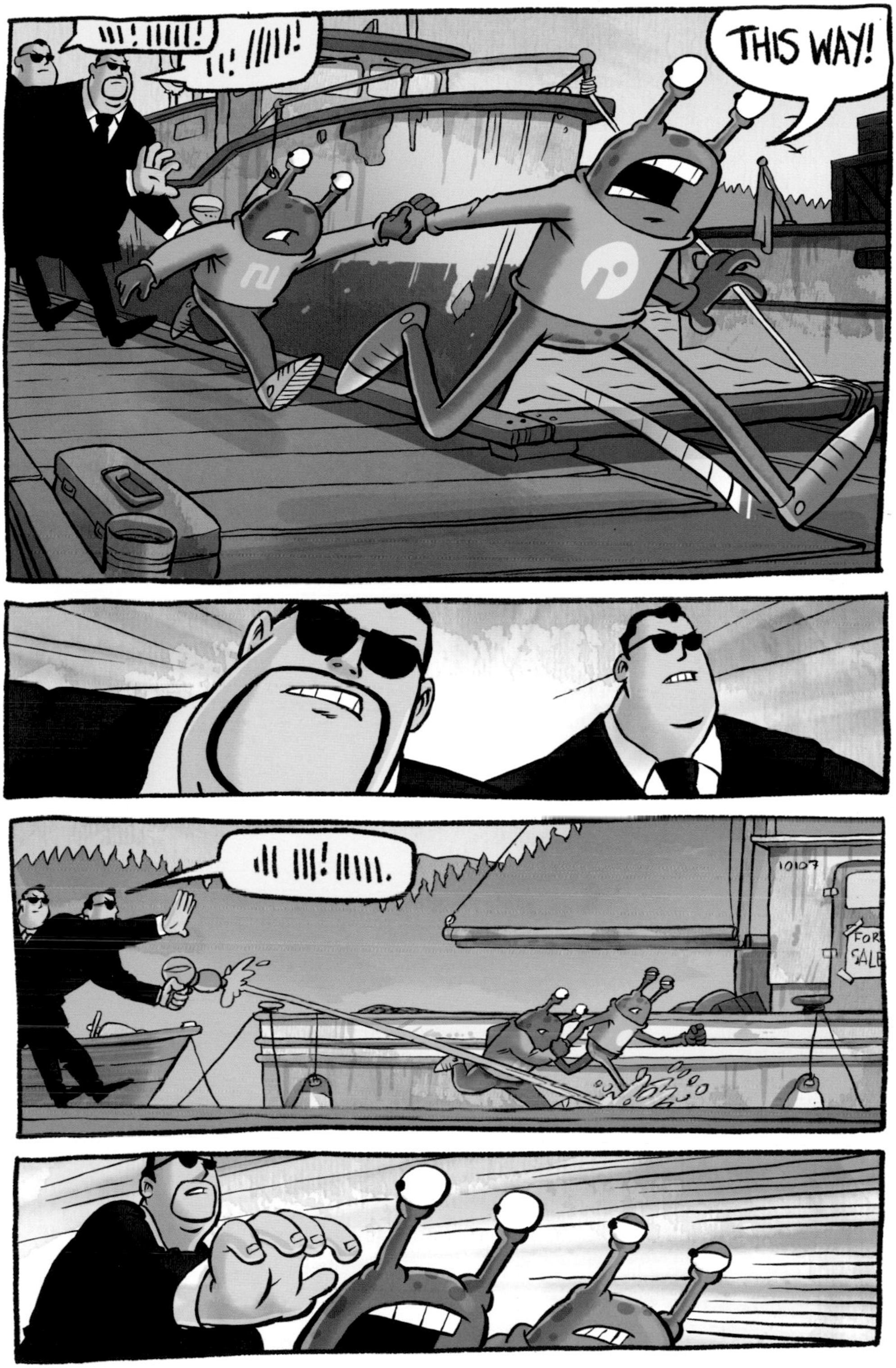
THIS WAY!
10107

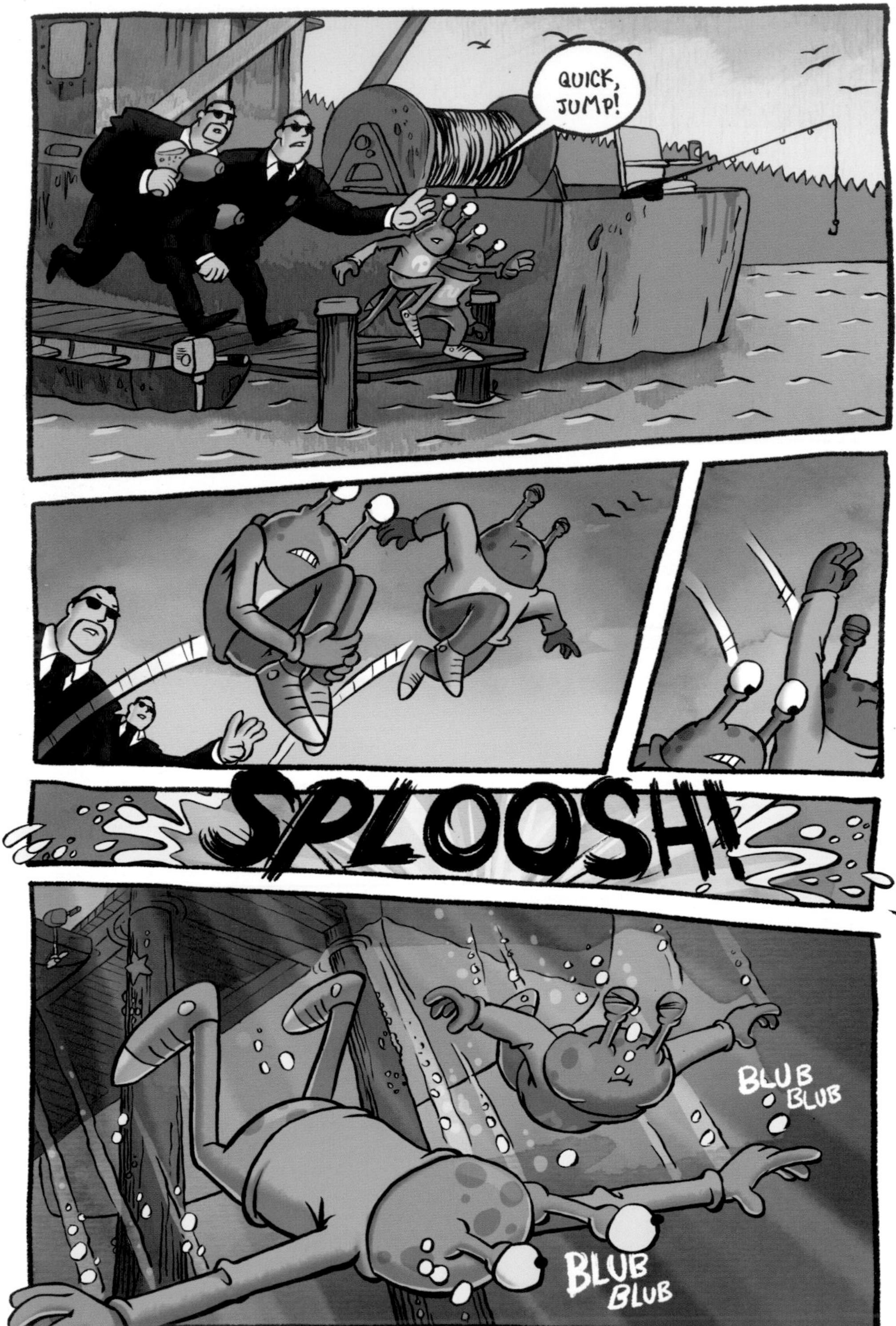
QUICK, JUMP!
SPLOOSH!
BLUB BLUB
BLUB BLUB

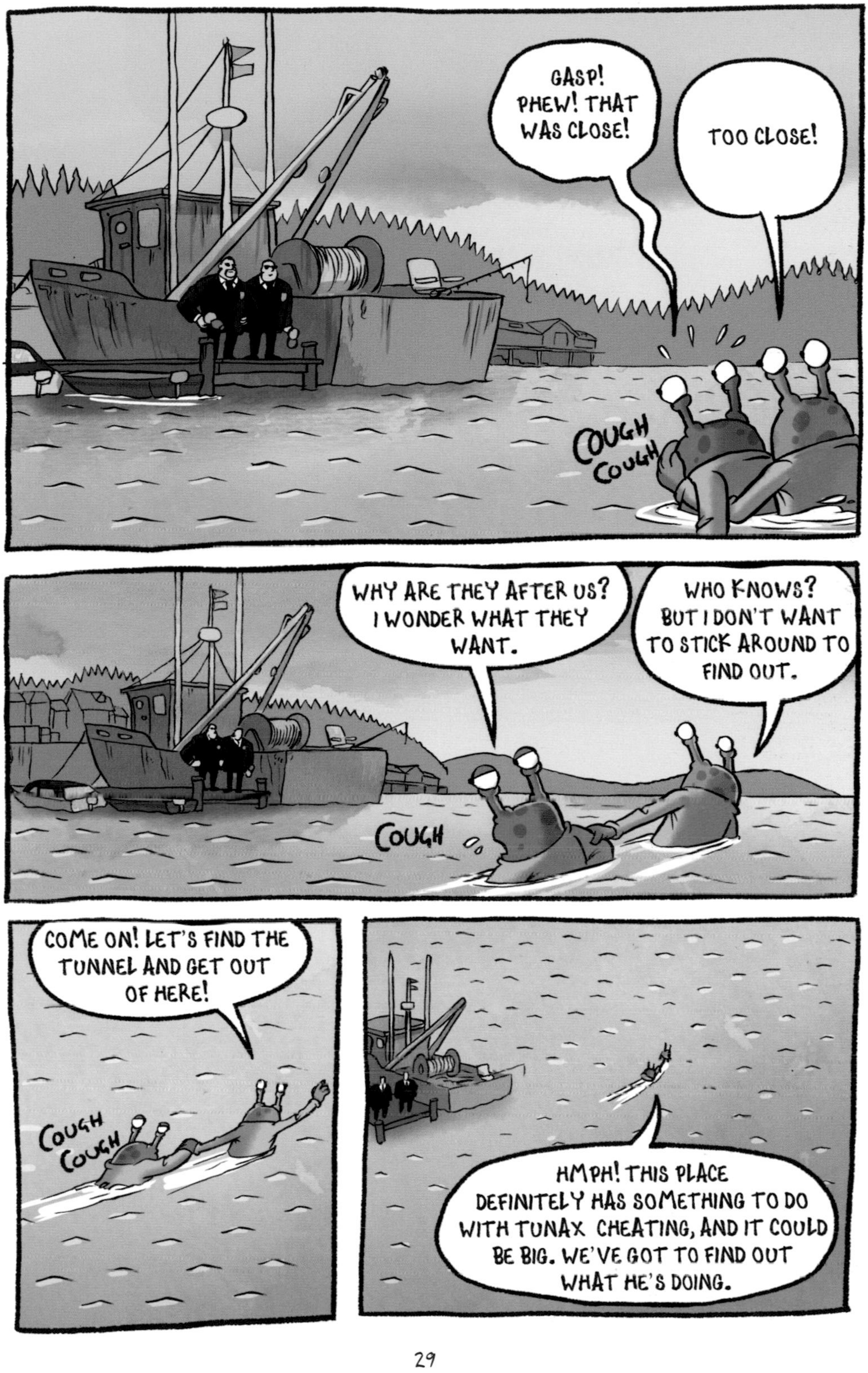
GASP! PHEW! THAT WAS CLOSE!
TOO CLOSE!
COUGH COUGH
WHY ARE THEY AFTER US? I WONDER WHAT THEY WANT.
WHO KNOWS? BUT I DON'T WANT TO STICK AROUND TO FIND OUT.
COUGH
COME ON! LET'S FIND THE TUNNEL AND GET OUT OF HERE!
COUGH COUGH
HMPH! THIS PLACE DEFINITELY HAS SOMETHING TO DO WITH TUNAX CHEATING, AND IT COULD BE BIG. WE'VE GOT TO FIND OUT WHAT HE'S DOING.

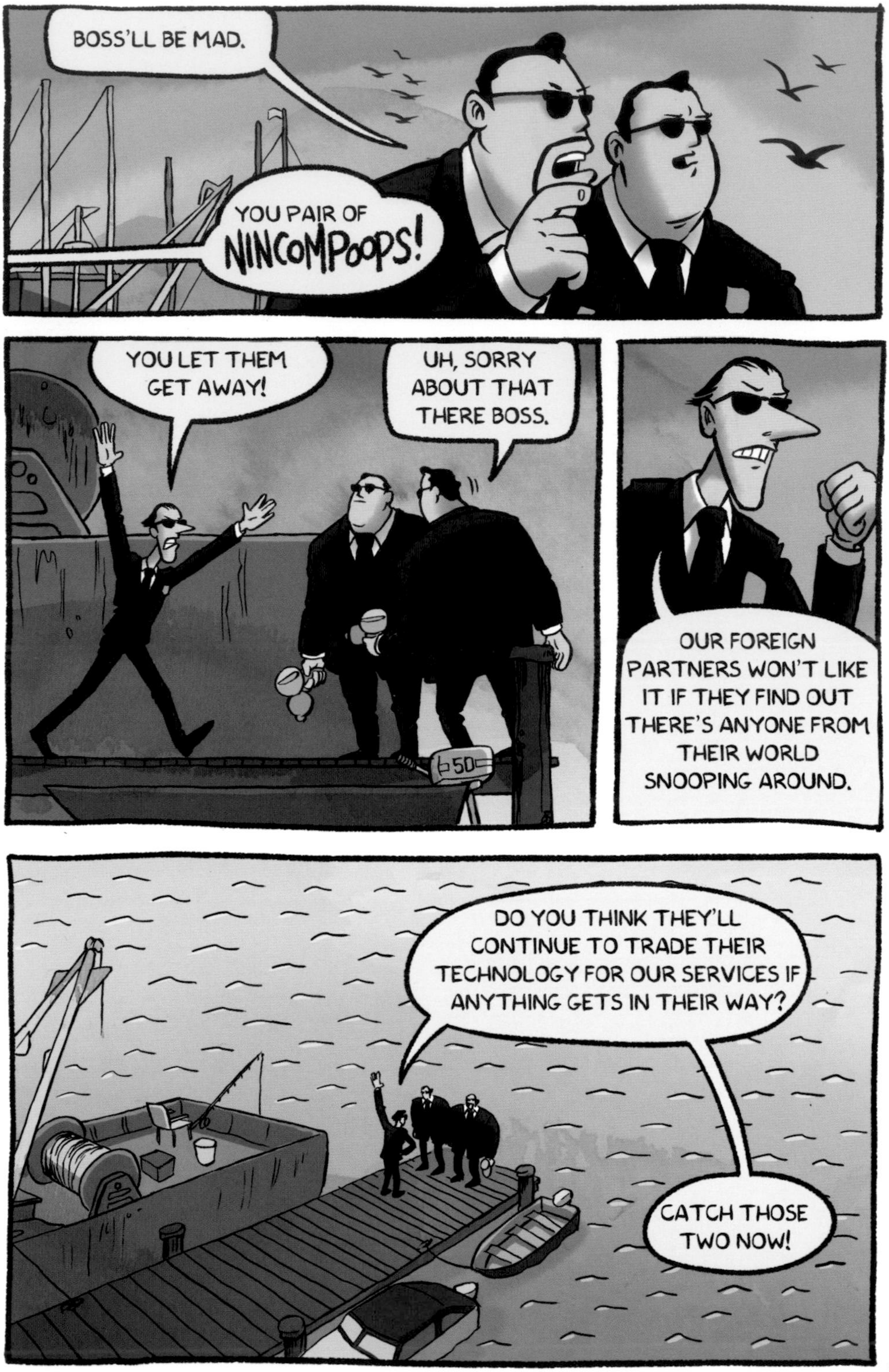
BOSS'LL BE MAD.
YOU PAIR OF NINCOMPOOPS!
YOU LET THEM GET AWAY!
UH, SORRY ABOUT THAT THERE BOSS.
OUR FOREIGN PARTNERS WON'T LIKE IT IF THEY FIND OUT THERE'S ANYONE FROM THEIR WORLD SNOOPING AROUND.
DO YOU THINK THEY'LL CONTINUE TO TRADE THEIR TECHNOLOGY FOR OUR SERVICES IF ANYTHING GETS IN THEIR WAY?
CATCH THOSE TWO NOW!

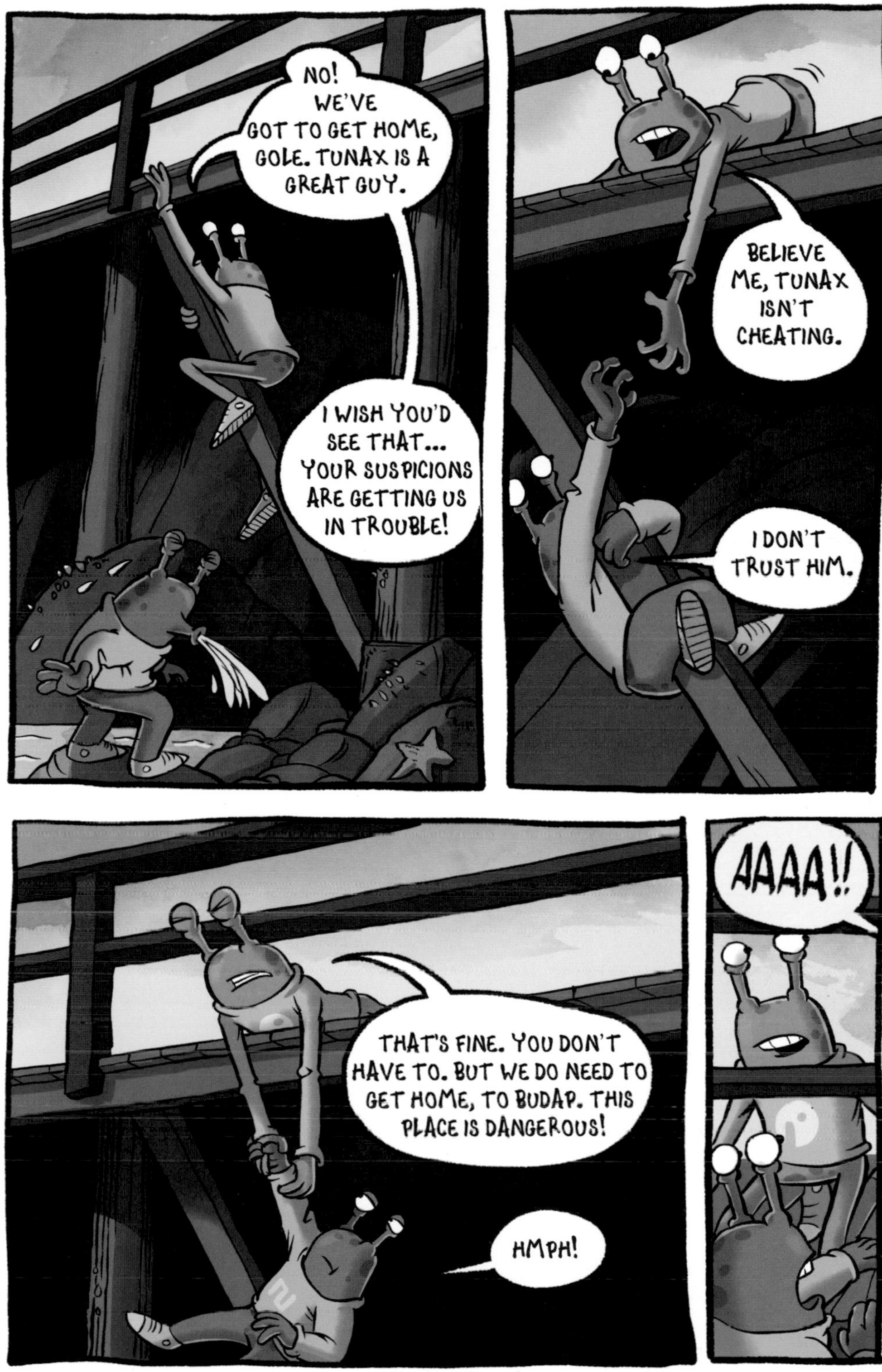
NO! WE'VE GOT TO GET HOME, GOLE. TUNAX IS A GREAT GUY.
I WISH YOU'D SEE THAT... YOUR SUSPICIONS ARE GETTING US IN TROUBLE!
BELIEVE ME, TUNAX ISN'T CHEATING.
I DON'T TRUST HIM.
THAT'S FINE. YOU DON'T HAVE TO. BUT WE DO NEED TO GET HOME, TO BUDAP. THIS PLACE IS DANGEROUS!
HMPH!
AAAA!!

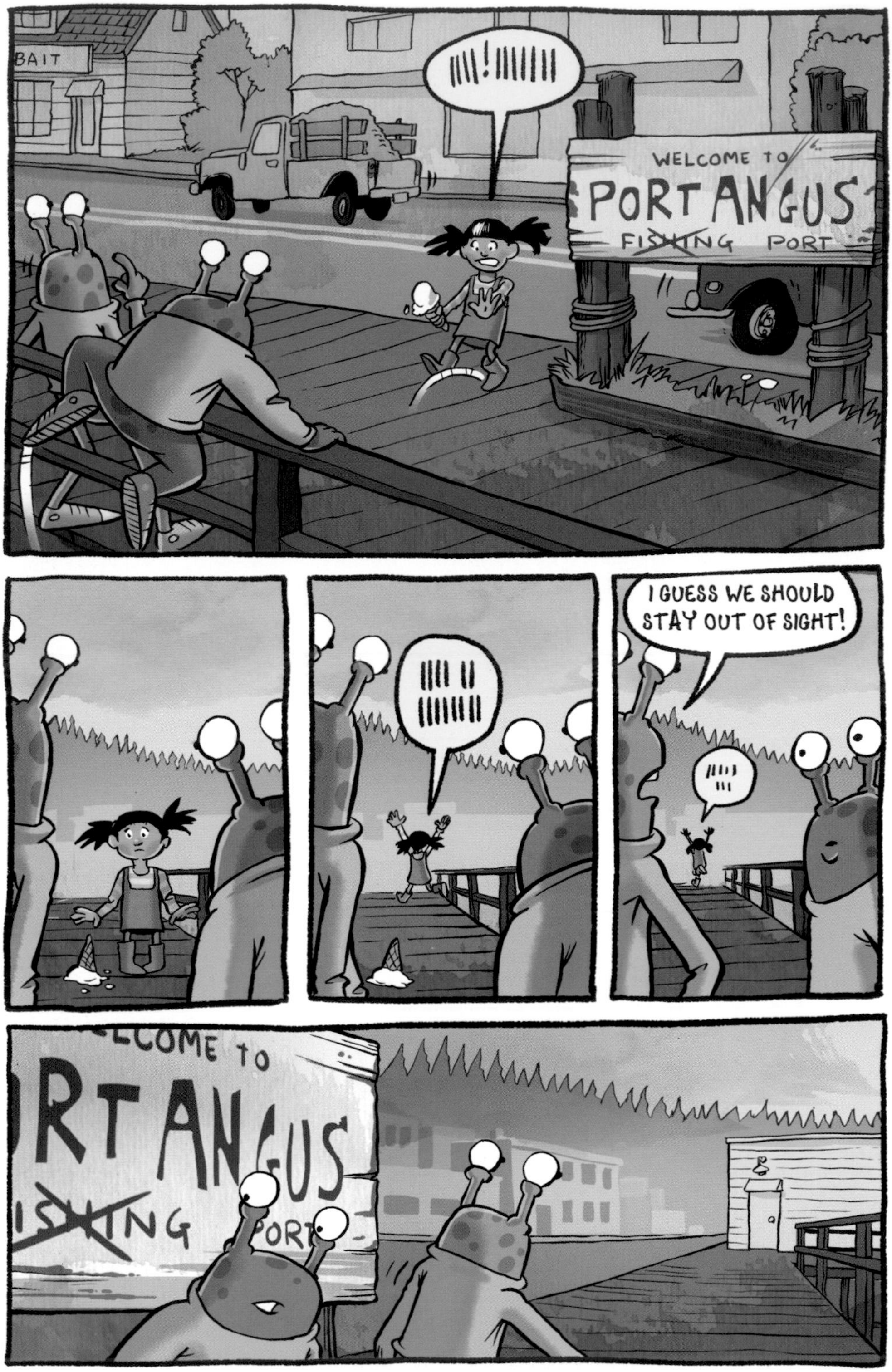
BAIT
WELCOME TO
PORT ANGUS
FISHING PORT
I GUESS WE SHOULD STAY OUT OF SIGHT!
WELCOME TO
RT ANGUS
ISHING PORT

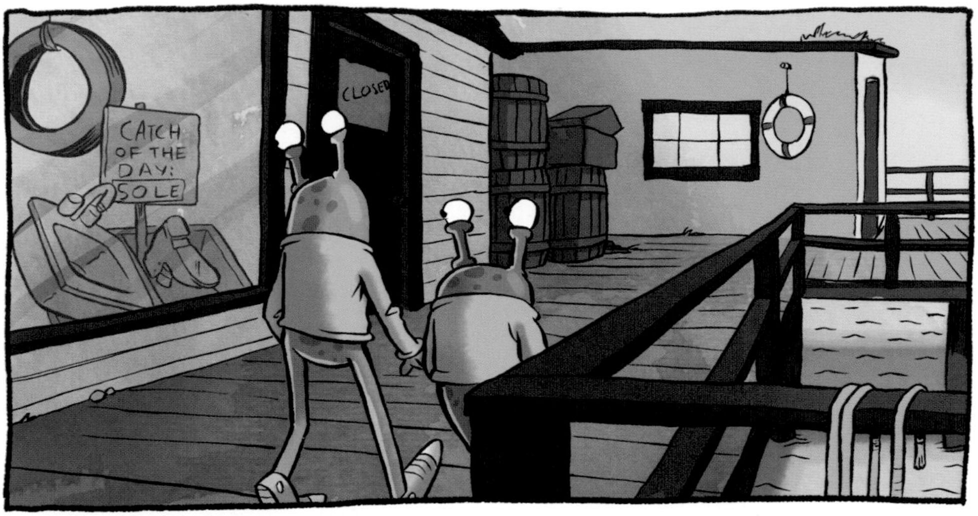
CLOSED
CATCH OF THE DAY: SOLE

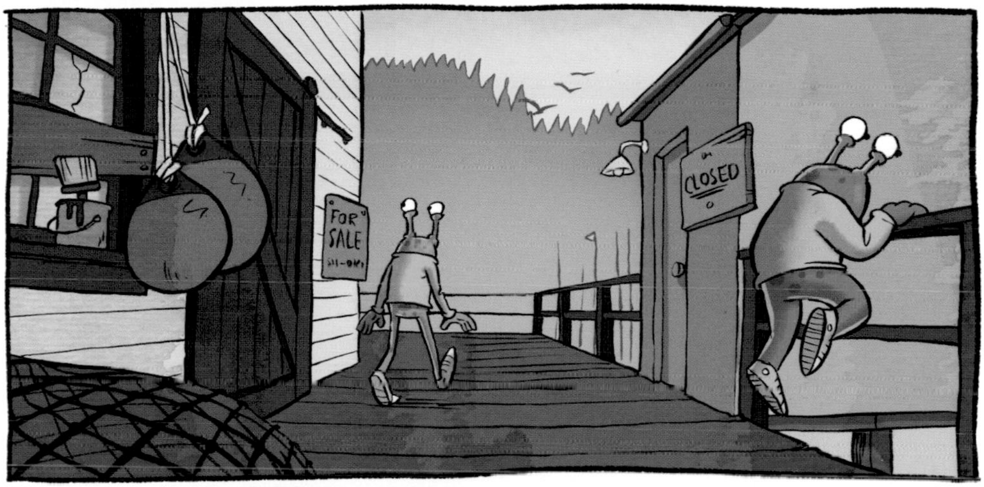
FOR SALE
CLOSED

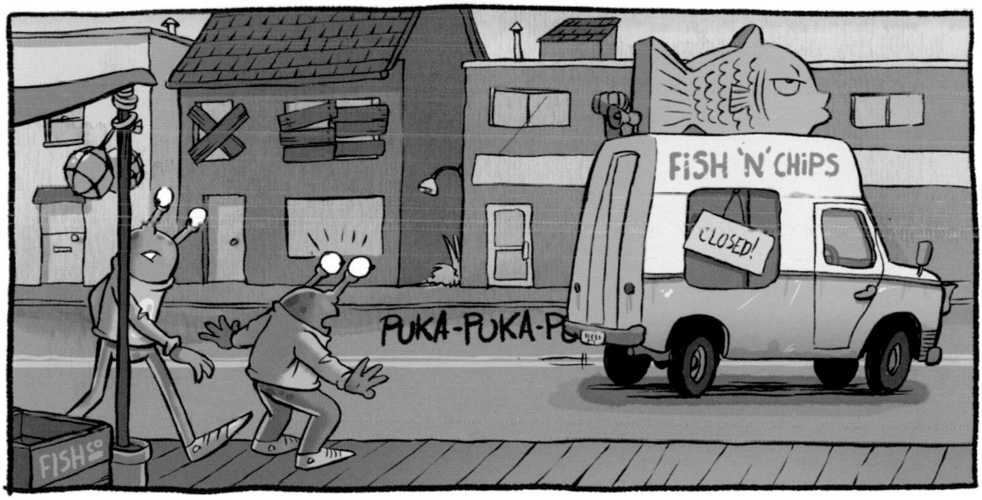
FISH 'N' CHIPS
CLOSED!
PUKA-PUKA-PU
FISH Co

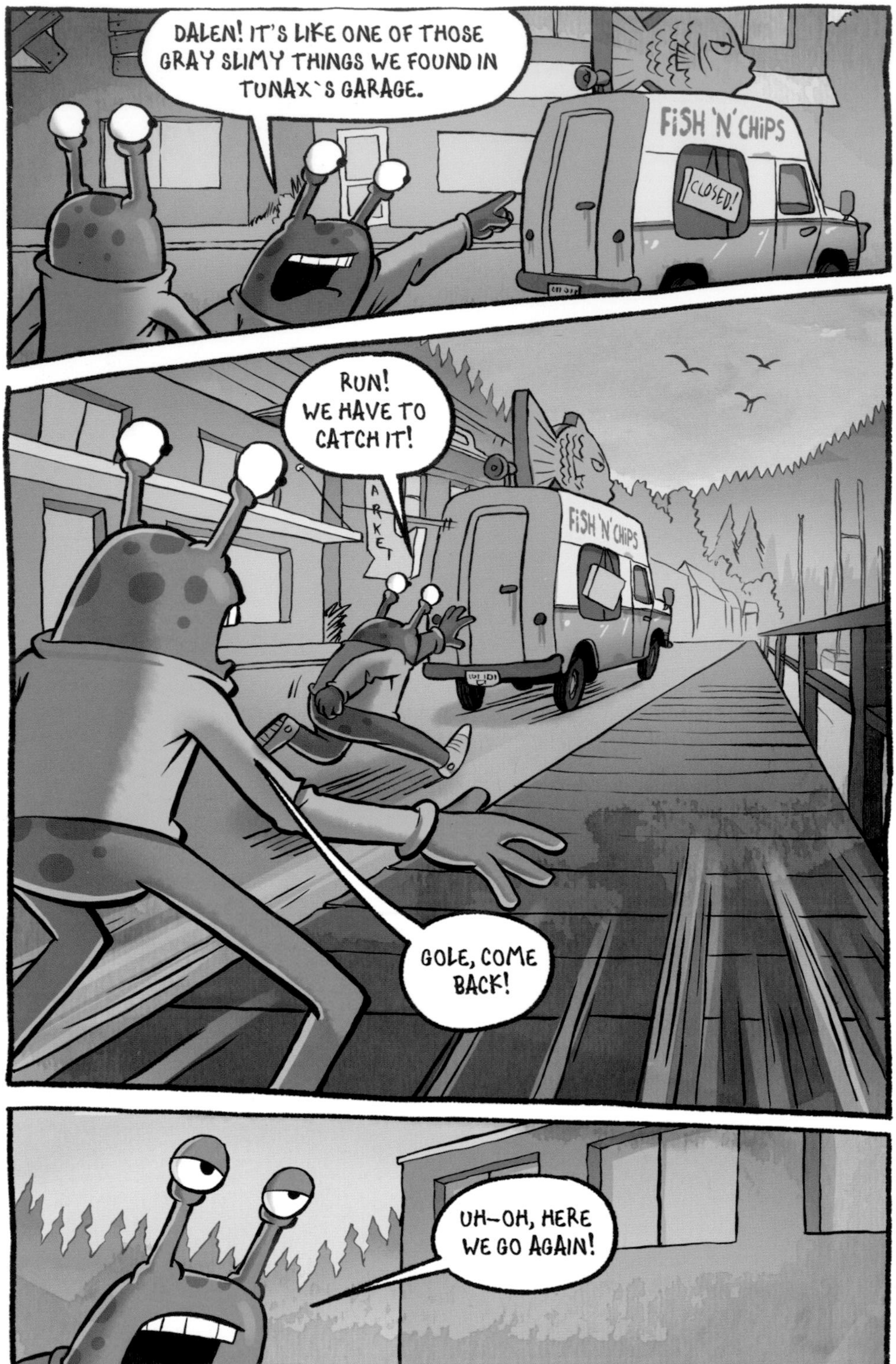
DALEN! IT'S LIKE ONE OF THOSE GRAY SLIMY THINGS WE FOUND IN TUNAX`S GARAGE.
FISH 'N' CHIPS
CLOSED!
RUN! WE HAVE TO CATCH IT!
MARKET
FISH 'N' CHIPS
GOLE, COME BACK!
UH-OH, HERE WE GO AGAIN!

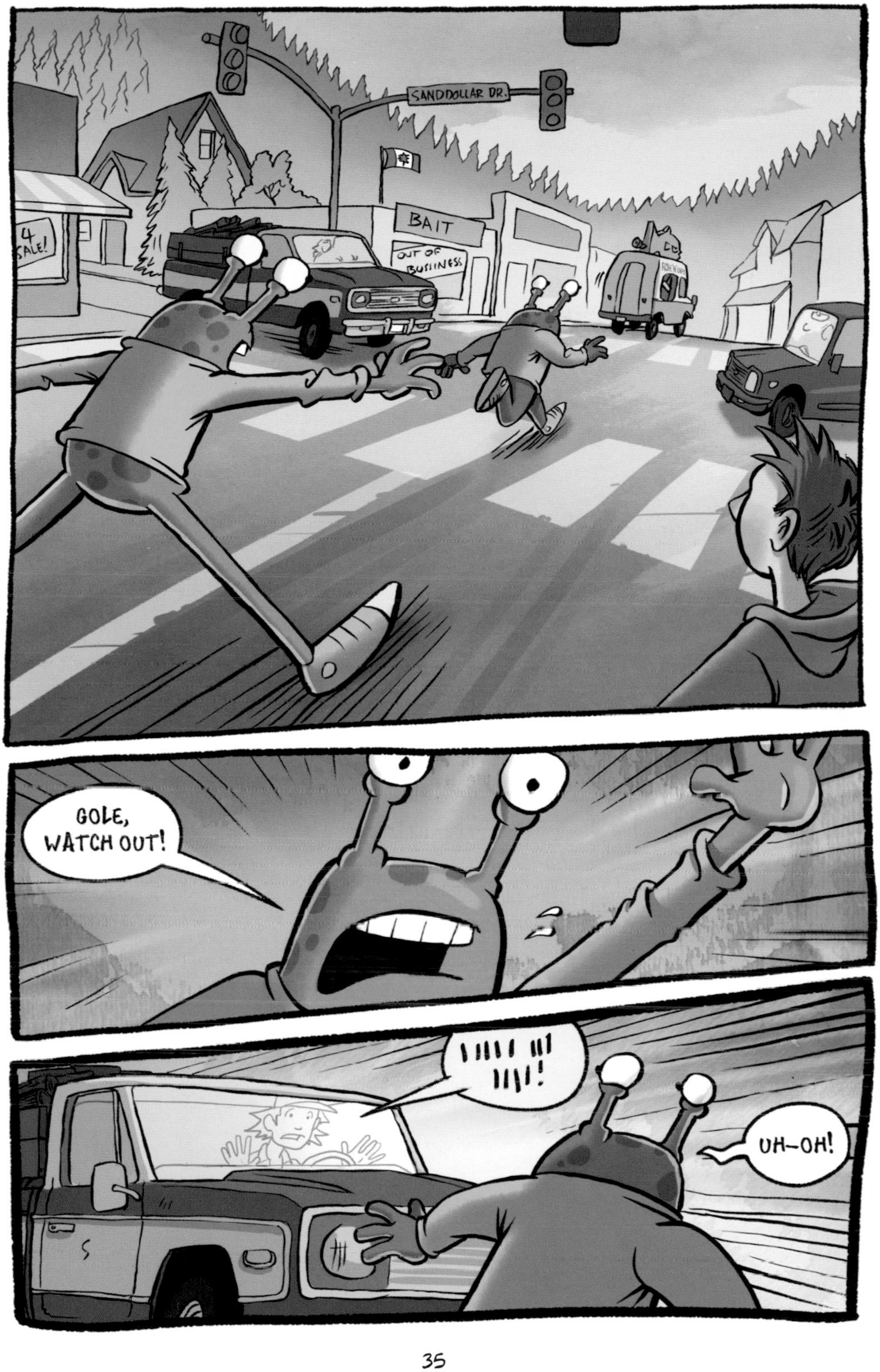
SANDDOLLAR DR.
BAIT
OUT OF BUSIINESS
4 SALE!
GOLE, WATCH OUT!
UH-OH!

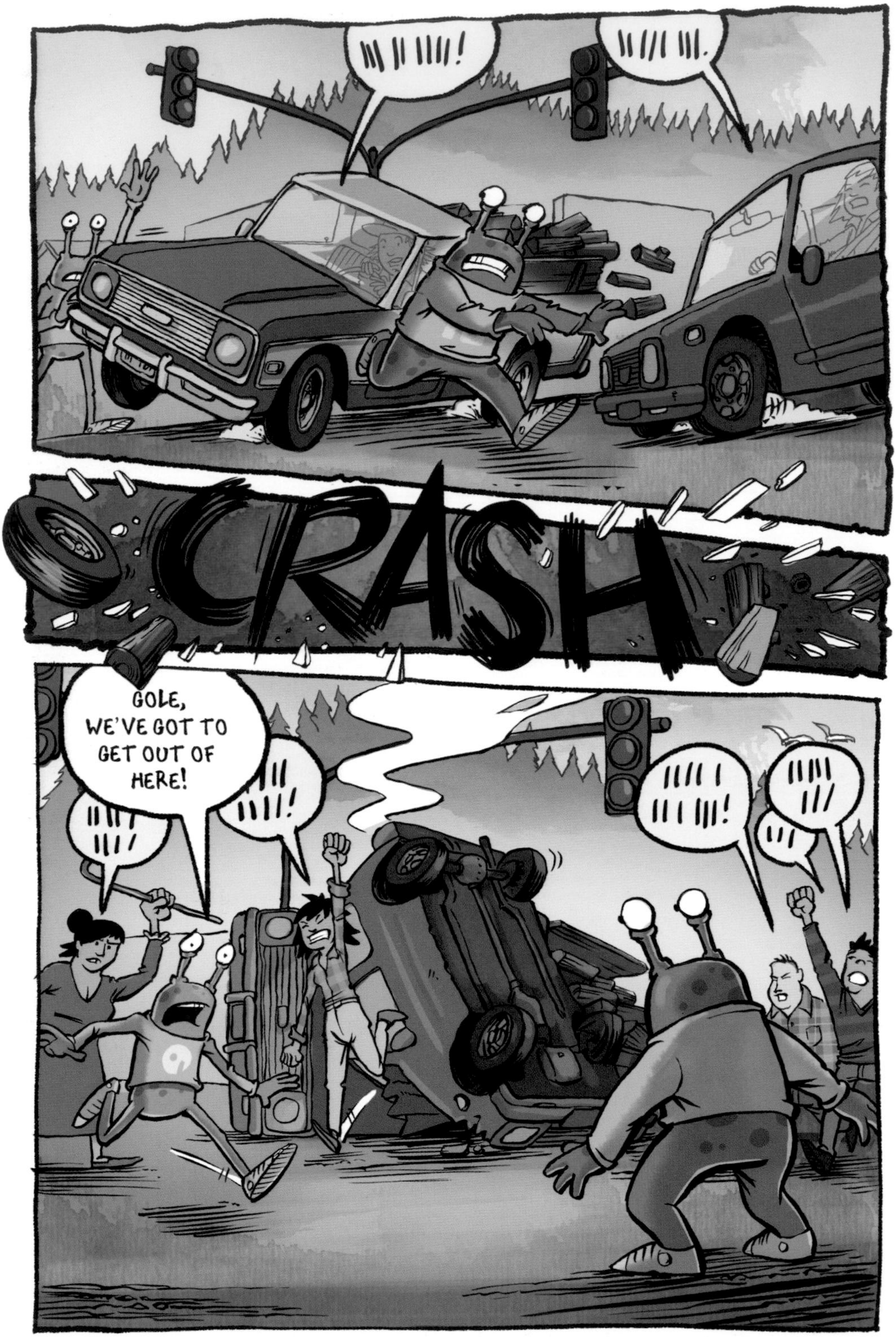
CRASH
GOLE, WE'VE GOT TO GET OUT OF HERE!

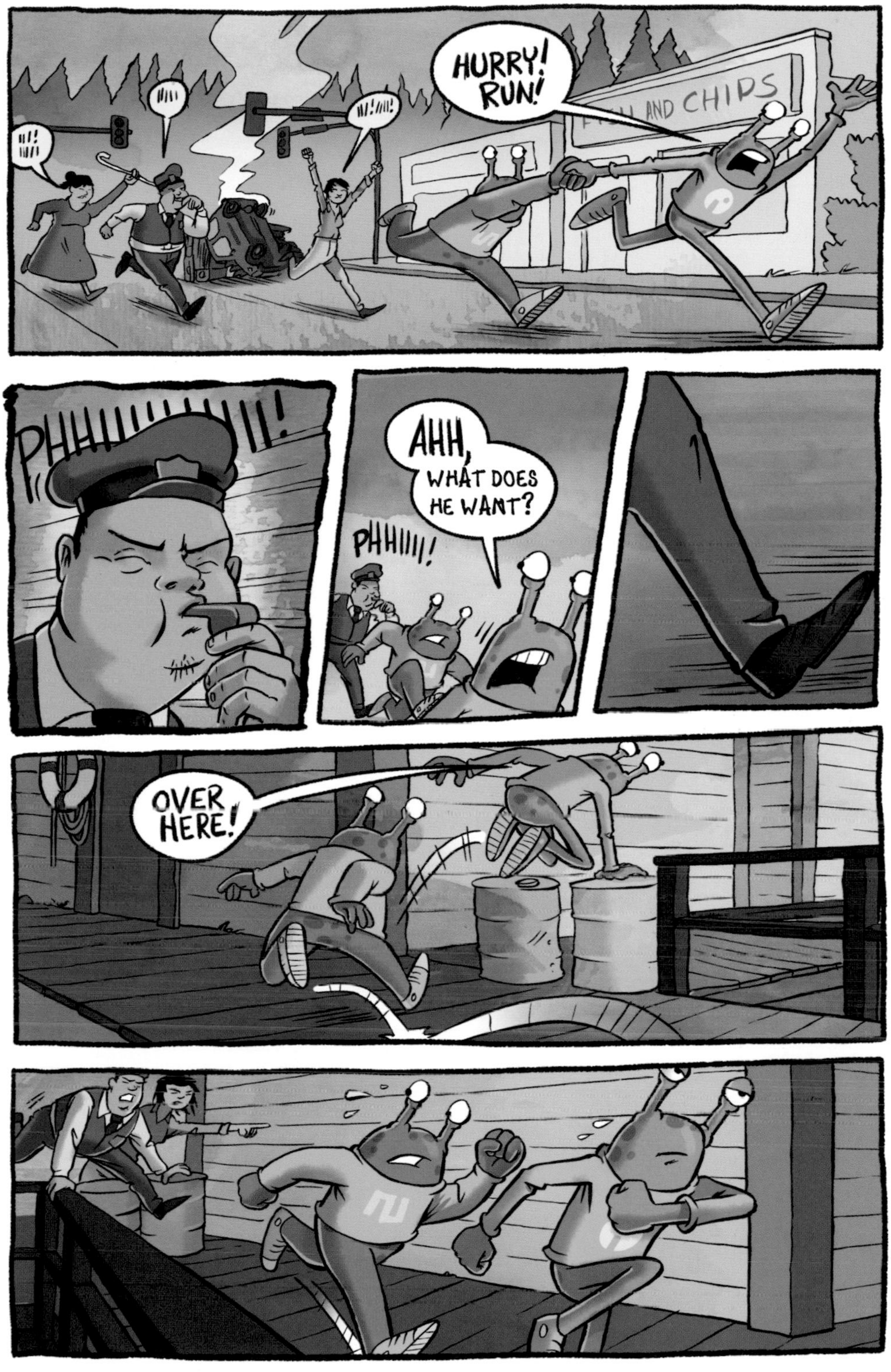
!!!!
!!!!
!!!!
!!!!
!!!
!!!!!!
HURRY! RUN!
AND CHIPS
PHHIIIIIIIIIIII!
AHH, WHAT DOES HE WANT?
PHHIIII!
OVER HERE!

IN HERE!
SPECIALS
• SEAWEED SANDWICH
• STEW DE LA WEED
MA'S
SEAFOOD CAFE
SEAWEED

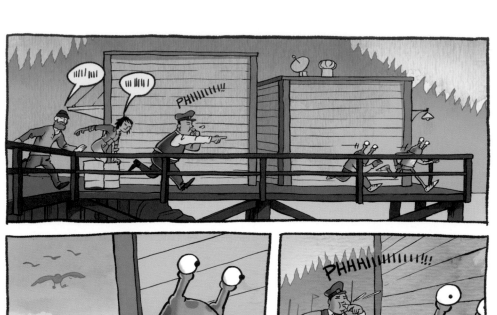

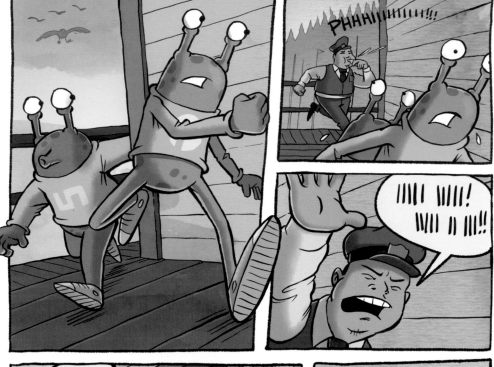

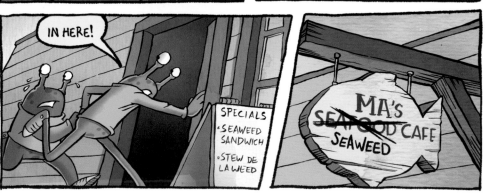

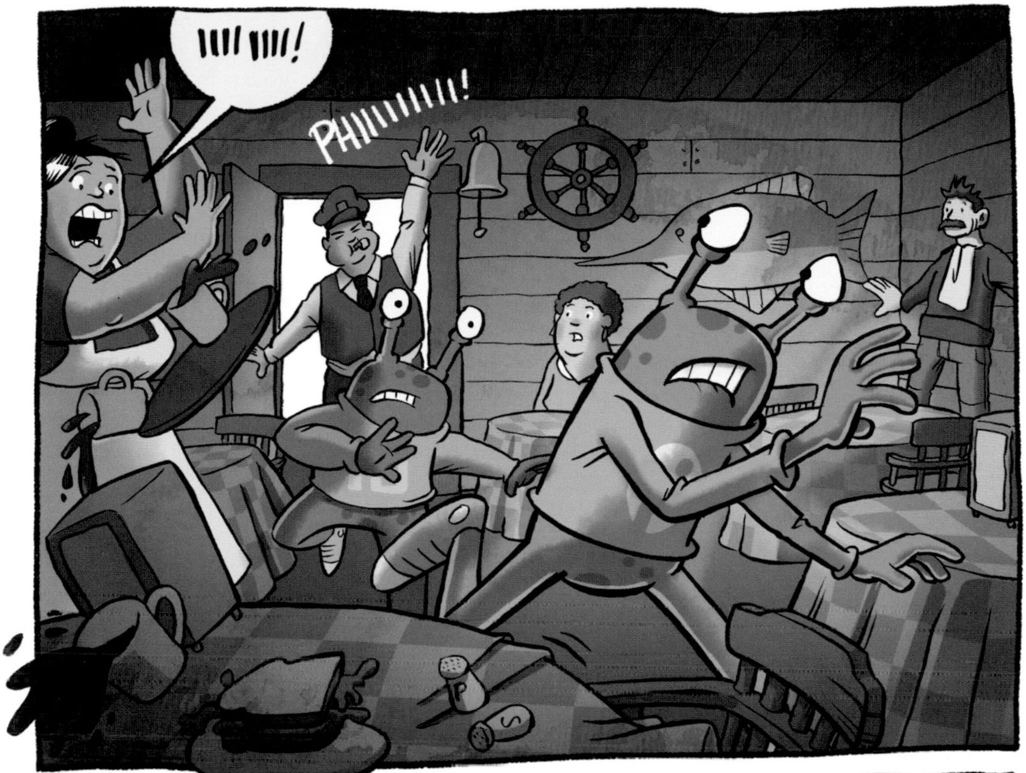
!!!! !!!!!!
PHIIIIIIII!

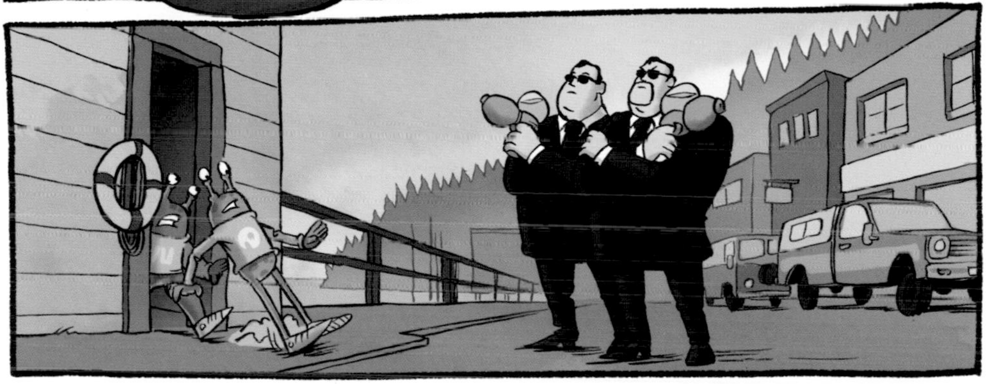

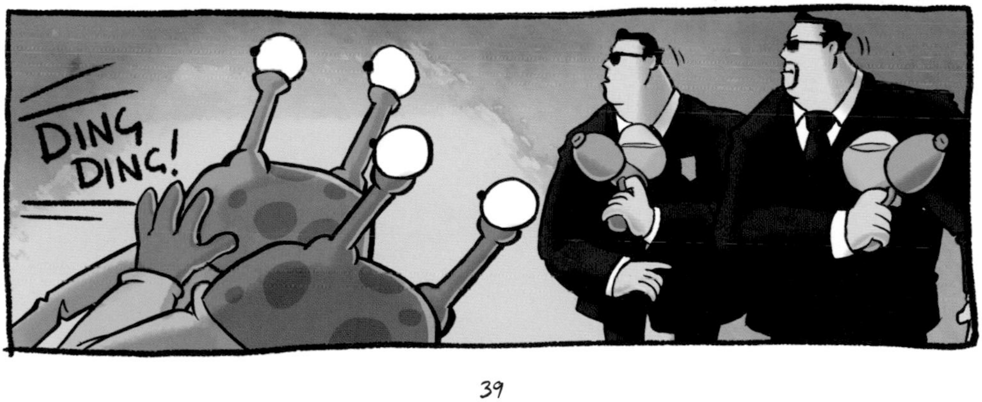
DING DING!

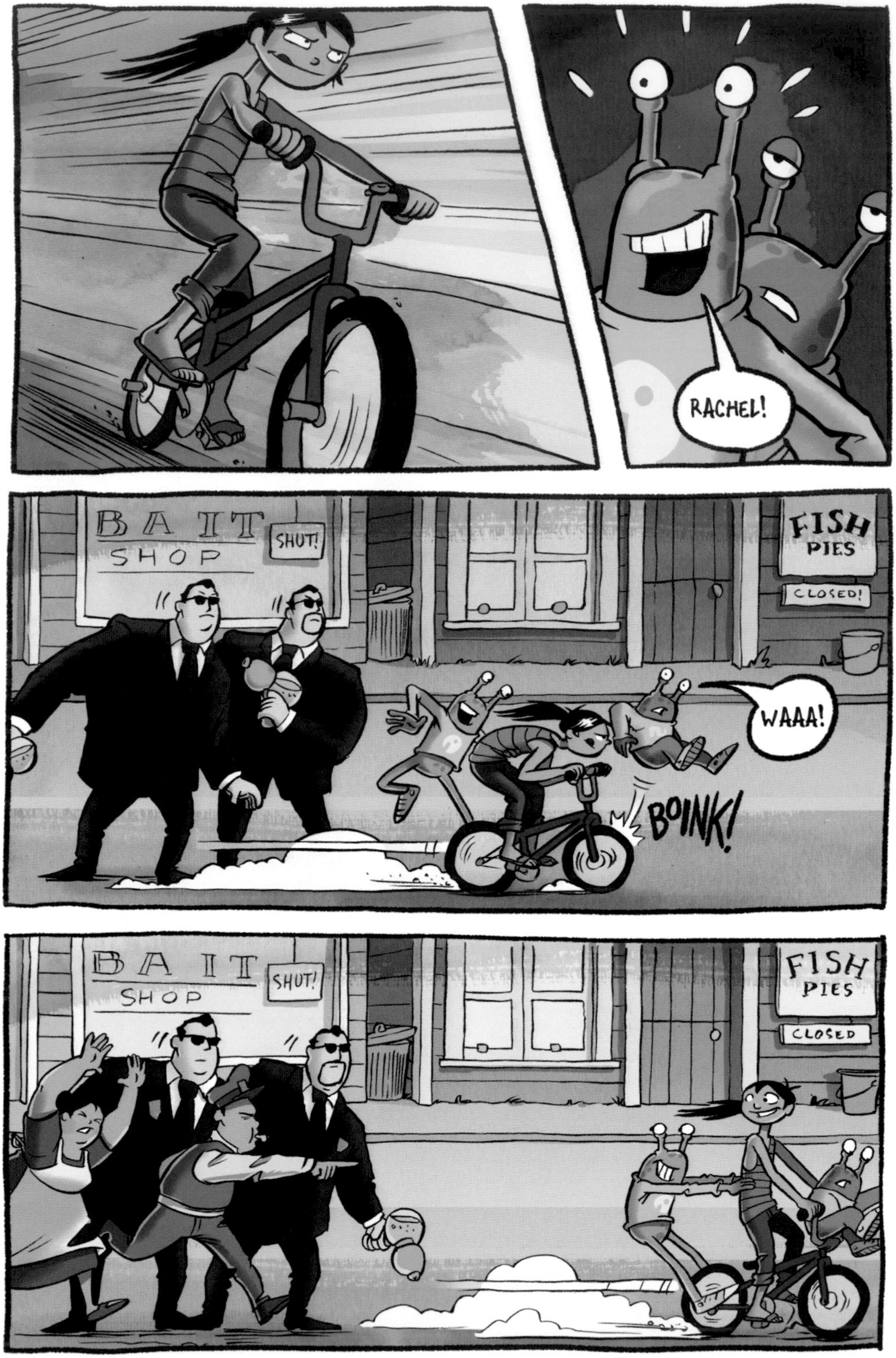
RACHEL!
BAIT SHOP
SHUT!
FISH PIES
CLOSED!
WAAA!
BOINK!
BAIT SHOP
SHUT!
FISH PIES
CLOSED

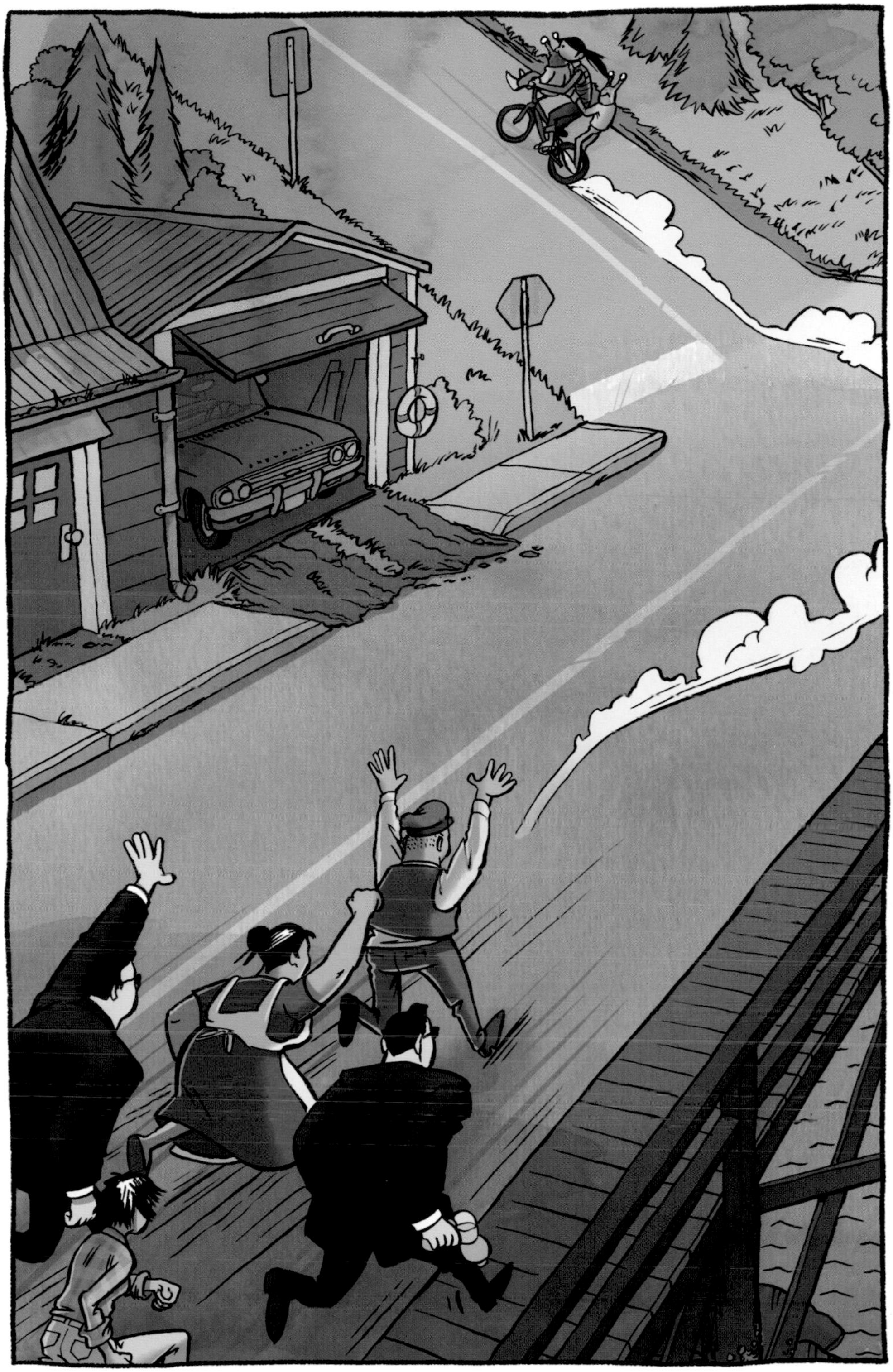

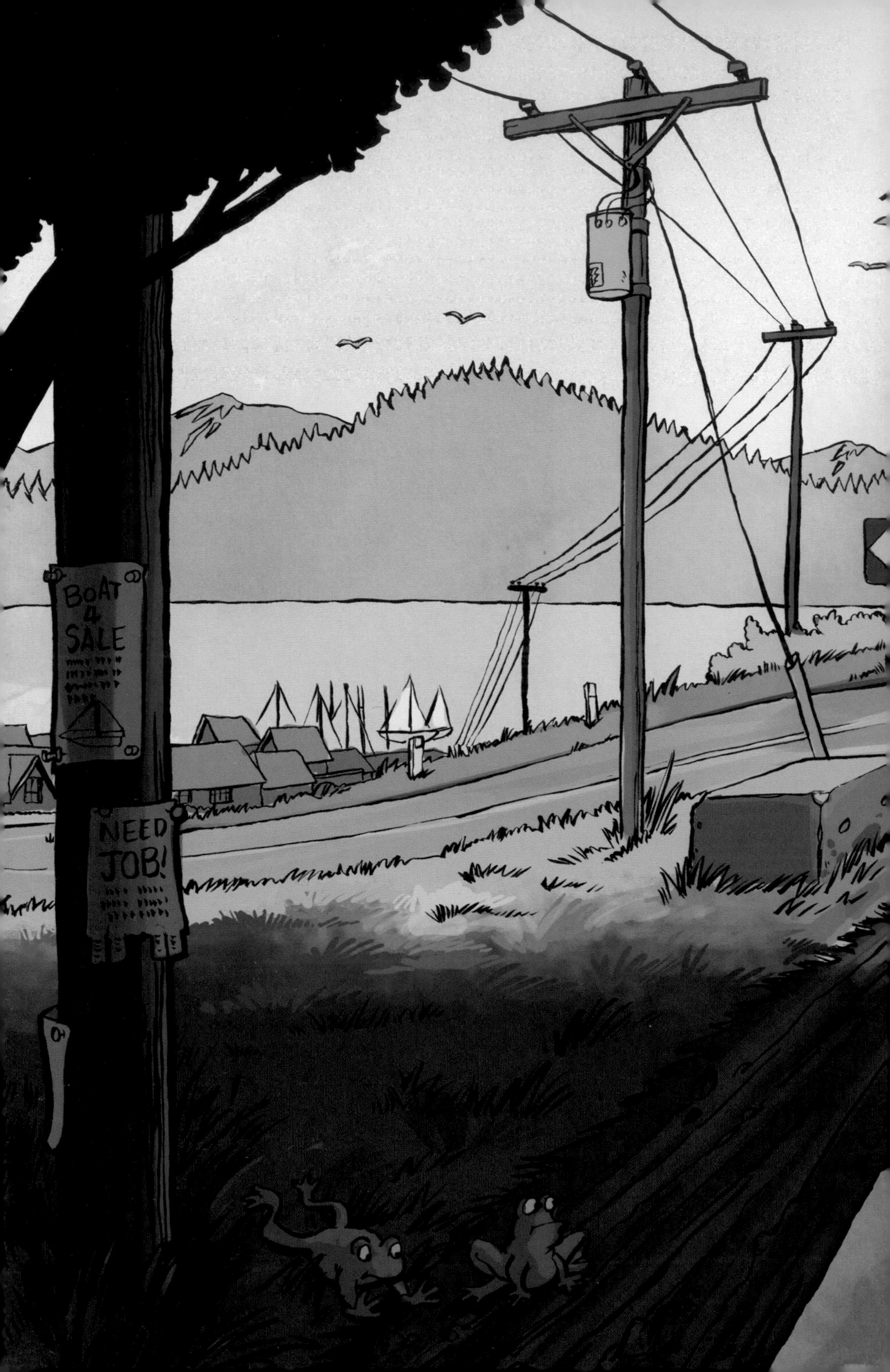
BOAT 4 SALE
NEED JOB!

CHAPTER 3

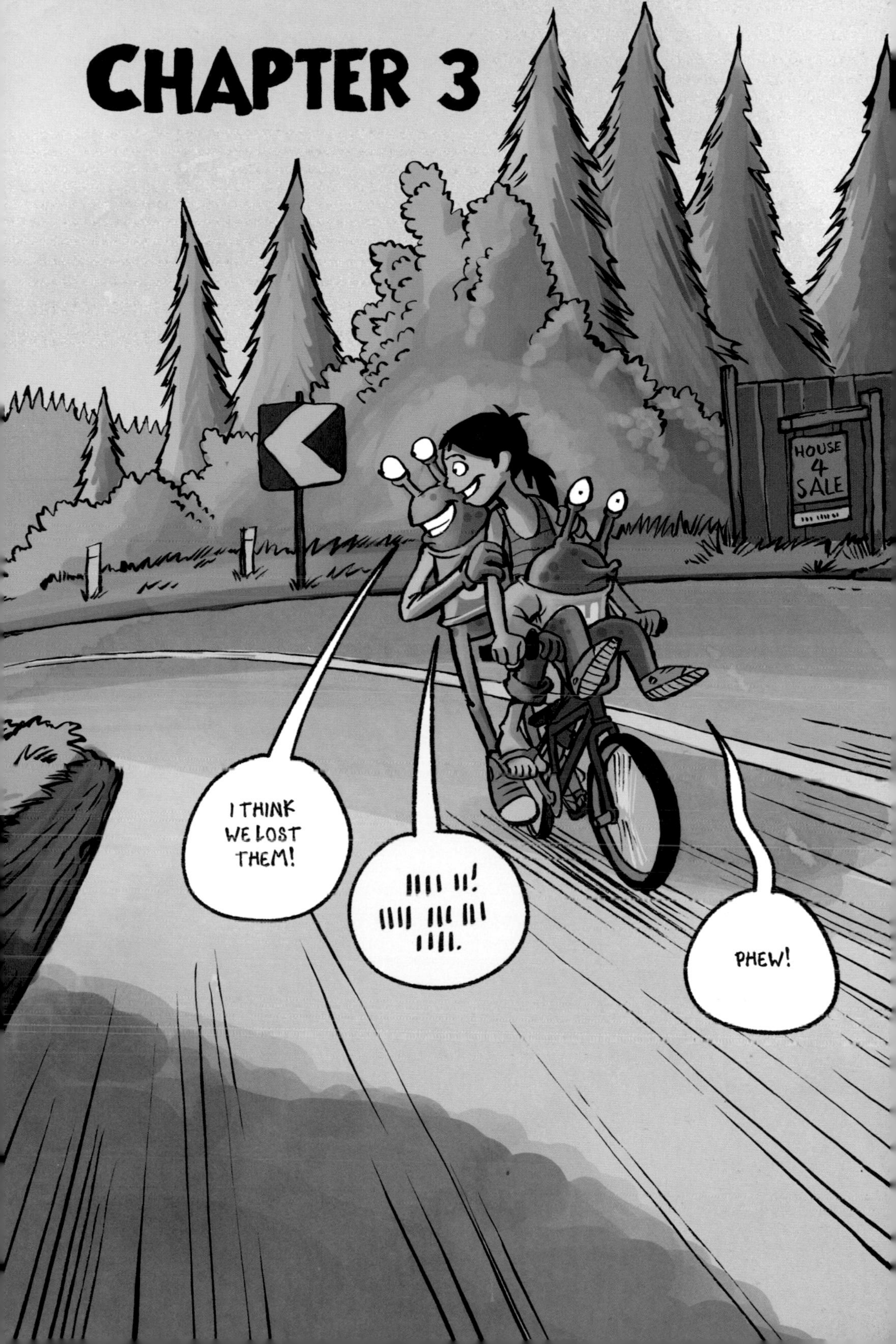
HOUSE 4 SALE
I THINK WE LOST THEM!
PHEW!

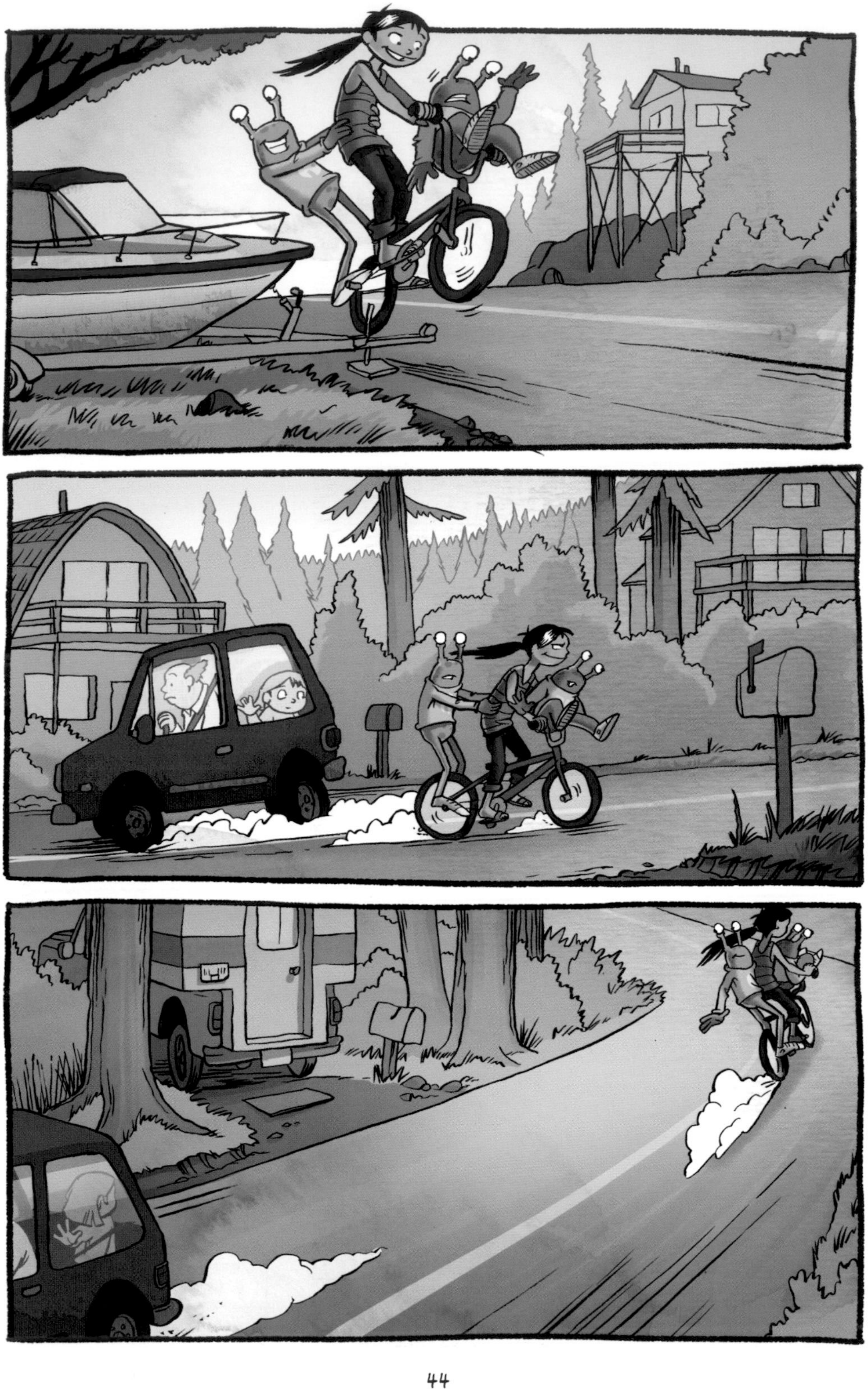

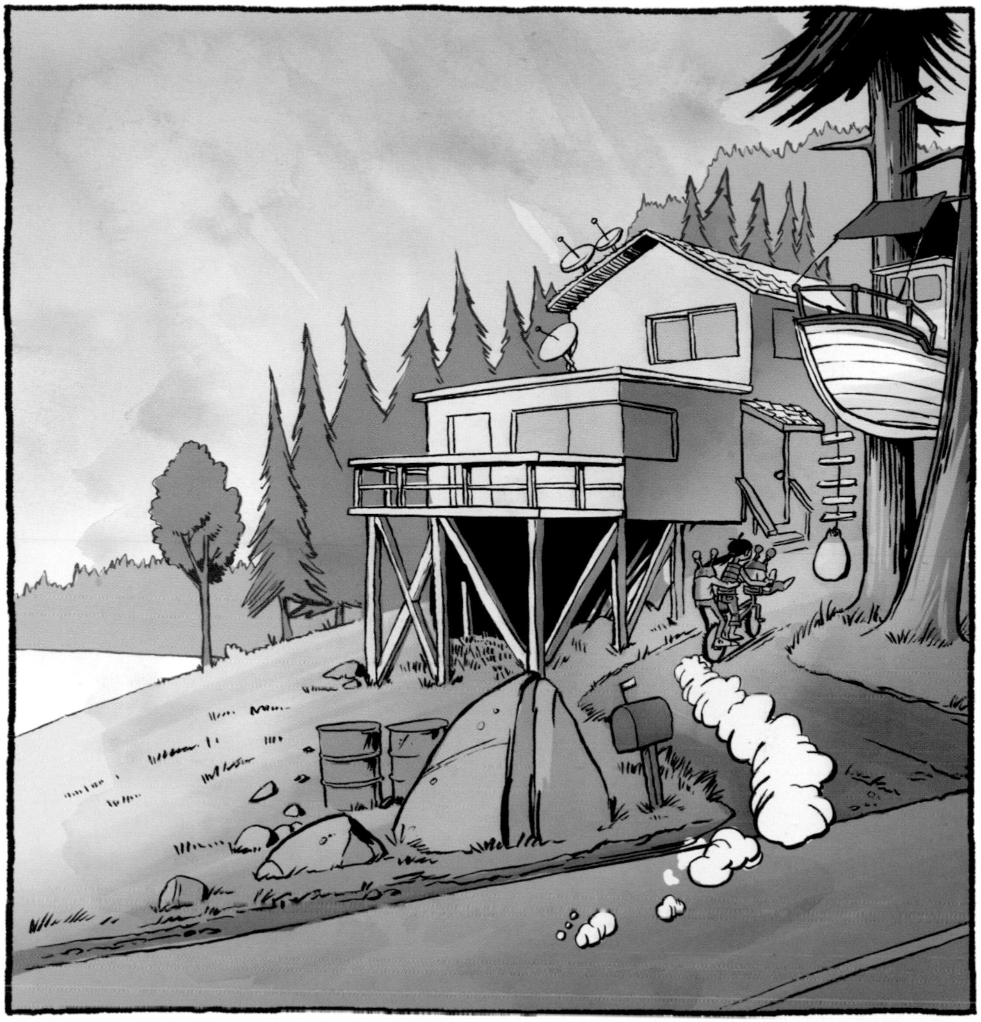

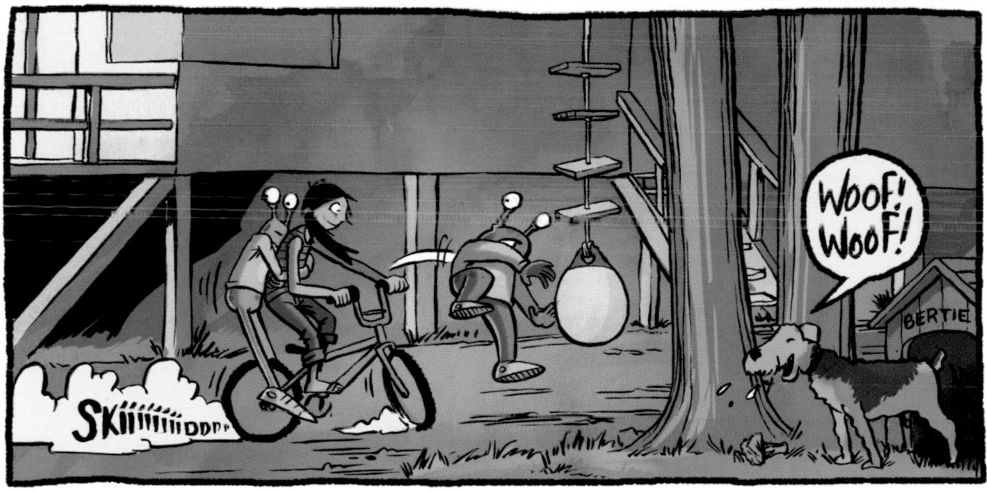
SKIIIIIIIIDDD
WOOF! WOOF!
BERTIE

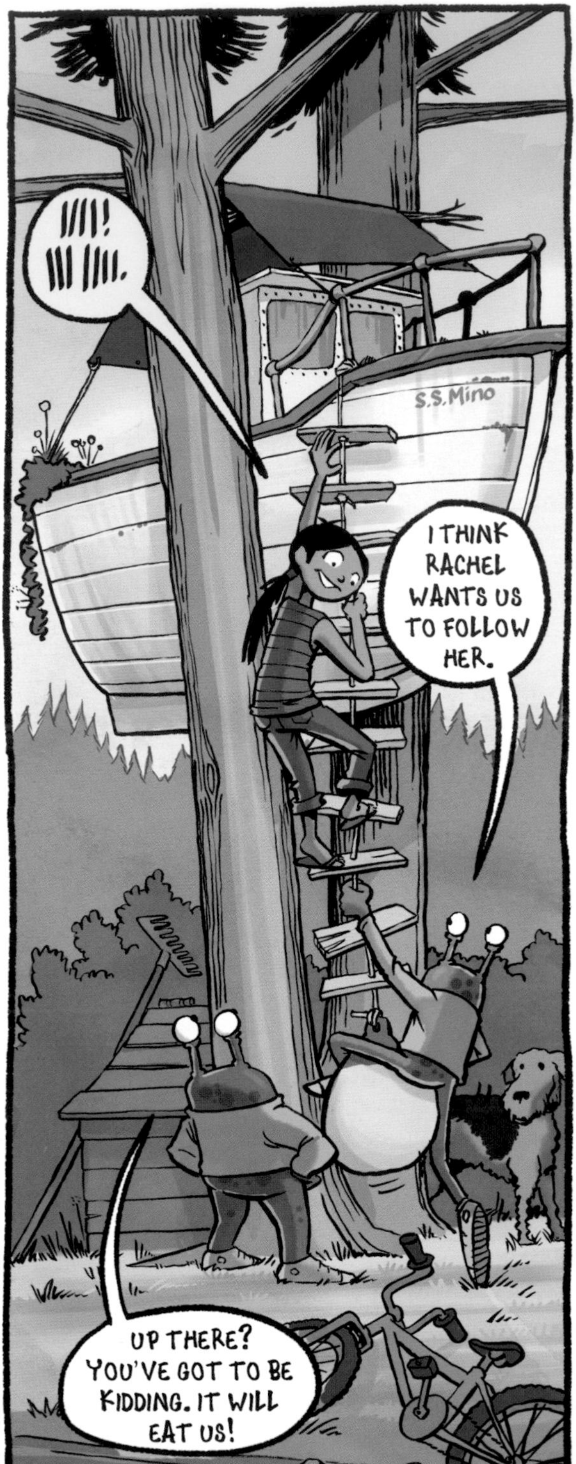

////! /// ////.
I THINK RACHEL WANTS US TO FOLLOW HER.
S.S. Mino
UP THERE? YOU'VE GOT TO BE KIDDING. IT WILL EAT US!

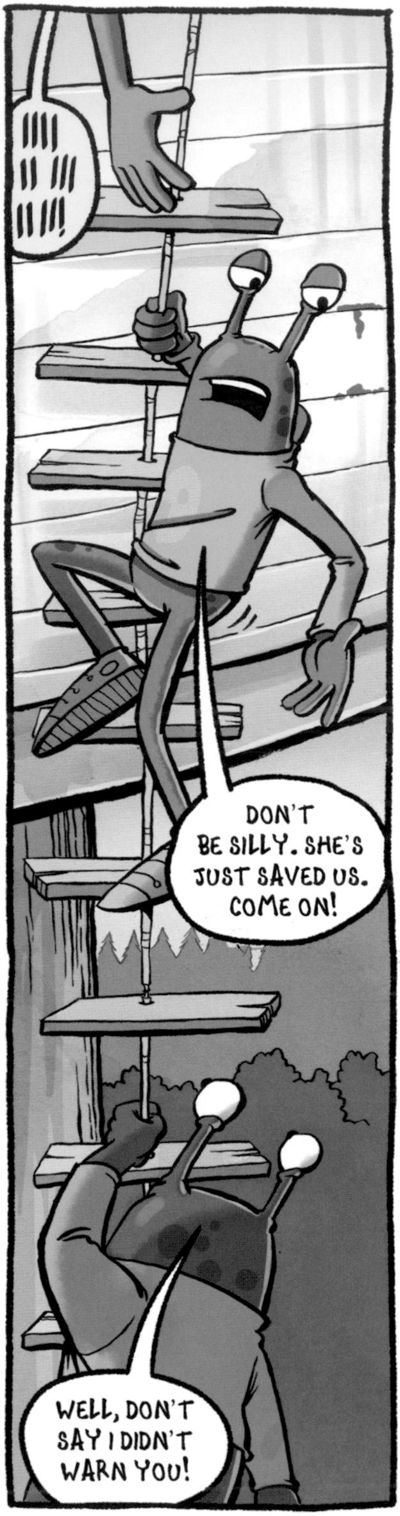

//// // /// ////!
DON'T BE SILLY. SHE'S JUST SAVED US. COME ON!
WELL, DON'T SAY I DIDN'T WARN YOU!

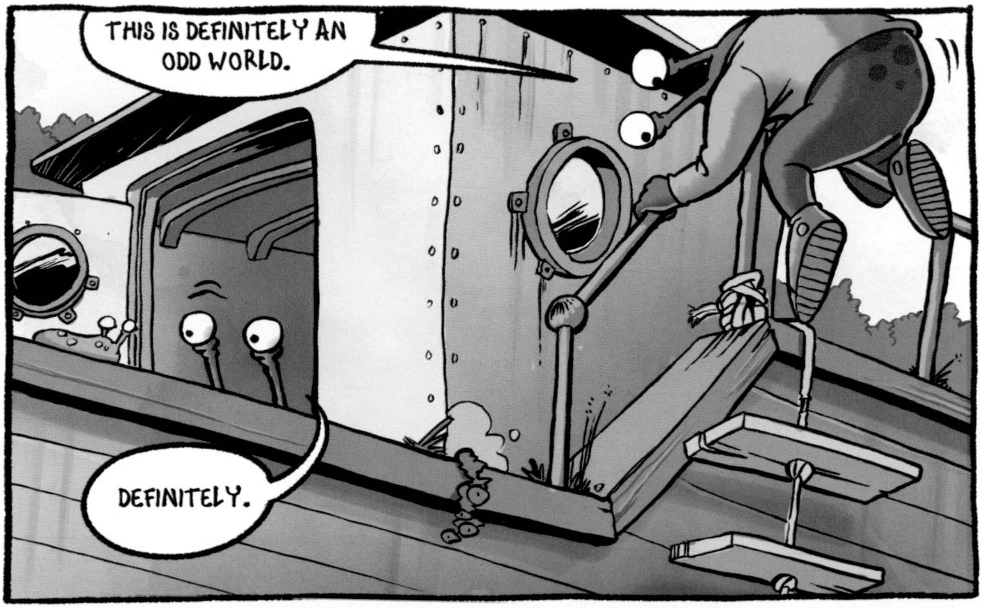
THIS IS DEFINITELY AN ODD WORLD.
DEFINITELY.

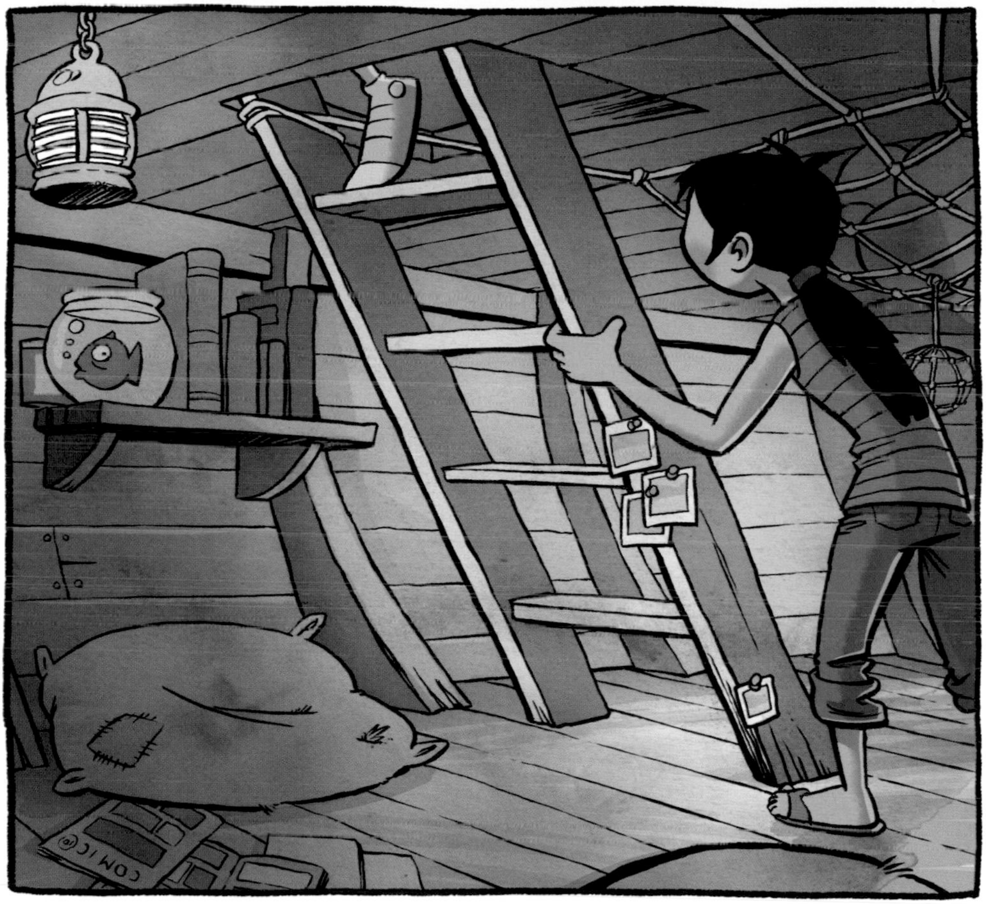
COMIC

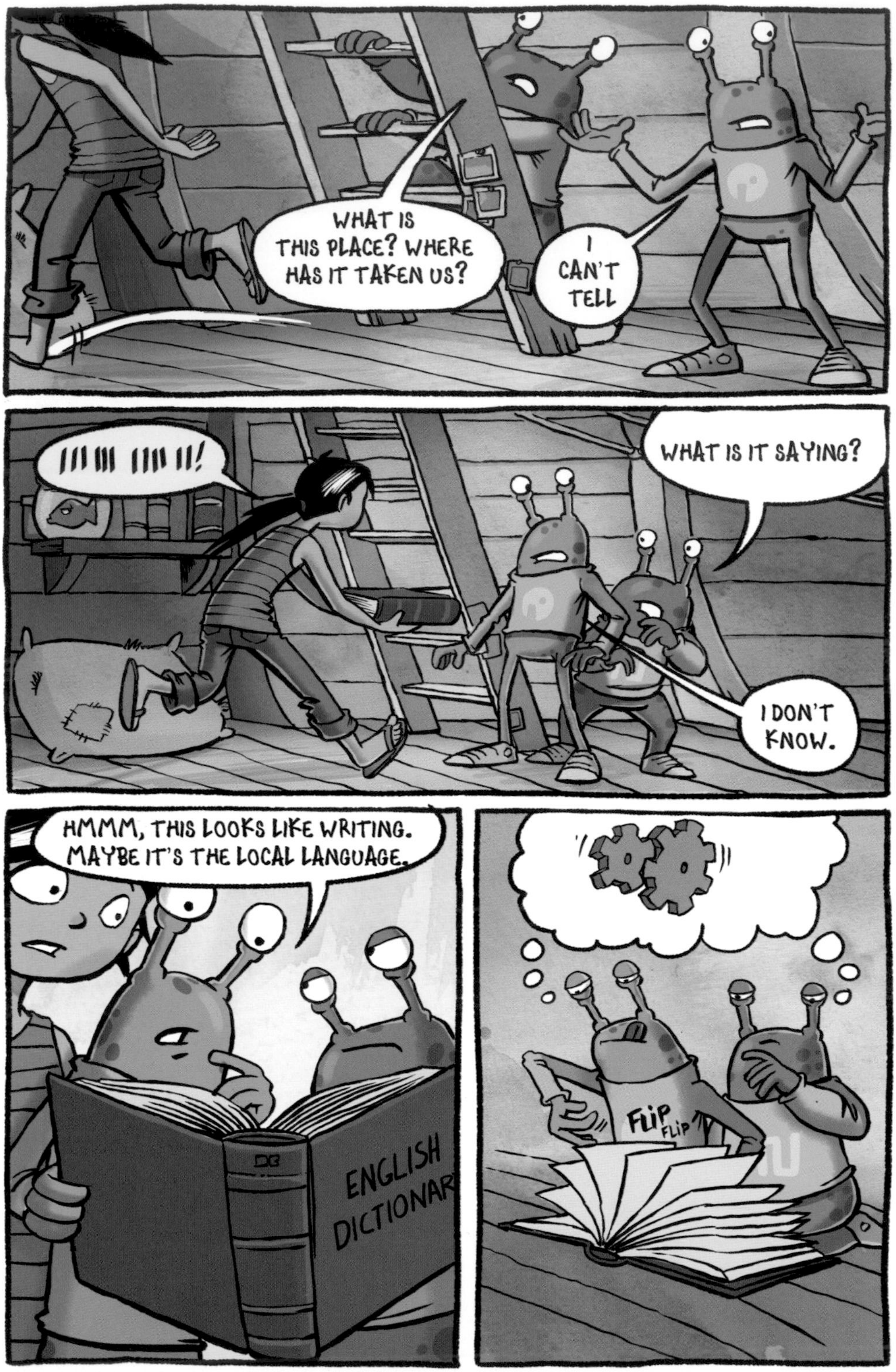
WHAT IS THIS PLACE? WHERE HAS IT TAKEN US?
I CAN'T TELL
||| ||| |||| ||!
WHAT IS IT SAYING?
I DON'T KNOW.
HMMM, THIS LOOKS LIKE WRITING. MAYBE IT'S THE LOCAL LANGUAGE.
ENGLISH DICTIONAR
FLIP FLIP

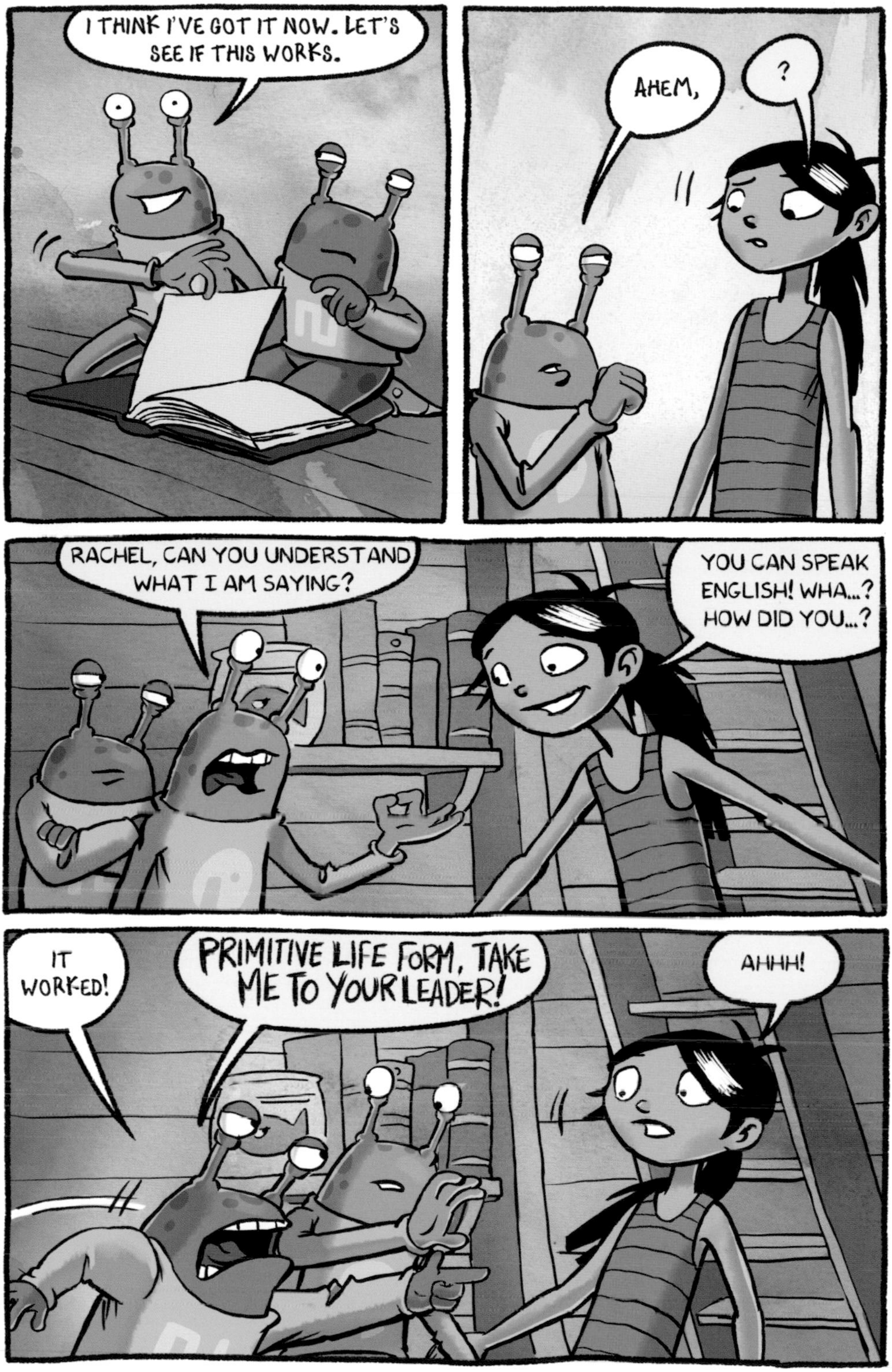
I THINK I'VE GOT IT NOW. LET'S SEE IF THIS WORKS.
AHEM,
?
RACHEL, CAN YOU UNDERSTAND WHAT I AM SAYING?
YOU CAN SPEAK ENGLISH! WHA...? HOW DID YOU...?
IT WORKED!
PRIMITIVE LIFE FORM, TAKE ME TO YOUR LEADER!
AHHH!

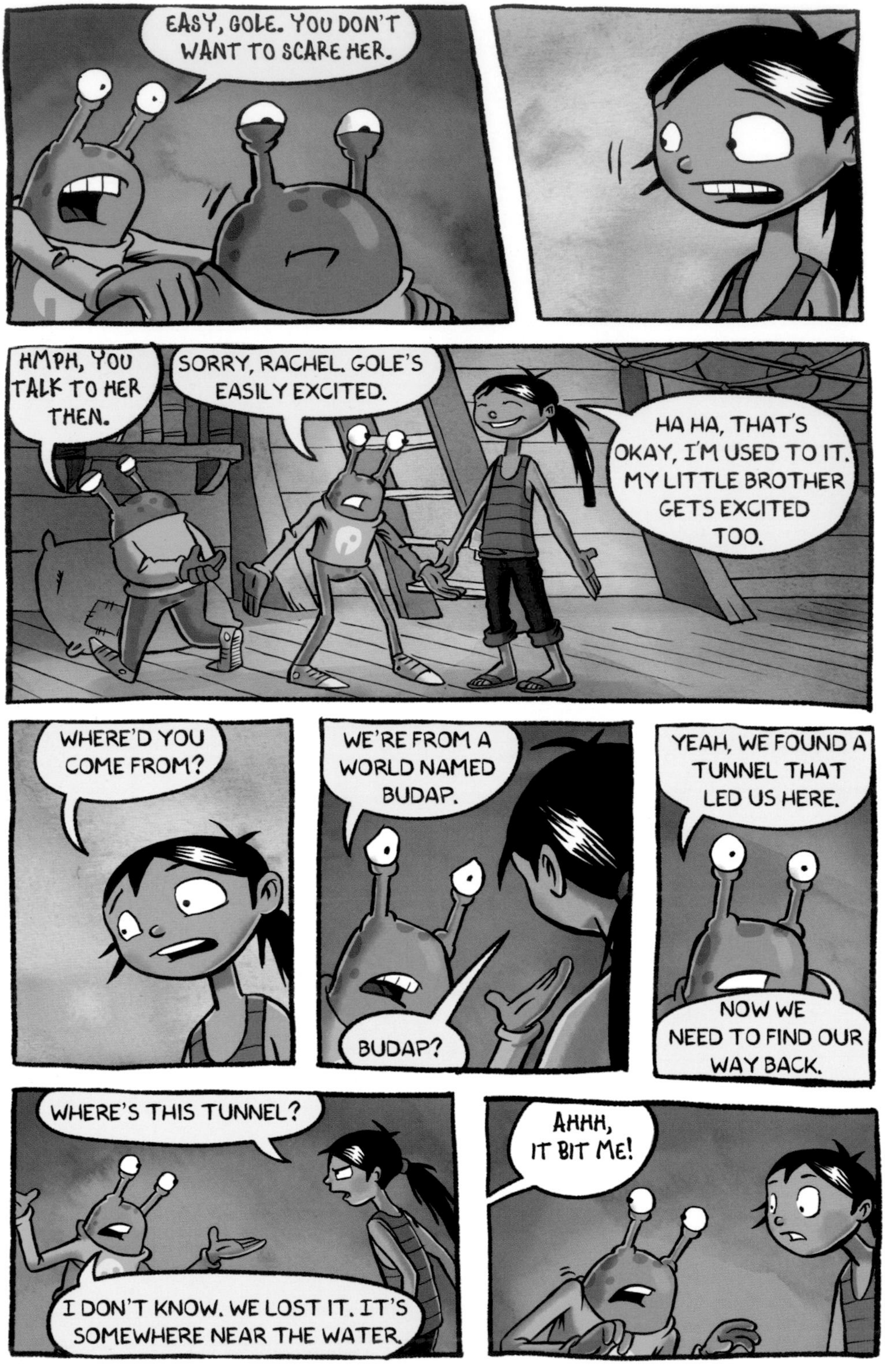
EASY, GOLE. YOU DON'T WANT TO SCARE HER.
HMPH, YOU TALK TO HER THEN.
SORRY, RACHEL. GOLE'S EASILY EXCITED.
HA HA, THAT'S OKAY, I'M USED TO IT. MY LITTLE BROTHER GETS EXCITED TOO.
WHERE'D YOU COME FROM?
WE'RE FROM A WORLD NAMED BUDAP.
BUDAP?
YEAH, WE FOUND A TUNNEL THAT LED US HERE.
NOW WE NEED TO FIND OUR WAY BACK.
WHERE'S THIS TUNNEL?
I DON'T KNOW. WE LOST IT. IT'S SOMEWHERE NEAR THE WATER.
AHHH, IT BIT ME!

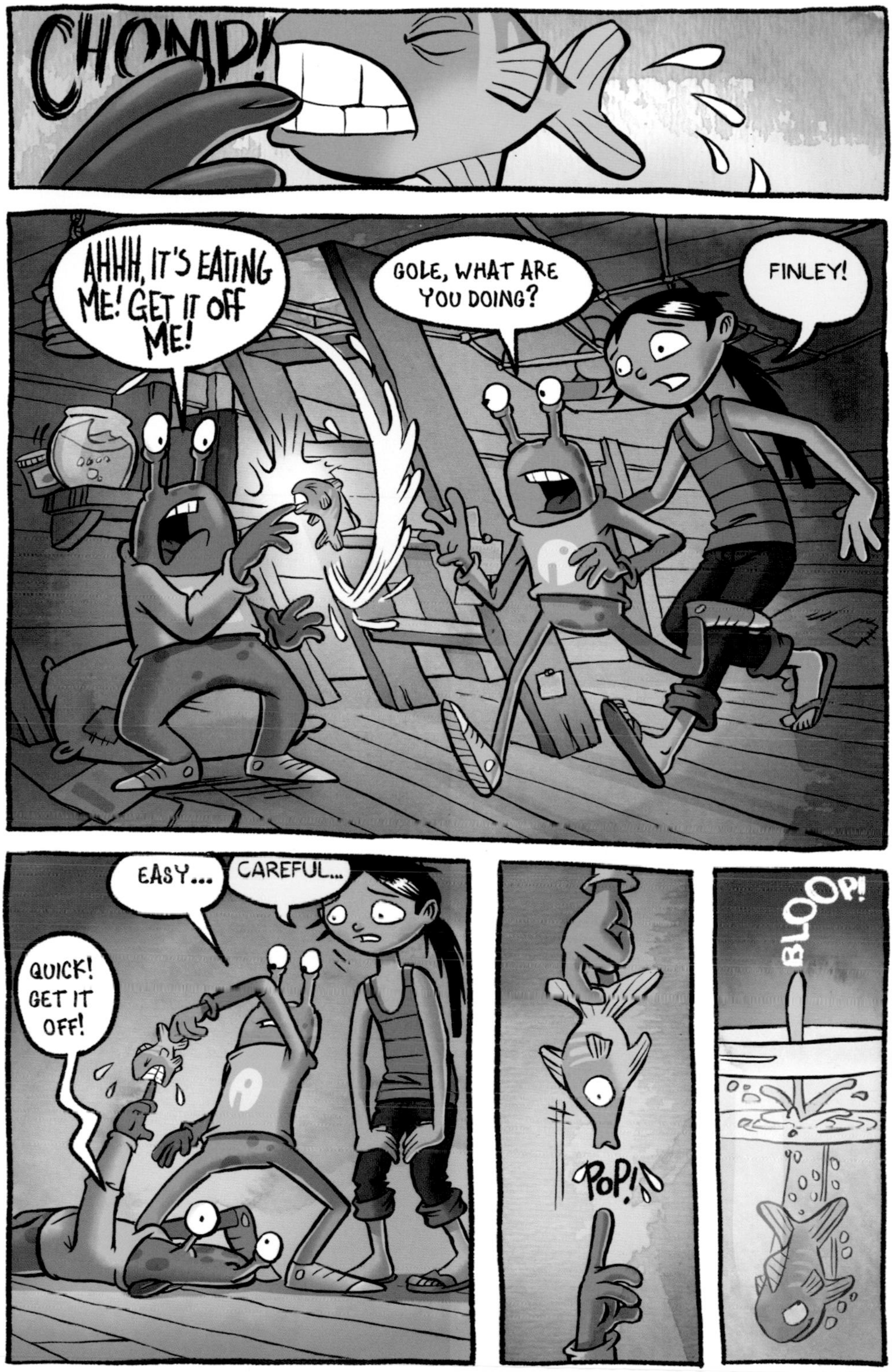
CHOMP!
AHHH, IT'S EATING ME! GET IT OFF ME!
GOLE, WHAT ARE YOU DOING?
FINLEY!
EASY...
CAREFUL...
QUICK! GET IT OFF!
POP!
BLOOP!

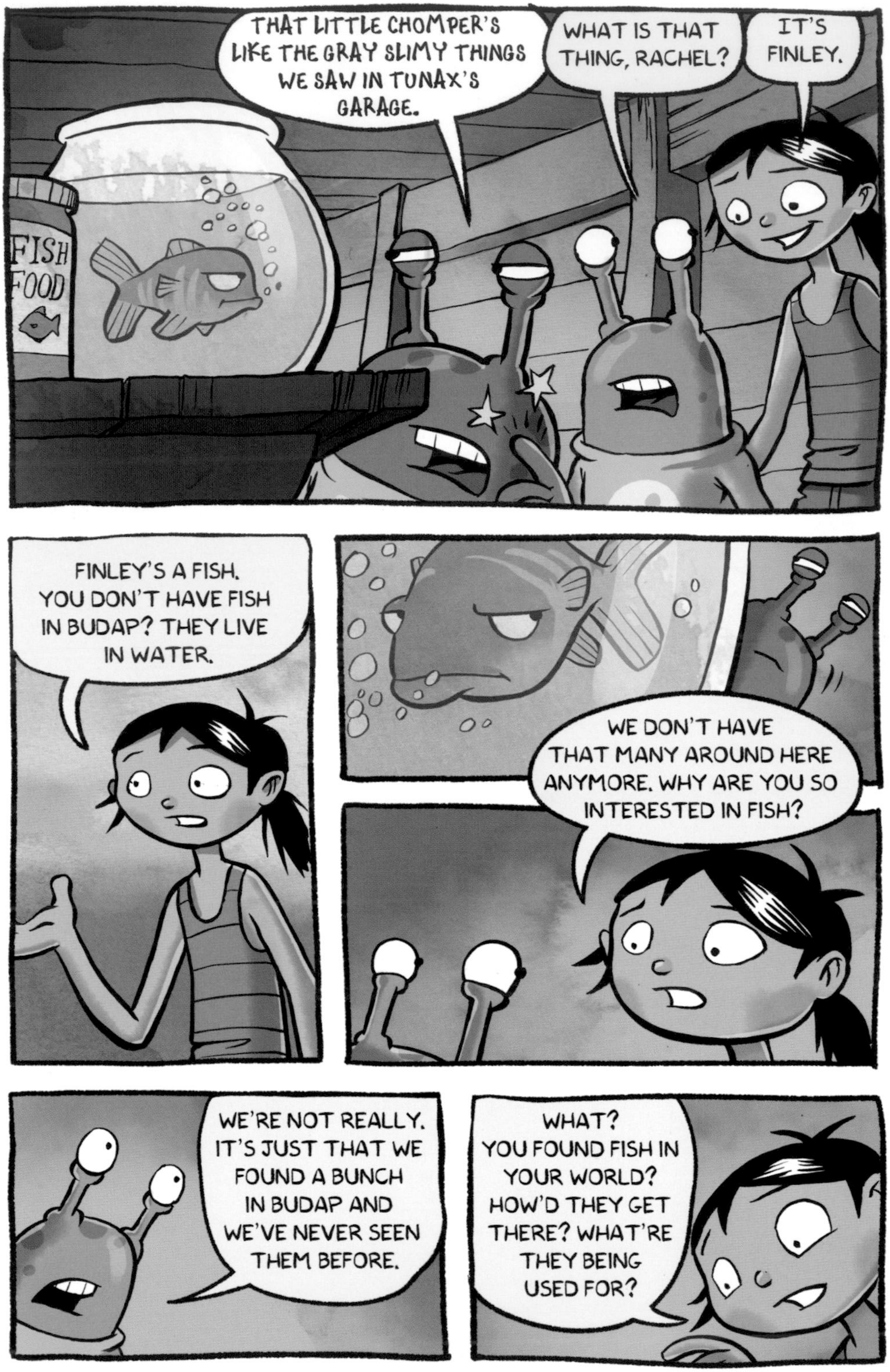
THAT LITTLE CHOMPER'S LIKE THE GRAY SLIMY THINGS WE SAW IN TUNAX'S GARAGE.
WHAT IS THAT THING, RACHEL?
IT'S FINLEY.
FISH FOOD
FINLEY'S A FISH. YOU DON'T HAVE FISH IN BUDAP? THEY LIVE IN WATER.
WE DON'T HAVE THAT MANY AROUND HERE ANYMORE. WHY ARE YOU SO INTERESTED IN FISH?
WE'RE NOT REALLY. IT'S JUST THAT WE FOUND A BUNCH IN BUDAP AND WE'VE NEVER SEEN THEM BEFORE.
WHAT? YOU FOUND FISH IN YOUR WORLD? HOW'D THEY GET THERE? WHAT'RE THEY BEING USED FOR?

YEAH, WE FOUND TONS OF THEM. I THINK THEY'RE BEING USED AS A FUEL!

WHAT? REALLY?

THIS TOWN, PORT ANGUS, MAKES ITS LIVING CATCHING AND SELLING FISH.

MY DAD IS A FISHERMAN. HE CATCHES FISH. THAT'S HOW HE SUPPORTS OUR FAMILY. BUT THEY'RE DISAPPEARING, AND NO ONE CAN FIGURE OUT WHERE THEY'RE GOING.

WHAT DO YOU DO WITH THESE FISH?

EAT THEM.

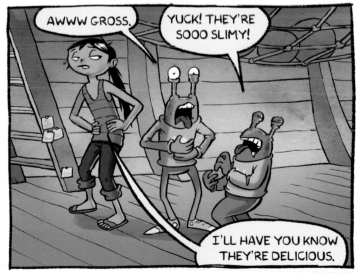

AWWW GROSS.

YUCK! THEY'RE SOOO SLIMY!

I'LL HAVE YOU KNOW THEY'RE DELICIOUS.

53

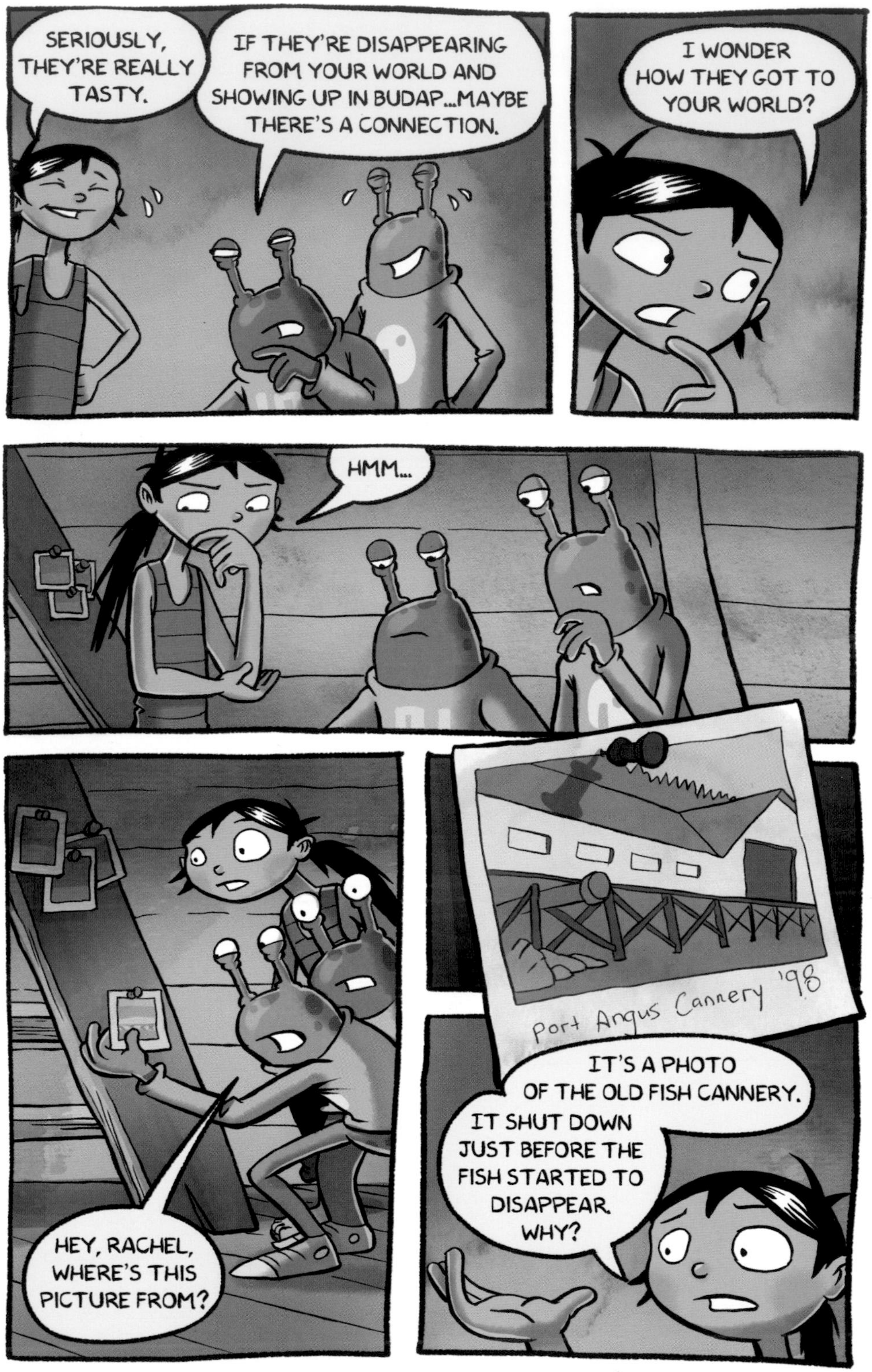
SERIOUSLY, THEY'RE REALLY TASTY.
IF THEY'RE DISAPPEARING FROM YOUR WORLD AND SHOWING UP IN BUDAP...MAYBE THERE'S A CONNECTION.
I WONDER HOW THEY GOT TO YOUR WORLD?
HMM...
HEY, RACHEL, WHERE'S THIS PICTURE FROM?
Port Angus Cannery '98
IT'S A PHOTO OF THE OLD FISH CANNERY.
IT SHUT DOWN JUST BEFORE THE FISH STARTED TO DISAPPEAR. WHY?

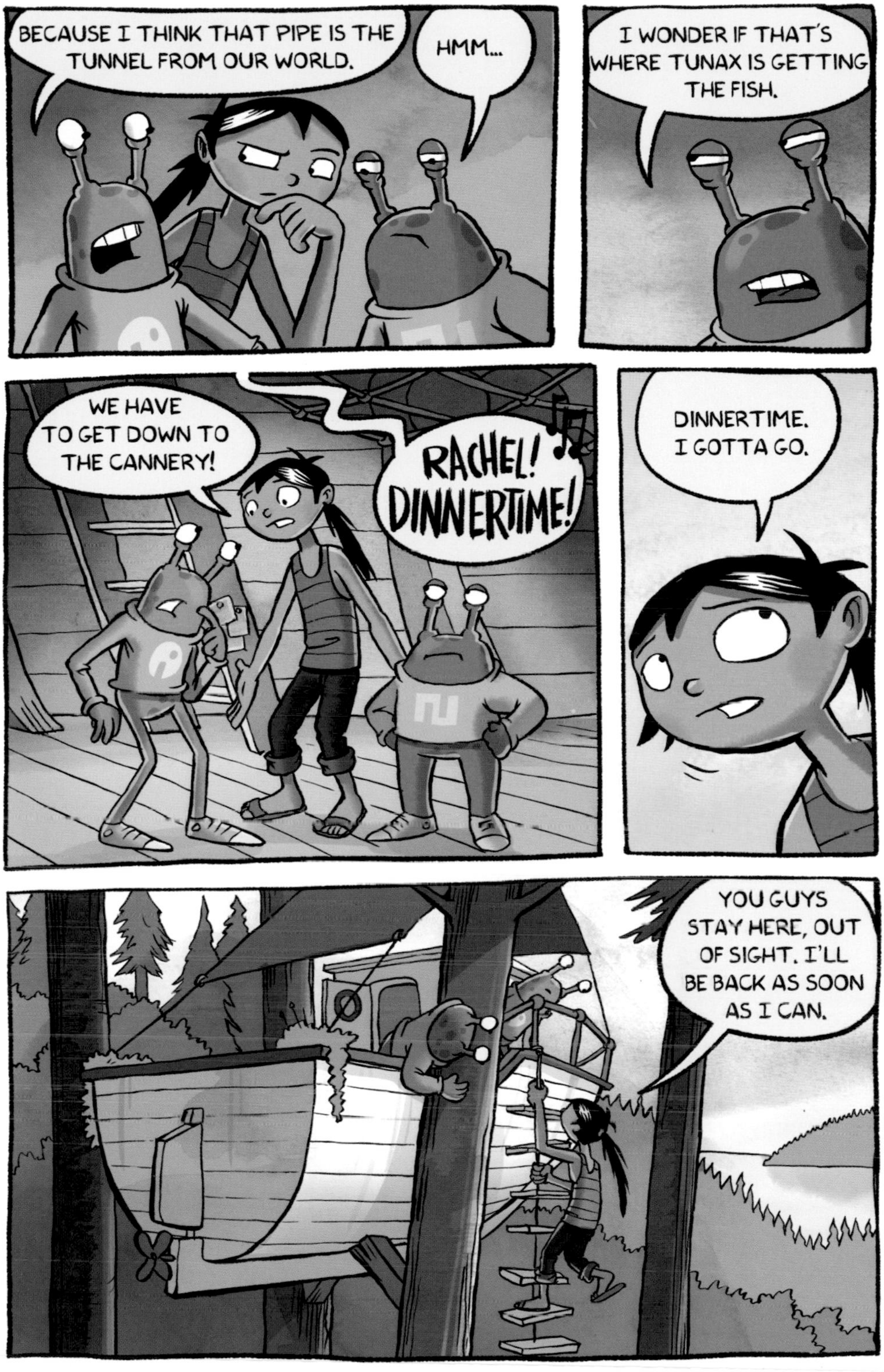
BECAUSE I THINK THAT PIPE IS THE TUNNEL FROM OUR WORLD.
HMM...
I WONDER IF THAT'S WHERE TUNAX IS GETTING THE FISH.
WE HAVE TO GET DOWN TO THE CANNERY!
RACHEL! DINNERTIME!
DINNERTIME. I GOTTA GO.
YOU GUYS STAY HERE, OUT OF SIGHT. I'LL BE BACK AS SOON AS I CAN.

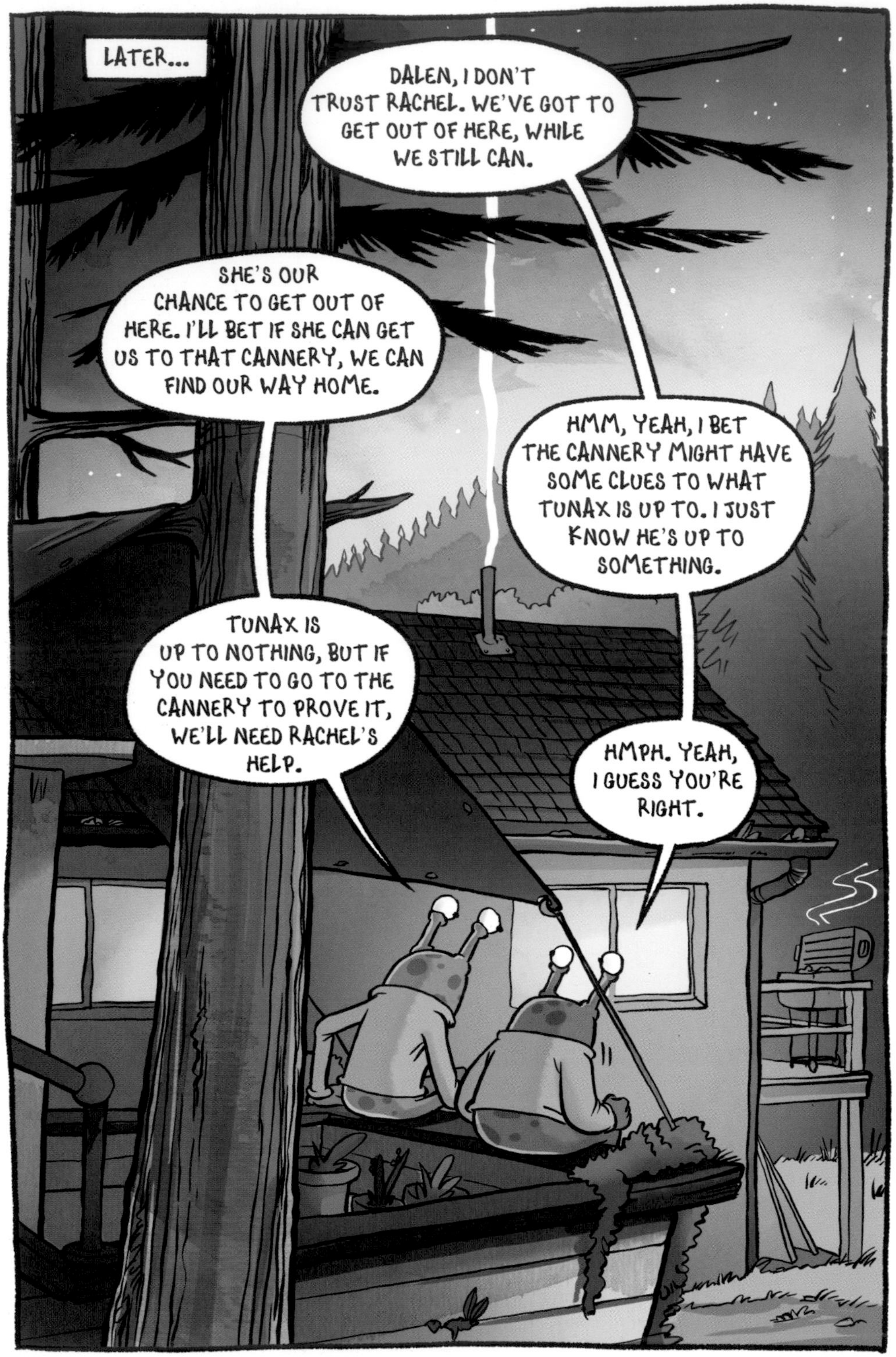
LATER...
DALEN, I DON'T TRUST RACHEL. WE'VE GOT TO GET OUT OF HERE, WHILE WE STILL CAN.
SHE'S OUR CHANCE TO GET OUT OF HERE. I'LL BET IF SHE CAN GET US TO THAT CANNERY, WE CAN FIND OUR WAY HOME.
HMM, YEAH, I BET THE CANNERY MIGHT HAVE SOME CLUES TO WHAT TUNAX IS UP TO. I JUST KNOW HE'S UP TO SOMETHING.
TUNAX IS UP TO NOTHING, BUT IF YOU NEED TO GO TO THE CANNERY TO PROVE IT, WE'LL NEED RACHEL'S HELP.
HMPH. YEAH, I GUESS YOU'RE RIGHT.

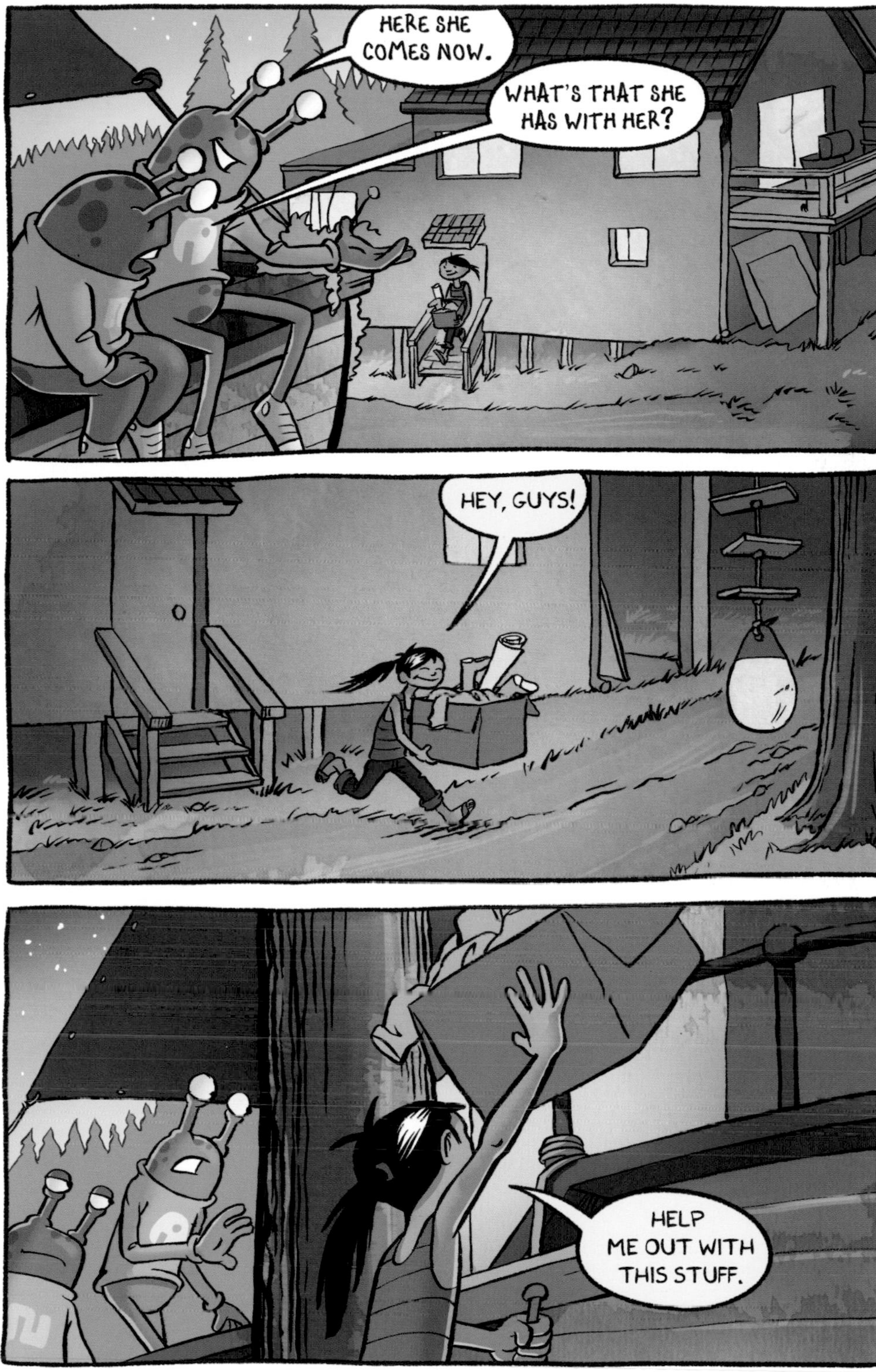
HERE SHE COMES NOW.
WHAT'S THAT SHE HAS WITH HER?
HEY, GUYS!
HELP ME OUT WITH THIS STUFF.

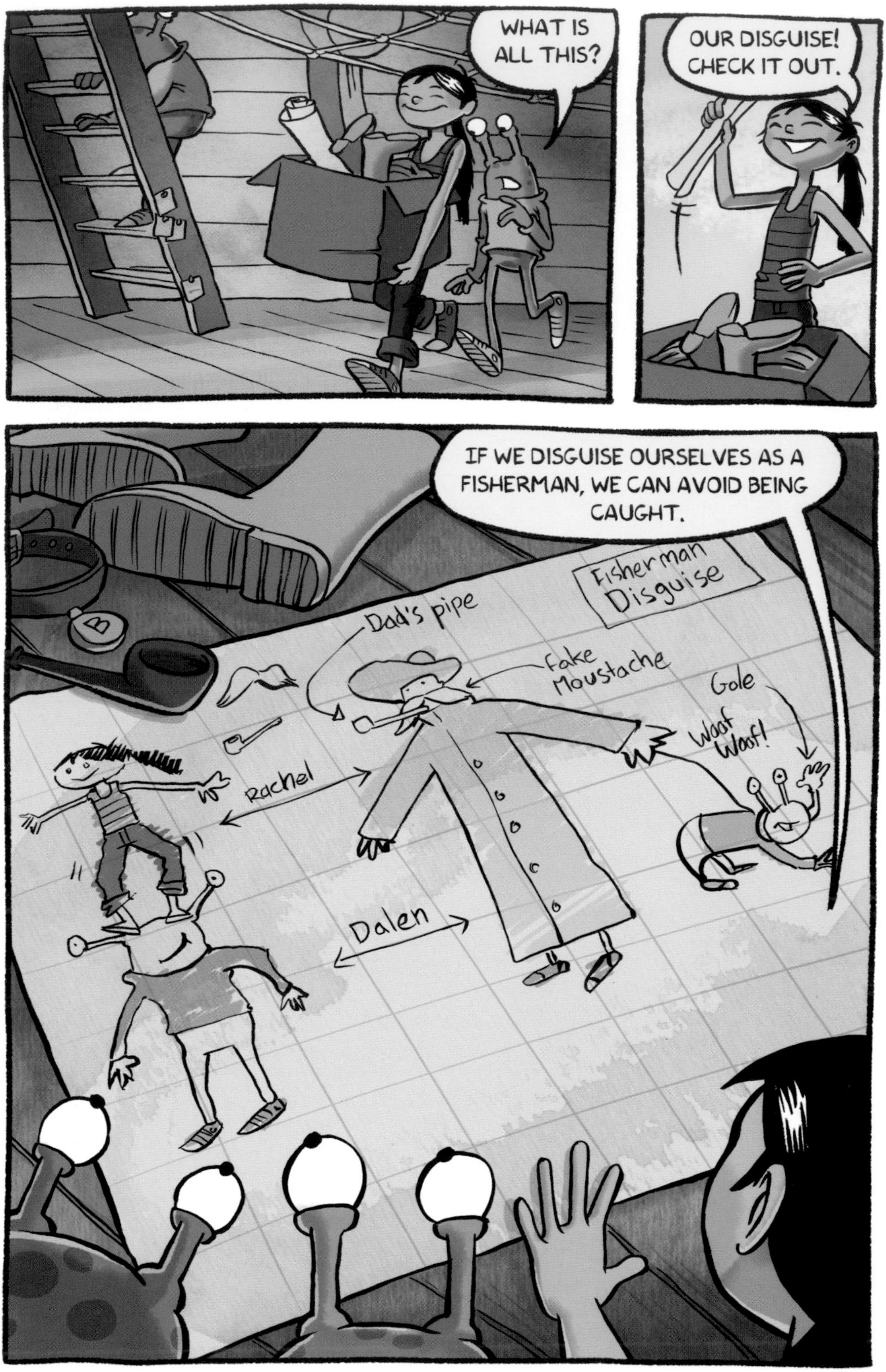
WHAT IS ALL THIS?
OUR DISGUISE! CHECK IT OUT.
IF WE DISGUISE OURSELVES AS A FISHERMAN, WE CAN AVOID BEING CAUGHT.
Fisherman Disguise
Dad's pipe
Fake Moustache
Gale
Woof Woof!
Rachel
Dalen

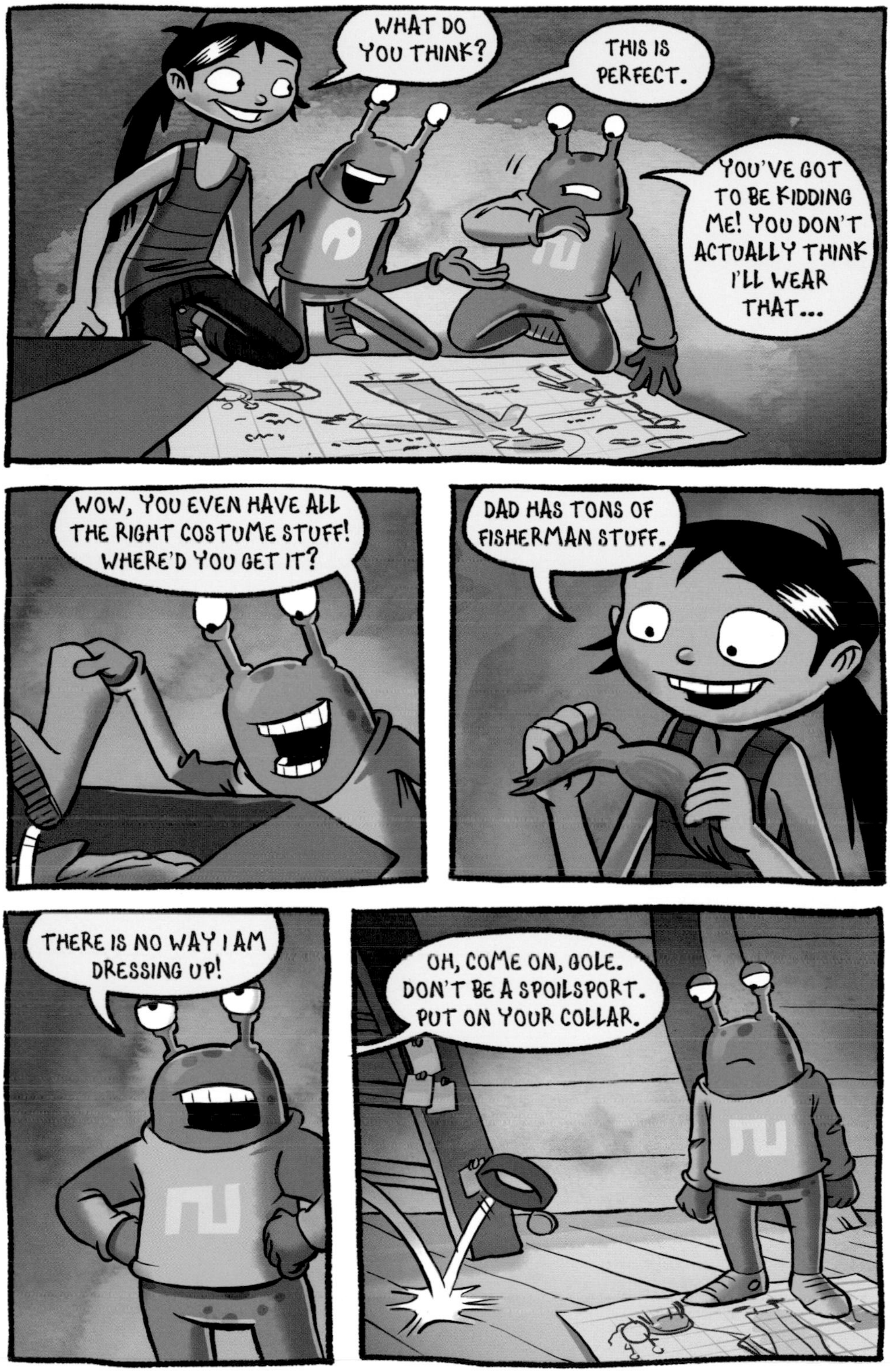
WHAT DO YOU THINK?
THIS IS PERFECT.
YOU'VE GOT TO BE KIDDING ME! YOU DON'T ACTUALLY THINK I'LL WEAR THAT...
WOW, YOU EVEN HAVE ALL THE RIGHT COSTUME STUFF! WHERE'D YOU GET IT?
DAD HAS TONS OF FISHERMAN STUFF.
THERE IS NO WAY I AM DRESSING UP!
OH, COME ON, GOLE. DON'T BE A SPOILSPORT. PUT ON YOUR COLLAR.

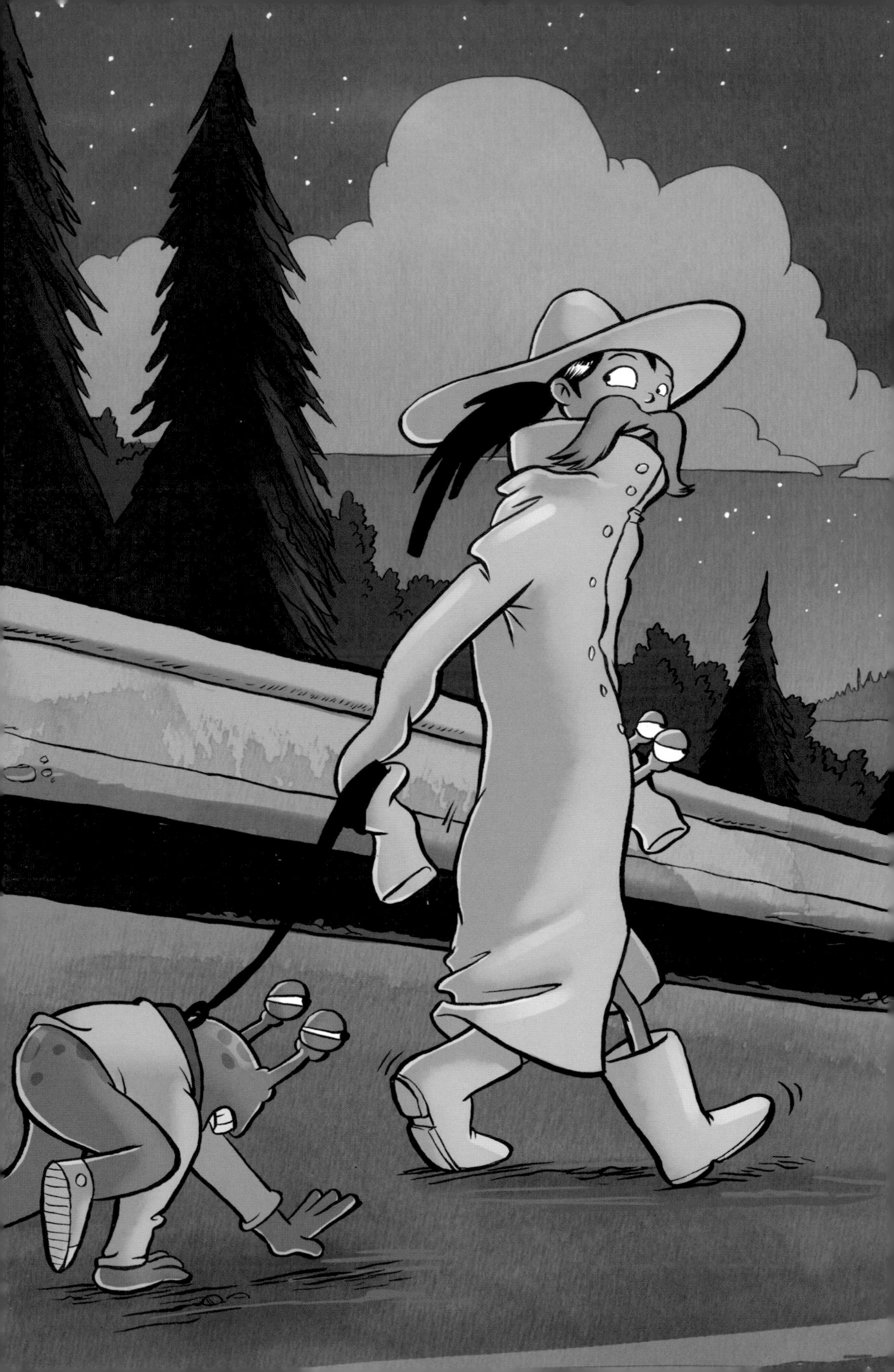

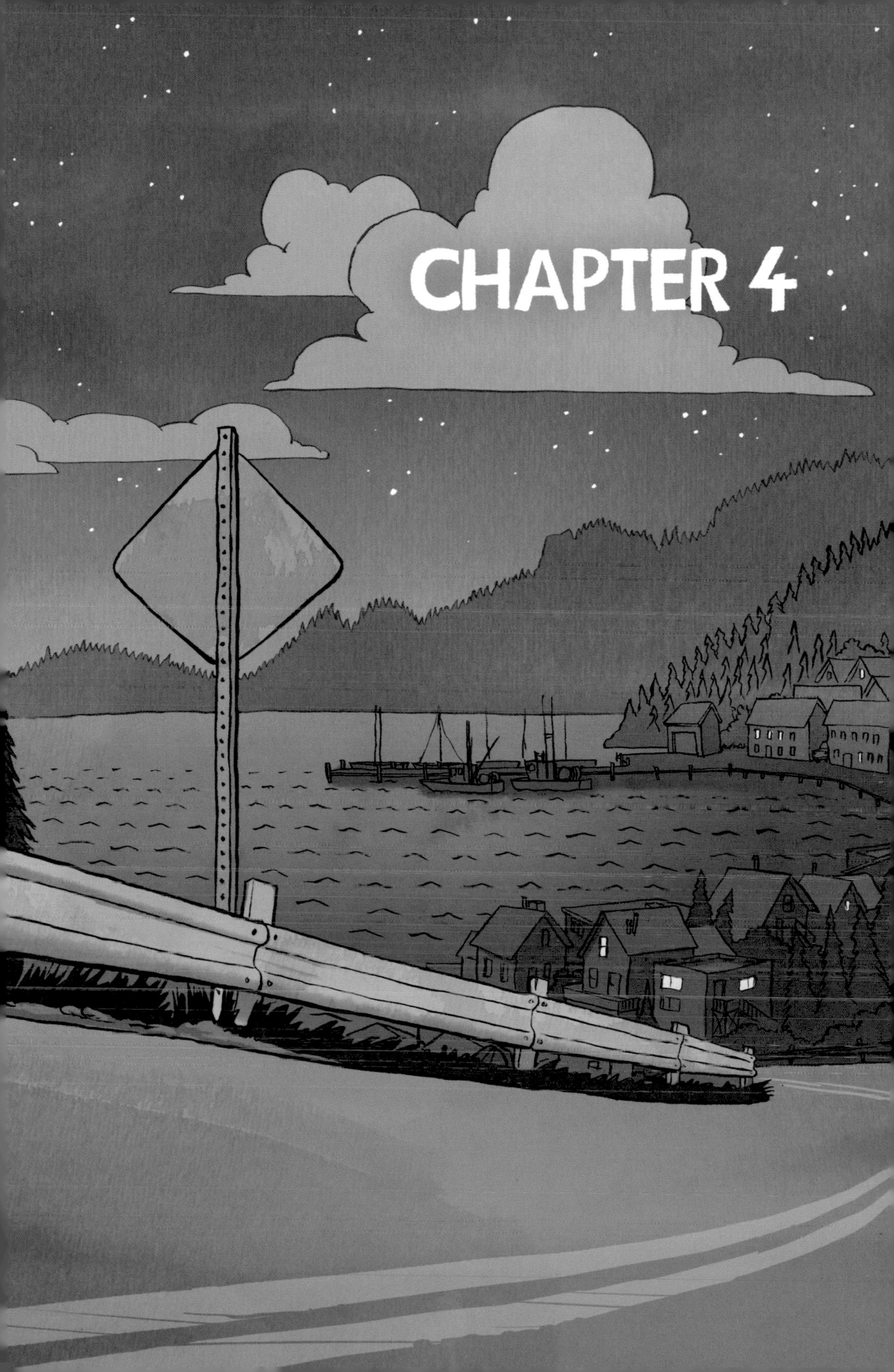
CHAPTER 4

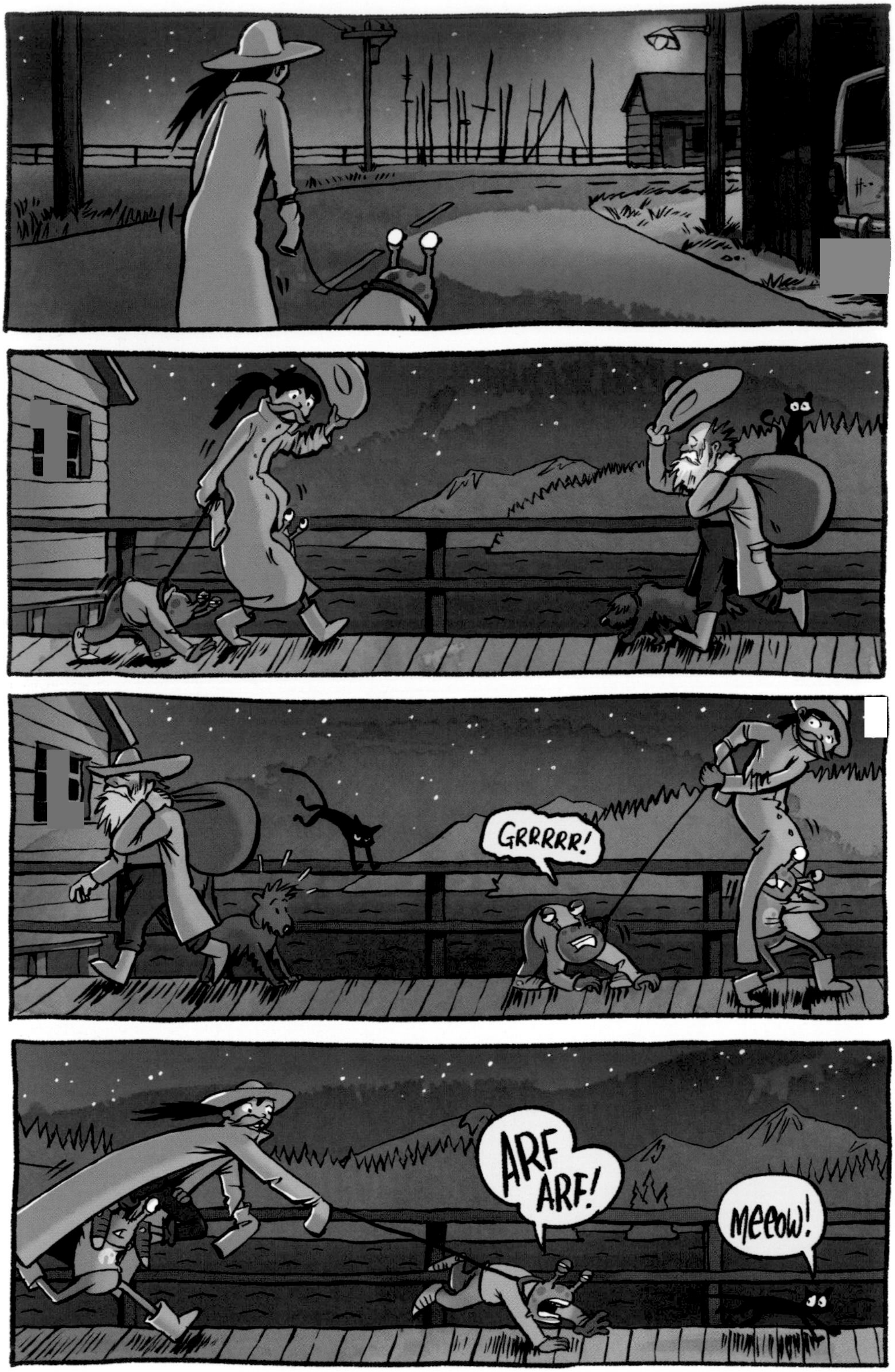
GRRRRR!
ARF ARF!
Meeow!

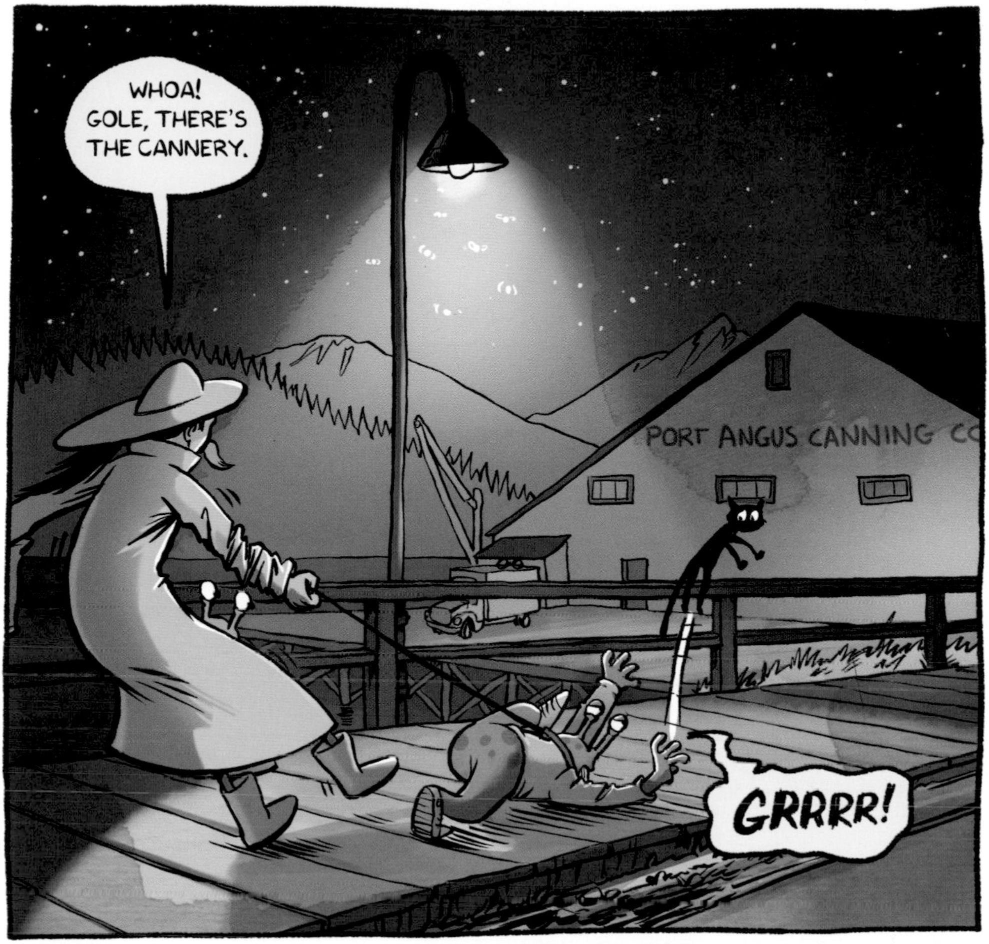
WHOA! GOLE, THERE'S THE CANNERY.
PORT ANGUS CANNING CO
GRRRR!

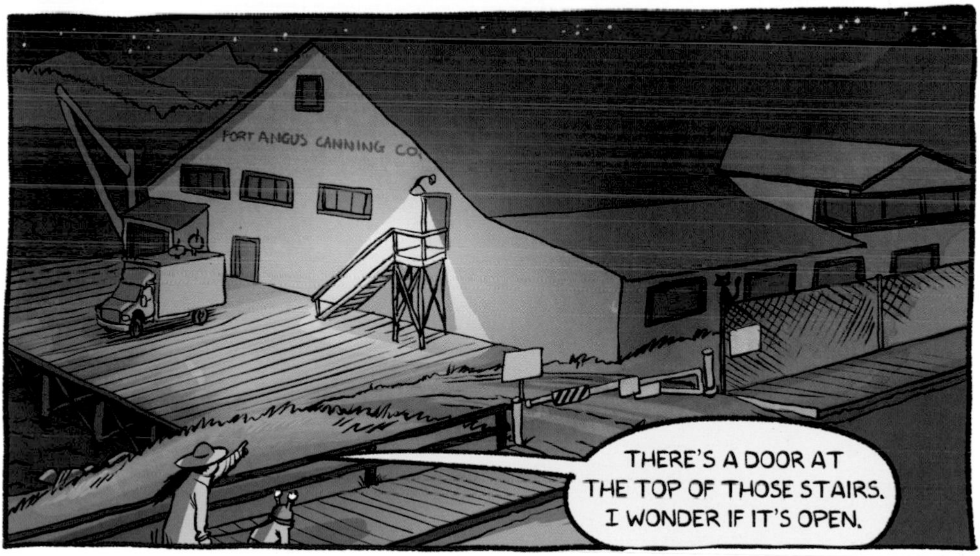
PORT ANGUS CANNING CO
THERE'S A DOOR AT THE TOP OF THOSE STAIRS. I WONDER IF IT'S OPEN.

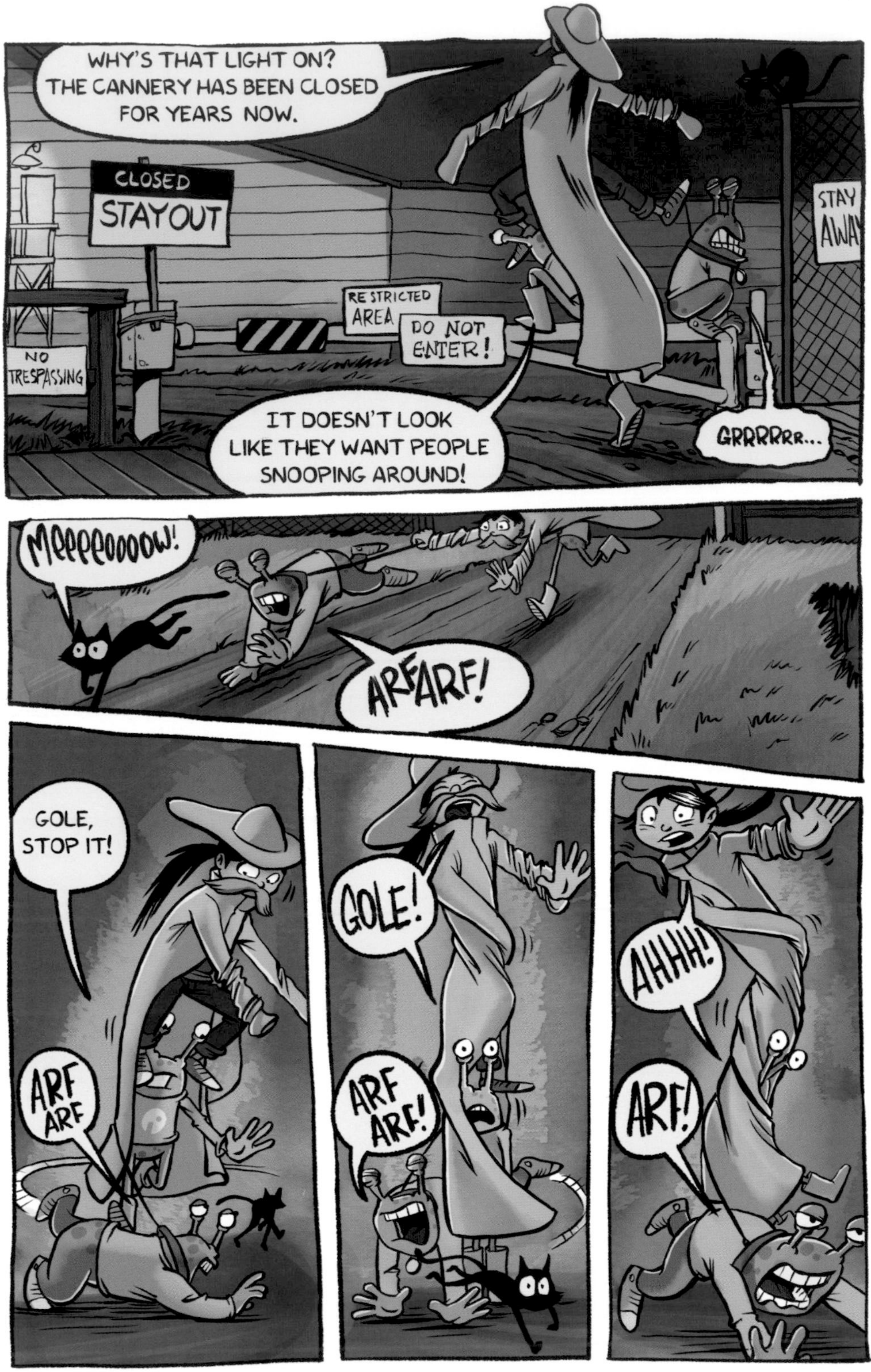
WHY'S THAT LIGHT ON? THE CANNERY HAS BEEN CLOSED FOR YEARS NOW.
CLOSED
STAY OUT
RESTRICTED AREA
DO NOT ENTER!
NO TRESPASSING
STAY AWAY
IT DOESN'T LOOK LIKE THEY WANT PEOPLE SNOOPING AROUND!
GRRRRRR...
MEEEOOOOW!
ARFARF!
GOLE, STOP IT!
ARF ARF
GOLE!
ARF ARF!
AHHH!
ARF!

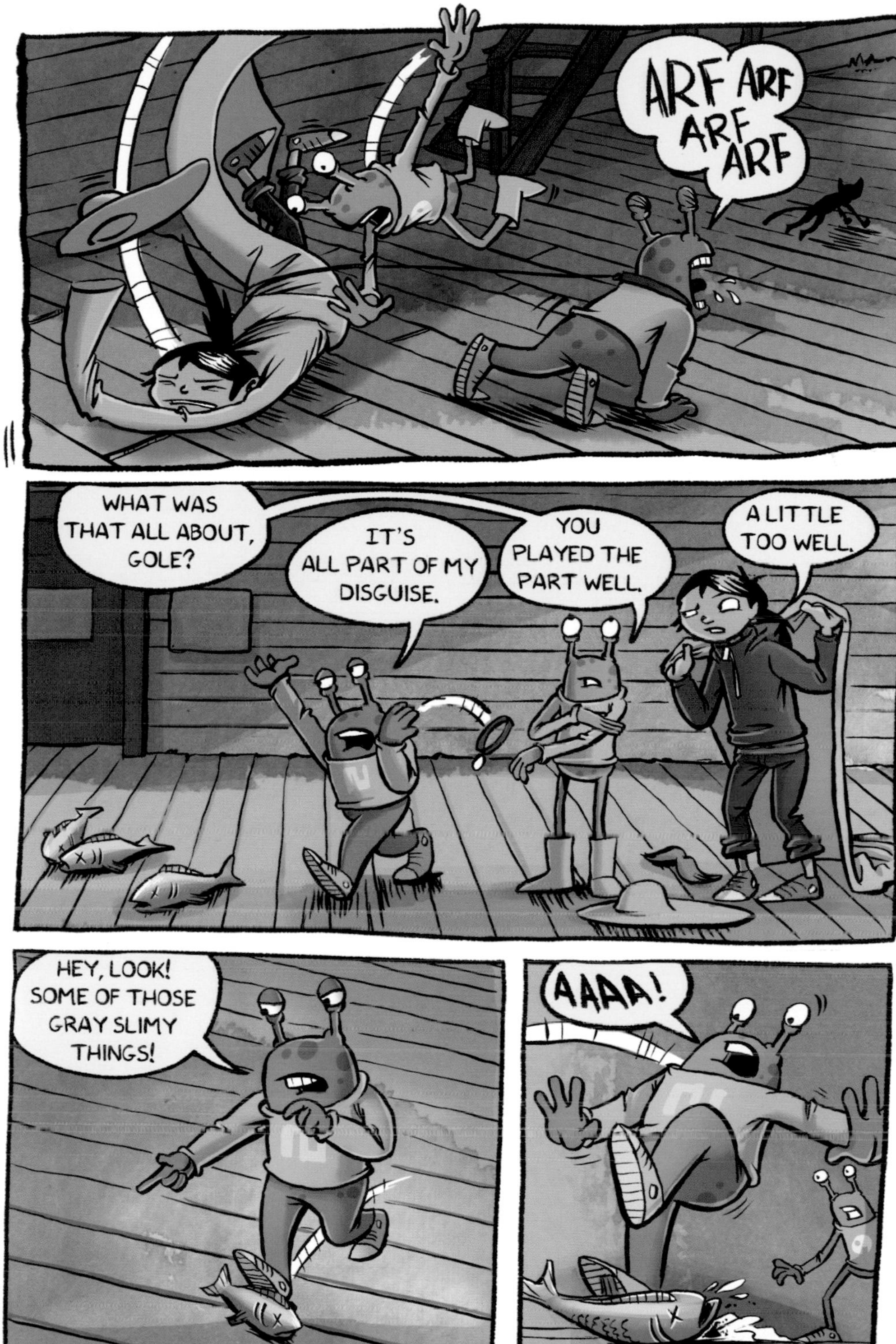
ARF ARF
ARF
ARF
WHAT WAS THAT ALL ABOUT, GOLE?
IT'S ALL PART OF MY DISGUISE.
YOU PLAYED THE PART WELL.
A LITTLE TOO WELL.
HEY, LOOK! SOME OF THOSE GRAY SLIMY THINGS!
AAAA!

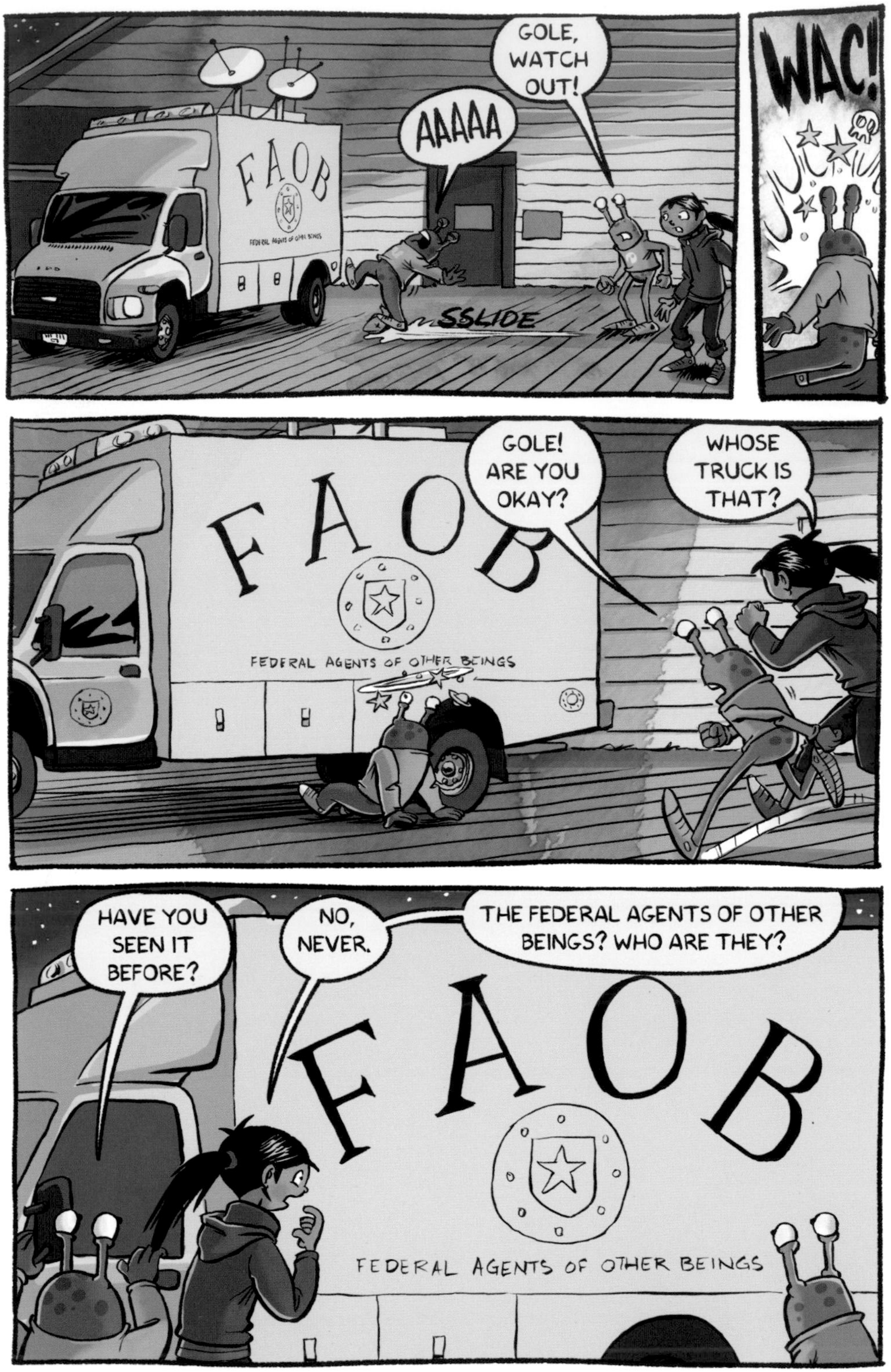
FAOB
AAAAA
GOLE, WATCH OUT!
SSLIDE
WAC!
FAOB
FEDERAL AGENTS OF OTHER BEINGS
GOLE! ARE YOU OKAY?
WHOSE TRUCK IS THAT?
HAVE YOU SEEN IT BEFORE?
NO, NEVER.
THE FEDERAL AGENTS OF OTHER BEINGS? WHO ARE THEY?
FAOB
FEDERAL AGENTS OF OTHER BEINGS

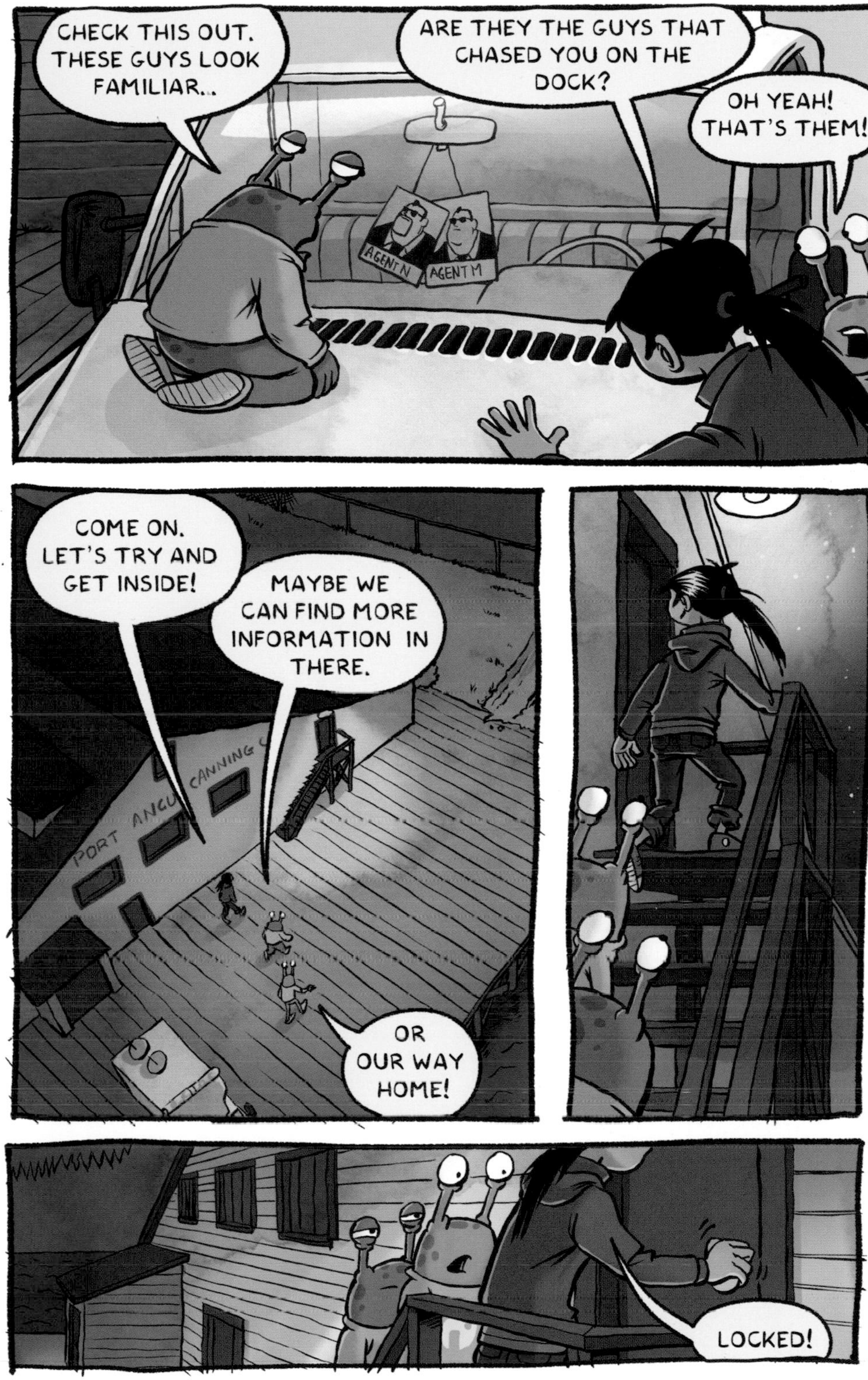
CHECK THIS OUT. THESE GUYS LOOK FAMILIAR...
ARE THEY THE GUYS THAT CHASED YOU ON THE DOCK?
OH YEAH! THAT'S THEM!
AGENT N
AGENT M
COME ON. LET'S TRY AND GET INSIDE!
MAYBE WE CAN FIND MORE INFORMATION IN THERE.
PORT ANGU CANNING
OR OUR WAY HOME!
LOCKED!

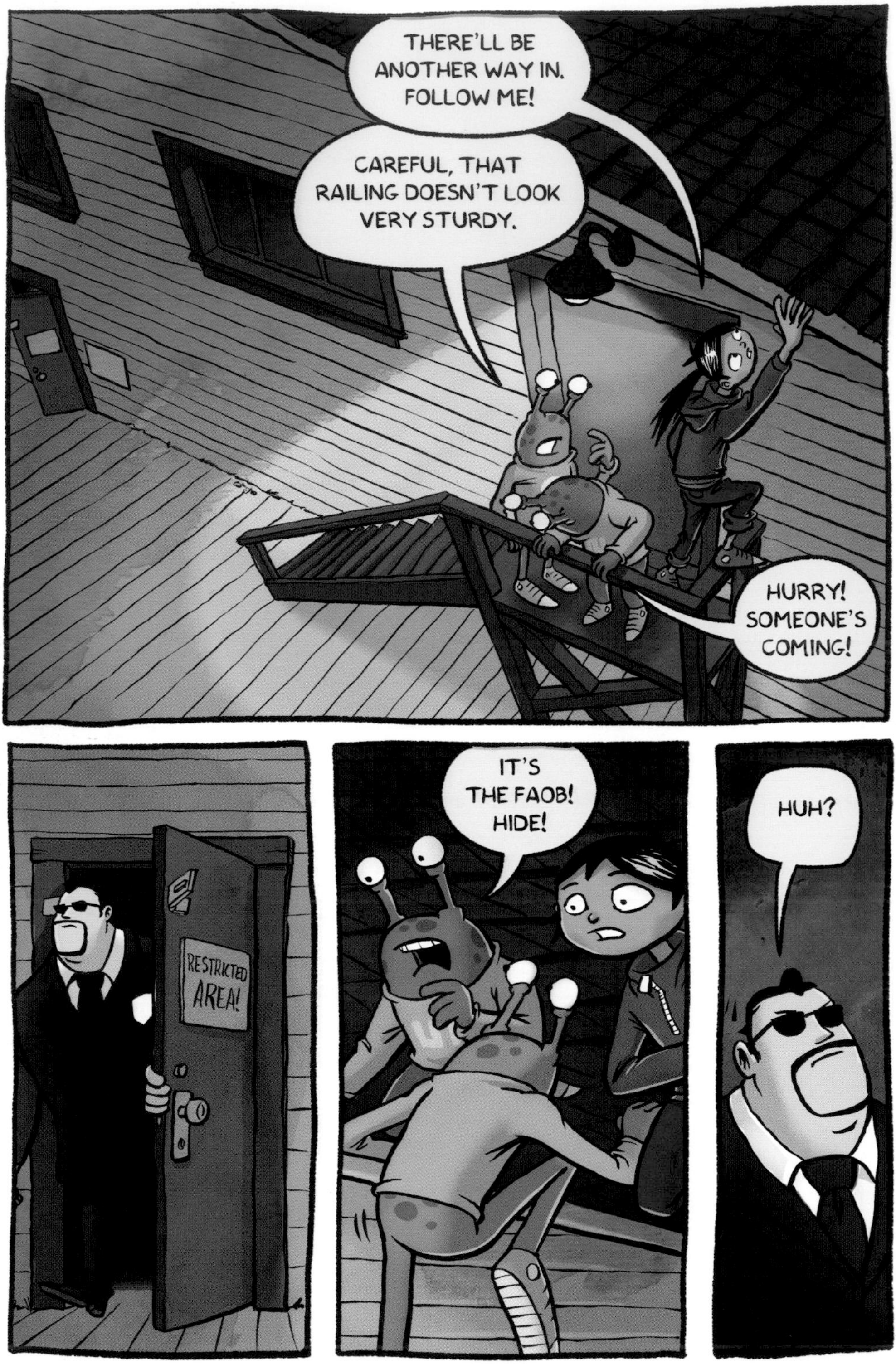
THERE'LL BE ANOTHER WAY IN. FOLLOW ME!
CAREFUL, THAT RAILING DOESN'T LOOK VERY STURDY.
HURRY! SOMEONE'S COMING!
RESTRICTED AREA!
IT'S THE FAOB! HIDE!
HUH?

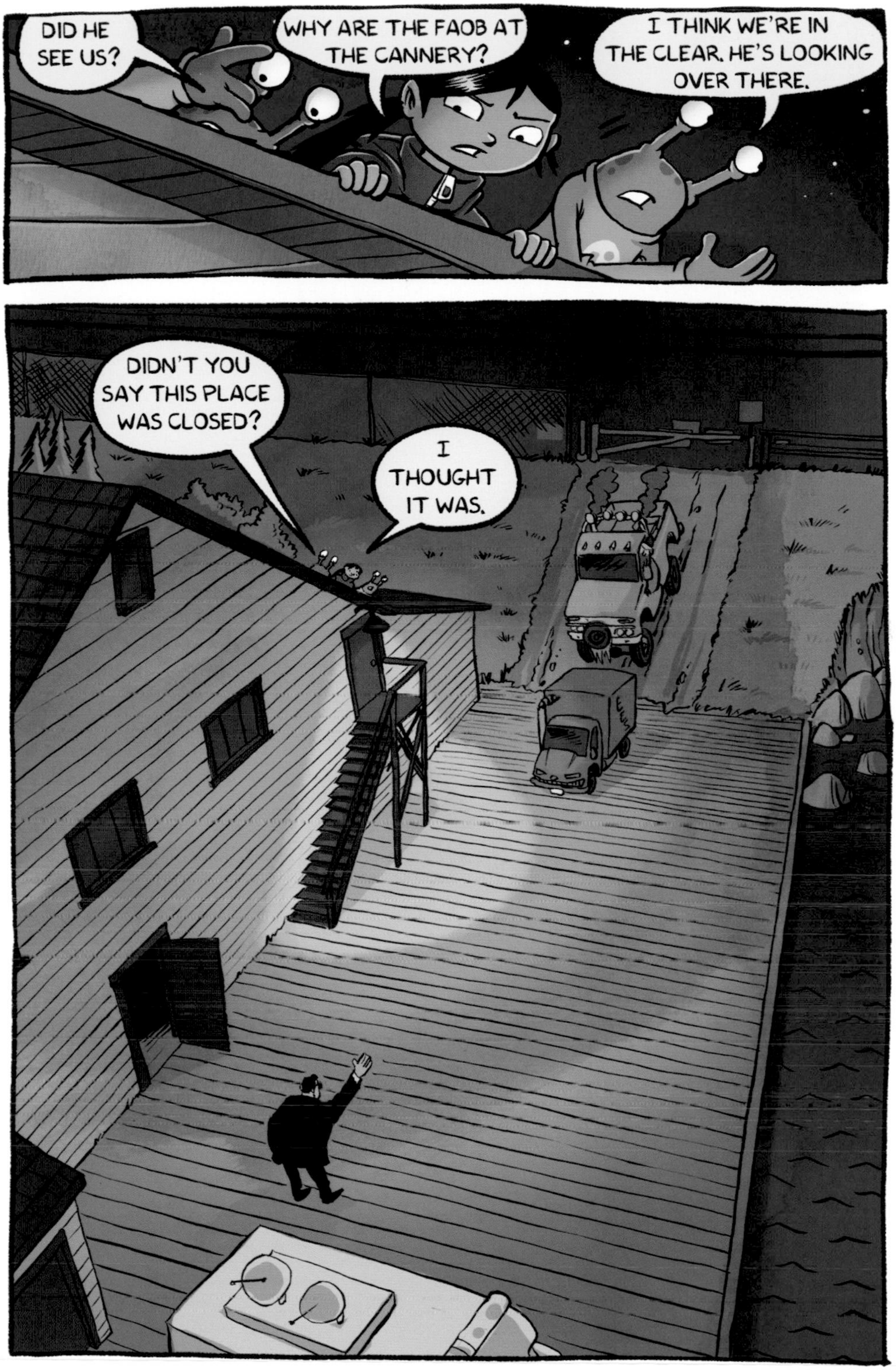
DID HE SEE US?
WHY ARE THE FAOB AT THE CANNERY?
I THINK WE'RE IN THE CLEAR. HE'S LOOKING OVER THERE.
DIDN'T YOU SAY THIS PLACE WAS CLOSED?
I THOUGHT IT WAS.

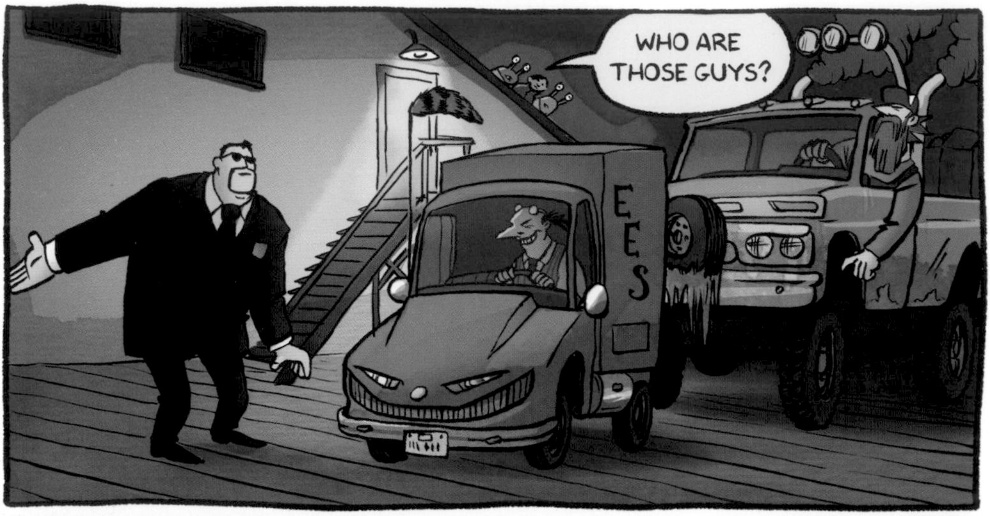
WHO ARE THOSE GUYS?
EES

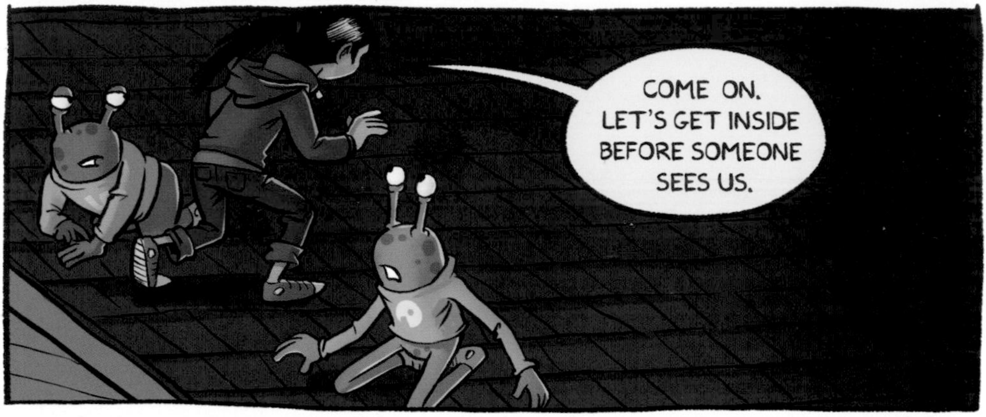
COME ON. LET'S GET INSIDE BEFORE SOMEONE SEES US.

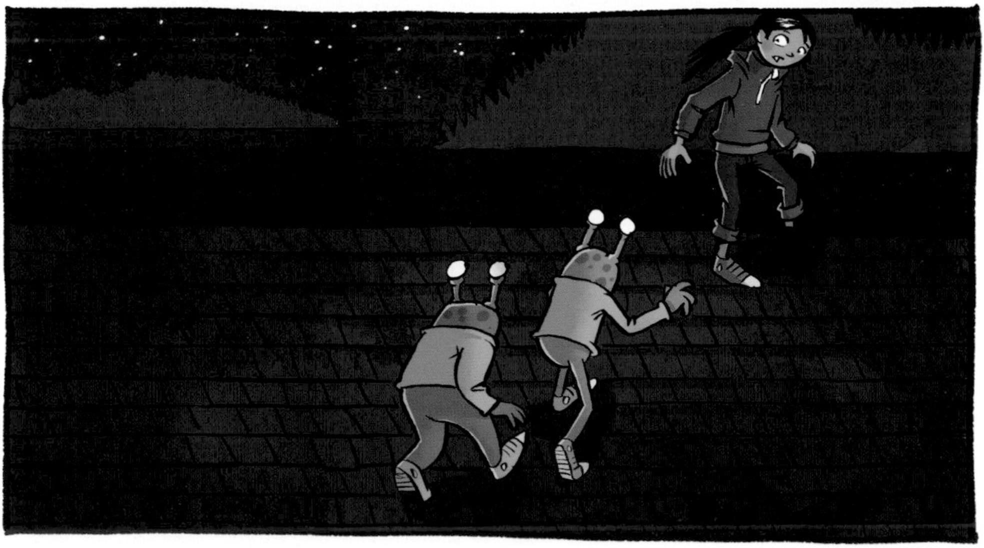

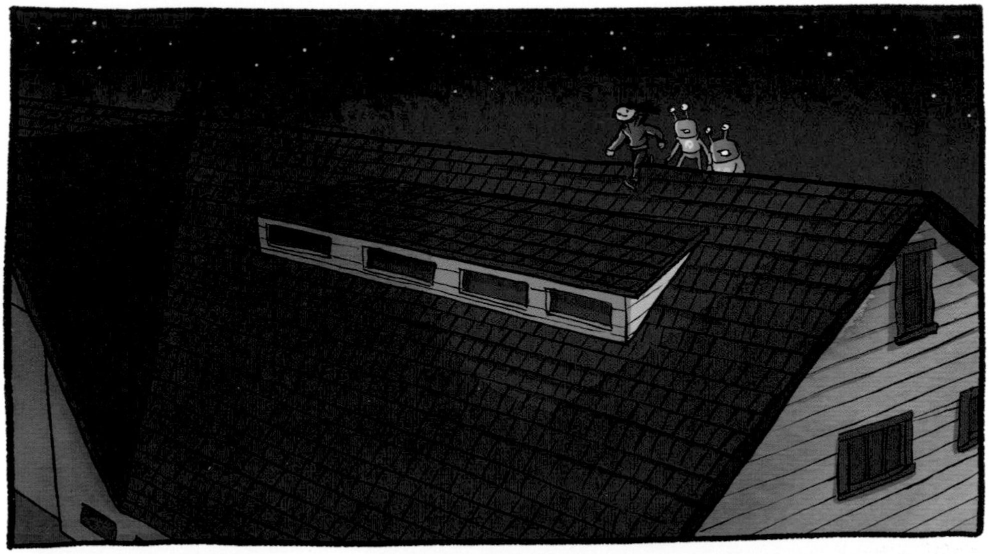

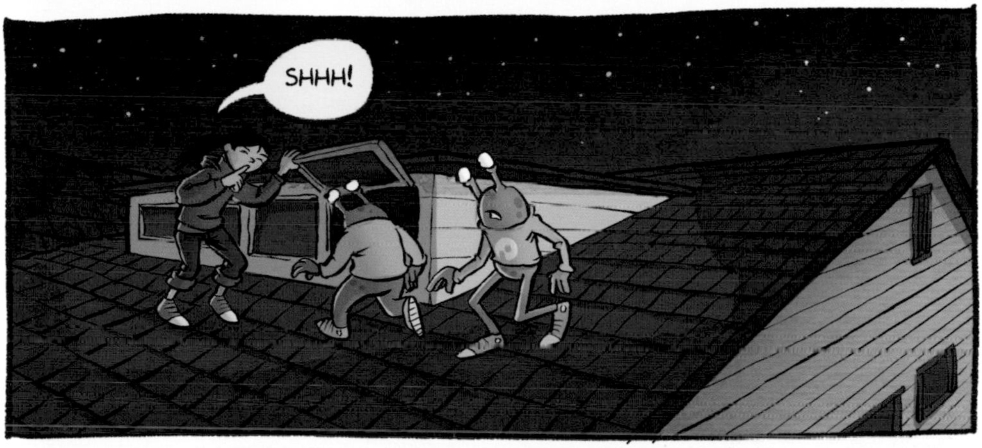
SHHH!

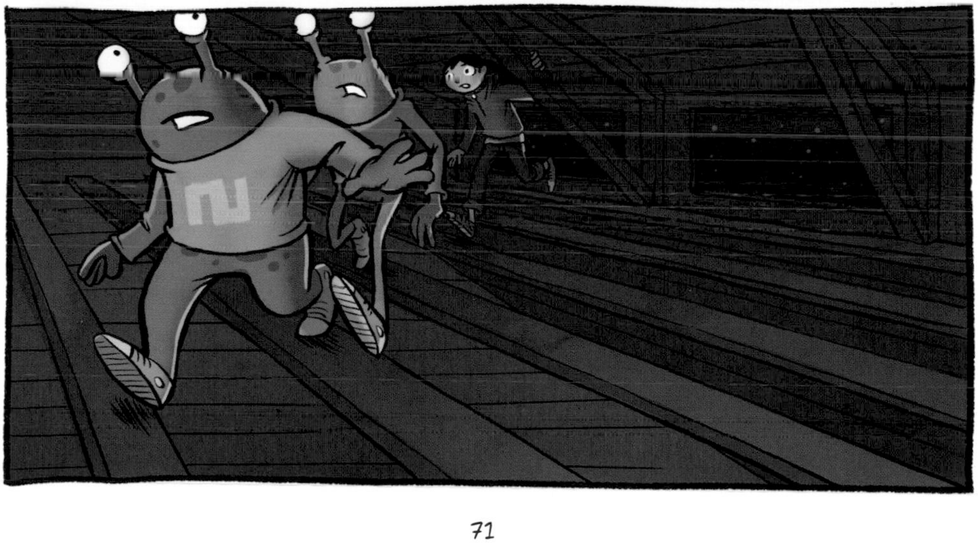

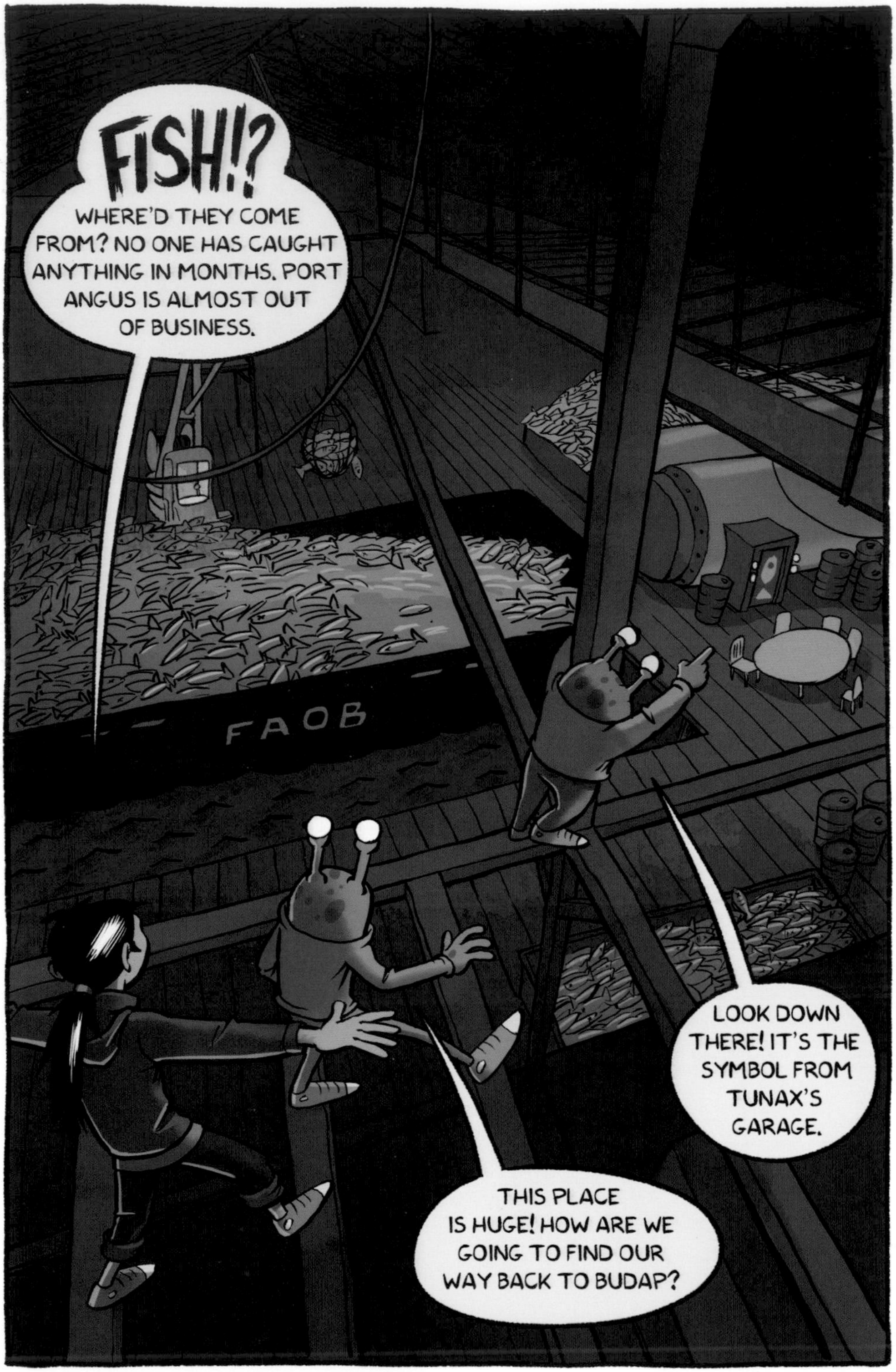
FISH!?
WHERE'D THEY COME FROM? NO ONE HAS CAUGHT ANYTHING IN MONTHS. PORT ANGUS IS ALMOST OUT OF BUSINESS.
FAOB
LOOK DOWN THERE! IT'S THE SYMBOL FROM TUNAX'S GARAGE.
THIS PLACE IS HUGE! HOW ARE WE GOING TO FIND OUR WAY BACK TO BUDAP?

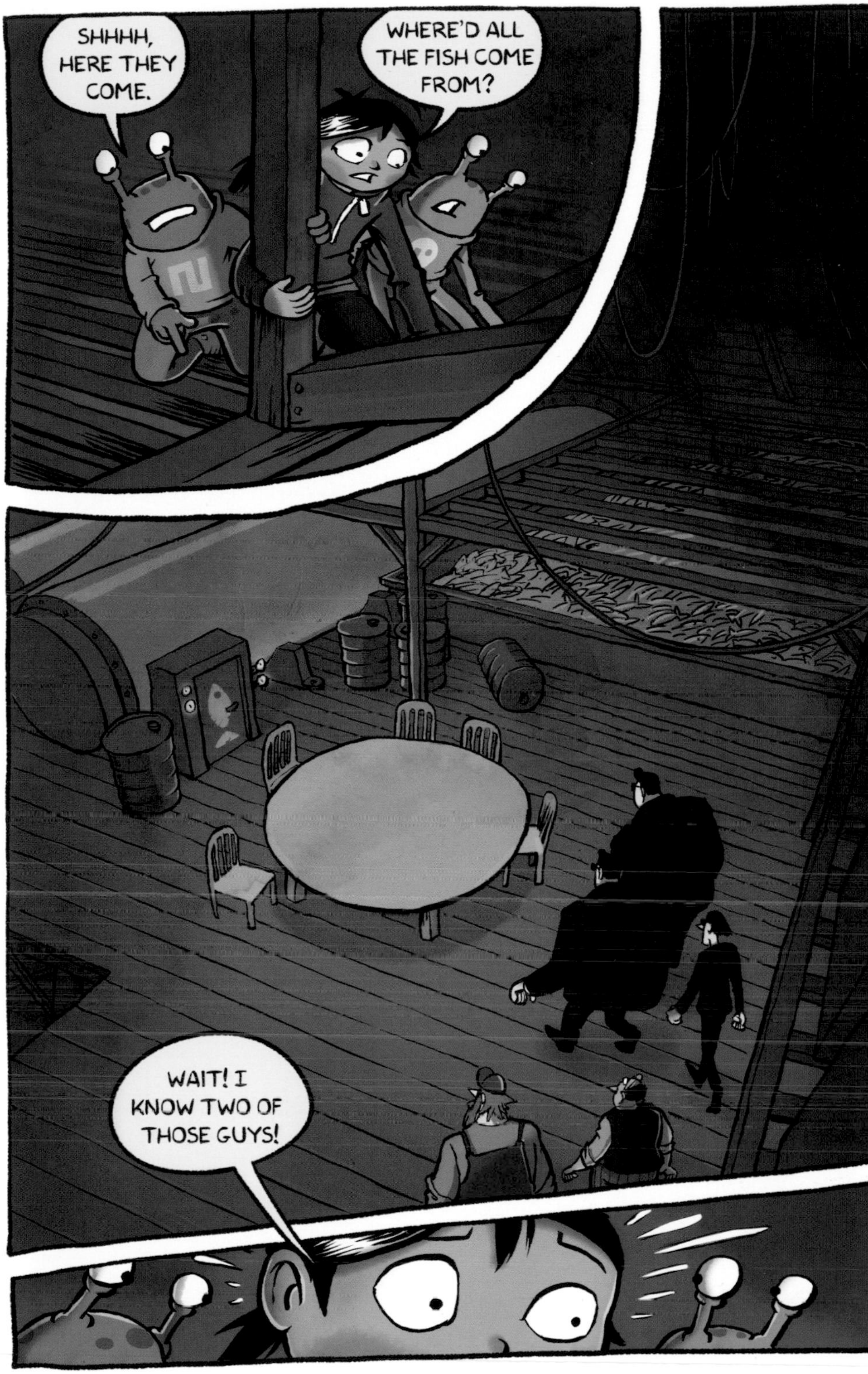
SHHHH, HERE THEY COME.
WHERE'D ALL THE FISH COME FROM?
WAIT! I KNOW TWO OF THOSE GUYS!

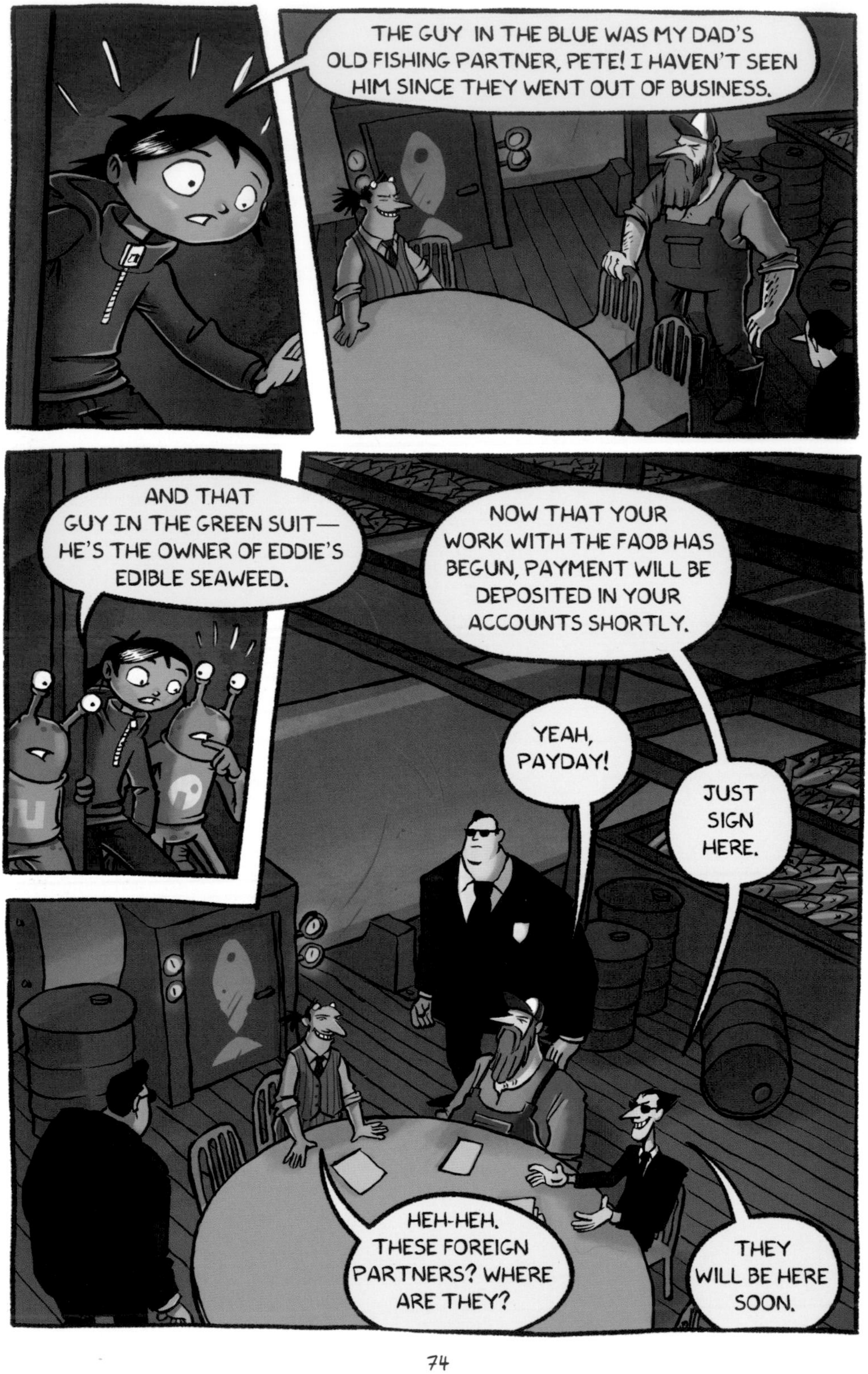
THE GUY IN THE BLUE WAS MY DAD'S OLD FISHING PARTNER, PETE! I HAVEN'T SEEN HIM SINCE THEY WENT OUT OF BUSINESS.
AND THAT GUY IN THE GREEN SUIT— HE'S THE OWNER OF EDDIE'S EDIBLE SEAWEED.
NOW THAT YOUR WORK WITH THE FAOB HAS BEGUN, PAYMENT WILL BE DEPOSITED IN YOUR ACCOUNTS SHORTLY.
YEAH, PAYDAY!
JUST SIGN HERE.
HEH-HEH. THESE FOREIGN PARTNERS? WHERE ARE THEY?
THEY WILL BE HERE SOON.

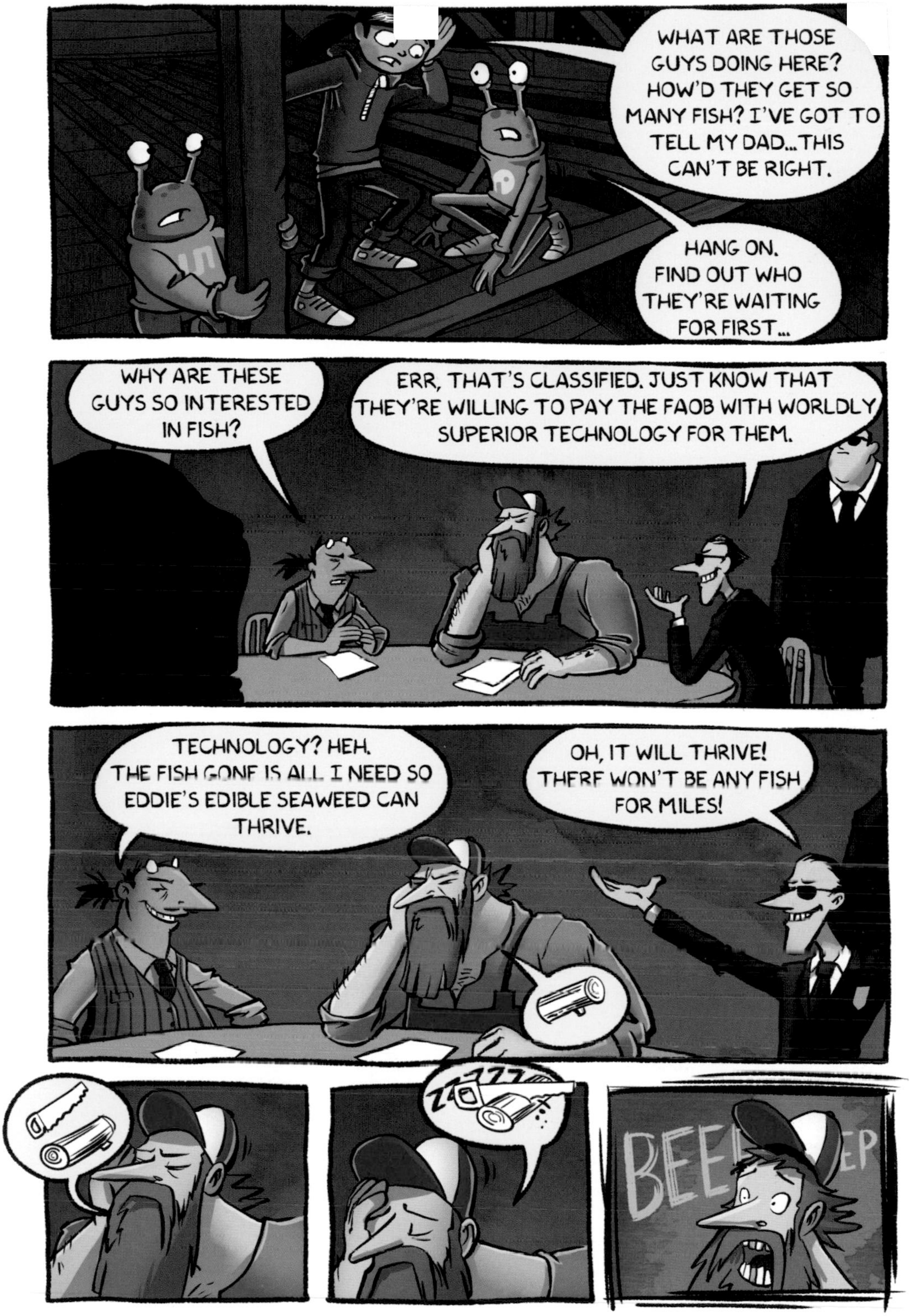

WHAT ARE THOSE GUYS DOING HERE? HOW'D THEY GET SO MANY FISH? I'VE GOT TO TELL MY DAD...THIS CAN'T BE RIGHT.
HANG ON. FIND OUT WHO THEY'RE WAITING FOR FIRST...
WHY ARE THESE GUYS SO INTERESTED IN FISH?
ERR, THAT'S CLASSIFIED. JUST KNOW THAT THEY'RE WILLING TO PAY THE FAOB WITH WORLDLY SUPERIOR TECHNOLOGY FOR THEM.
TECHNOLOGY? HEH. THE FISH GONE IS ALL I NEED SO EDDIE'S EDIBLE SEAWEED CAN THRIVE.
OH, IT WILL THRIVE! THERE WON'T BE ANY FISH FOR MILES!
BEEP

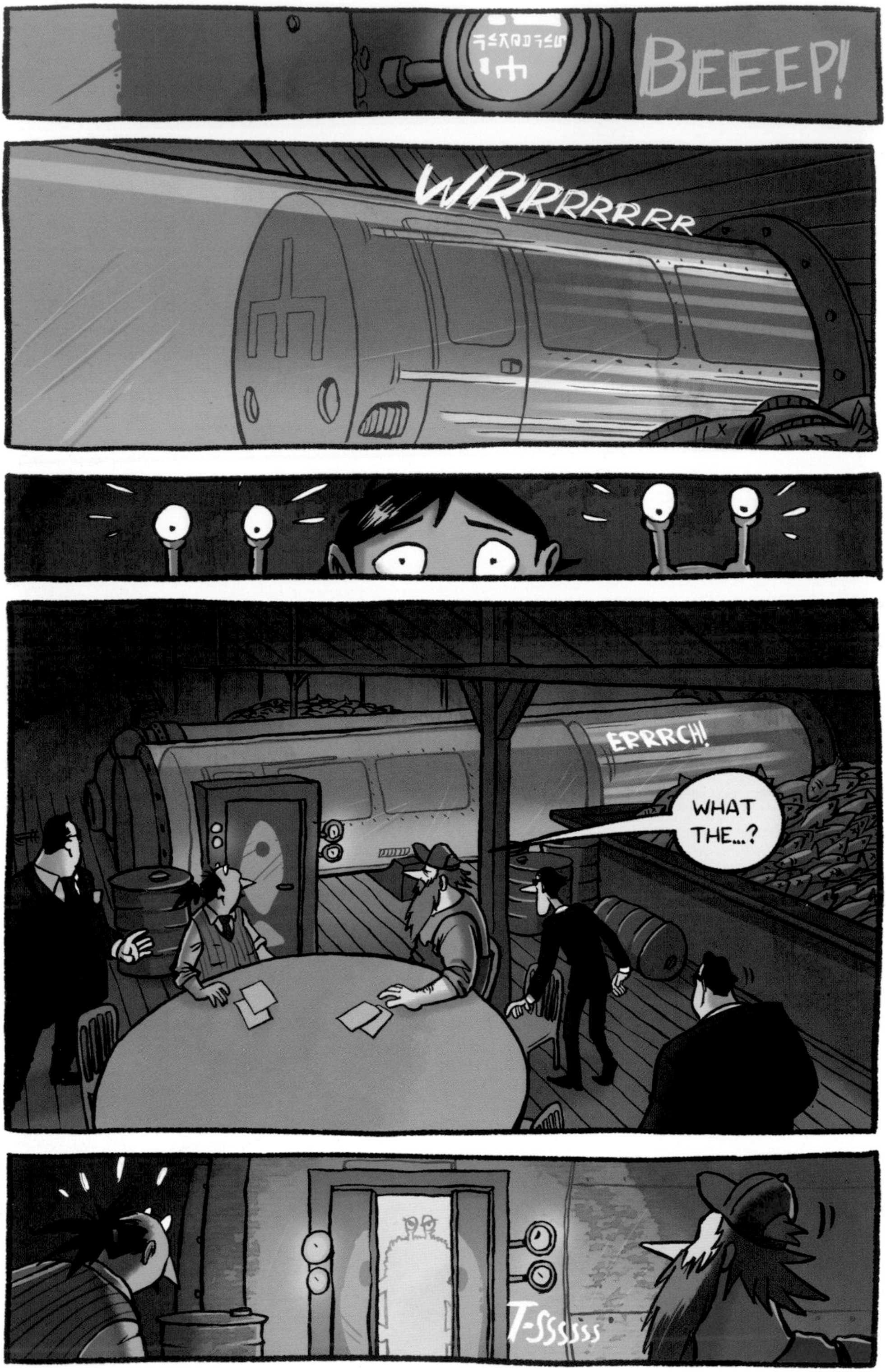
BEEEP!
WRRRRRRRR
ERRRCH!
WHAT THE...?
T-SSSSSS

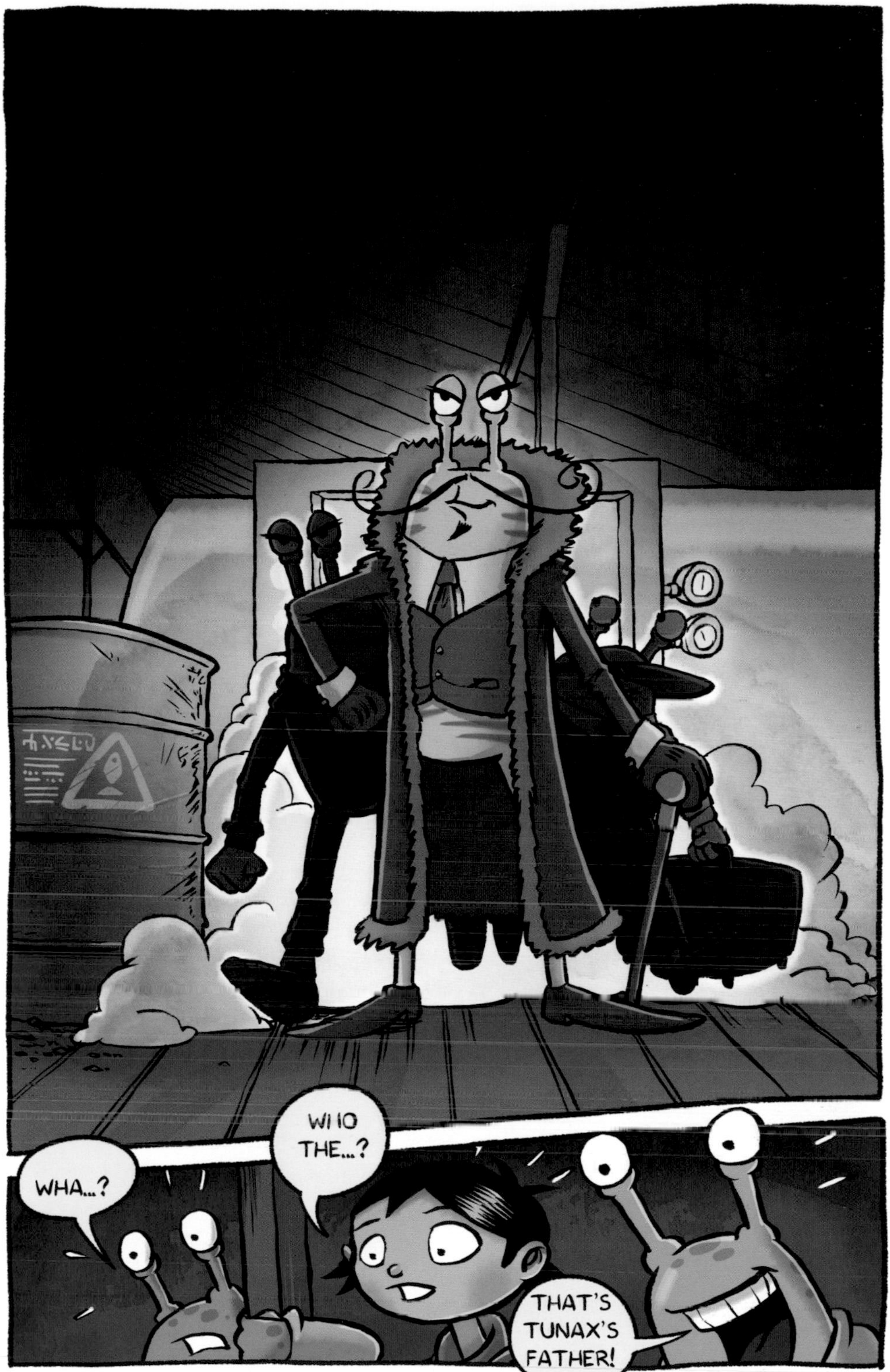
WHA...?
WHO THE...?
THAT'S TUNAX'S FATHER!

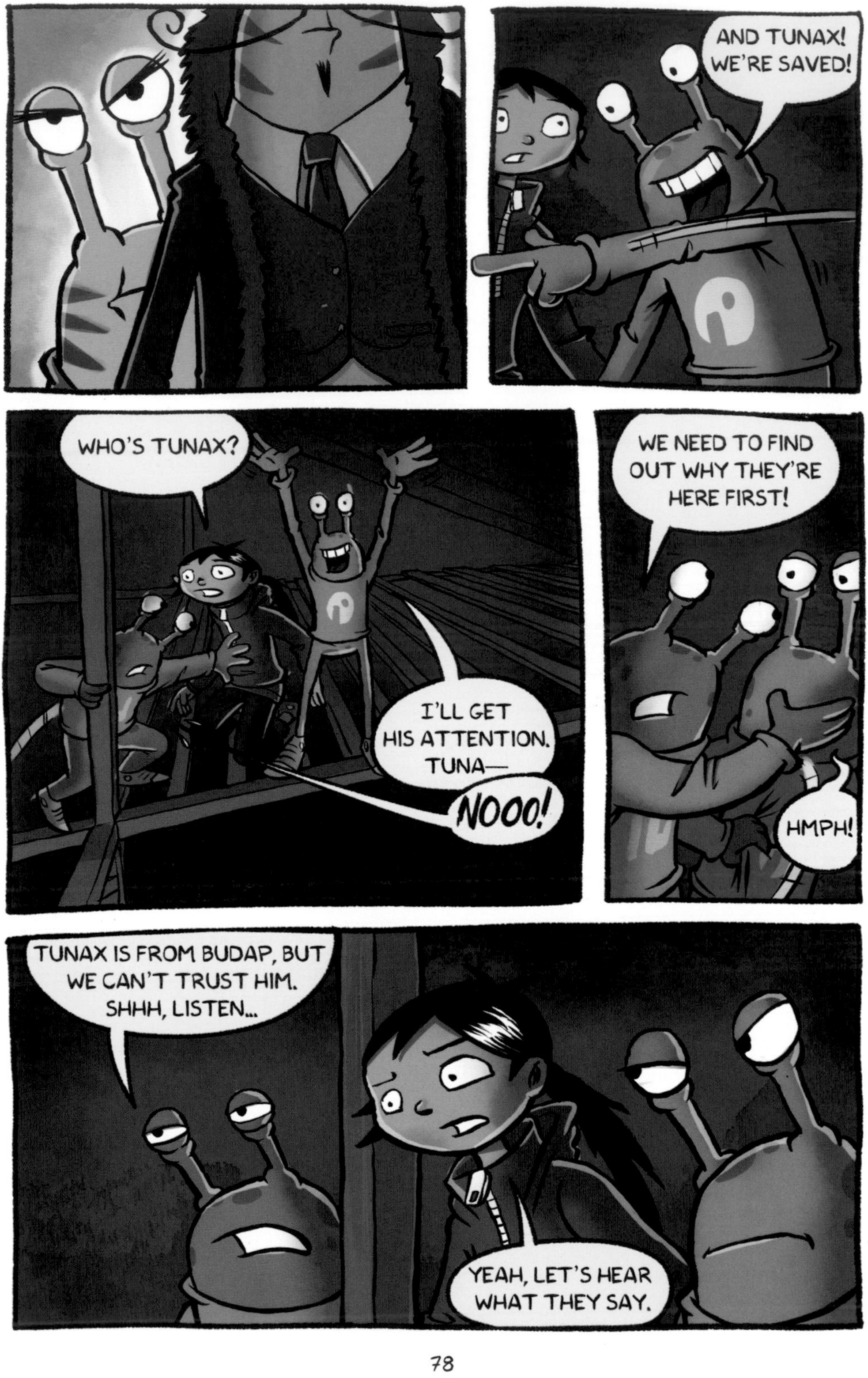

AND TUNAX! WE'RE SAVED!
WHO'S TUNAX?
I'LL GET HIS ATTENTION. TUNA—
NOOO!
WE NEED TO FIND OUT WHY THEY'RE HERE FIRST!
HMPH!
TUNAX IS FROM BUDAP, BUT WE CAN'T TRUST HIM. SHHH, LISTEN...
YEAH, LET'S HEAR WHAT THEY SAY.

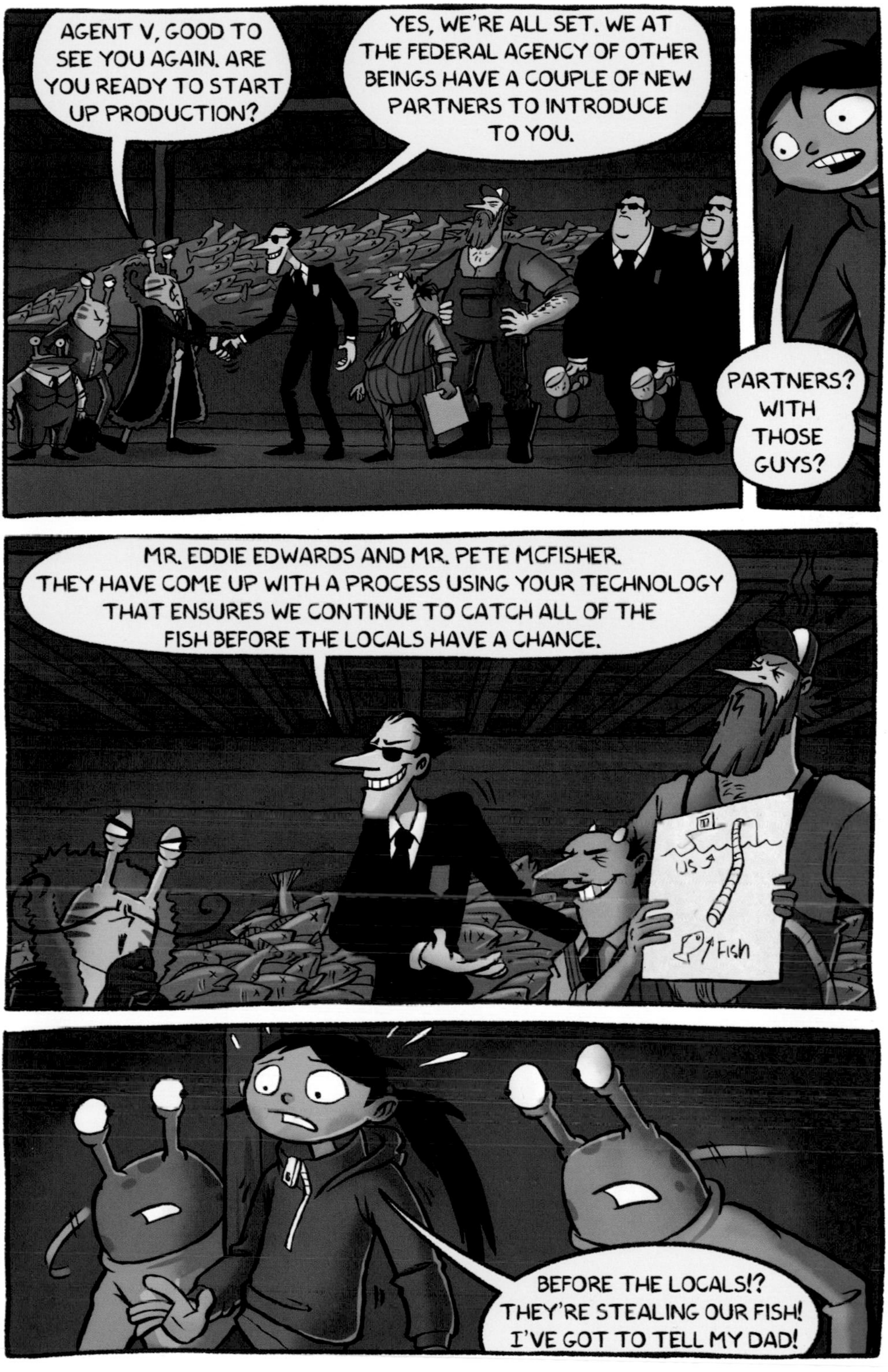
AGENT V, GOOD TO SEE YOU AGAIN. ARE YOU READY TO START UP PRODUCTION?
YES, WE'RE ALL SET. WE AT THE FEDERAL AGENCY OF OTHER BEINGS HAVE A COUPLE OF NEW PARTNERS TO INTRODUCE TO YOU.
PARTNERS? WITH THOSE GUYS?
MR. EDDIE EDWARDS AND MR. PETE MCFISHER. THEY HAVE COME UP WITH A PROCESS USING YOUR TECHNOLOGY THAT ENSURES WE CONTINUE TO CATCH ALL OF THE FISH BEFORE THE LOCALS HAVE A CHANCE.
US
Fish
BEFORE THE LOCALS!? THEY'RE STEALING OUR FISH! I'VE GOT TO TELL MY DAD!

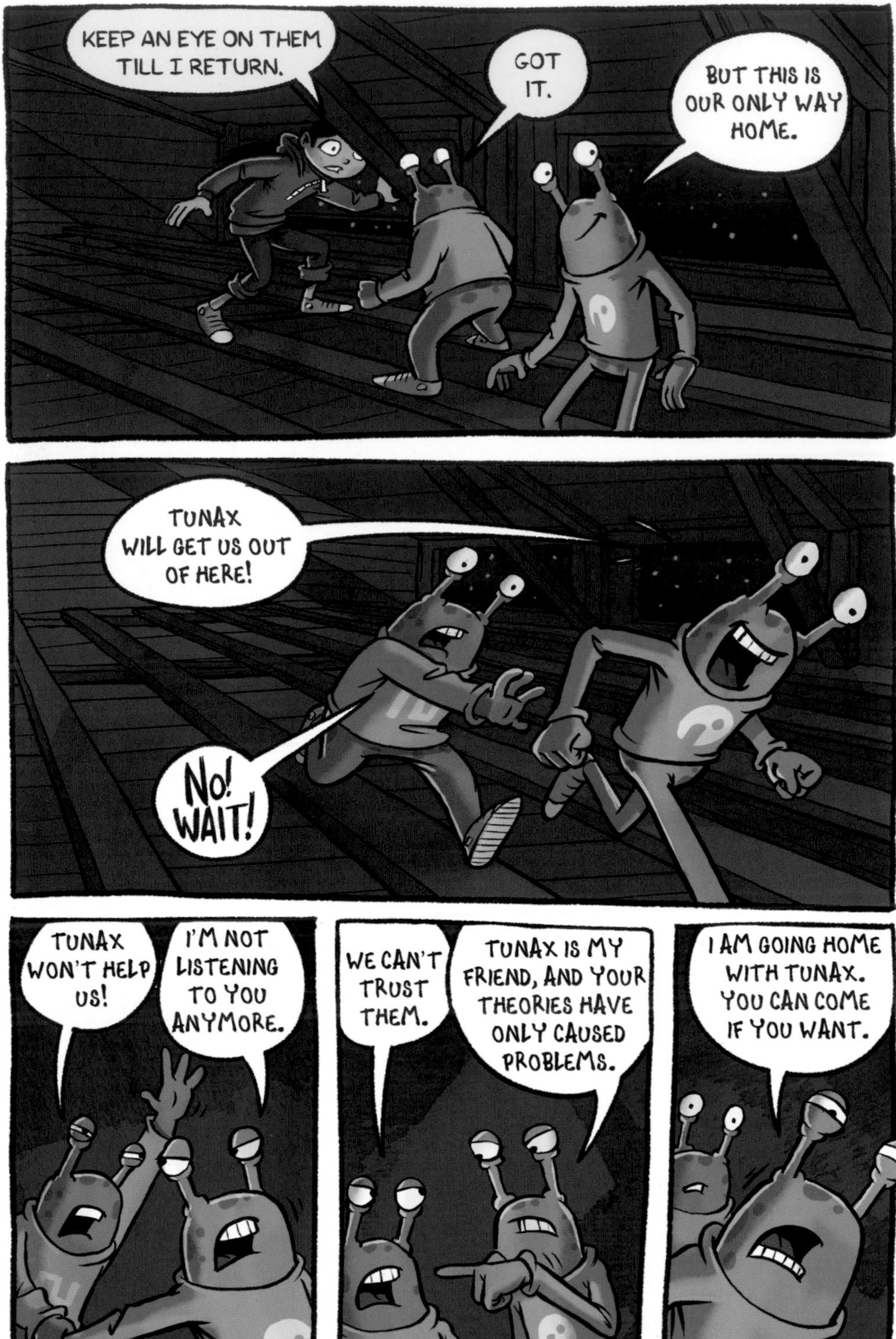
KEEP AN EYE ON THEM TILL I RETURN.
GOT IT.
BUT THIS IS OUR ONLY WAY HOME.
TUNAX WILL GET US OUT OF HERE!
NO! WAIT!
TUNAX WON'T HELP US!
I'M NOT LISTENING TO YOU ANYMORE.
WE CAN'T TRUST THEM.
TUNAX IS MY FRIEND, AND YOUR THEORIES HAVE ONLY CAUSED PROBLEMS.
I AM GOING HOME WITH TUNAX. YOU CAN COME IF YOU WANT.

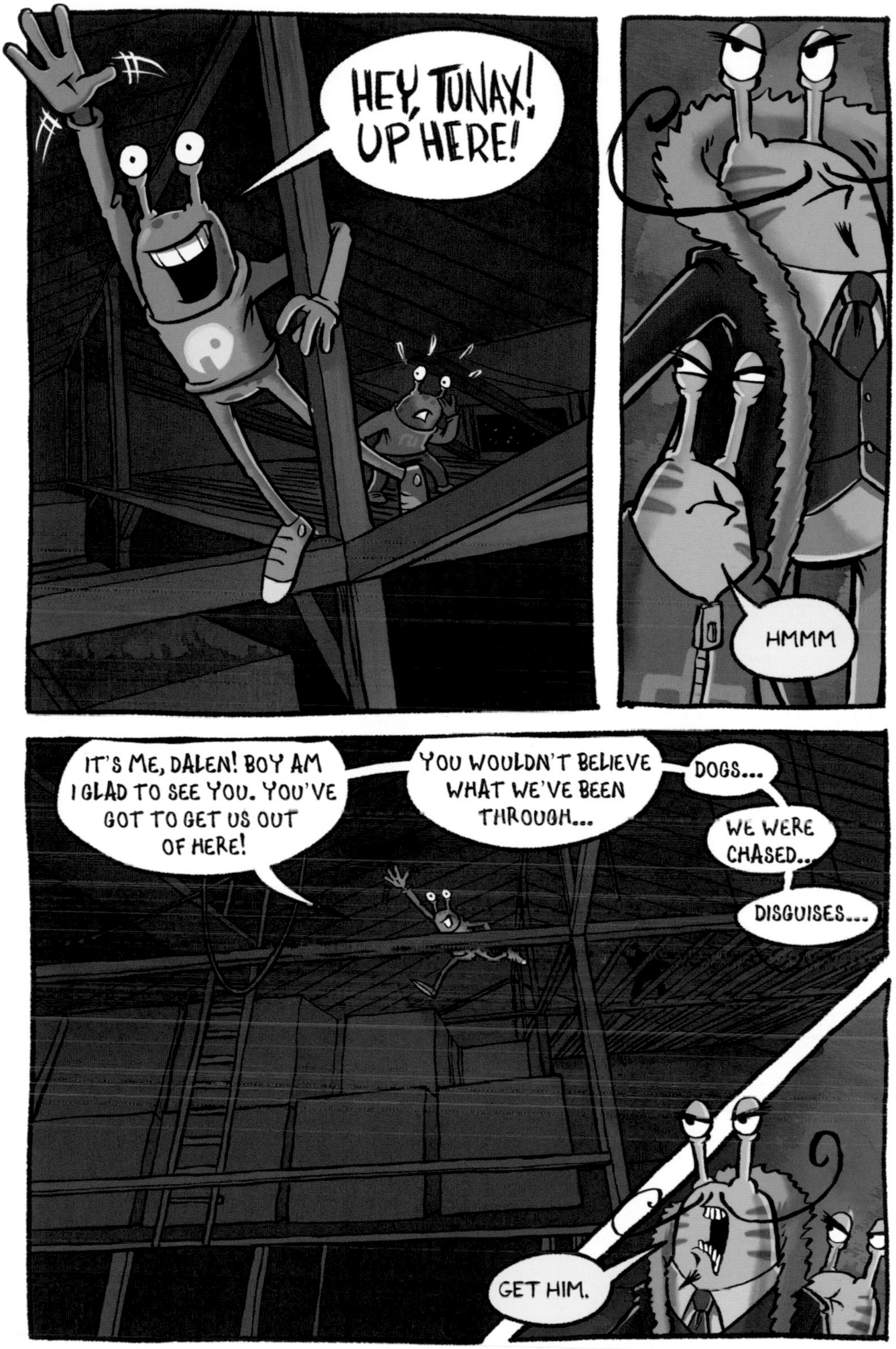
HEY, TUNAX! UP HERE!
HMMM
IT'S ME, DALEN! BOY AM I GLAD TO SEE YOU. YOU'VE GOT TO GET US OUT OF HERE!
YOU WOULDN'T BELIEVE WHAT WE'VE BEEN THROUGH...
DOGS...
WE WERE CHASED...
DISGUISES...
GET HIM.

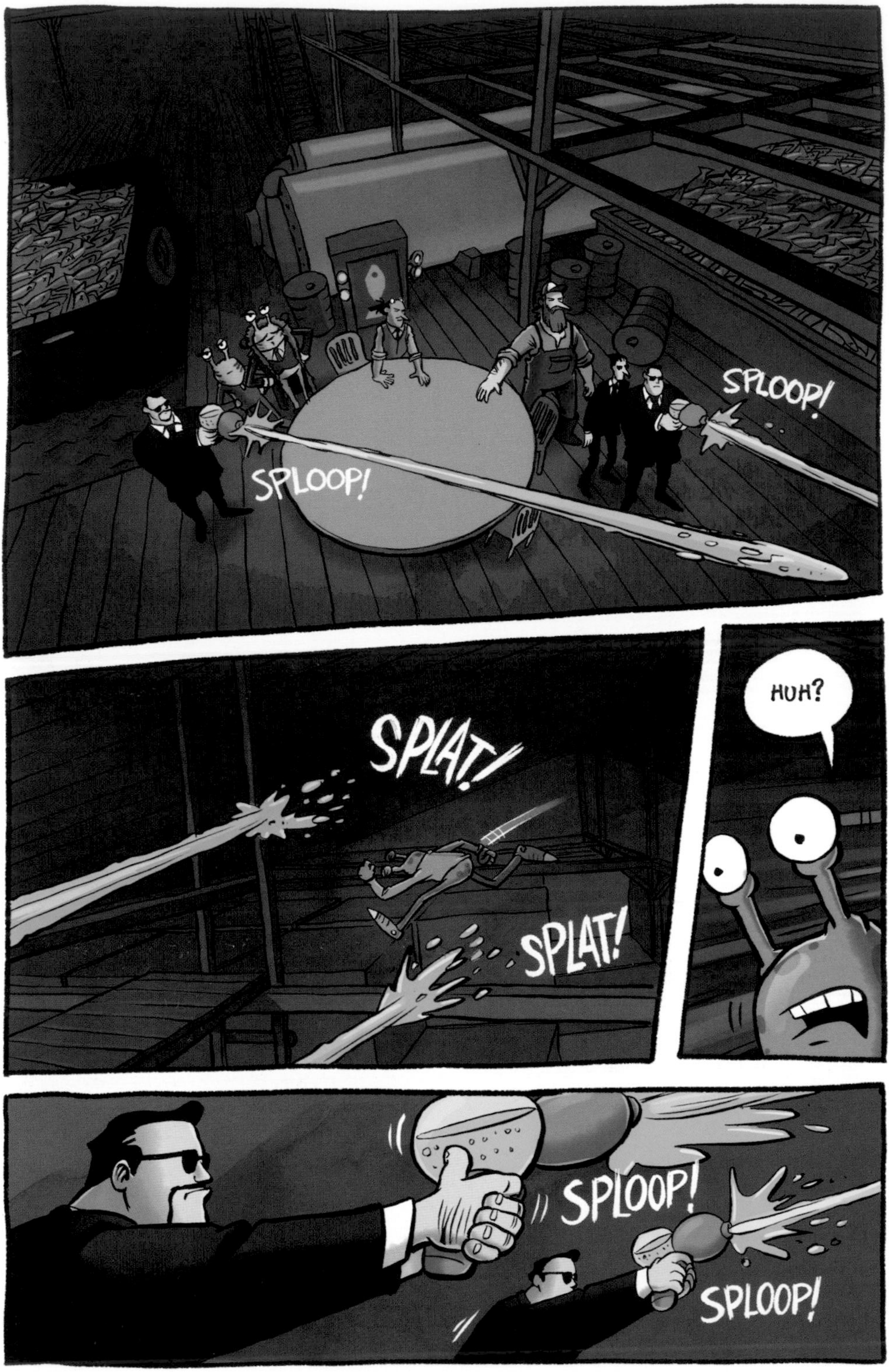
SPLOOP!
SPLOOP!
SPLAT!
SPLAT!
HUH?
SPLOOP!
SPLOOP!

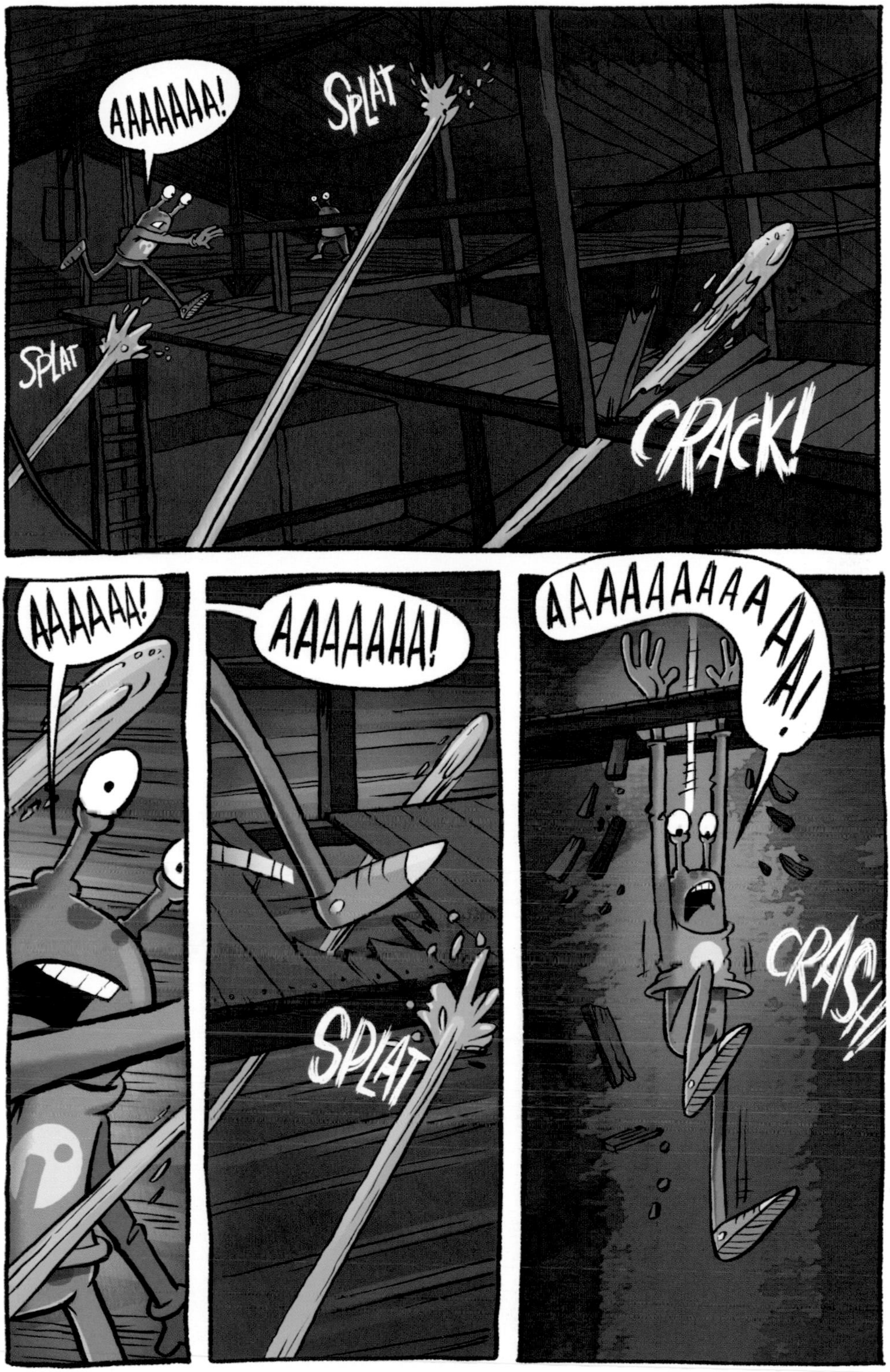
AAAAAAA!
SPLAT
SPLAT
CRACK!
AAAAAA!
AAAAAAA!
SPLAT
AAAAAAAAAAAA!
CRASH!

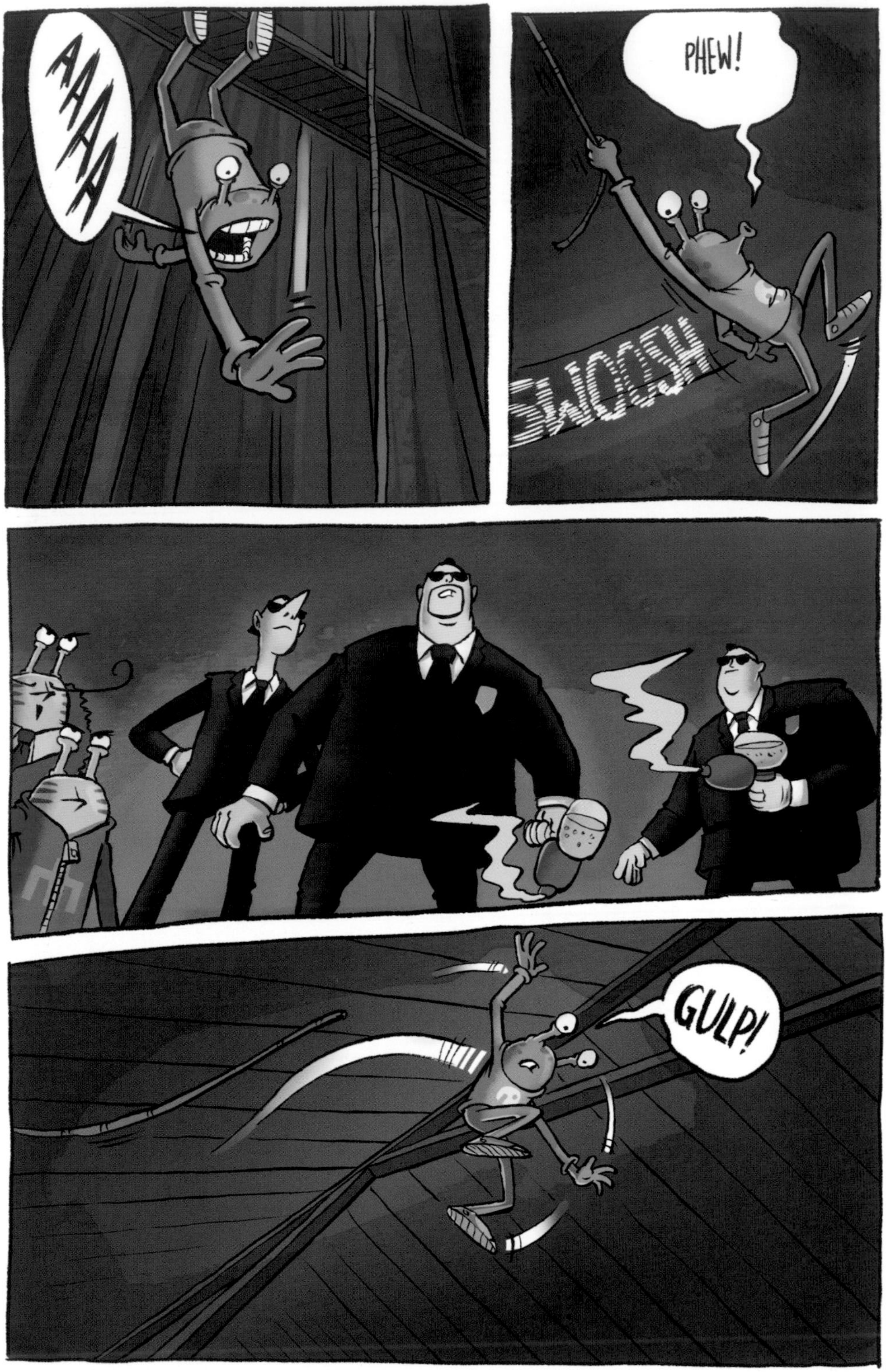
AAAAA
PHEW!
SWOOSH
GULP!

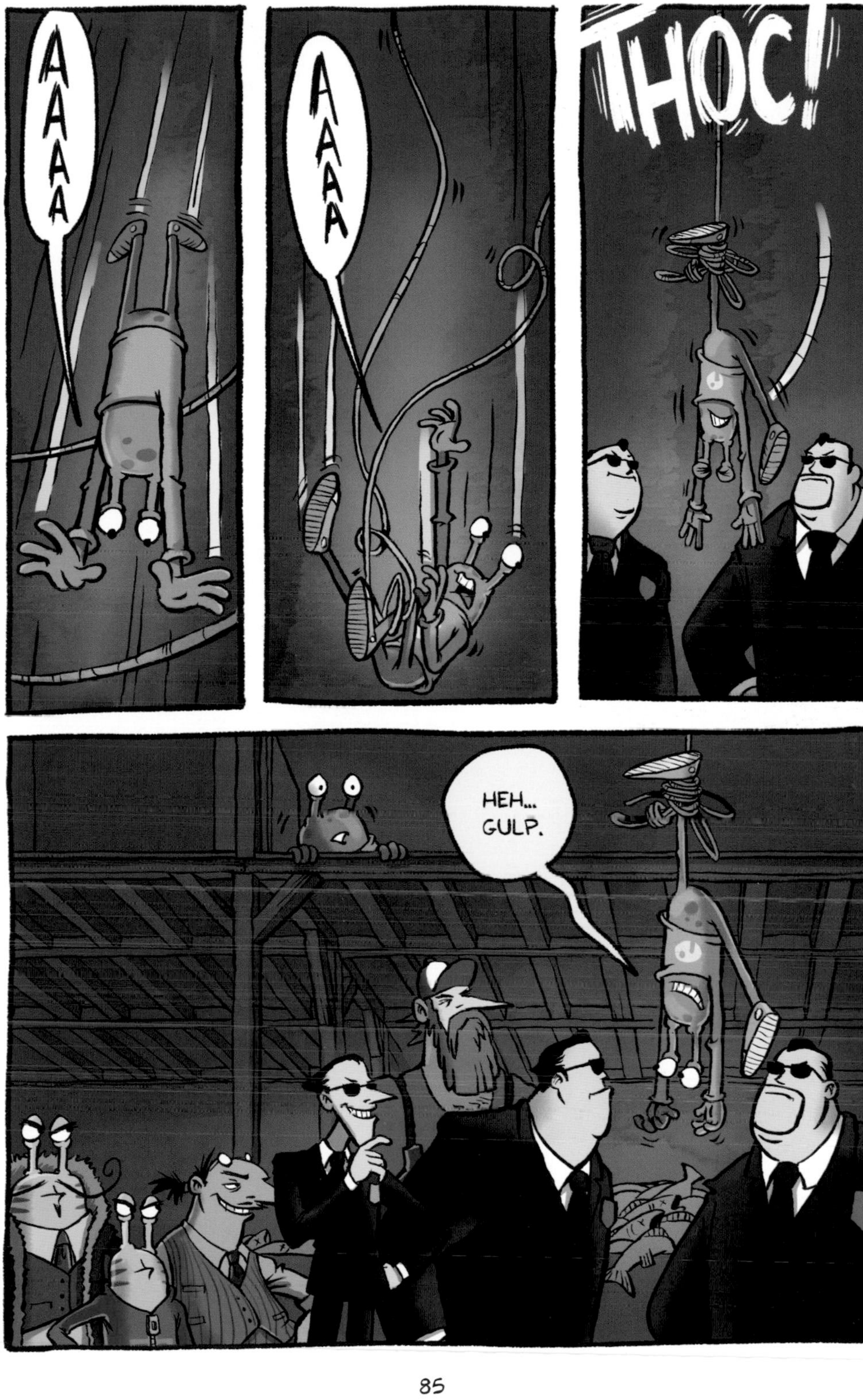
AAAAA
AAAAA
THOC!
HEH... GULP.

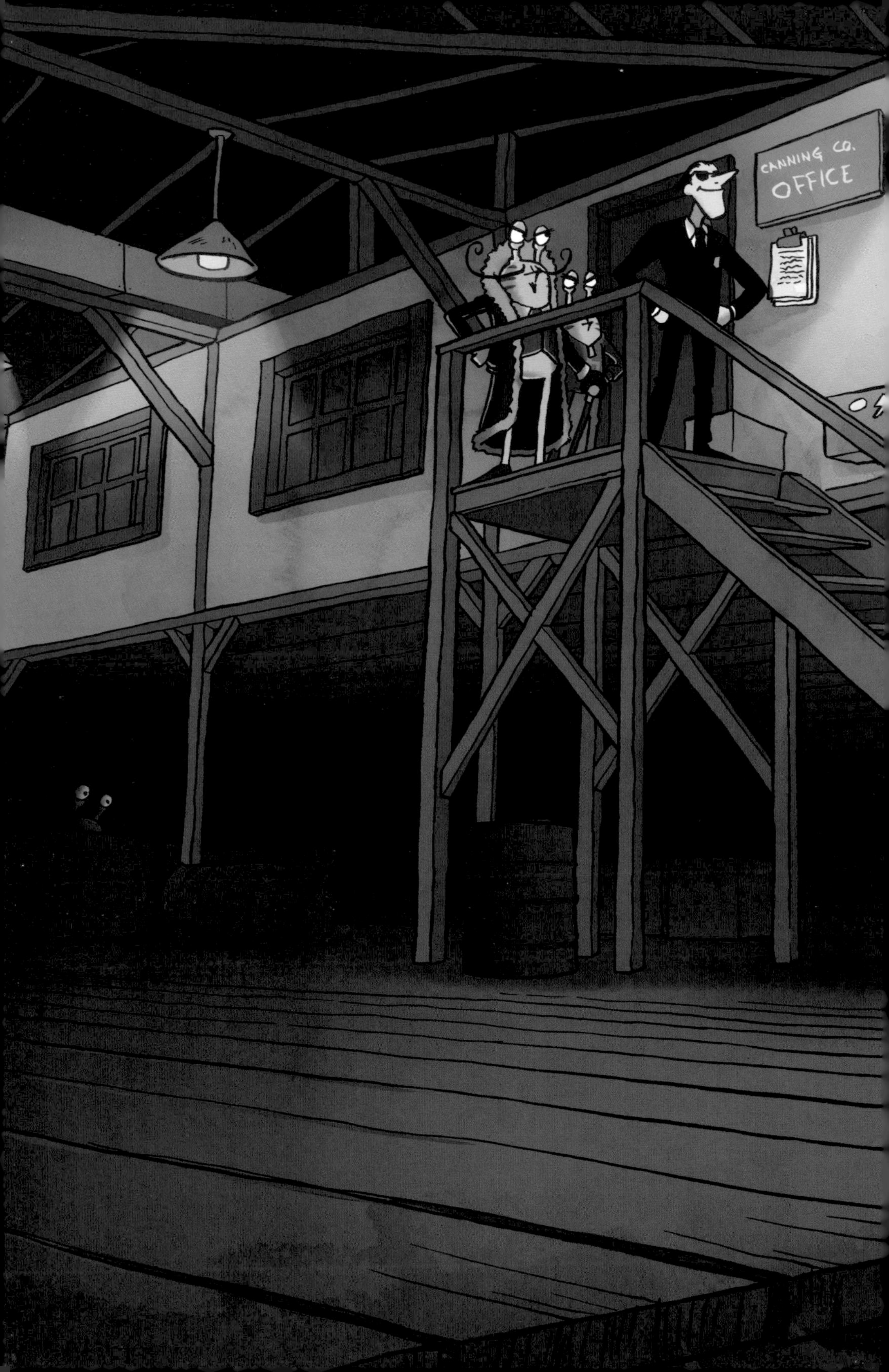
CANNING CO.
OFFICE

CHAPTER 5

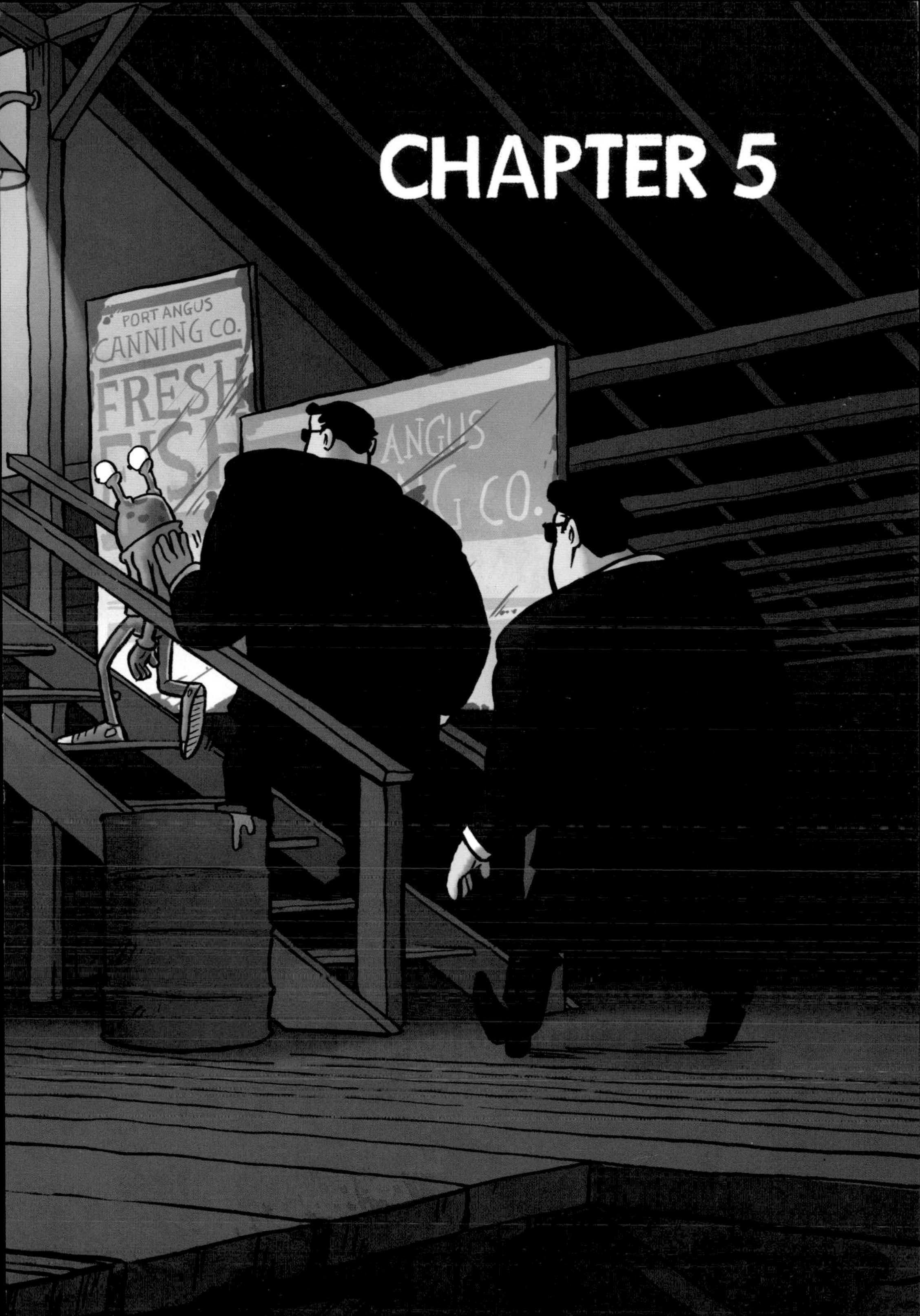
PORT ANGUS
CANNING CO.
FRESH

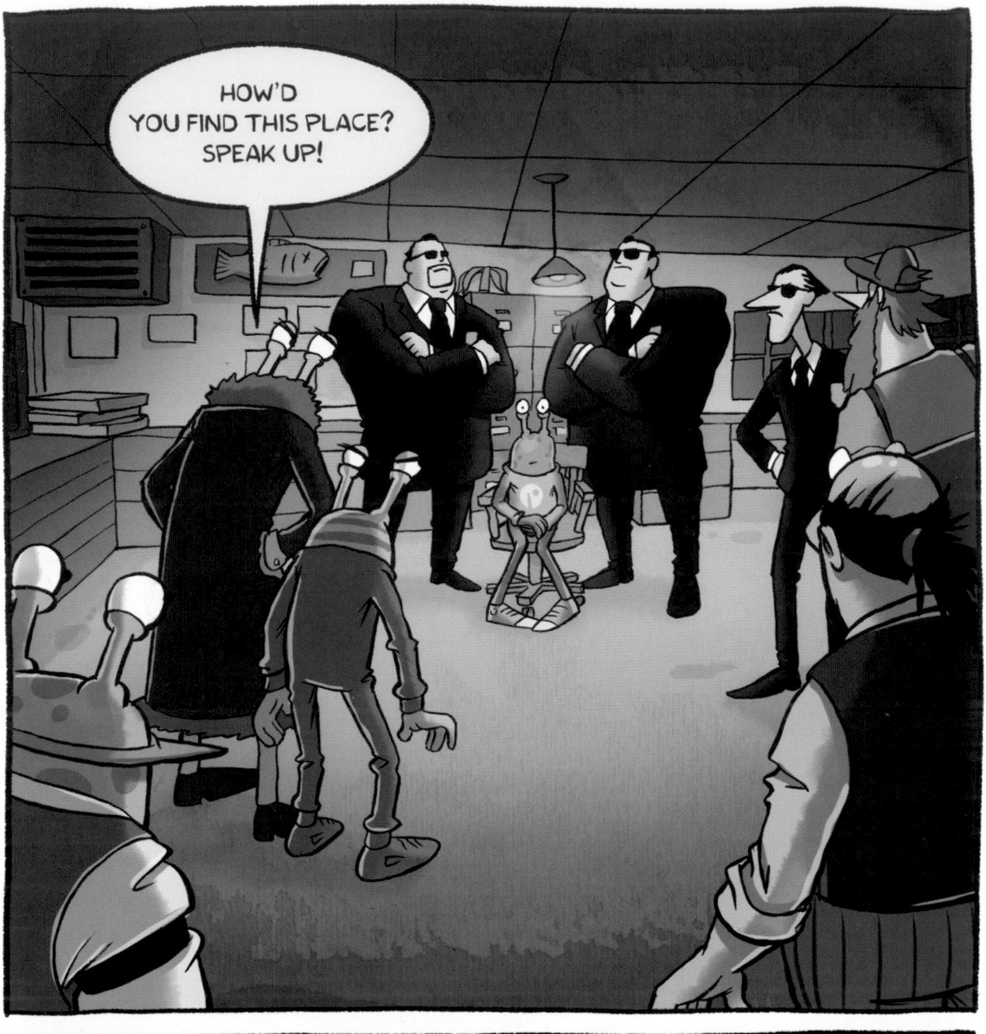
HOW'D YOU FIND THIS PLACE? SPEAK UP!

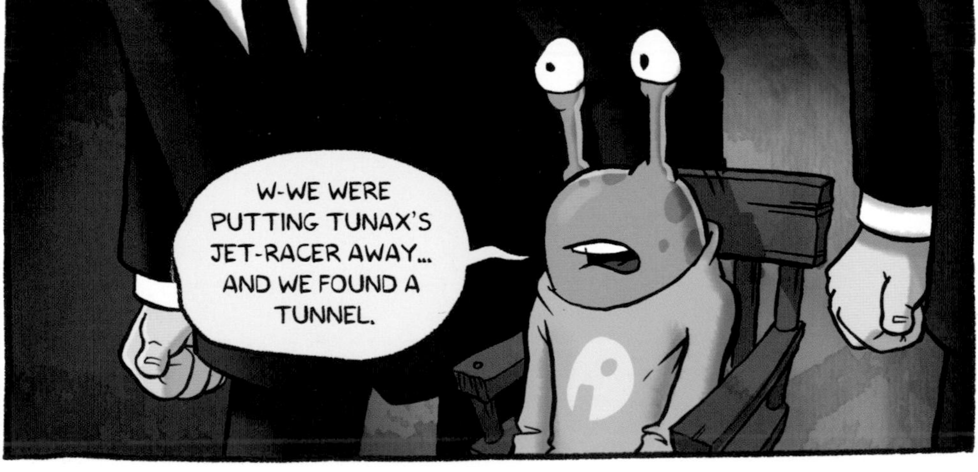
W-WE WERE PUTTING TUNAX'S JET-RACER AWAY... AND WE FOUND A TUNNEL.

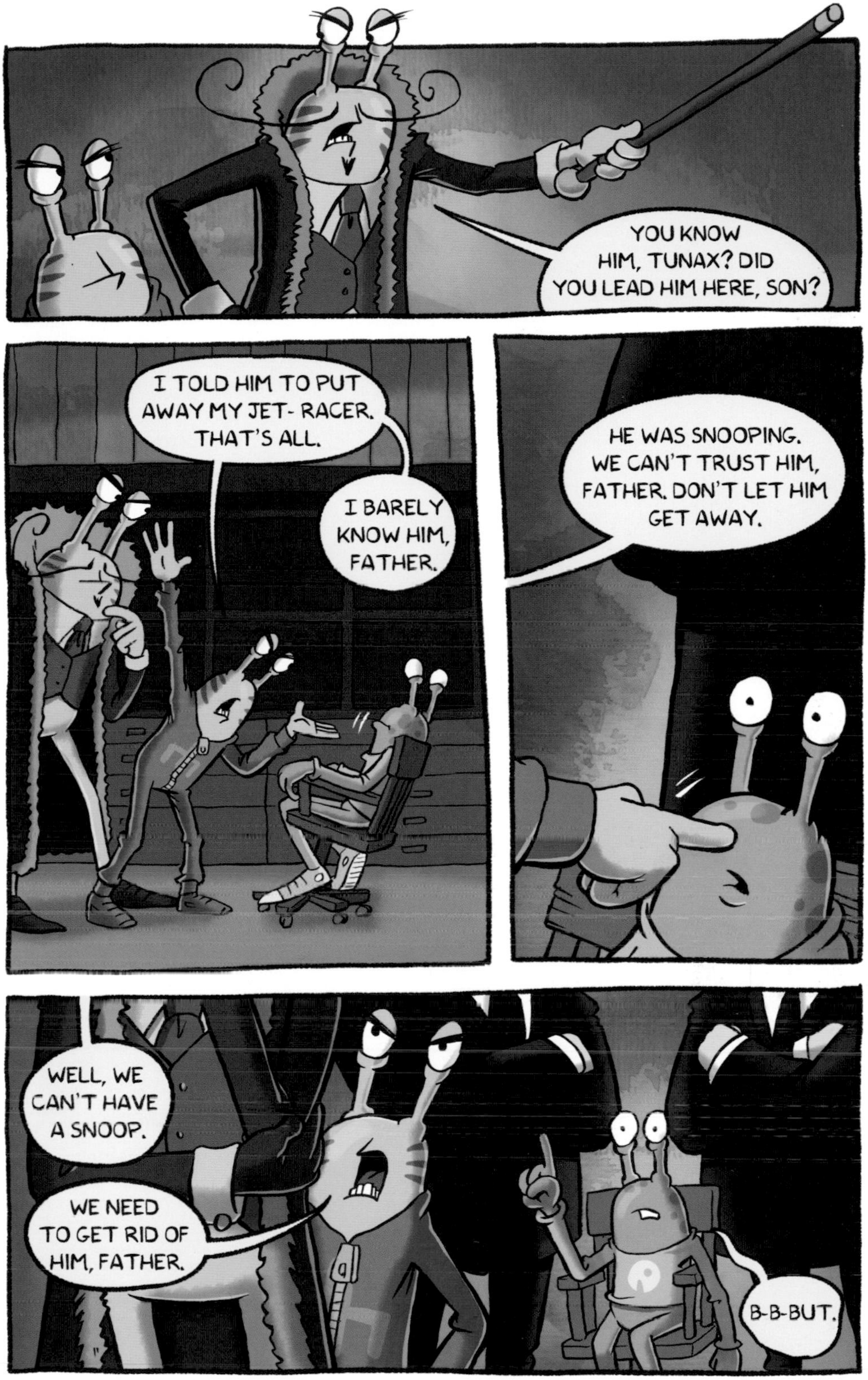
YOU KNOW HIM, TUNAX? DID YOU LEAD HIM HERE, SON?
I TOLD HIM TO PUT AWAY MY JET- RACER. THAT'S ALL.
I BARELY KNOW HIM, FATHER.
HE WAS SNOOPING. WE CAN'T TRUST HIM, FATHER. DON'T LET HIM GET AWAY.
WELL, WE CAN'T HAVE A SNOOP.
WE NEED TO GET RID OF HIM, FATHER.
B-B-BUT.

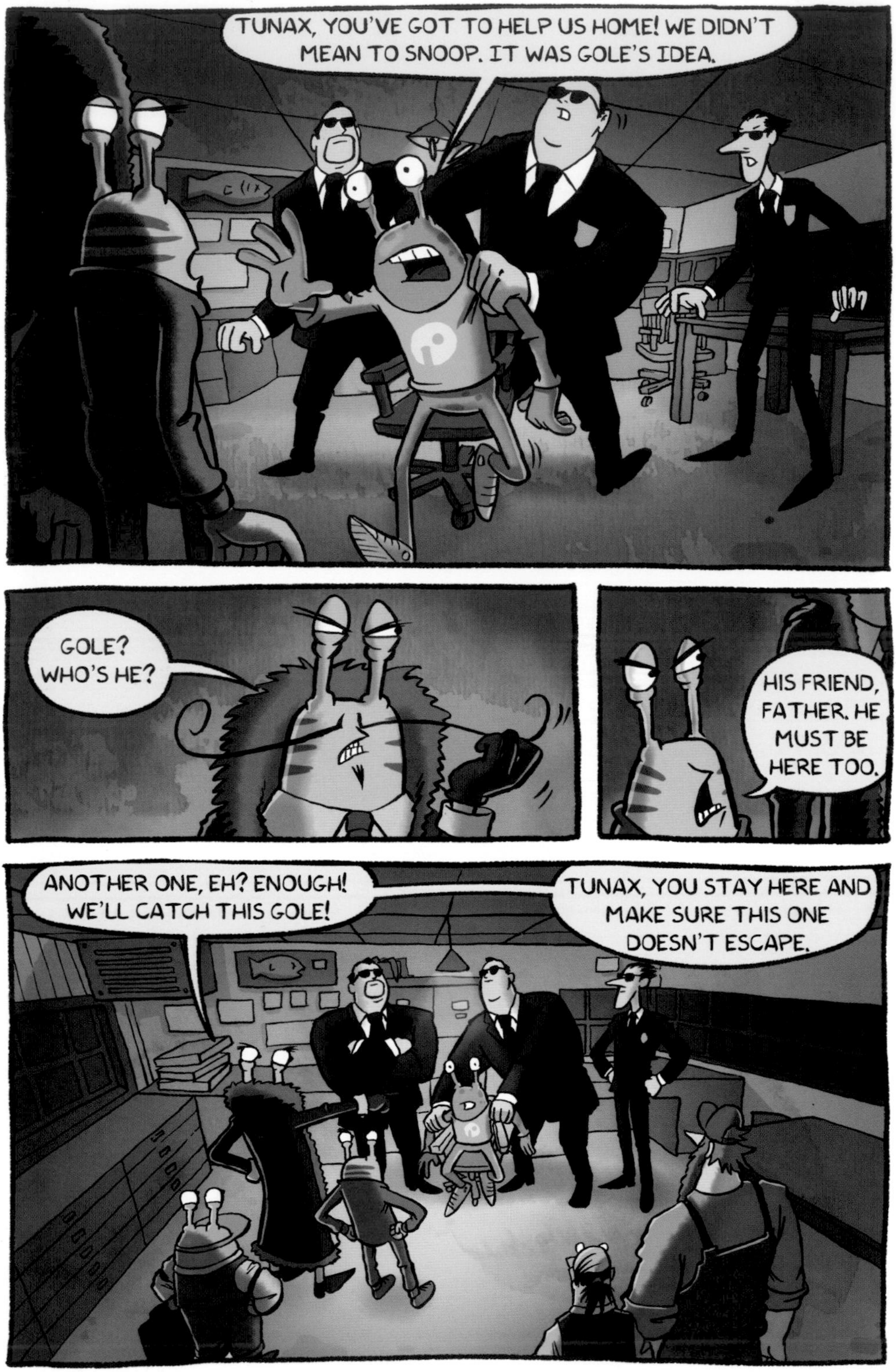
TUNAX, YOU'VE GOT TO HELP US HOME! WE DIDN'T MEAN TO SNOOP. IT WAS GOLE'S IDEA.
GOLE? WHO'S HE?
HIS FRIEND, FATHER. HE MUST BE HERE TOO.
ANOTHER ONE, EH? ENOUGH! WE'LL CATCH THIS GOLE!
TUNAX, YOU STAY HERE AND MAKE SURE THIS ONE DOESN'T ESCAPE.

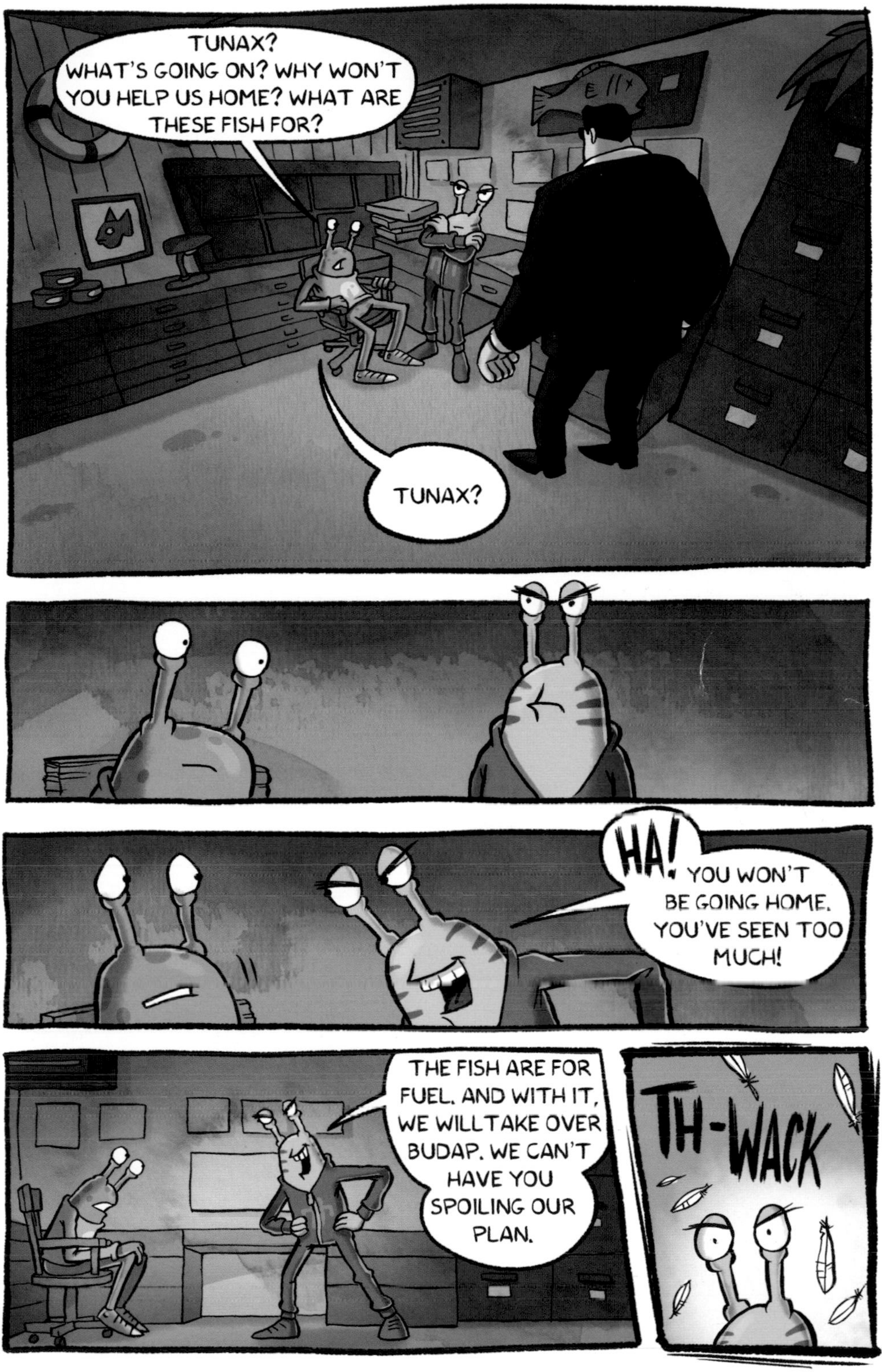
TUNAX? WHAT'S GOING ON? WHY WON'T YOU HELP US HOME? WHAT ARE THESE FISH FOR?
TUNAX?
HA! YOU WON'T BE GOING HOME. YOU'VE SEEN TOO MUCH!
THE FISH ARE FOR FUEL. AND WITH IT, WE WILLTAKE OVER BUDAP. WE CAN'T HAVE YOU SPOILING OUR PLAN.
TH-WACK

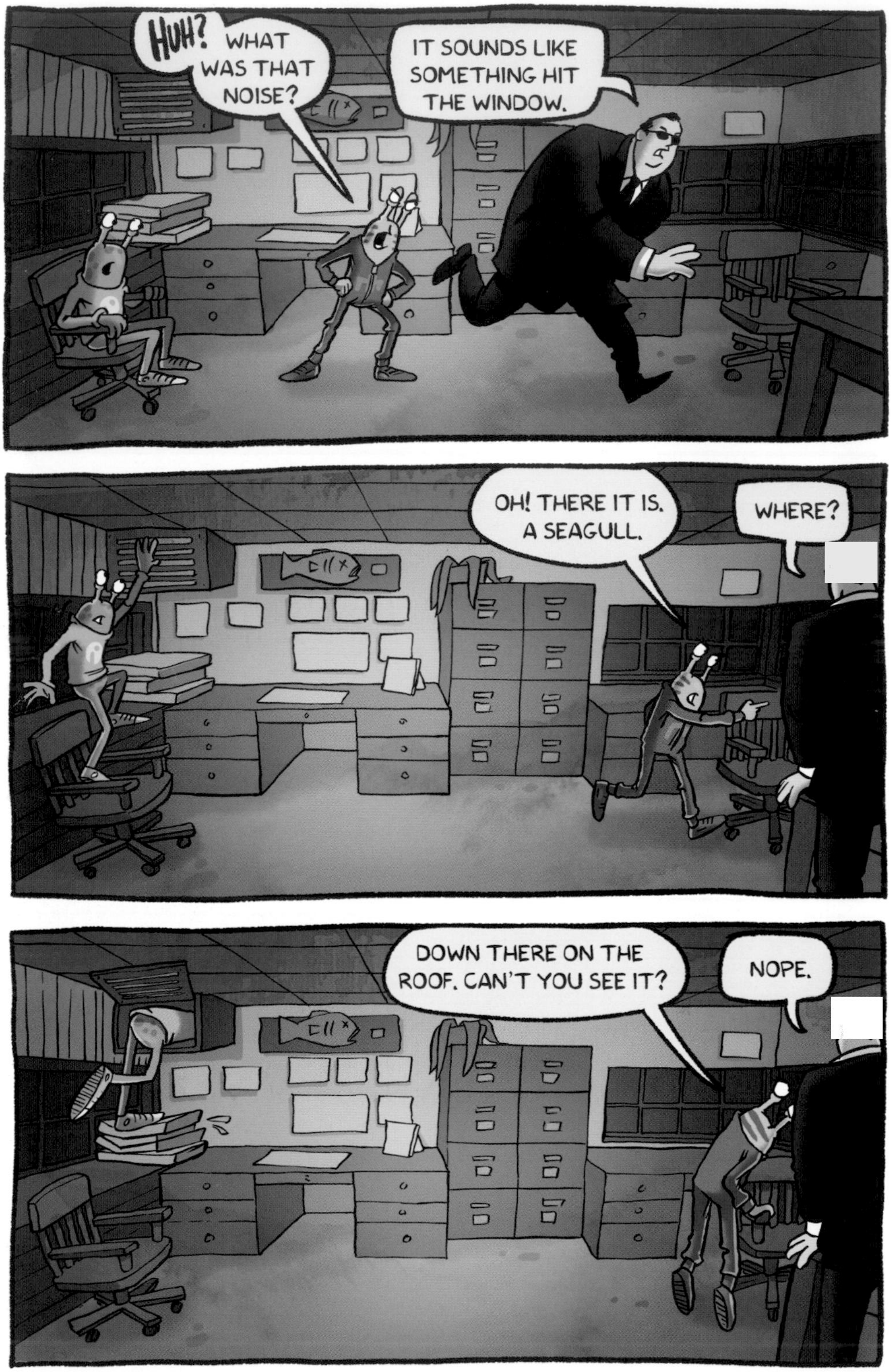
HUH?
WHAT WAS THAT NOISE?
IT SOUNDS LIKE SOMETHING HIT THE WINDOW.
OH! THERE IT IS. A SEAGULL.
WHERE?
DOWN THERE ON THE ROOF. CAN'T YOU SEE IT?
NOPE.

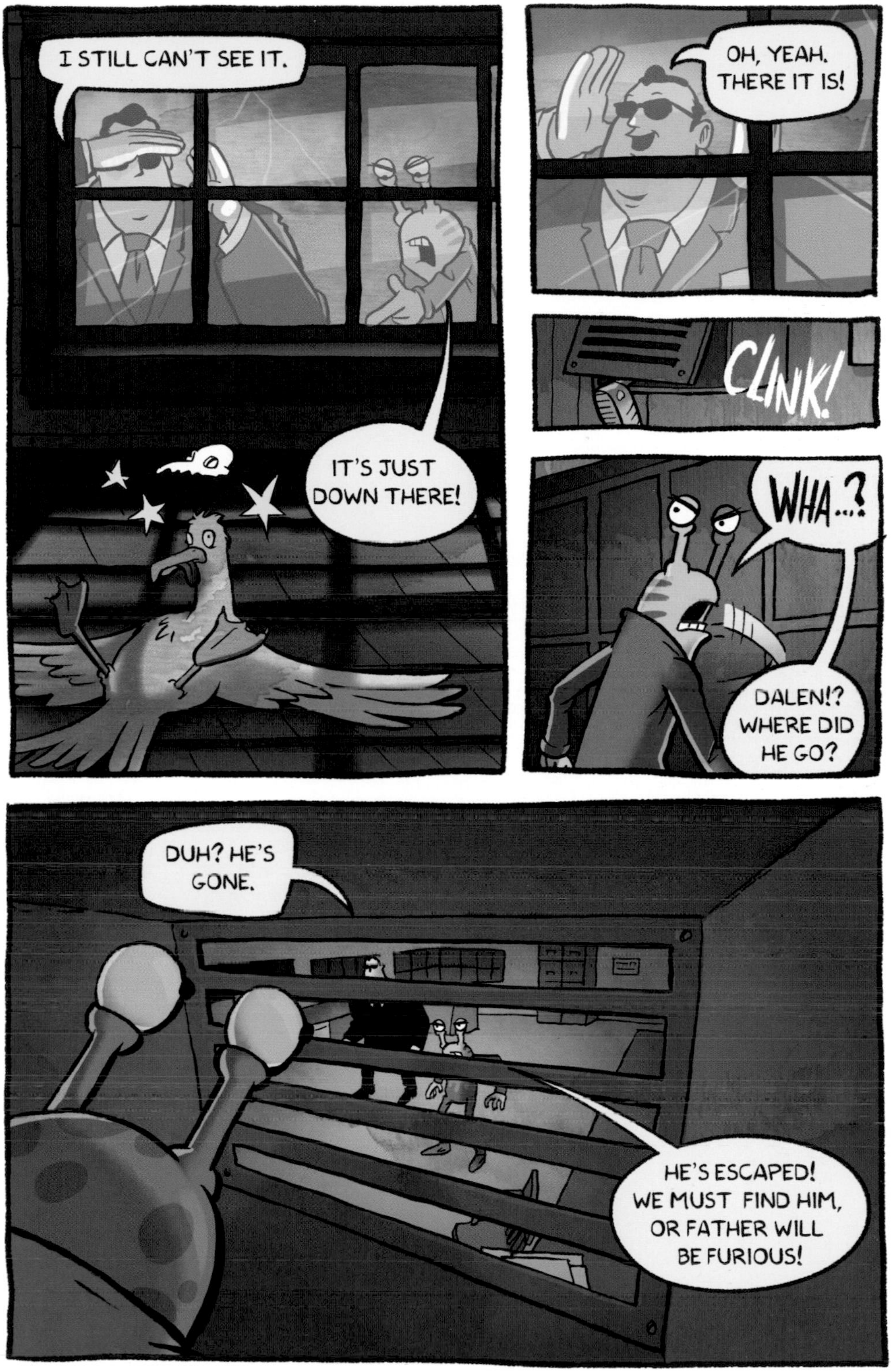
I STILL CAN'T SEE IT.
IT'S JUST DOWN THERE!
OH, YEAH. THERE IT IS!
CLINK!
WHA...?
DALEN!? WHERE DID HE GO?
DUH? HE'S GONE.
HE'S ESCAPED! WE MUST FIND HIM, OR FATHER WILL BE FURIOUS!

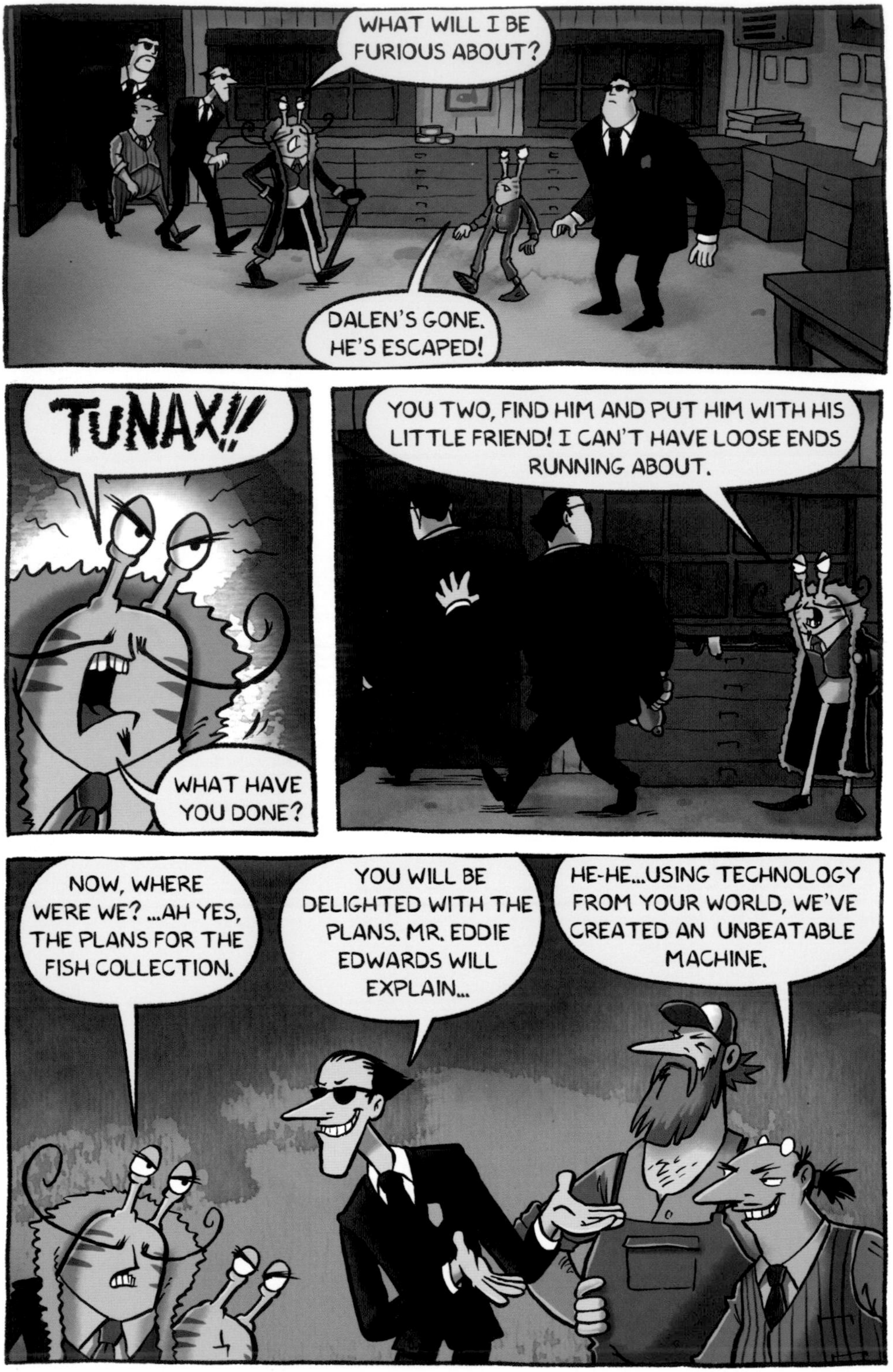
WHAT WILL I BE FURIOUS ABOUT?
DALEN'S GONE. HE'S ESCAPED!
TUNAX!!
WHAT HAVE YOU DONE?
YOU TWO, FIND HIM AND PUT HIM WITH HIS LITTLE FRIEND! I CAN'T HAVE LOOSE ENDS RUNNING ABOUT.
NOW, WHERE WERE WE? ...AH YES, THE PLANS FOR THE FISH COLLECTION.
YOU WILL BE DELIGHTED WITH THE PLANS. MR. EDDIE EDWARDS WILL EXPLAIN...
HE-HE...USING TECHNOLOGY FROM YOUR WORLD, WE'VE CREATED AN UNBEATABLE MACHINE.

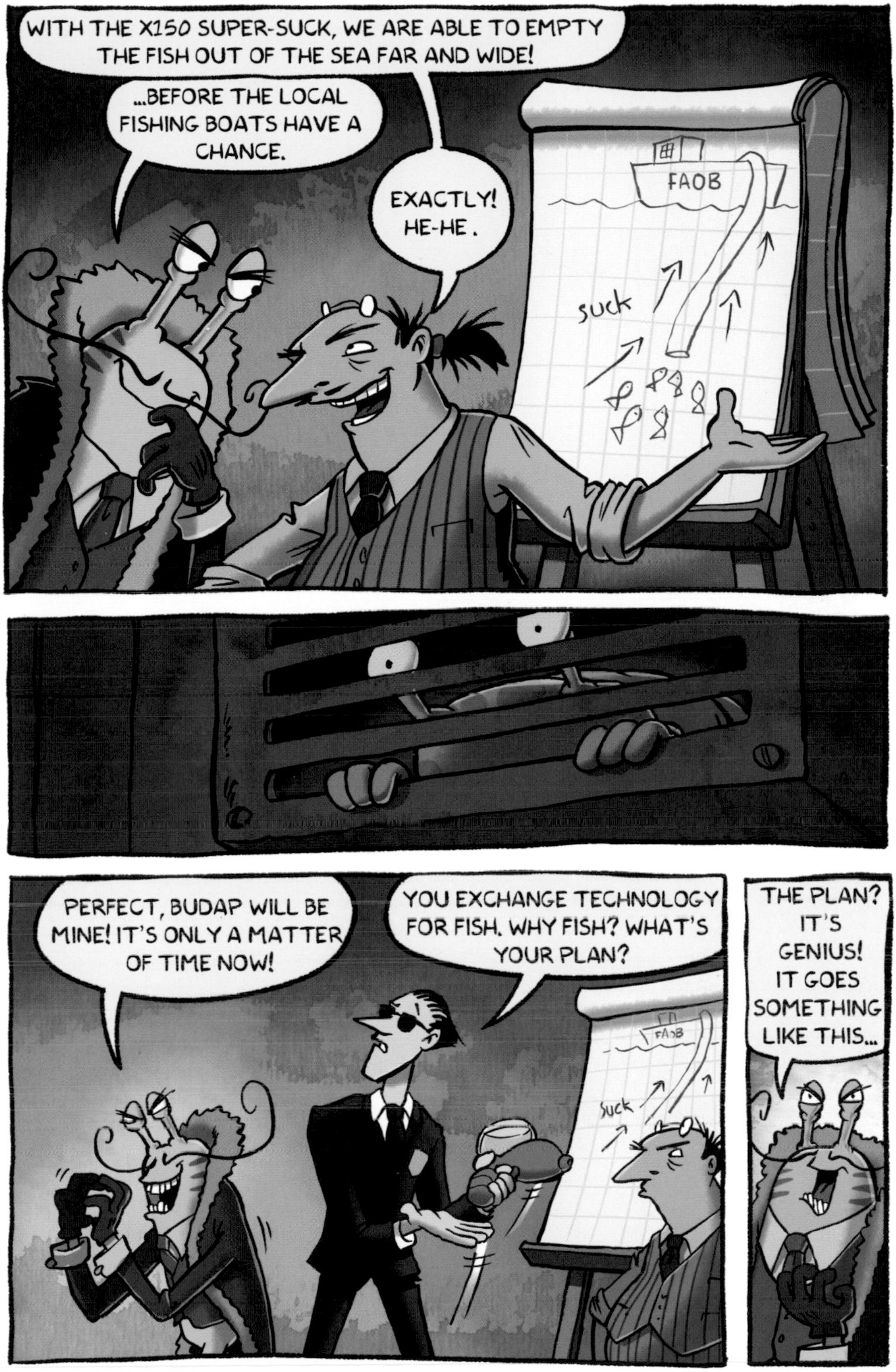
WITH THE X150 SUPER-SUCK, WE ARE ABLE TO EMPTY THE FISH OUT OF THE SEA FAR AND WIDE!
...BEFORE THE LOCAL FISHING BOATS HAVE A CHANCE.
EXACTLY! HE-HE.
FAOB
SUCK
PERFECT, BUDAP WILL BE MINE! IT'S ONLY A MATTER OF TIME NOW!
YOU EXCHANGE TECHNOLOGY FOR FISH. WHY FISH? WHAT'S YOUR PLAN?
THE PLAN? IT'S GENIUS! IT GOES SOMETHING LIKE THIS...

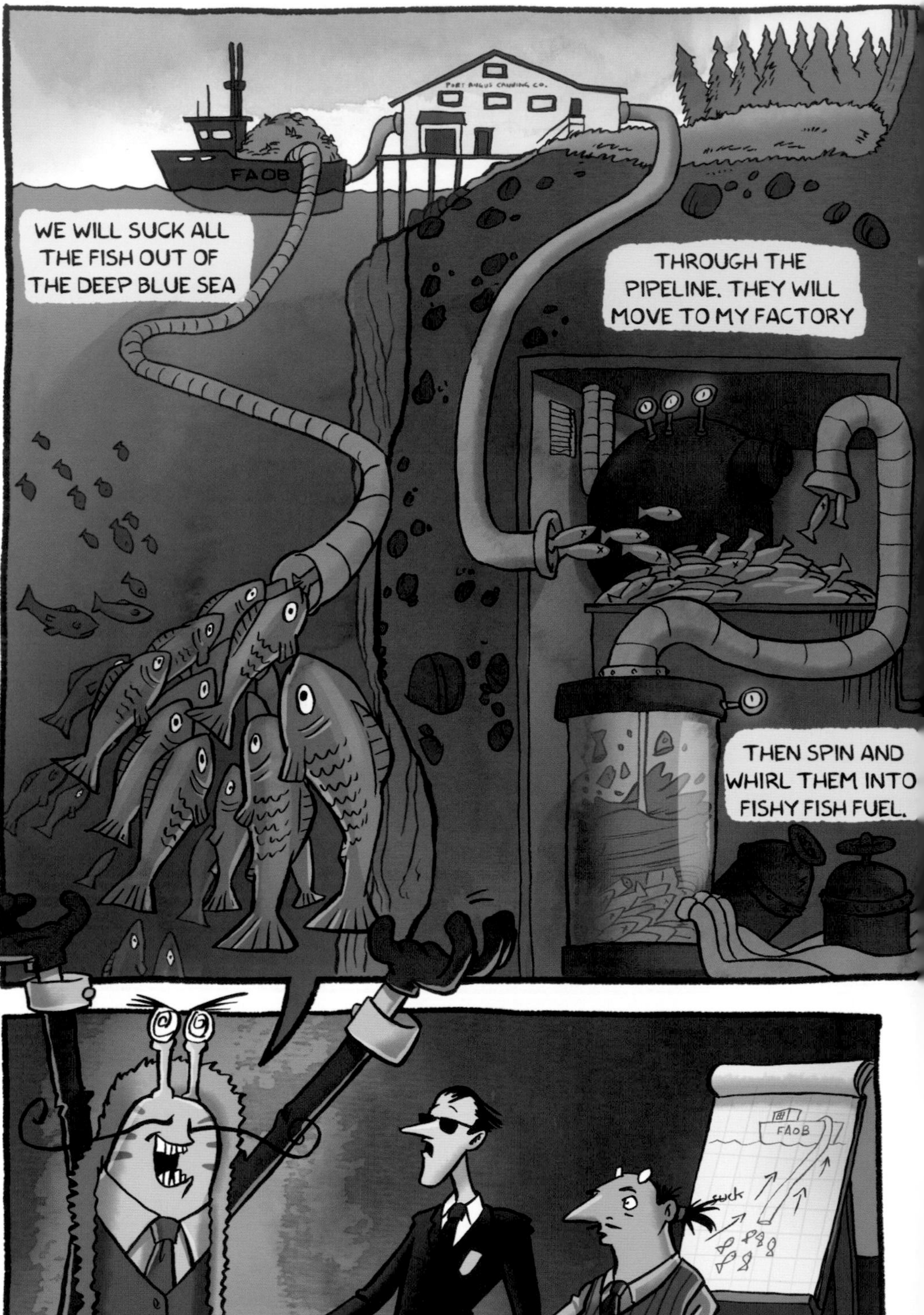

FAOB
PORT ANGUS CANNING CO.
WE WILL SUCK ALL THE FISH OUT OF THE DEEP BLUE SEA
THROUGH THE PIPELINE. THEY WILL MOVE TO MY FACTORY
THEN SPIN AND WHIRL THEM INTO FISHY FISH FUEL.
FAOB
suck

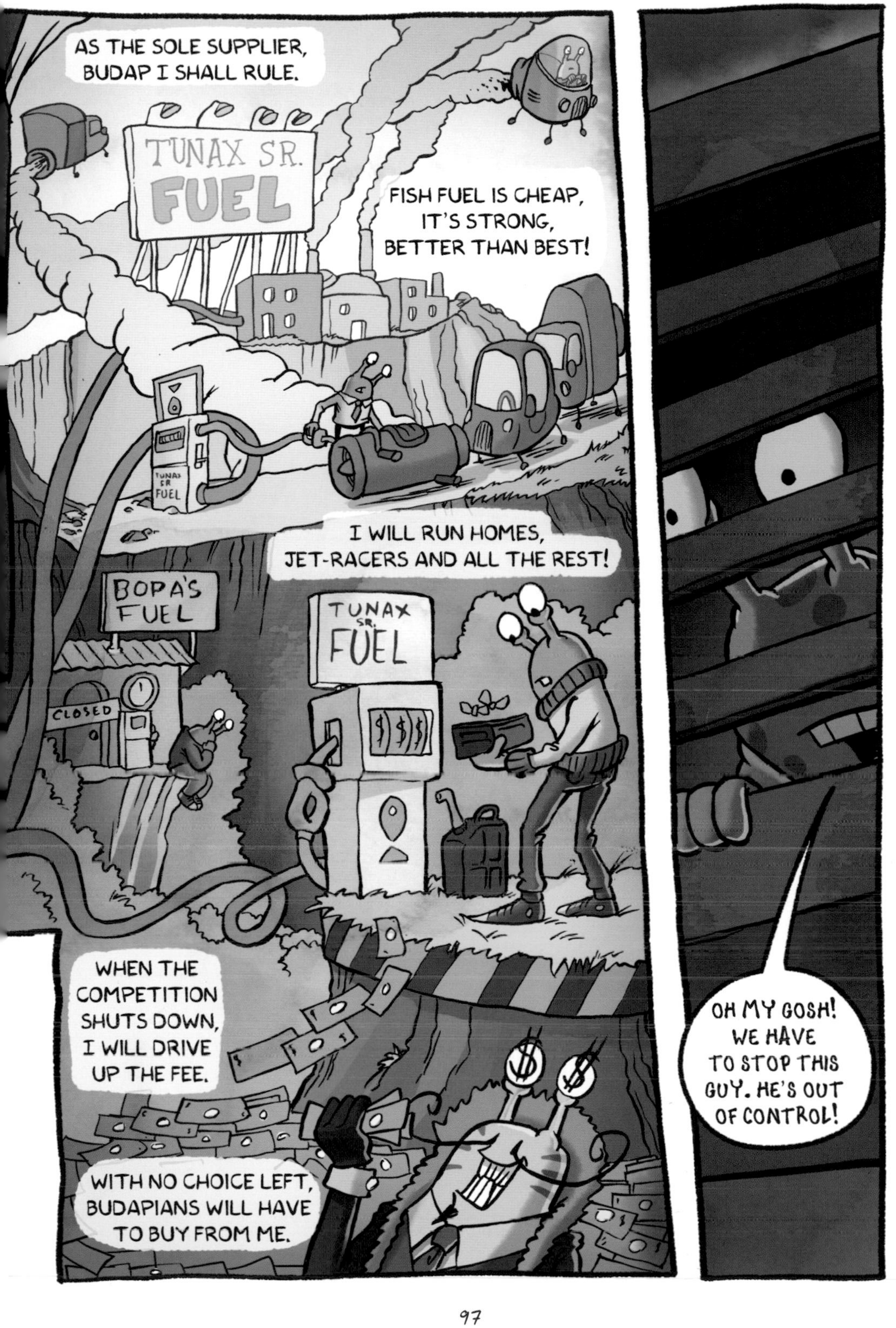
AS THE SOLE SUPPLIER, BUDAP I SHALL RULE.
TUNAX SR. FUEL
FISH FUEL IS CHEAP, IT'S STRONG, BETTER THAN BEST!
TUNAX SR FUEL
I WILL RUN HOMES, JET-RACERS AND ALL THE REST!
BOPA'S FUEL
CLOSED
TUNAX SR. FUEL
WHEN THE COMPETITION SHUTS DOWN, I WILL DRIVE UP THE FEE.
WITH NO CHOICE LEFT, BUDAPIANS WILL HAVE TO BUY FROM ME.
OH MY GOSH! WE HAVE TO STOP THIS GUY. HE'S OUT OF CONTROL!

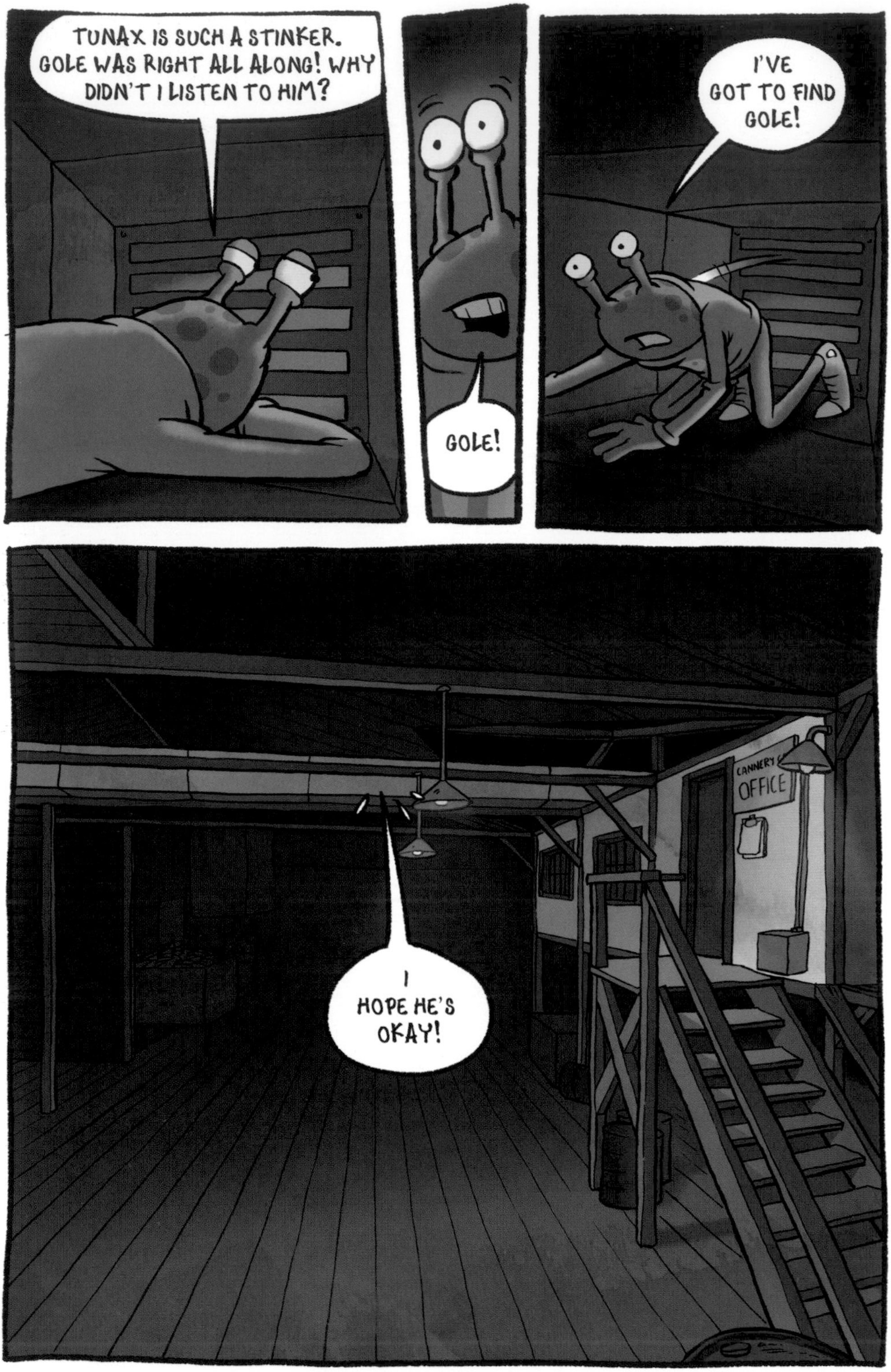
TUNAX IS SUCH A STINKER. GOLE WAS RIGHT ALL ALONG! WHY DIDN'T I LISTEN TO HIM?
GOLE!
I'VE GOT TO FIND GOLE!
CANNERY
OFFICE
I HOPE HE'S OKAY!

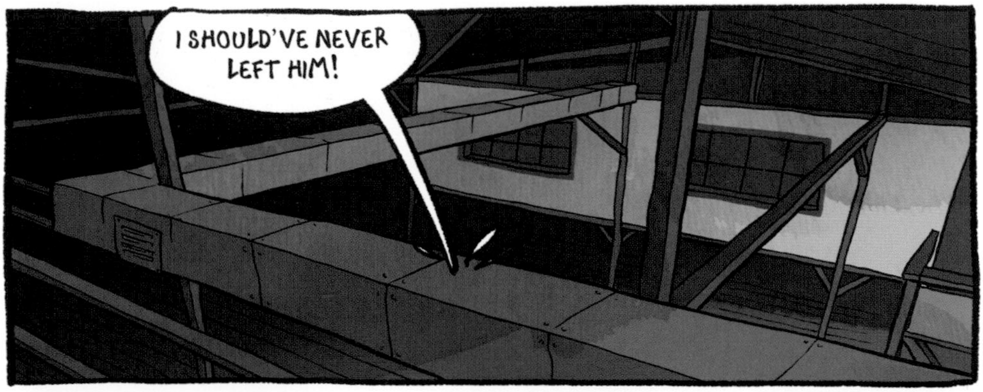
I SHOULD'VE NEVER LEFT HIM!

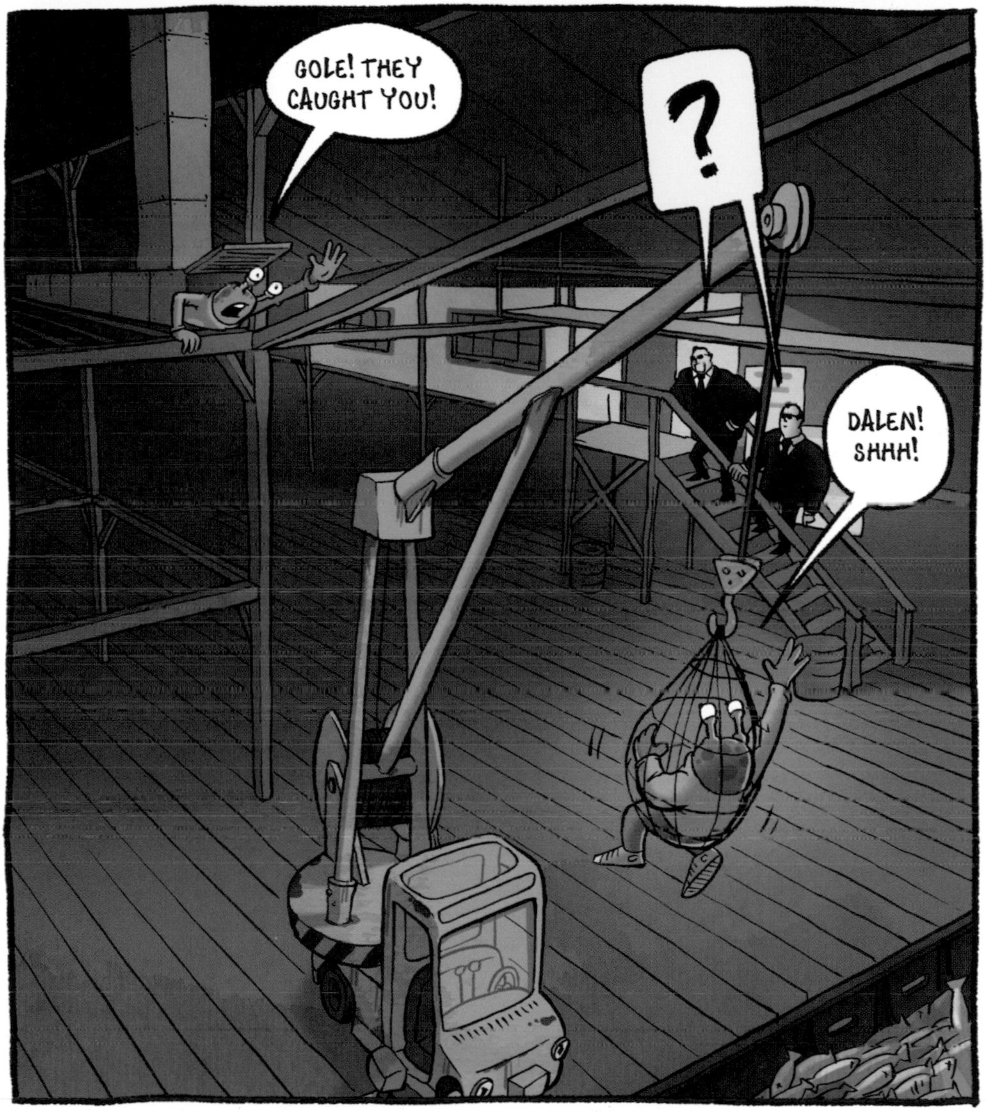
GOLE! THEY CAUGHT YOU!
?
DALEN! SHHH!

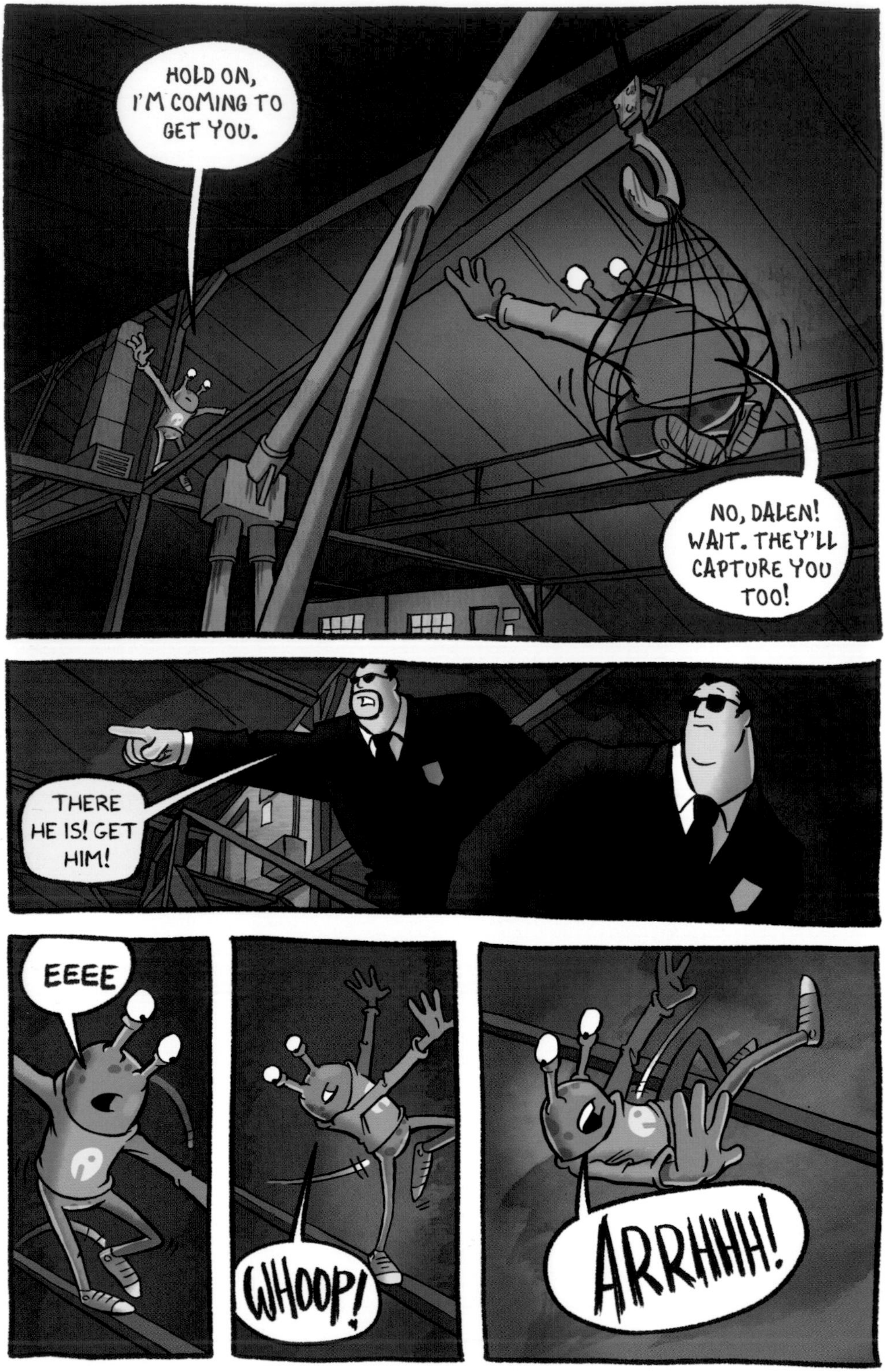
HOLD ON, I'M COMING TO GET YOU.
NO, DALEN! WAIT. THEY'LL CAPTURE YOU TOO!
THERE HE IS! GET HIM!
EEEE
WHOOP!
ARRHHH!

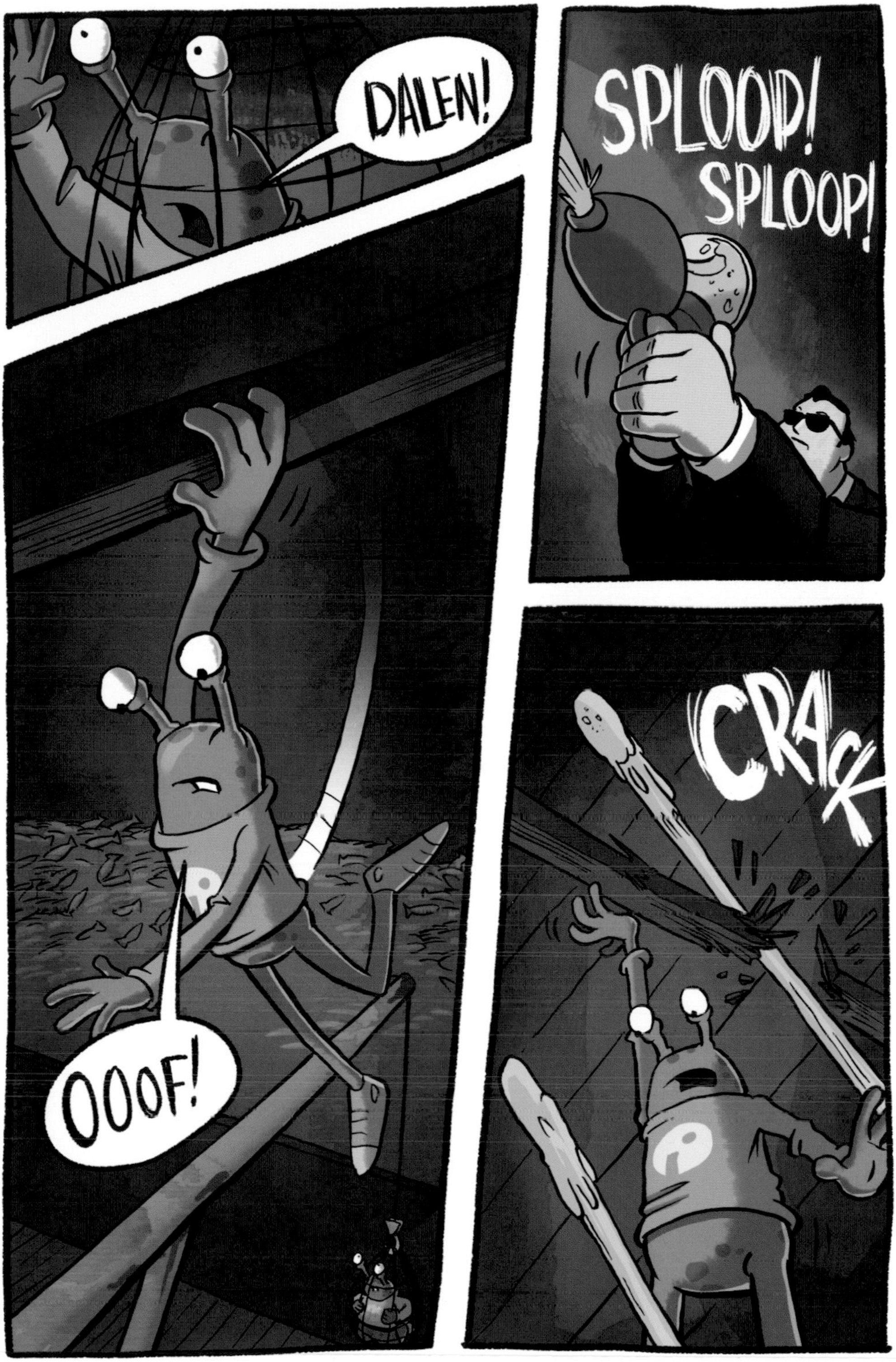
DALEN!
SPLOOP!
SPLOOP!
OOOF!
CRACK

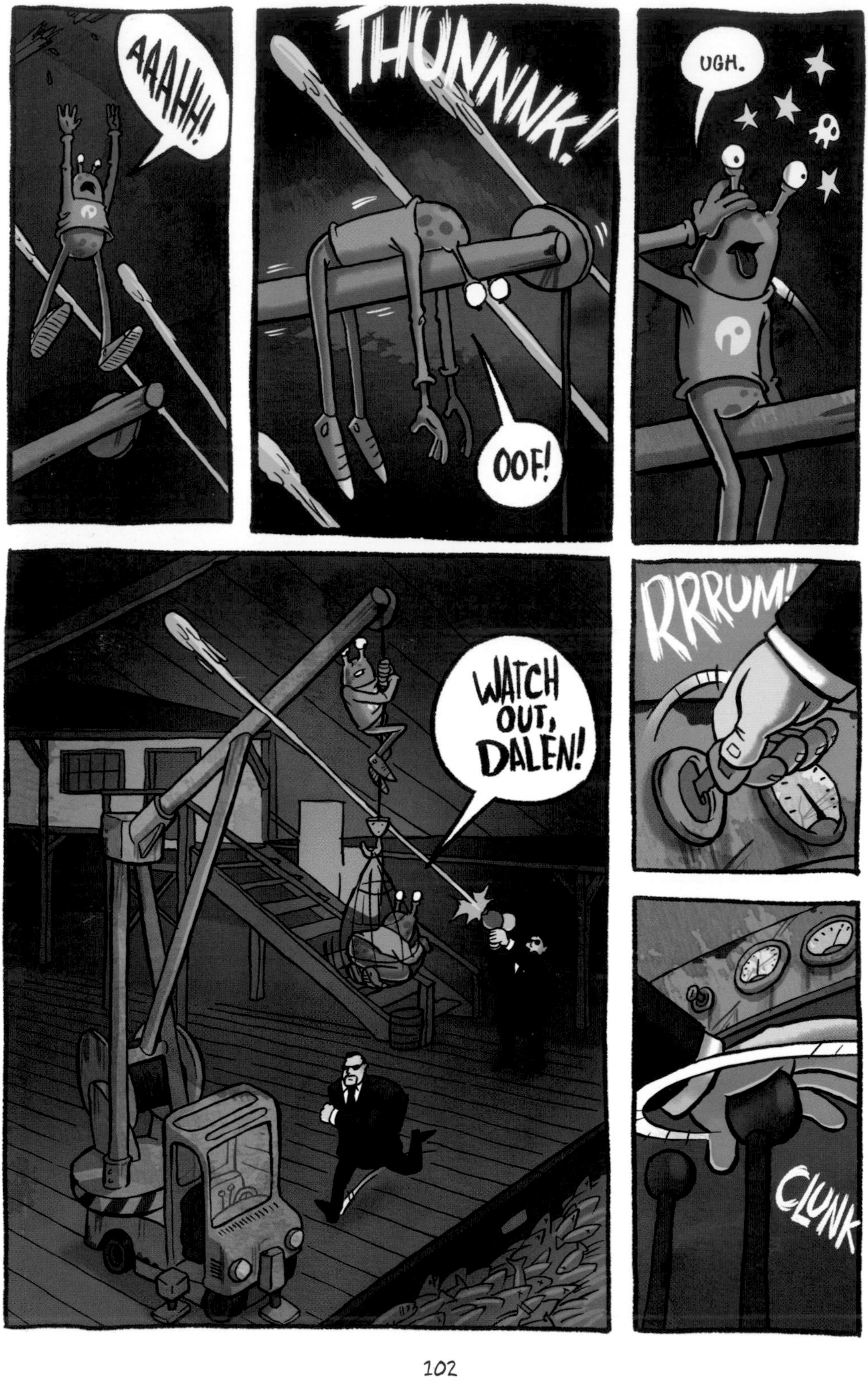
AAAHH!
THUNNNK!
OOF!
UGH.
WATCH OUT, DALEN!
RRRUM!
CLUNK

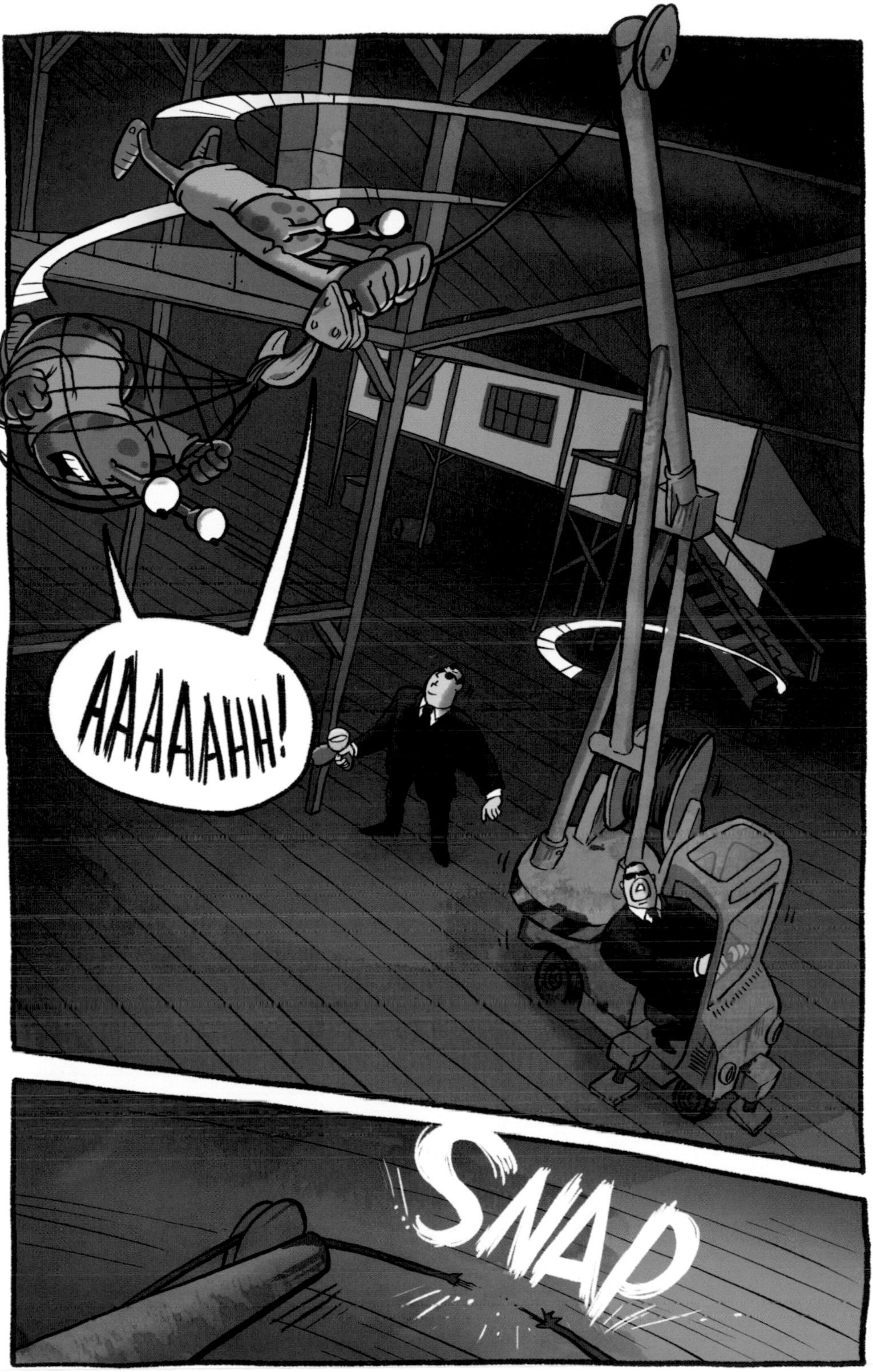
AAAAAHH!
SNAP

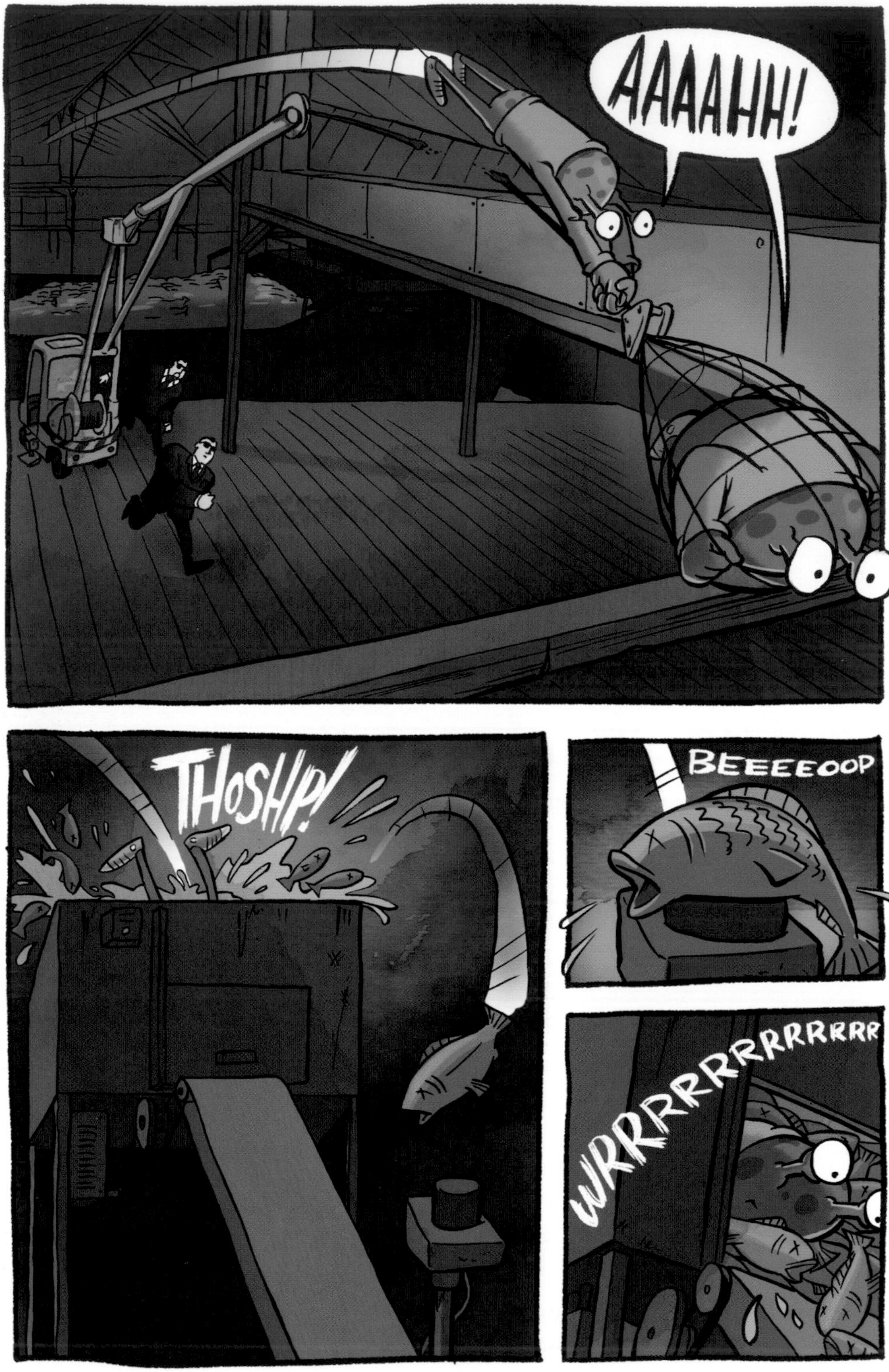
AAAAHH!
THOSHP!
BEEEEEOOP
WRRRRRRRRRRRR

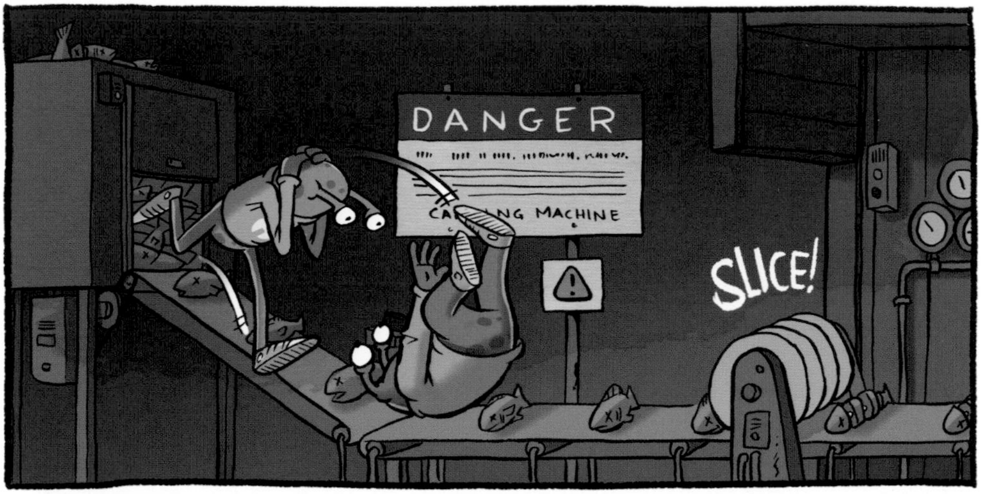
DANGER
CANNING MACHINE
SLICE!

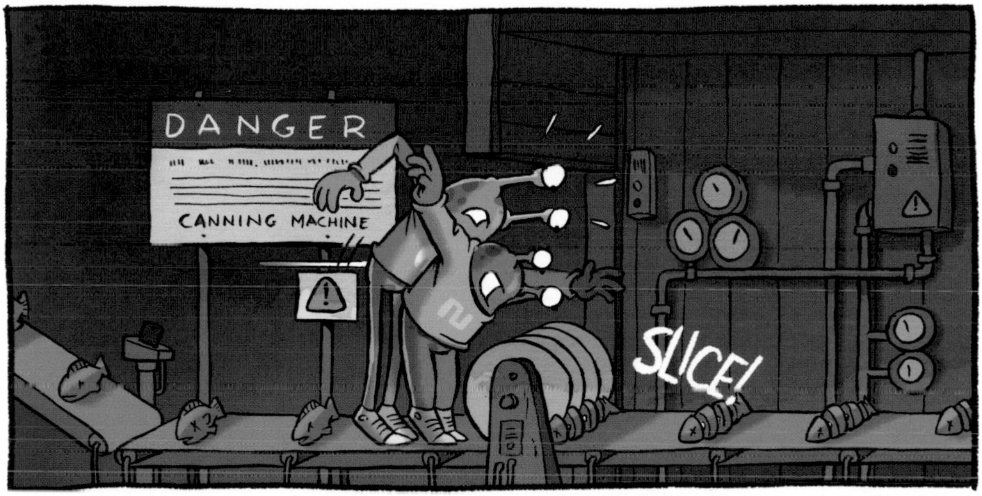
DANGER
CANNING MACHINE
SLICE!

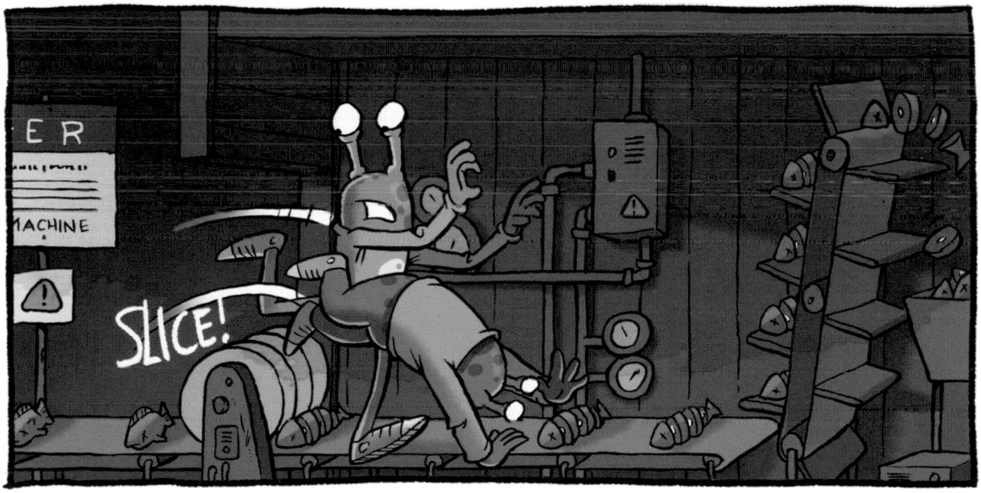
ER
MACHINE
SLICE!

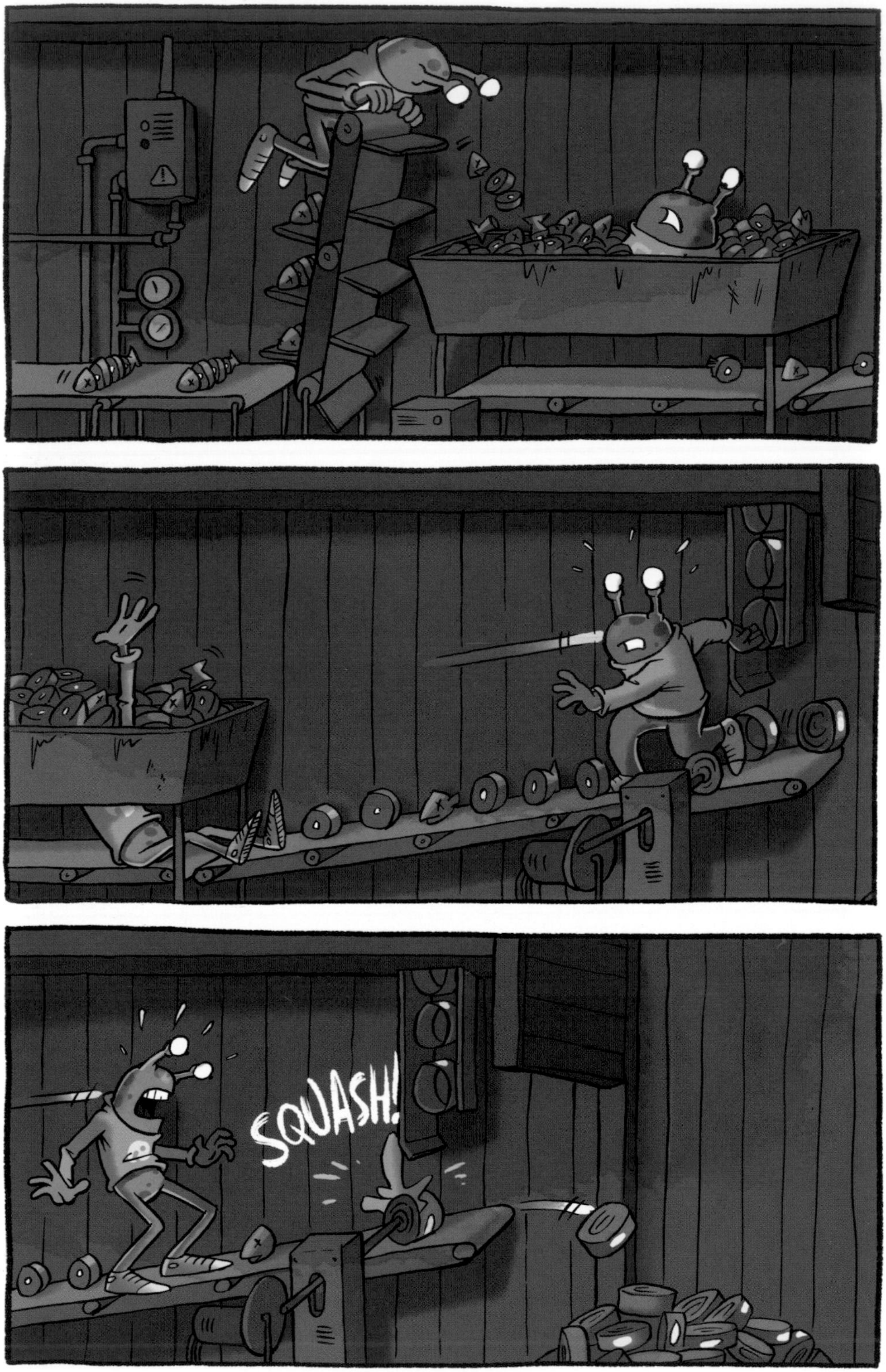
SQUASH!

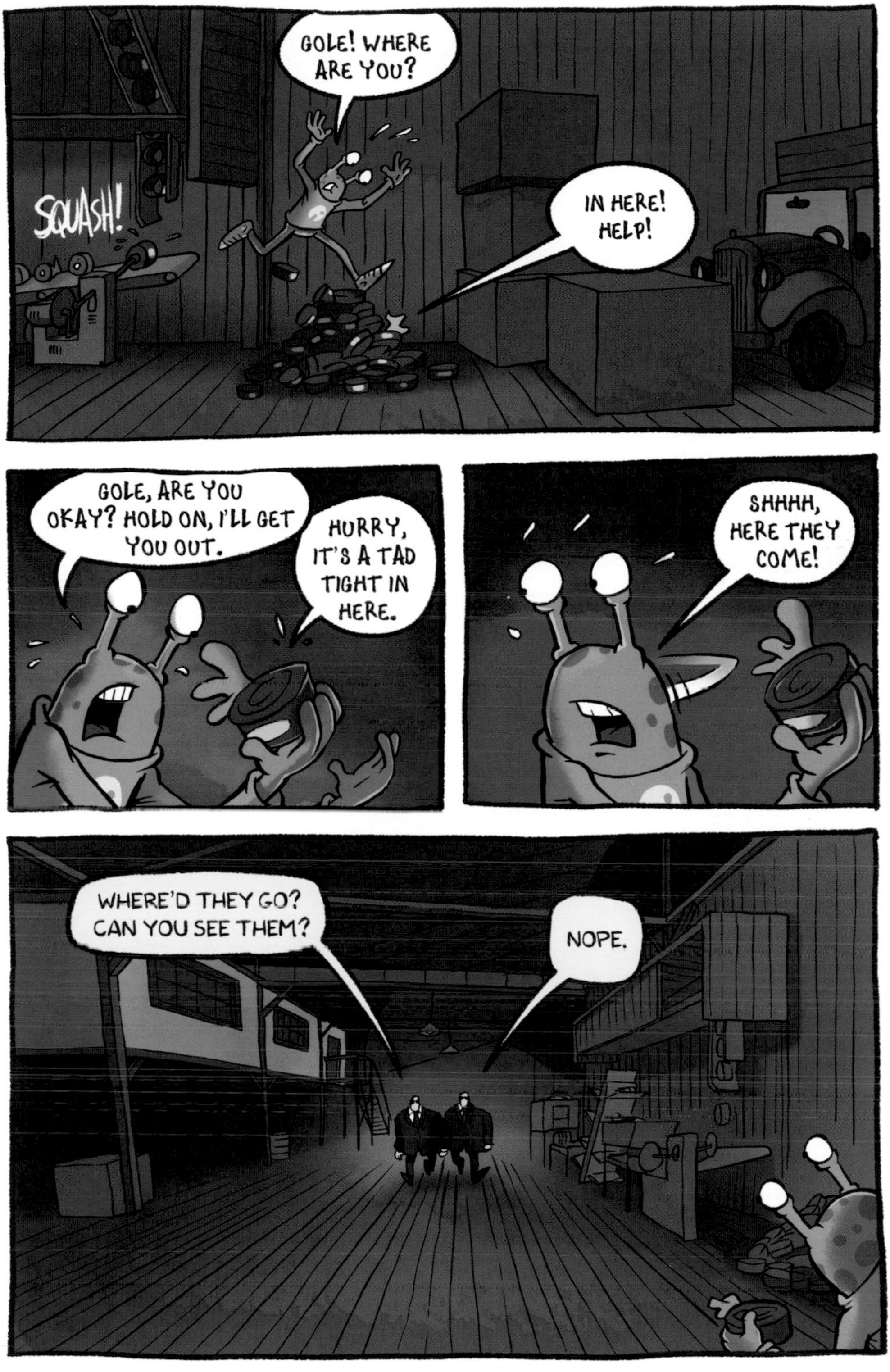
GOLE! WHERE ARE YOU?
SQUASH!
IN HERE! HELP!
GOLE, ARE YOU OKAY? HOLD ON, I'LL GET YOU OUT.
HURRY, IT'S A TAD TIGHT IN HERE.
SHHHH, HERE THEY COME!
WHERE'D THEY GO? CAN YOU SEE THEM?
NOPE.

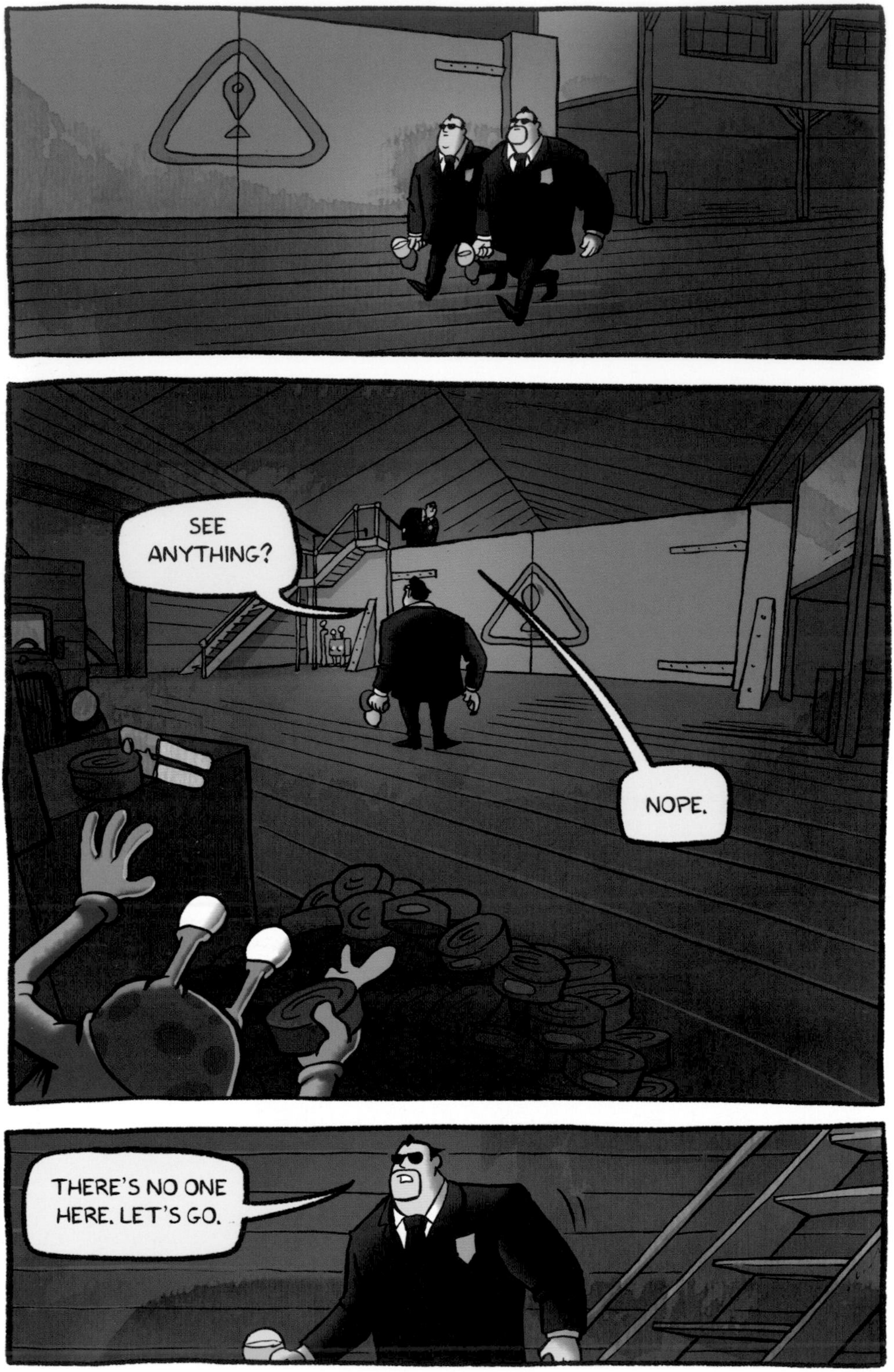
SEE ANYTHING?
NOPE.
THERE'S NO ONE HERE. LET'S GO.

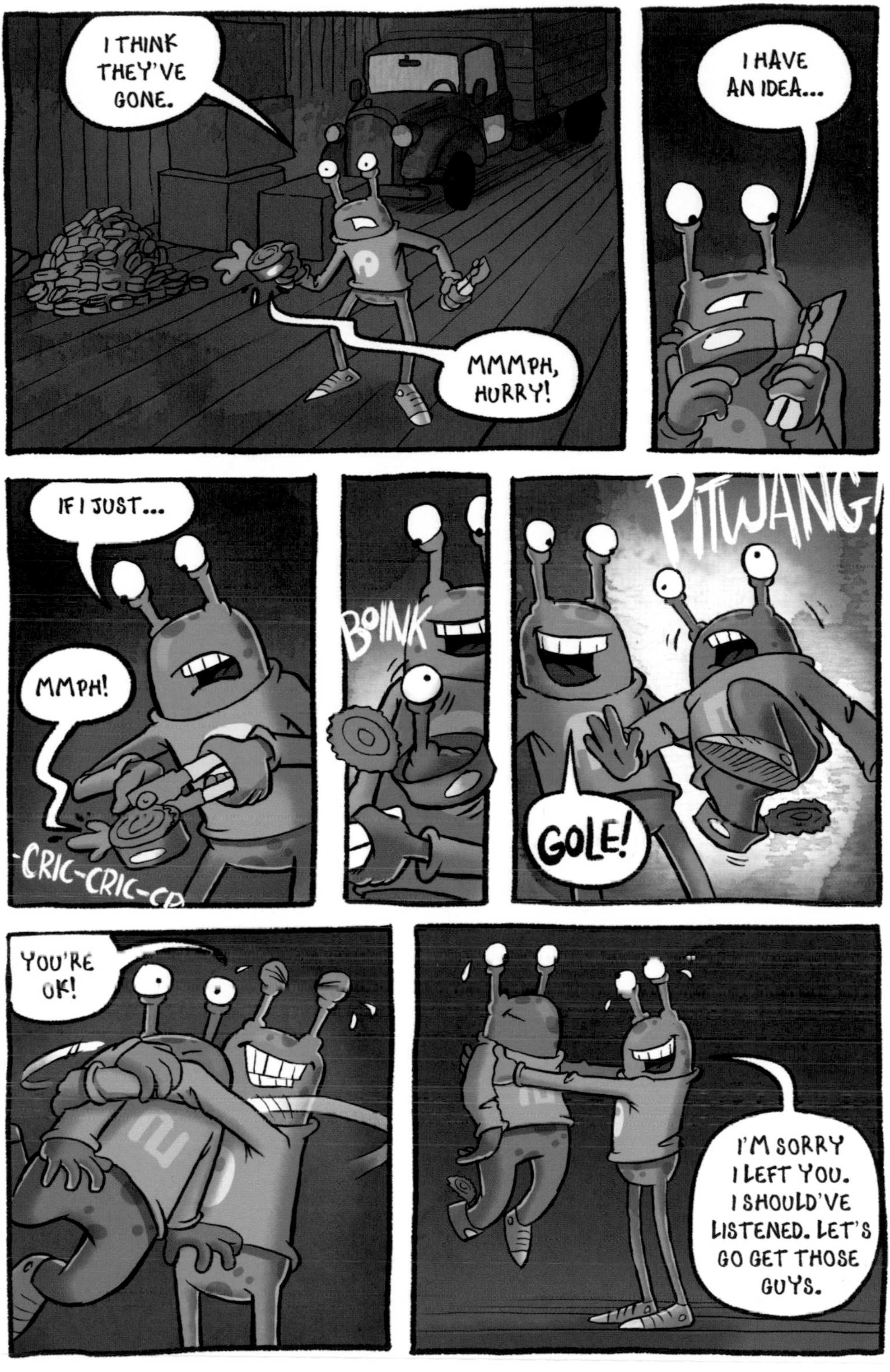
I THINK THEY'VE GONE.
MMMPH, HURRY!
I HAVE AN IDEA...
IF I JUST...
MMPH!
-CRIC-CRIC-CR
BOINK
PITWANG!
GOLE!
YOU'RE OK!
I'M SORRY I LEFT YOU. I SHOULD'VE LISTENED. LET'S GO GET THOSE GUYS.

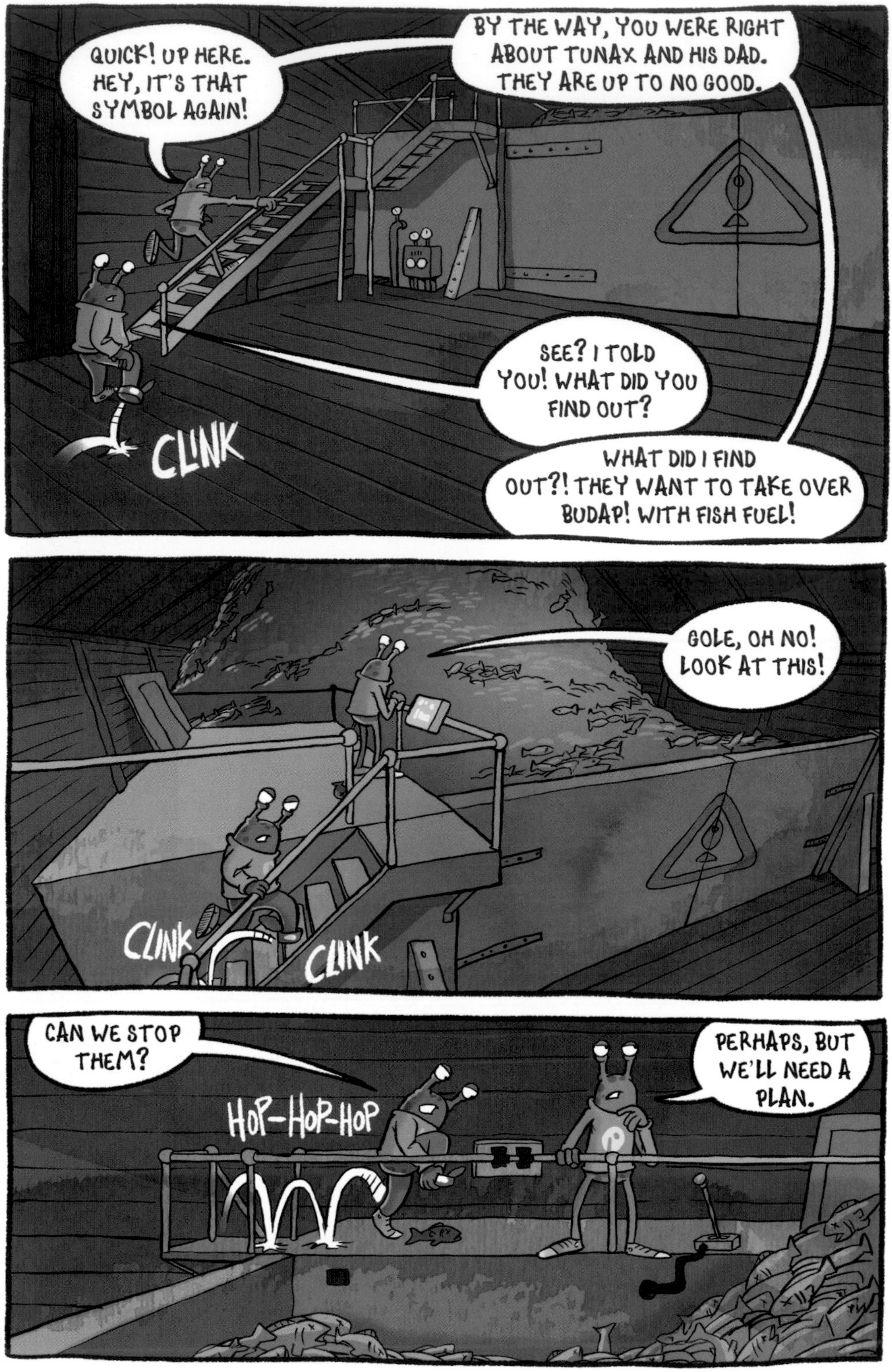
QUICK! UP HERE. HEY, IT'S THAT SYMBOL AGAIN!
BY THE WAY, YOU WERE RIGHT ABOUT TUNAX AND HIS DAD. THEY ARE UP TO NO GOOD.
CLINK
SEE? I TOLD YOU! WHAT DID YOU FIND OUT?
WHAT DID I FIND OUT?! THEY WANT TO TAKE OVER BUDAP! WITH FISH FUEL!
GOLE, OH NO! LOOK AT THIS!
CLINK
CLINK
CAN WE STOP THEM?
HOP-HOP-HOP
PERHAPS, BUT WE'LL NEED A PLAN.

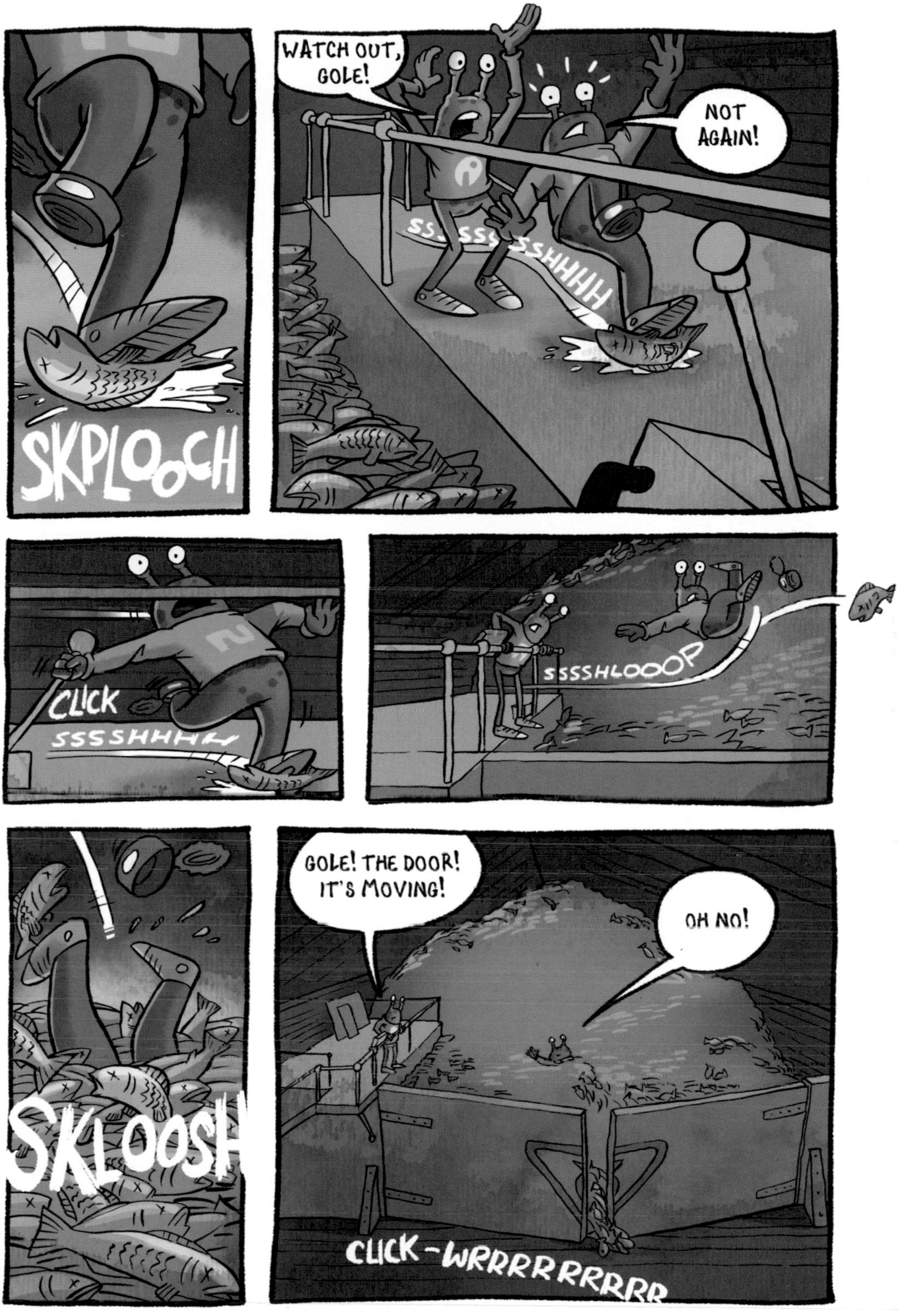
SKPLOOCH
WATCH OUT, GOLE!
NOT AGAIN!
SSSSSSSSHHHHH
CLICK
SSSSHHHH
SSSSHLOOOP
SKLOOSH
GOLE! THE DOOR! IT'S MOVING!
OH NO!
CLICK-WRRRRRRRRR

MEANWHILE, ON THE OTHER SIDE OF THE CANNERY...
OKAY, START SUCKING THIS LOAD OF FISH THROUGH.
YOU GOT IT.
BEEP
SUUUUCK!
SUUUCK!

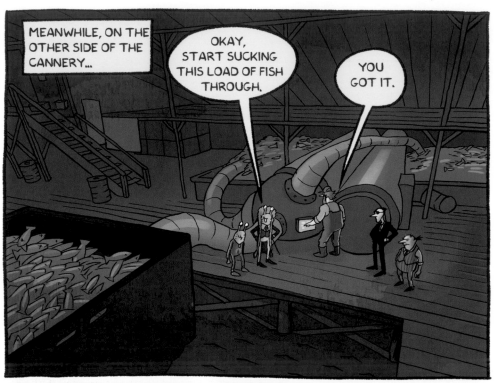

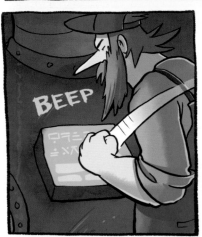

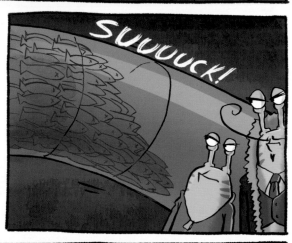

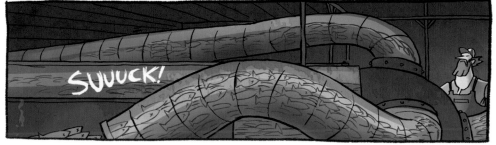

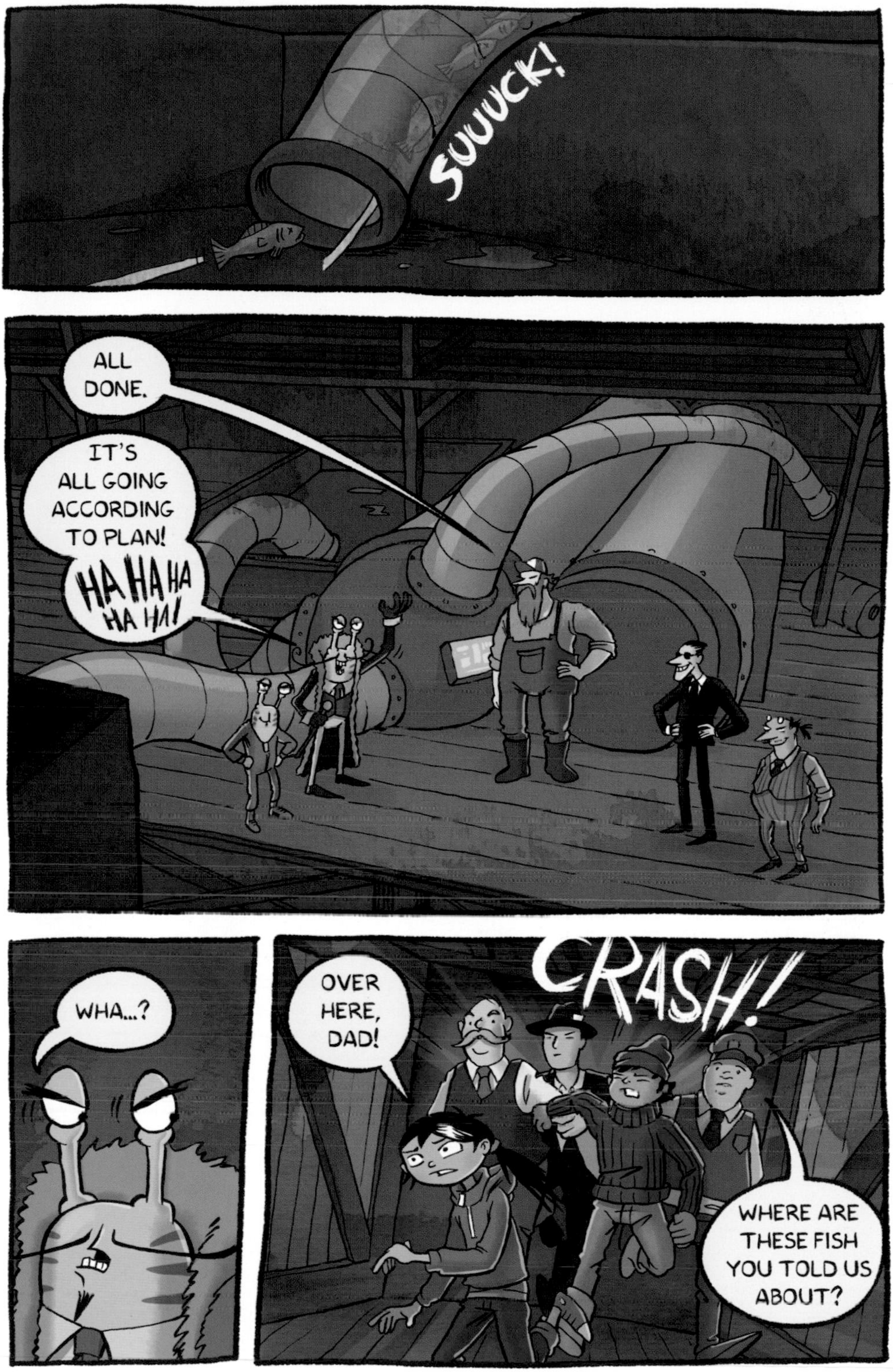
SUUUCK!
ALL DONE.
IT'S ALL GOING ACCORDING TO PLAN!
HA HA HA HA HA!
WHA...?
CRASH!
OVER HERE, DAD!
WHERE ARE THESE FISH YOU TOLD US ABOUT?

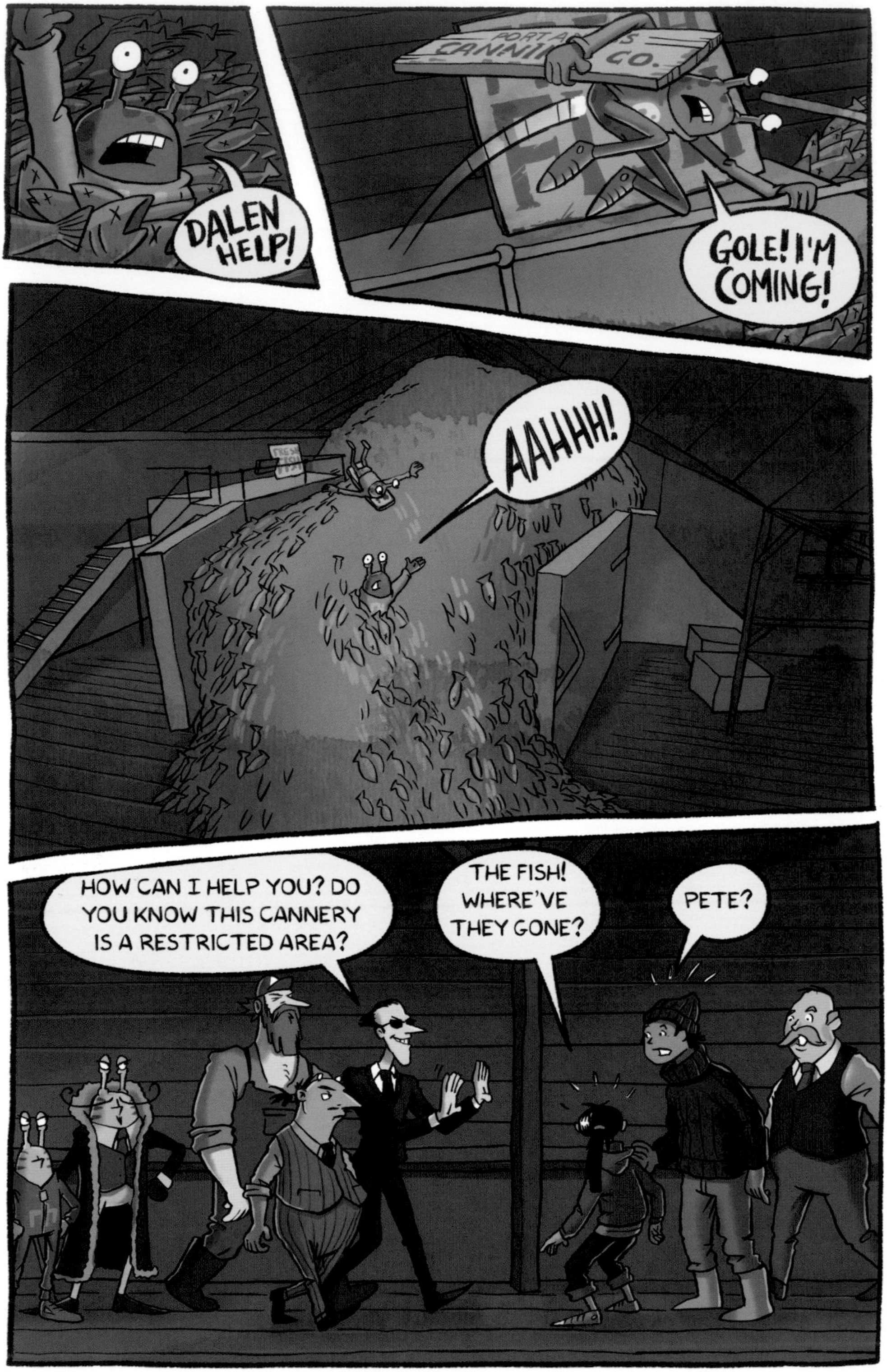
DALEN HELP!
GOLE! I'M COMING!
AAHHH!
HOW CAN I HELP YOU? DO YOU KNOW THIS CANNERY IS A RESTRICTED AREA?
THE FISH! WHERE'VE THEY GONE?
PETE?

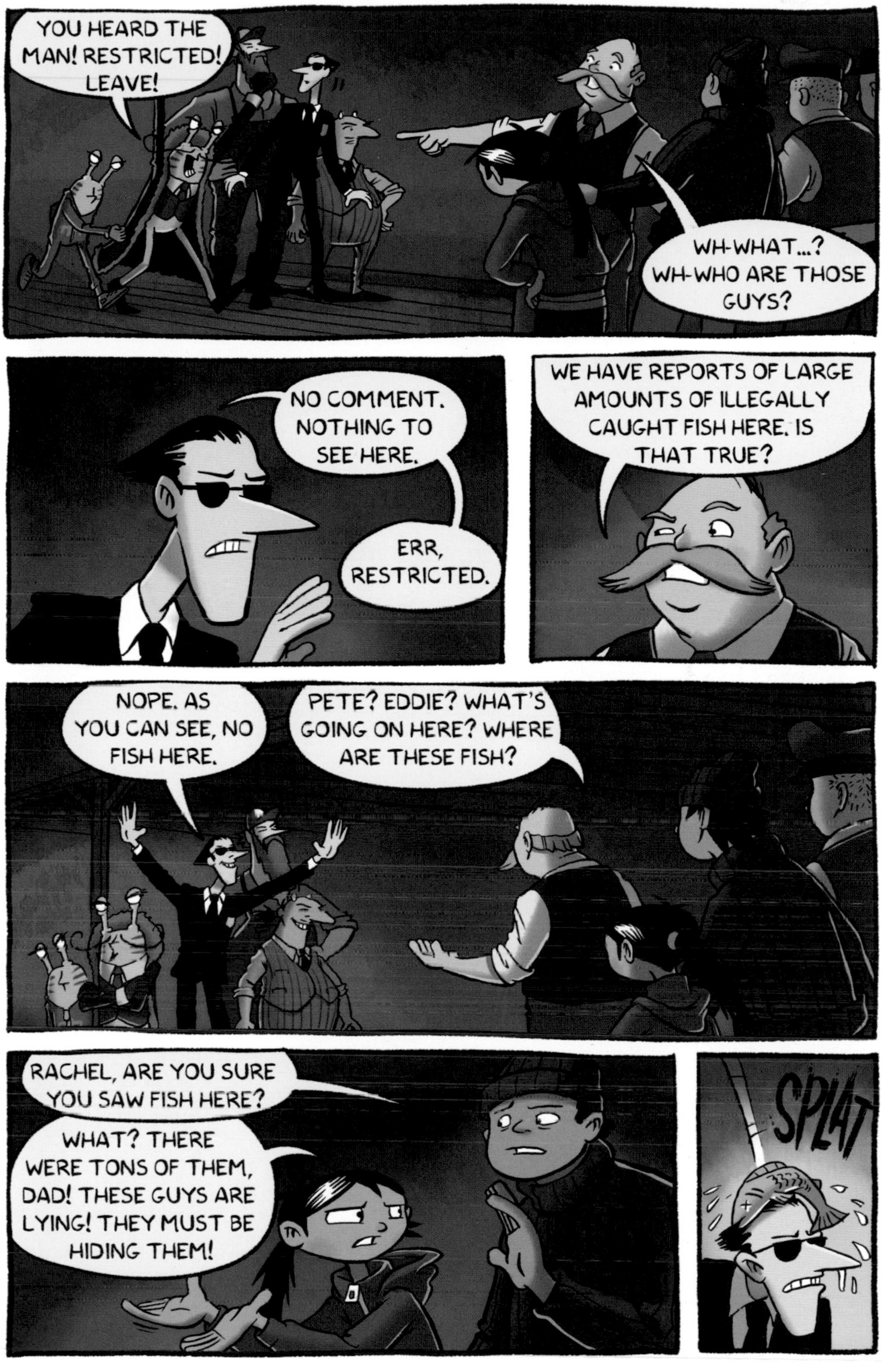

YOU HEARD THE MAN! RESTRICTED! LEAVE!
WH-WHAT...? WH-WHO ARE THOSE GUYS?
NO COMMENT. NOTHING TO SEE HERE.
ERR, RESTRICTED.
WE HAVE REPORTS OF LARGE AMOUNTS OF ILLEGALLY CAUGHT FISH HERE. IS THAT TRUE?
NOPE. AS YOU CAN SEE, NO FISH HERE.
PETE? EDDIE? WHAT'S GOING ON HERE? WHERE ARE THESE FISH?
RACHEL, ARE YOU SURE YOU SAW FISH HERE?
WHAT? THERE WERE TONS OF THEM, DAD! THESE GUYS ARE LYING! THEY MUST BE HIDING THEM!
SPLAT

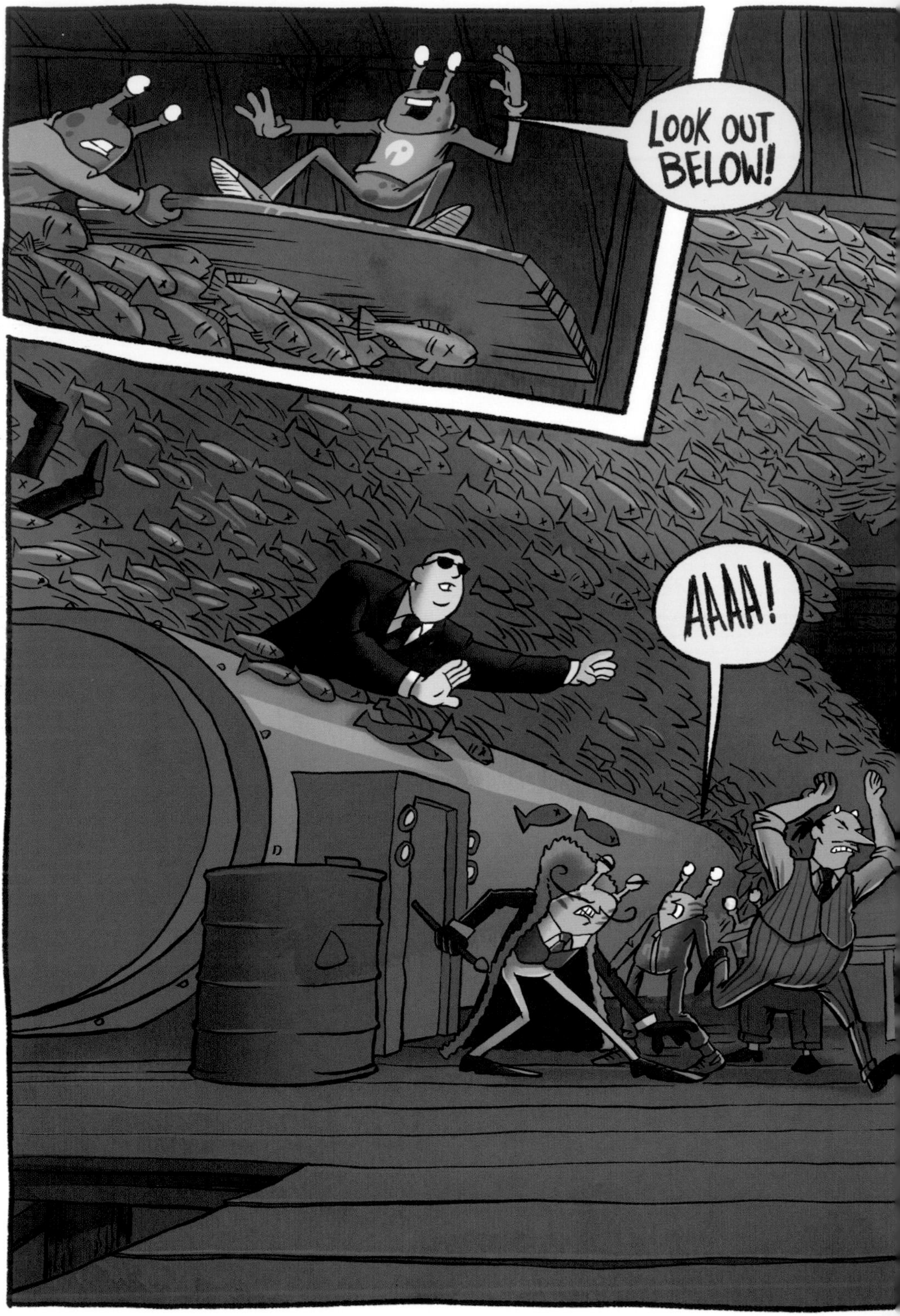
LOOK OUT BELOW!
AAAA!

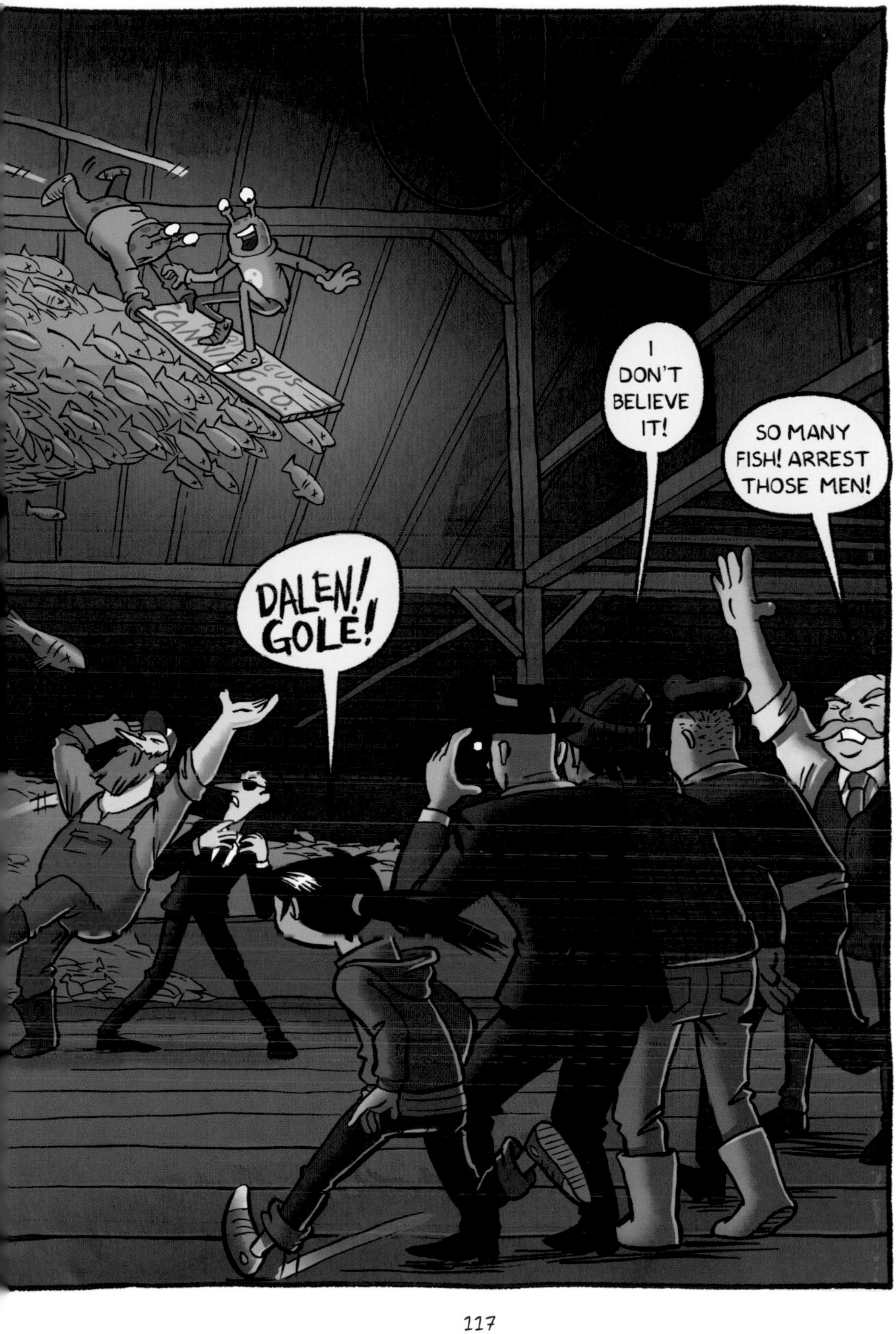
CANNING CO.
DALEN! GOLE!
I DON'T BELIEVE IT!
SO MANY FISH! ARREST THOSE MEN!

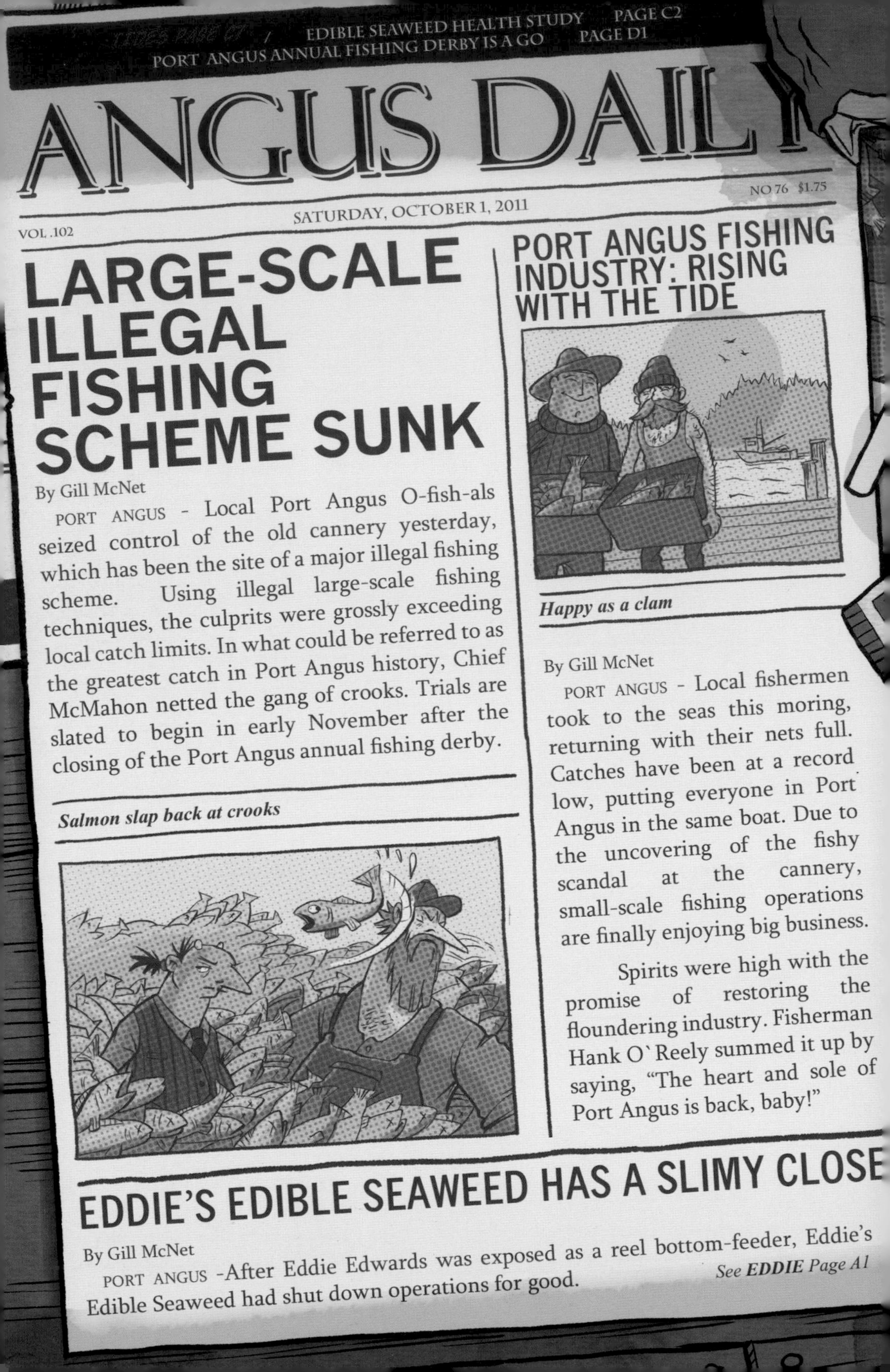

TIDES PAGE C7 / EDIBLE SEAWEED HEALTH STUDY PAGE C2
PORT ANGUS ANNUAL FISHING DERBY IS A GO PAGE D1

ANGUS DAILY

VOL .102 SATURDAY, OCTOBER 1, 2011 NO 76 $1.75

LARGE-SCALE ILLEGAL FISHING SCHEME SUNK

By Gill McNet

PORT ANGUS - Local Port Angus O-fish-als seized control of the old cannery yesterday, which has been the site of a major illegal fishing scheme. Using illegal large-scale fishing techniques, the culprits were grossly exceeding local catch limits. In what could be referred to as the greatest catch in Port Angus history, Chief McMahon netted the gang of crooks. Trials are slated to begin in early November after the closing of the Port Angus annual fishing derby.

Salmon slap back at crooks

PORT ANGUS FISHING INDUSTRY: RISING WITH THE TIDE

Happy as a clam

By Gill McNet

PORT ANGUS - Local fishermen took to the seas this moring, returning with their nets full. Catches have been at a record low, putting everyone in Port Angus in the same boat. Due to the uncovering of the fishy scandal at the cannery, small-scale fishing operations are finally enjoying big business.

Spirits were high with the promise of restoring the floundering industry. Fisherman Hank O`Reely summed it up by saying, "The heart and sole of Port Angus is back, baby!"

EDDIE'S EDIBLE SEAWEED HAS A SLIMY CLOSE

By Gill McNet

PORT ANGUS -After Eddie Edwards was exposed as a reel bottom-feeder, Eddie's Edible Seaweed had shut down operations for good.

*See **EDDIE** Page A1*

CHAPTER 6

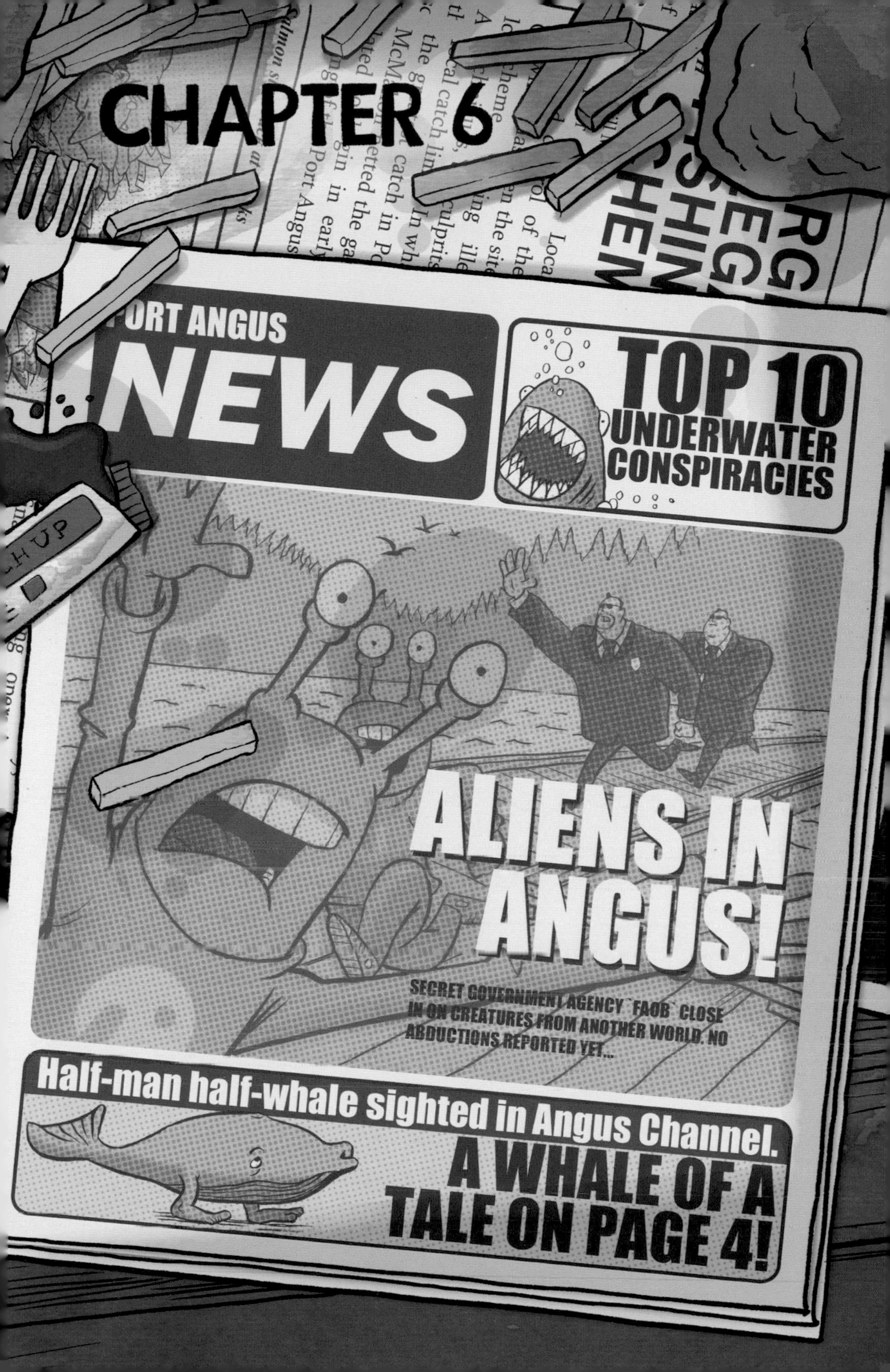
PORT ANGUS
NEWS
TOP 10
UNDERWATER
CONSPIRACIES
ALIENS IN ANGUS!
SECRET GOVERNMENT AGENCY `FAOB` CLOSE IN ON CREATURES FROM ANOTHER WORLD. NO ABDUCTIONS REPORTED YET...
Half-man half-whale sighted in Angus Channel.
A WHALE OF A TALE ON PAGE 4!

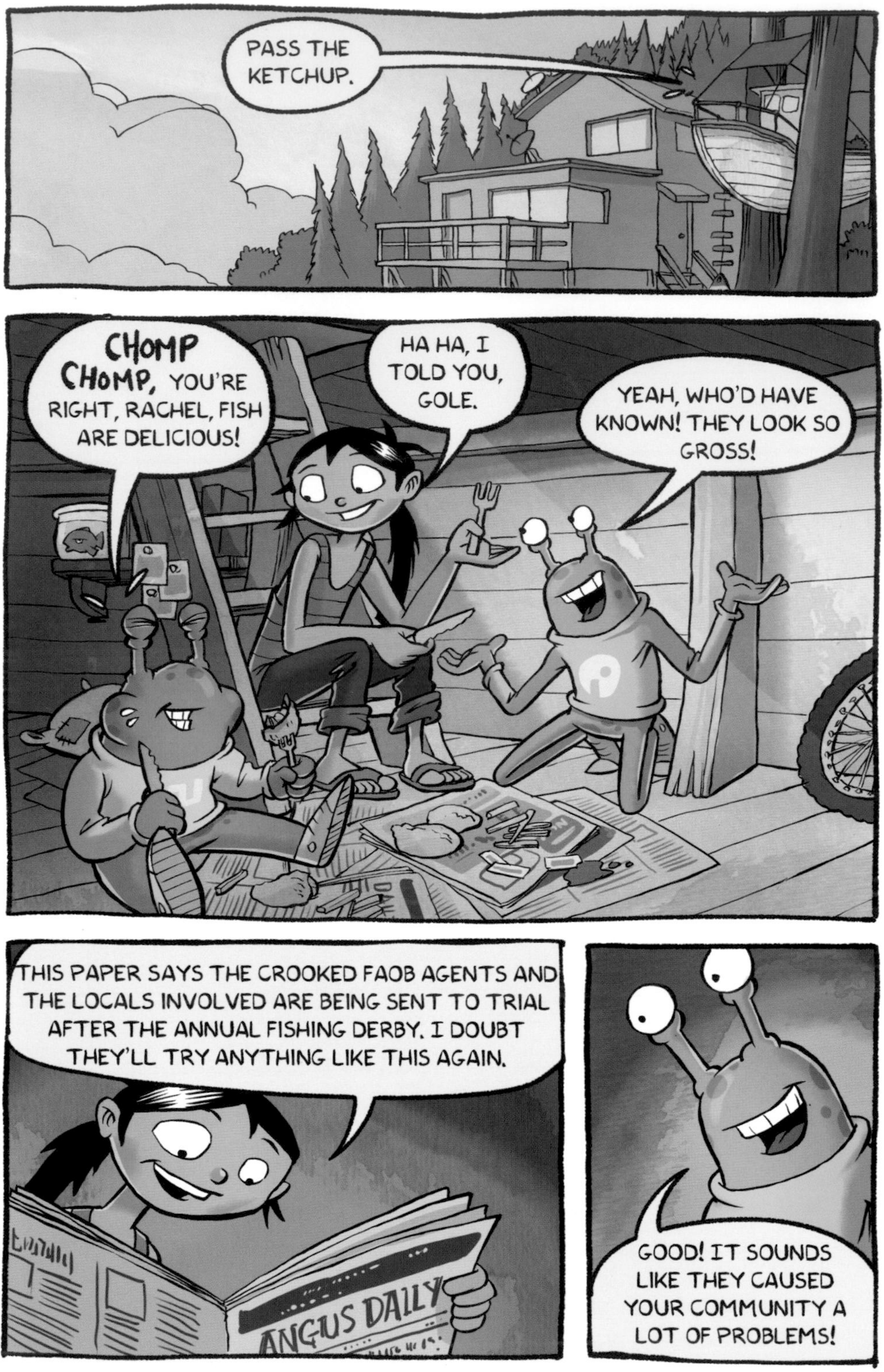
PASS THE KETCHUP.
CHOMP CHOMP, YOU'RE RIGHT, RACHEL, FISH ARE DELICIOUS!
HA HA, I TOLD YOU, GOLE.
YEAH, WHO'D HAVE KNOWN! THEY LOOK SO GROSS!
THIS PAPER SAYS THE CROOKED FAOB AGENTS AND THE LOCALS INVOLVED ARE BEING SENT TO TRIAL AFTER THE ANNUAL FISHING DERBY. I DOUBT THEY'LL TRY ANYTHING LIKE THIS AGAIN.
ANGUS DAILY
GOOD! IT SOUNDS LIKE THEY CAUSED YOUR COMMUNITY A LOT OF PROBLEMS!

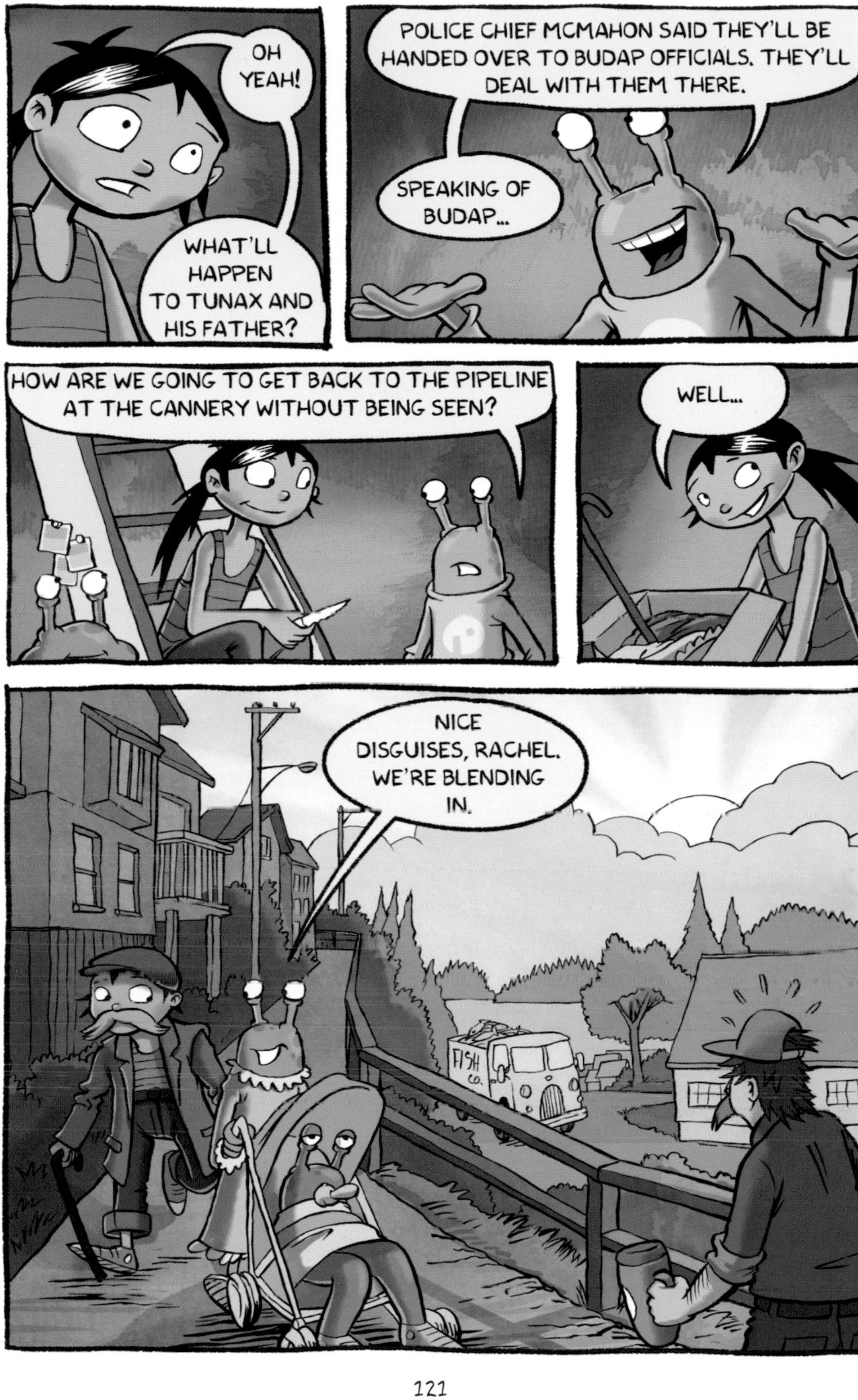
OH YEAH!
WHAT'LL HAPPEN TO TUNAX AND HIS FATHER?
POLICE CHIEF MCMAHON SAID THEY'LL BE HANDED OVER TO BUDAP OFFICIALS. THEY'LL DEAL WITH THEM THERE.
SPEAKING OF BUDAP...
HOW ARE WE GOING TO GET BACK TO THE PIPELINE AT THE CANNERY WITHOUT BEING SEEN?
WELL...
NICE DISGUISES, RACHEL. WE'RE BLENDING IN.
FISH CO.

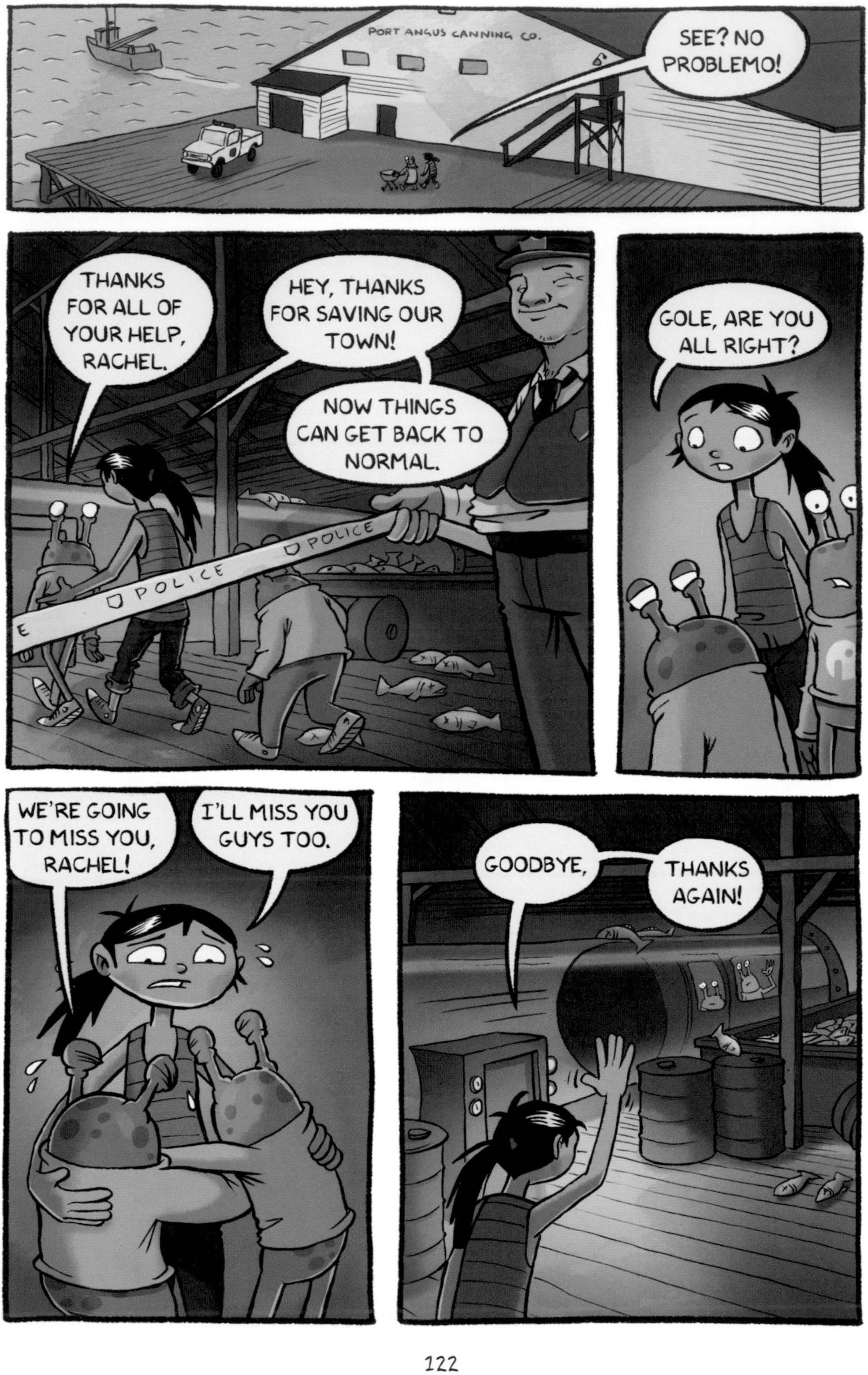
PORT ANGUS CANNING CO.
SEE? NO PROBLEMO!
THANKS FOR ALL OF YOUR HELP, RACHEL.
HEY, THANKS FOR SAVING OUR TOWN!
NOW THINGS CAN GET BACK TO NORMAL.
POLICE
POLICE
GOLE, ARE YOU ALL RIGHT?
WE'RE GOING TO MISS YOU, RACHEL!
I'LL MISS YOU GUYS TOO.
GOODBYE,
THANKS AGAIN!

ONE YEAR LATER, BACK IN THE WORLD OF BUDAP...
ANOTHER GREAT LETTER FROM RACHEL. SOUNDS LIKE PORT ANGUS IS BACK IN BUSINESS.
YEAH!
DALEN, DO YOU THINK WE'LL EVER SEE HER AGAIN?
I DON'T KNOW, BUT I DO KNOW ONE THING!
WHAT'S THAT?
WE HAVE A GOOD CHANCE AT WINNING THE JUNIOR JET-RACER COMPETITION THIS YEAR!
YEAH, NO PURPLE SMOKE!
THE END

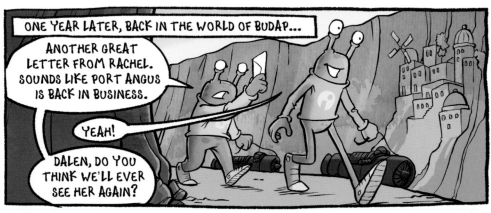

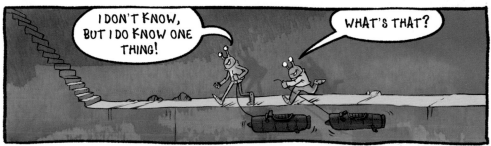

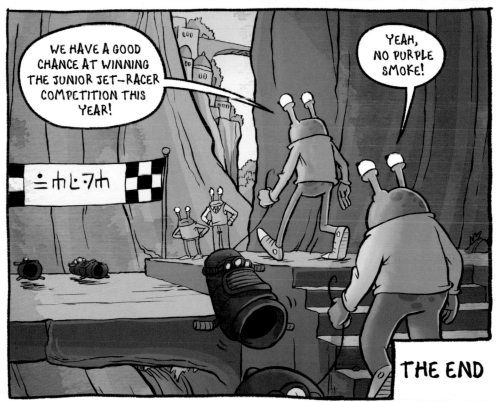

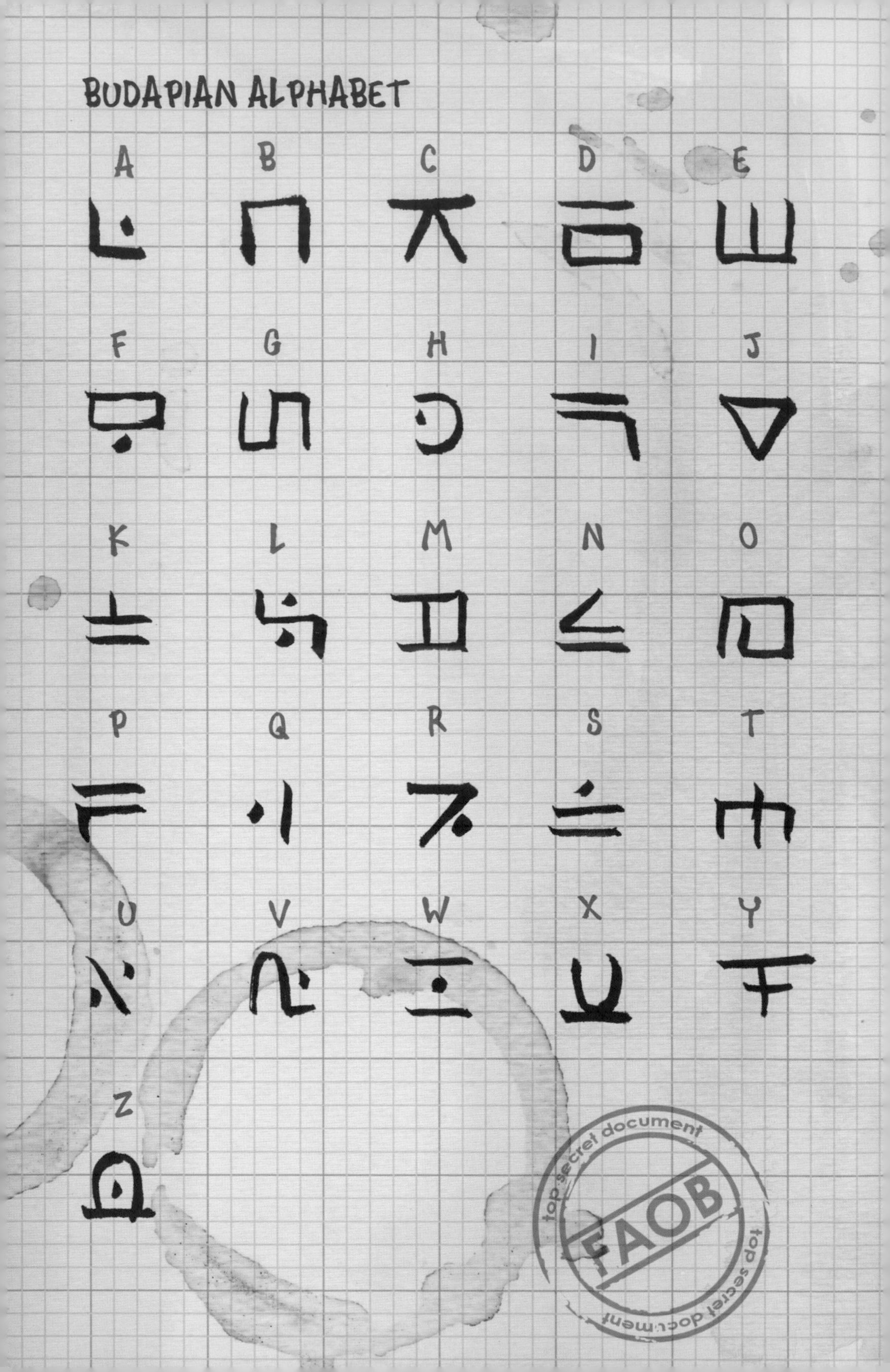
BUDAPIAN ALPHABET
A
B
C
D
E
F
G
H
I
J
K
L
M
N
O
P
Q
R
S
T
U
V
W
X
Y
Z
top secret document
FAOB
top secret document

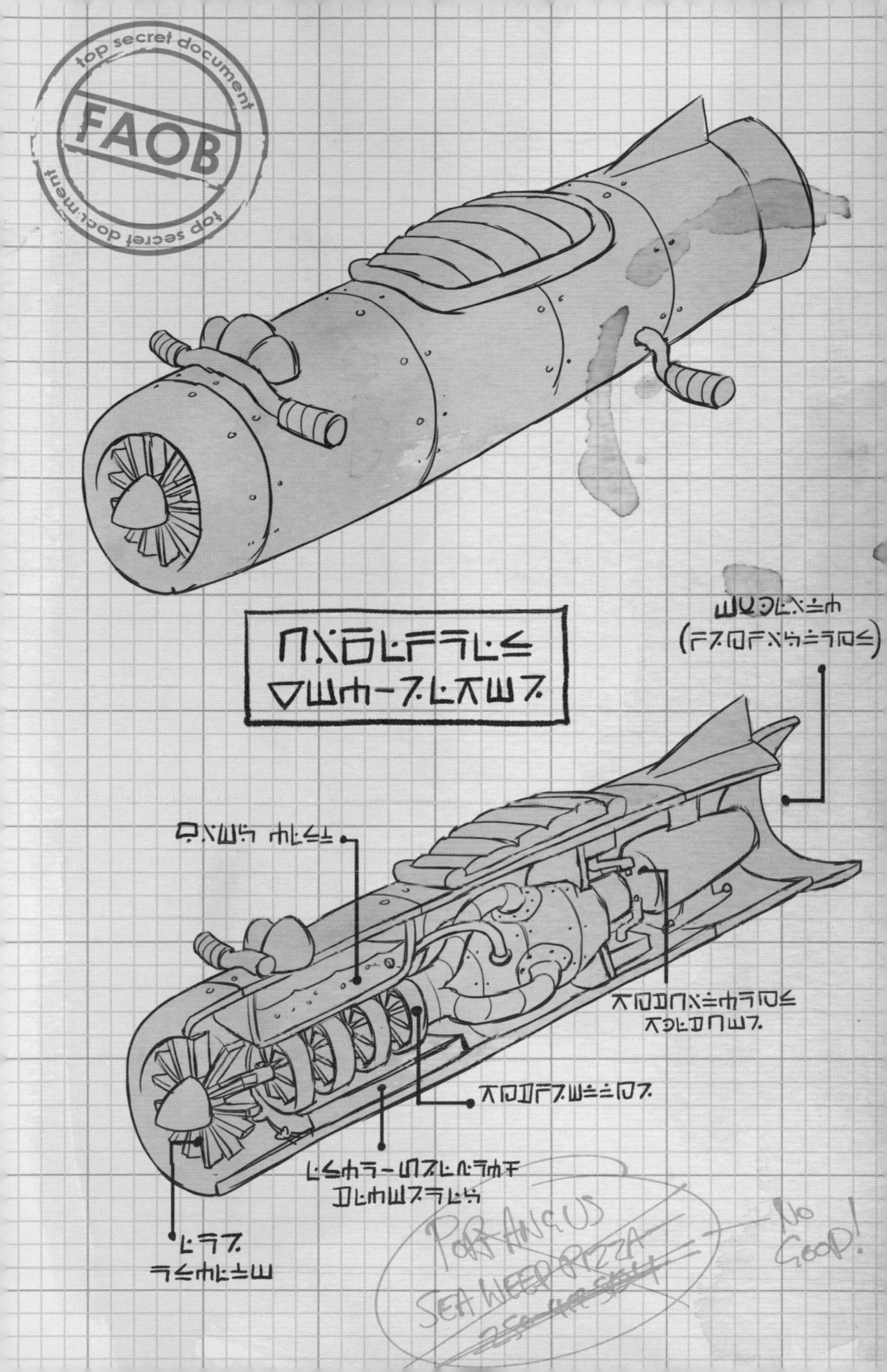
top secret document
FAOB
top secret document
SEA WEED PIZZA
NO GOOD!

MIKE DEAS is a talented illustrator in a number of different genres. He graduated from Capilano College's Commercial Animation program and has worked as a game developer. Mike is the illustrator of the Graphic Guide Adventures series, written by Liam O'Donnell, and is at work on a new graphic novel for teen readers. Mike lives in Victoria, British Columbia. More information about Mike is available at WWW.DEASILLUSTRATION.COM.